D0631711

PROJECT GEMINI

MISSION 2: OKINAWA

JILL WILLIAMSON

Project Gemini
Copyright © 2013 by Jill Williamson. All rights reserved.

This book or parts thereof may not be reproduced in any form, stored in a
retrieval system, or transmitted in any form by any means—electronic,
mechanical, photocopy, recording, or otherwise—without prior written
permission of the publisher, except as provided by United States of America
copyright law.

This is a work of fiction. Names, characters, places, and incidents are
products of the author's imagination or are used fictitiously. Any similarity
to actual people, organizations, and/or events is purely coincidental.

Scriptures taken from the Holy Bible, New International Version®, NIV®.
Copyright © 1973, 1978, 1984, 2011 by Biblica, Inc.™ Used by permission of
Zondervan. All rights reserved worldwide. www.zondervan.com. The "NIV"
and "New International Version" are trademarks registered in the United
States Patent and Trademark Office by Biblica, Inc.™

The author is represented by MacGregor Literary Inc. of Hillsboro, OR.

Cover Designer: Kirk DouPonce
Editor: Jeff Gerke
All other miscellaneous images: Jill Williamson

Library of Congress Cataloging-in-Publication Data
An application to register this book for cataloging has been filed with the
Library of Congress.

International Standard Book Number: 978-0-9962945-7-7

Printed in the United States of America

RESTRICTED ACCESS

YOU HAVE ACCESSED THE
INTERNATIONAL SERVER FOR
THE MISSION LEAGUE.

THESE FILES CONTAIN CLASSIFIED INFORMATION
ON THE ORGANIZATION, AGENTS, CRIMINALS, PROCEDURES,
TRAININGS AND MISSIONS.

GOD HAS CALLED. YOU HAVE ANSWERED.

Other books by Jill Williamson

The Mission League series
The New Recruit
Chokepoint
Project Gemini
Ambushed
Broken Trust
The Profile Match

The Blood of Kings trilogy
By Darkness Hid
To Darkness Fled
From Darkness Won

The Kinsman Chronicles
King's Folly
King's Blood
King's War

The Safe Lands series
Captives
Outcasts
Rebels

RoboTales
Tinker
Mardok and the Seven Exiles
The Tiny Cyborg

Stand-Alone Titles
Replication: The Jason Experiment

Nonfiction
Go Teen Writers: How to Turn Your First Draft into a Published Book
Storyworld First: Creating a Unique Fantasy World for Your Novel

To Kim Titus for being Bob to my Bill,
for going to Okinawa with me,
and for being the best friend a girl could have.

Love you!

CLASSIFIED MISSION BRIEFING

JUVENILE MISSION BACKGROUND REPORT

SUBMITTED BY: Agent-in-Training Spencer Garmond

A LITTLE LESS THAN ONE YEAR AGO I was recruited into the Agent Development program of the Mission League, a secret branch of INTERPOL, whose primary objective is to follow the will of God in collecting, analyzing, evaluating, and disseminating intelligence against the rulers, the authorities, the powers of this dark world, and the spiritual forces of evil in the heavenly realms.

Yeah, I know what you're thinking: churchers. And I thought the same at first. But then I found out that my real name is Jonas Wright and I'm in a witness protection program of sorts, hiding out from my criminal dad, who was responsible for my mom's death. Real nice, huh?

So I went on a training mission to Moscow and met this woman, Anya Vseveloda, who was working with the Russian mob to get people hooked on drugs and into a cult called Bratva. I'd been having dreams about her for years and found out I was gifted in prophecy. I went after her, figuring that's what God wanted me to do. Wrongo. Got suspended from extracurricular training activities until I get my points up.

When I got back to California and started my sophomore year at Pilot Point Christian School, Beth Watkins offered to teach me League Combat Training (LCT) on her own time, which was awesome because I had a thing for her. But then Prière showed up—he's the official intercessor for our group of agents-in-training. He told me that I matched the profile for a sixty-year-old prophecy and that some bad guys were after me because of what I did in Moscow. So some agents started following me everywhere to keep me safe. Two guys, Blaine and Tito, they guy-napped me after Homecoming last year, and Nick Muren and Katie Lindley helped them. Real nice to have such friends, right?

But even though the agents nabbed Blain and Tito, there was still a traitor on the inside, so Prière asked me to enter the Regional LCT event—as *bait* to help catch the guy. And that's where Beth humiliated me. But I did manage to figure out that the traitor was one of my bodyguards, the guy I called Gardener. But now he's not talking, so we're back to square one as to who is after me.

Things have quieted down some for the past few weeks. I'm studying Japanese for this coming summer's training mission, and I'm nearing the end of the basketball season. We're poised to make the state game this year. [fingers crossed]

So that's the scoop on my life. Thrilling, I know. And if you really want to know more, read on.

Spencer Garmond
Agent-in-training
Pilot Point Mission League

REPORT NUMBER: 1

REPORT TITLE: I Find Out My Friends Are Psychopaths
SUBMITTED BY: Agent-in-Training Spencer Garmond
LOCATION: Grandma Alice's House, Pilot Point, California, USA
DATE AND TIME: Wednesday, February 25, 5:14 p.m.

I'D ALWAYS LOVED THE RUSH that came from being where I wasn't supposed to be.

Grandma's bedroom smelled like lilac powder, Vicks VapoRub, and dust. I stood on the braided rug that took up what little open floor space was left, what with the double bed, two dressers, a file cabinet, and piles of fabric that lined every inch of the baseboard. The walls were painted dirty pink. Mauve, Grandma called it. She had white curtains with pink and red roses on them. I felt weird standing in there. I couldn't remember the last time I'd even crossed the threshold.

The last few months had been intense with basketball, but finally the season was almost over. Today had been the first time I'd been home without Grandma here to keep me from

3

snooping in her room. I didn't know where she was, either—
she could be home any moment—so I needed to move fast.

I pulled open the top drawer of the file cabinet and studied
the tabs on the folders inside: bank, credit card, electric,
insurance, pay stubs, phone, retirement, taxes, water. I read
them all twice. None looked like a folder that might contain a
picture of my mom.

The second drawer contained nothing but quilting books
and patterns. The third drawer, more fabric.

I sighed, scanning the room for other places Grandma
might hide sentimental things. The closet? It was a two-walled
walk-in filled with clothing, Grandma's on the right, Grandpa's
on the left. She'd gotten rid of most his stuff after he'd died,
but she'd hung on to his fancy suits. I spotted the one I'd worn
to the homecoming dance last fall and shuddered at the
memory of how Blaine and Tito had nearly gotten away with
guy-napping me, and how for five hundred bucks my date had
naively helped them do it.

Couldn't really blame Katie. For that kind of money, I
probably would've helped too.

I still wasn't convinced that Nick had told Prière everything
about his involvement with those creepers, though. But that
was a problem for another time.

I looked up at the shelves above the closet rods. Clear
plastic Rubbermaid containers were stacked like bricks. I
moved them around, glad I could see through their sides. They
held things like thread, yarn, fabric paint, beads and bows,
shoes, my old Thomas the Train set, and some Hot Wheels.

Come on. Grandma kept all my old junk but nothing of my
mom's? No way.

I searched the top shelf on the other side. It was more of

the same. I found one container of pictures, but they were all of me. Little me. Ginger-haired kindergartener holding a basketball that was bigger than my head. Sitting on Santa's lap. Holding my finger on a quilt tie for Mrs. Daggett. The other picture packets showed older versions of me, but no Mom.

I finished my search of the closet and walked back into the bedroom. There had to be another place to stash things. Under the bed?

Nothing but dust bunnies and eight pairs of house slippers.

Might as well try the dressers. I rummaged through Grandma's clothes, wincing at the drawers that contained undergarments. So very eww.

After I struck out in the drawers, I inspected the clutter on top. A couple of baskets with perfumes and powders. And on the big dresser, Grandma had an old wooden jewelry box with glass doors and two drawers. Nothing but a lot of bling tangled in knots. But there was a good three inches on the bottom that seemed like it should have another drawer. I pulled the jewelry box out and turned it, revealing a drawer on the bottom of the back.

A secret drawer!

A rush of heat ran over me. Come on, baby, give me what I need. I pulled open the drawer and found it filled with pictures. Score! A shiver ran up my arms as I gathered the photos into my hands. The first was of a little blond girl with pigtails, hugging a stuffed cat. Same girl a few years older, playing a clarinet. The next was a picture of a basketball team. Nice. The blond girl was kneeling on the end of the front row. Looked to be in about eighth grade. Then a young Grandpa Earl holding a baby. Another baby picture.

I'd found it. These had to be pics of my mom.

The last one was half of a wedding photo. It had been torn down the center. Of the groom, only the hands were still visible, clasped with the woman's. She looked about twenty-two. Pretty. All fancied up and in the white dress, she looked like the chick that played Galadriel in *The Lord of the Rings*. Pale. Blond. Regal. Had my nose.

Or I had hers. Whatever.

It was her, though. The ache in my gut was all the proof I needed. Mommy dearest.

A distant bang made me jump. Screen door. Grandma.

I returned all but the wedding picture to the drawer and twisted the jewelry box back into place. I booked it out of Grandma's room and into my own, carefully closing the door behind me.

"Spencer? You home?"

"Yeah!" I sat on the edge of my bed and studied my mom's face in the photo. She looked really happy. Blissful, actually. But something had gone wrong in her life. Big time. Kimbal had said my dad was a traitor. Then later he'd said that everyone had liked my dad. But even I knew that no loving husband would let his wife get killed. None of this added up, and I was sick of it.

But I didn't want to just sit there and stew, so I turned on my MacBook and opened my file on prophecy. I'd been studying the subject, trying to figure out how it worked. There wasn't much to go on. Forget current day stuff. Everything online was either New Age garbage, wacko psychics peddling their ability to "see," or doomsayers who either claimed that anything bad that happened was God punishing people for their sins or a sign that we were in the last days, as prophesied in the book of Revelation.

So I focused on the old stuff. The stuff from the Bible. There were a lot of symbolic prophecies back then. I'd never experienced anything like that. And no messengers had ever appeared to me, either. Unless Viktor, that mysterious guy in Moscow, had really been an angel . . .

Me? I just saw the future. In biblical times, God had used visions and dreams to deliver messages to people back then. I guessed that was sort of the same thing for me, because Prière had told me that my prophecies were to be considered warnings. First John 4:1 said that prophets were supposed to test their prophecies, which was what the whole intercession report system in the Mission League was for. Prière had taught me how to keep my intercession journal and submit reports to Mr. S, who sent them to the international office.

But that didn't tell me anything about what I was supposed to do with these visions. How was I supposed to know when God wanted me to sit back and when He wanted me to act?

I had no clue. And everyone I'd asked had said the same thing: Pray.

Which was something I sucked at, apparently, because God never answered me.

• • •

Rock Academy in San Diego had invited some bigger schools to their basketball tournament, including our hometown rivals, Pilot Point High. PPH wasn't as big of a threat to us though. But the Rock Academy "Drillers" not only looked like a bunch of guys who worked on an oil rig, they fought like it too.

After a traveling call, their point guard threw the ball at me, and I jammed my fingers trying to catch it. The same guy—

who didn't know how to steal without fouling—also gave me a set of scratches down my arm. I scored twelve points off bonus free throws, though, so I was good with it.

Mike had a black eye from their center's elbow. Kip sprained his knee. And Desh got thrown out of the game on his second technical foul for pushing one of their players.

Despite how hard we fought, they beat us in the opening game, which knocked us into the loser's bracket. So sad.

That night, we camped out in a math classroom to sleep. I rolled out my sleeping bag in the far corner underneath a pi poster. We might not be able to win the tournament now, but we still had a chance at fourth, and I still had a chance at an all-star trophy, so I wanted to get some sleep.

Some of the guys were wound up, though, trading dirty jokes and stories of their dating conquests. I popped in my ear buds and dozed off.

"Let her go. Please?" I say. My hands are trapped. I'm trapped.

Anya Vseveloda steps into my vision. She's dressed all in white. A fancy suit of some kind. Her hair is down and wild. Her lips are blood red. They twist into a smile as she raises a knife to my face. She's enjoying this. "Just seeing how much you want this delights me. I think she will help us get information from you. Yes. I think she will be very helpful."

I glance over and see two girls in a restaurant booth: one is the Asian swimmer I've dreamed of before, the other is slumped over the table, curly brown hair in a ponytail. Is she bleeding? I can't see her face.

I awoke, my heart thumping hard, irregularly, reminding me of that old Morse code stuff. Did some hearts beat harder than others? Was that normal? Maybe I had some sort of heart malfunction . . .

I lay there wondering if I was going to die, but then I woke up enough to gather my senses. Voices. Laughing and whispering. I could barely see the poster of pi on the wall in the darkness. Right. We were in San Diego at the tournament. It had been a dream. Duh.

I rolled over and dug my intercession journal out of my backpack. It had been a few weeks since I'd had something to log. Prière had taught me how to keep track of the glimpses and dreams I had. A "glimpse" was a prophecy that came when I was awake, while a "dream," obviously, was a prophecy that came when I was asleep. A dream as freaky as the one about Anya torturing me and some half-dead girl was going to have to go into an official report too. Nothing like getting the Mission League bigwigs focused on little old me again. I only hoped the dream would act as a warning and not actually happen at some point.

But the pretty Asian girl . . . I'd seen her before in my dreams. Swimming in the ocean. Was I going to see her this summer? Couldn't say that I'd mind *that*.

I sat up inside my sleeping bag and used *My Precious*—my iPhone—as a flashlight as I jotted down the facts of the dream. The air conditioning kicked on, rumbling in the ceiling and blowing a gust of chilled air down on me. I wasn't wearing a shirt, so I shivered.

Desh's honking laugh pulled my gaze across the room. Kip, Desh, Chaz, Mike, and Wyatt were sitting in a group by the door, their faces lit by cell phones and Mike's 3DS screen. The rest of the guys were asleep.

"Let's go, then." Desh pushed up to a squatting position. "You guys coming?"

Mike shut his 3DS. "I'm in."

"We'll get busted," Wyatt said.

"Not if we're quick." This from Kip. He looked at his phone, then leaned back and shoved it into his front pants pocket. "Megan said they've got a lookout."

Megan. Gag me. Kip and his girlfriend were like a pair of neodymium magnets.

Kip saw me then and smiled. He got up and stepped over Alex's sleeping form, then Dan's. His foot whacked Dan's leg. Dan groaned and rolled over. Kip froze until he saw that Dan was still again, then continued across the room and crouched beside my sleeping bag. His shaggy dark hair hung in his eyes. "We're going to hang with some cheerleaders and the girls' team," Kip said. "The coaches are in a meeting. Come with us."

I looked at my iPhone. It was 1:36 a.m. "Dude, we have a game at eight." Why were the coaches still up? Why was anybody up?

Kip snorted. "Just Bishop. We can't win the tournament anymore, anyway. Come on. It'll be fun."

"We still need to play our best." Don't get me wrong, I liked girls as much as the next guy, but time and place, man. We were here to play ball. And if these knuckleheads messed up tomorrow's game—and my chance at an all-star trophy—I was going to kick some heads.

"Don't be lame," Kip said. "It's just until the coaches' meeting is over."

I said what I hoped would get rid of Kip. "Yeah, I'll catch

up with you. I'm not dressed."

"'Kay. Room 127." Kip made his way back to the door where Desh, Mike, Wyatt, and Chaz were now standing. They all took off down the hall, whispering and punching each other. Morons.

I rolled over and went back to sleep.

"Let's go! Let's go! Let's go!"

Light flooded the room. I jerked awake, recoiling at the brightness. I pushed up onto one elbow and shielded my eyes with my other hand. Everyone was scrambling around, putting on shoes. I checked the time on my iPhone—2:43 a.m.? That couldn't be right. There was no blaring alarm, though, so the place couldn't be on fire.

"Garmond. Shoes. Now." Coach Van Buren, standing in the doorway, face flushed, eyes like *PoP* lasers ready to fire. He was ticked off. Great.

I rolled my body toward my backpack and grabbed my shoes. Beside me, Dan sat on top of his sleeping bag, looking half dead.

"What's up?" I whispered.

"Coach busted some of the guys for being in one of the girls' rooms. But no one will confess, so he's making us all run."

Those idiots.

"Move it," Coach yelled. "To the gym. Now!"

The guys scrambled out the door. I was still sitting on top of my sleeping bag, holding my shoes in my lap.

"Today, Garmond," Coach said.

I groaned and pushed to standing, still dizzy with sleep. I set one shoe on the floor and stepped into it, then stumbled to the door, stomping my bare foot into the thing, the laces trailing. I hugged the other shoe. "I was sleeping, Coach. I didn't—"

"Don't want to hear it, Garmond. Gym. Move."

One shoe on, one off, I jogged down the dark hallway and into the gymnasium. It was dark too, with only three lights buzzing overhead. I stepped into my other shoe and crouched to tie my laces. I shivered and rubbed the goosebumps on my arms, wishing I'd grabbed a shirt.

We lined up along the base line.

Coach strode into the gym, pacing back and forth in front of us at the free throw line, his eyes angry and glaring. "I am *appalled*. We represent a *Christian* school, for Pete's sake! And we're here to play ball, not screw around with cheerleaders. Killers. Go."

Killers: Coach's favorite torture device. I began to run. To the free throw line and back to the baseline.

"Cheerleaders are here to *cheer* for you," Coach said. "To encourage the crowd to *cheer* for you. Which should help you play better. Frankly, I could care less if they're here or not. And once Principal McKaffey gets wind of this, they might not be here ever again. You're lucky I don't make you all sleep in the parking lot. Is that clear?"

The gym was silent but for the sound of sneakers plodding and squeaking over the floor. Baseline to half court and back, then out to the far free throw line and back.

"Is. That. Clear?" Coach yelled.

"Yes, Coach," we replied, a monotone dirge.

"I don't know whose bright idea it was to *pretend* to attack some poor girl, but I'll tell you this: Rape is not funny. It's not something to pretend or threaten or joke about. It's a crime, and only lowlife scum mess around with it. Is that clear?"

"Yes, Coach," the guys said.

My eyes bulged as I headed to the opposite baseline. I glanced at Kip's back, in front on my left. What had those morons done?

"If I ever hear one of you say the word *rape* again, you're off the team. Is that clear?"

"Yes, Coach."

"And I don't want to see any of you so much as look at a cheerleader for the rest of this trip. Is *that* clear?"

"Yes, Coach."

When I finished my killer, I ran into the mats that were hanging on the baseline wall. My side ached. I panted, walking it off in little circles while the rest of the team finished. As usual, we were waiting for Desh. By the time the *slowest runner who ever lived* crossed the baseline, my heart rate had slowed. I glanced at Kip again, wondering what had happened, knowing he'd tell me later.

"Let's go again," Coach said, pointing to the other end of the gym.

I stifled a groan and jogged out to the free throw line.

Coach made us run for a half hour. Desh fell over long before that, and Coach let him sit. Kip wanted to shower when we were done, but Coach said he may as well smell like scum if he was going to act like scum. Touché. I'd never seen the man so angry. Not even when Mike made that lay-up on the wrong end of the court to win the game for Culver City Christian last week.

No one talked about what had happened—not then, not in the morning when we got ready to play, not when we lost our other games, and not when I *didn't* get a trophy because the guys were all too tired to catch my passes. But on the bus ride home that night, it all came out. Coach segregated us: Cheerleaders and the girls' basketball team in the front of the bus, guys in the back, coaches in the middle. Chaz and Desh were in the back right seat, Mike and Wyatt were in front of them. Kip and Dan had the left back seat, and I had a seat to myself in front of Kip.

"We were playing spin the lotion bottle," Chaz said when I asked for the whole story. He was a pretty-boy surfer with bleached hair, who was so tan he looked Polynesian.

"Wow. How very junior high of you," I said.

"You're just jealous," Desh said. "It was worth the killers."

"Like you can talk, fool," Kip said. "You only ran two before you passed out."

"I have a low metabolism." Desh. A guy more suited for heavyweight wrestling than basketball, a guy with no neck who shaved his head bald on purpose and had a face that looked like he'd gotten hit by a bus. *That* was Desh.

"*Anyway* . . ." Chaz glared at Desh then turned back to me, his feet in the aisle. "It was Desh's turn, but the bottle pointed to this girl who wasn't playing. I don't know her name."

"Cute little freshman thing," Kip said. "I think she's from Pilot Point High."

"Wait. The PPH cheerleaders were there?" I asked. "I thought it was just girls from our school."

"We were all in the PPH cheerleaders' room," Kip said. "Megan's cousin invited everyone."

Jasmine. The girl Kip and Megan kept trying to set me up

with even though she already had a boyfriend.

"Get back to the story," Chaz said.

"Okay, so this girl was reading a *Bible* with a flashlight." Desh honked his obnoxious laugh.

"There's nothing wrong with reading a Bible," Dan said, glaring at Desh.

"Shut up," Desh said, standing up in the seat he shared with Chaz.

Chaz pushed him back. "So the girls say to spin again."

Desh slapped the top of Mike's seat. "But I said, 'No way. The lotion bottle has spoken.'" His eyes were wild and borderline psychotic as he relived the moment in his mind.

I wrinkled my nose. Desh was a freak.

"And the moron went over and told her she *had* to kiss him," Kip said. "And she told him to get lost, of course, because he's a creeper."

"She was breaking the rules of the game," Desh said.

"Then the creeper grabbed her," Kip said.

Desh lifted his hands. "I was *just* joking."

"He was," Kip said, "but it freaked her out, so she kicked him in the—"

"Nailed him!" Chaz said.

"I saw red, man." Desh shook his head in slow motion. "So I thought I'd give her a little scare, you know? Payback for dissing the Desh in public."

I glanced at Dan, not sure I wanted to hear the rest.

"Chaz ran over and started to chant," Kip said. "You know, the now-forbidden word."

"*I* didn't say it," Chaz said. "It was Mike. Then a bunch of us joined in."

"And some of the girls flipped and went and got their

coaches," Kip said.

"It was a joke!" Desh said again. "We were just messing around."

Wow. "You guys are sick," I said. "Keep it up and they'll reopen Alcatraz just for you people."

Desh guffawed as if I'd meant that as a compliment. I shook my head and enjoyed a moment of silent appreciation for the poor cheerleader who'd been brave enough to take on Desh. And I wondered yet again why I was hanging around with these morons.

● ● ●

Monday, as Gabe and I made our way through the lunch line, I couldn't help thinking about how life was ticking me off lately. Here was why:

1. The torture dream with Anya. But I didn't really want to think about that.
2. The whole thing with my mom. I'd managed to learn her real name—Lisa Wright, which meant my real name was Jonas Wright—but I still couldn't figure out what had really happened when she'd been killed.
3. I'd struck out big time when I'd tried to kiss Beth. Now she hated me. And she'd practically cheated to beat me in our finals match at the Regional LCT—League Combat Training—event. So now I despised her right back, but I couldn't stop thinking about her. Stupid brain, anyway.
4. Kip and Megan had taken their relationship to the schmoopie level, adding nauseating baby talk to their endless bouts of PDA. Which made my having struck out

with Beth all the more painful.

5. Gabe had picked me to be his sympathetic listener as he went on and on about how he'd lost Isabel to Nick, a task for which I was totally unqualified. Besides, I knew Isabel was on a surveillance mission to follow Nick. So her "dating" him was a total sham. But I wasn't supposed to know, so I couldn't tell Gabe. And there you have the hardest part of being a spy: keeping your big mouth shut.

6. I'd risked my life to set a trap for Gardener—one of my former bodyguards—who turned out to be working for the baddies. But the traitor wasn't talking, and Prière kept threatening to relocate me, give me a new name and fake parents to keep me safe. But I didn't want to move. I wanted to stay here and play basketball and earn a college scholarship. Witness protection programs were *not* going to help that dream become a reality. Besides, Kimbal and Sasquatch were still following me around everywhere, though I did ask Sasquatch to stop tailing me into the bathrooms. I mean, come on.

7. In three weeks we'd be playing basketball regionals, and we truly had a shot at making it to state. But my team was constantly risking our success with their stupidity. I mean, couldn't they wait until the season ended to break the law? *I* could.

8. And to make it all worse, today's lunch was the Pilot Point Christian School cafeteria's version of beef stroganoff. So nasty.

Gabe and I were the first to arrive at the table formally designated for the basketball team. About this time last year the churchers I'd met in the Mission League had invaded our territory, completely destroying PPCS lunch table hierarchy. But Gabe still looked out of place. I mean, at six foot four, I was by far the tallest guy on the team. The other guys were big too—except Chaz, who was only five ten. Gabe was maybe five eight. He had short, ringlet curls, braces, and wore black Buddy Holly glasses.

"There they are," Gabe said, his head turning slowly to follow pretty boy Nick Muren and the goddess Isabel Rodriguez as they headed for one of the cozy round tables on the perimeter of the cafeteria where couples liked to sit and *not* eat. The only reason Kip and Megan didn't sit over there was because Kip liked to brag.

"Get over it," I said, choking down a glob of grisly fake-steak. Smooth, I know. But I had my own problems.

Gabe released a sigh that could fill a balloon. "I'm trying."

And he was. The guy was practically a saint. Gabe's intense jealousy over Isabel "dating" Nick was a new phase in his life: self-indulgence. I couldn't blame him. I'd once worshipped the Cuban goddess *Ee-sabel* myself, but I'd backed off when I'd realized that Gabe had a thing for her.

"It won't last," I said. "Nick can't hide his true self forever. She'll see his dark side eventually." Or the mission would end. As long as Nick was destroyed, either worked for me.

Kip and Megan arrived then. Kip held both their trays, which allowed Megan to keep her hand in his back pocket. I know, I know. TMI.

"Dude, why haven't you signed up for camp yet?" Kip asked me, shaking his hair out of his eyes. "Coach said you're the only one who hasn't. What's the deal?"

Basketball camp. Add that to my list of drama. The deal was: I couldn't go. Not if I was going to Japan with The

Mission League. Worlds were colliding in a big way. Again. And I hadn't broken it to the team yet. Or Coach. I just didn't know how.

"Is basketball camp this summer?" Gabe asked.

"All summer," Kip said. "Why?"

"Did you see the Lakers game yesterday?" I asked in a desperate attempt to change the subject before Gabe spilled the beans.

But Kip was on to me. He held his hand in front of my face. "Gabe?"

Gabe picked at his braces. "Spencer is going to Japan."

"*Japan?*" Kip dropped his hand to the table, slapping the surface. "Are you kidding me?"

"Thanks a lot," I said to Gabe, then shoveled a forkful of fake-steak into my mouth.

"Dude, Coach is going to flip," Kip said.

I wanted to say, "Tell me about it," but I just gnawed on the fake steak and avoided Kip's glare.

"I'll still see you this summer, right?" Megan asked Kip.

Her pouty tone distracted my best friend from me. He looked at her, and his eyes lost focus. "Every night, girl."

"Oh, baby." She grabbed Kip's ears and pulled his lips to hers as if he was on today's lunch menu and not the stroganoff.

Gag. I pried my eyes from the PDA. Why were there never any teachers around when Kip and Megan got going?

Arianna Sloan arrived then, smelling of herbal tea and wearing a floor-length navy blue skirt that looked like a feather duster. She was the only girl in school who got away with a modified school uniform because Principal McKaffey had given her special permission when she'd protested the immodesty of the knee-length skirt.

True story.

Her unibrow sank as she frowned at Kip and Megan, who were still making out. "How are you today, Megan?" she asked, arranging her lunch on the table.

Megan ran her hands up into Kip's hair and grabbed two fistfuls, somehow seeming to pull him closer to her, though it already looked like she was eating his face.

Arianna tried again. "Megan, did you get all the notes down in Mr. Olson's class?"

Megan emitted a soft hum.

"Hey, Spencer," Gabe said, "my sister started basketball."

I was glad for a reason to look away from the Kip-Megan creature. Gabe's sisters were in middle school, if I remembered right. Mary was the athlete. "She any good?"

"I don't know. I guess. She plays a lot."

"What position?"

Gabe winced. "Uh . . . she dribbles the ball down the court like you."

"She's point guard?" Mary's stock rose a few points in my mind.

"Spencer, you should volunteer to ref or coach an elementary school team," Arianna said. "It would be the perfect way for you to serve the community."

"Mary's in seventh grade," Gabe told Arianna. "And this is the regular school season."

"I know," Arianna said. "But the elementary schools need volunteers for their Little Dribblers program."

"I don't have time to volunteer for squat," I said. "Do you know how busy I am?" Between LCT and basketball practices, my own personal workouts, and my investigation into my mom's death, I could just about pass for a zombie on *The*

Walking Dead.

"You need to rely on others more, Spencer," Arianna said. "My word for this year is 'listen.' And you inspired it."

"Is that a fact?" I didn't want to hear how I'd inspired such a thing, but I knew Arianna would tell me anyway.

"You said I nagged people, so I'm trying to listen this year, and not talk so much, so I can hear the needs of those around me. What I'm hearing from you is that you're exhausted."

"Amazing deduction, Sherlock. And you think coaching a kids' basketball team will help me relax?"

"Forget I said it." Arianna removed an apple from her lunch bag and polished it on her skirt. "I'm just saying, we're your friends. Let us help. You can't do everything on your own. The Bible says two are better than one. Pity anyone who falls and has no one to help him."

"I'm not going to fall," I said, then I threw a quote back at Arianna. "'The weak die out and the strong survive.'" I'd heard it in English class. I couldn't remember what from, but it was true. I was a survivor. And it felt good to one-up her quote too.

"'Arrogance does not see itself,'" Gabe said, sounding like his dad.

Clearly I was outmatched. "Why are you people picking on me? Basketball is almost over, then we'll be off to Japan where I won't have basketball *or* LCT practice."

"So you're really going to Japan with the missionaries instead of summer camp and conditioning. Again?" Kip asked.

I turned to face him. "I'm sorry, are you speaking to me? I hadn't realized you'd come up for air."

Kip smirked. "Jealous much?"

Totally. Desperately. Painfully. "Puh-lease."

REPORT NUMBER: 2

REPORT TITLE: I Get a Warning, a Kiss, and a Punch in the Face
SUBMITTED BY: Agent-in-Training Spencer Garmond
LOCATION: Pilot Point Christian School, Pilot Point,
California, USA
DATE AND TIME: Monday, March 9, 5:06 p.m.

DESH'S WHOLE "ATTACK THE CHEERLEADER" incident had me worried that hanging with the guys just might get me arrested. I'd been arrested twice before in middle school. It wasn't fun. And getting arrested now would kill the rest of my basketball season and maybe ruin my chance at a college scholarship.

I couldn't risk that until the season was over, so I decided to spend some time with Gabe. Grandma would be so pleased.

Practice was early this week and ended about the same time as afternoon Mission League. I had LCT at six, so when basketball practice was over, I didn't bother changing out of my workout clothes. I just put on my old Lakers cap and headed outside to meet Gabe and his mom in front of the school. Sasquatch, as always, was right behind me.

I had bodyguards because of some old prophecy. International had this mysterious "profile match" narrowed down to me and fourteen other guys around the world. But because of Anya Vseveloda's odd interest in me in Moscow, Prière was convinced I was the match.

Too bad no one would tell me what this *match* was supposed to do.

Kimbal's sedan was idling out front, right behind the Stopplecamps' silver Honda minivan.

"I'm going to Gabe's," I told my bodyguard as he headed for the black car. Sasquatch flashed me a thumbs up. The man had a sweet European accent, but I could rarely get him to talk.

Kerri rolled down the passenger window of the minivan and waved me over. Gabe was in the driver's seat. "Right here, Spencer!"

Like I could miss them. Kerri Stopplecamp, Gabe's mom and Mr. S's wife. Picture a kindergarten teacher who was always smiling and had the kind of voice that could coax a cat out of a tree. And no, she didn't teach kindergarten. That was just her natural charm.

Gabe and his sisters all had their mom's curly dark hair. Mr. S was 100 percent bald.

I climbed into the middle row of the minivan. "Wait. Gabe is driving?" I clutched the back of the passenger's seat with mock fear.

"Gabriel is an excellent driver," Kerri said, as Gabe steered the van out of the school lot. "He's taking Defensive Driving."

The Mission League taught several upper division courses for agents-in-training who were in good standing. Sophomores were eligible for LCT, which I had somewhat mastered, and juniors were eligible for Defensive Driving. I was taking Driver's Ed in school, but I was starting to doubt that Grandma would ever let me drive anywhere.

Gabe's mom was right, of course: The Boy Scout was an excellent driver and would soon be learning to drive backward with one eye blindfolded. The lucky dog.

The city of Pilot Point had four classes of housing. Rich people like Kip and Nick lived up on Snob Hill. The upper middle class lived along the base of Snob Hill in what people called First Base. In the Neighborhood, the middle class owned old houses that had been there since the fifties and before. And the apartments in downtown and near the train tracks were referred to as either Downtown or Ghettoside, in mockery of the Meadowside Apartment complex.

Gabe's house was on Rose Street just north of Eighth, which put it in First Base. The house reflected that. It was big—not a mansion like Kip's or Nick's, but twice the size of Grandma's two-bedroom in the Neighborhood. It had a big, grassy front yard, neatly mowed, with thick flowerbeds lining the house front. Stakes with pink and yellow Easter eggs had been stabbed into the grass. More colorful eggs adorned the front door and windows too, some of them exclaiming "Happy Easter" and "He is Risen."

Inside, the place smelled like cookies and something meaty. Most everything was decorated in brown or green. Dark wood cabinets in the kitchen, dark wood floor, green counters. Green carpet in the living room, brown leather sofa and matching recliners. Mr. S sat at the baby grand piano in the corner, tinkling away at a worship piece. He smiled as we passed by, never missing a note.

I followed Gabe down a short hallway covered with the same thick green carpet. Family photos lined the walls with hundreds of happy Stopplecamp faces. No wall of fame in this house.

Gabe pushed open the door on the left at the end of the hall. "The Mini Ms will be home soon so we'd better stay in here."

"Mini Ms?"

"My sisters."

"Right." Mary and Martha, Gabe's identical twin sisters, had gone with us to Moscow, though I'd hardly seen them, since Kerri always segregated them from us.

Gabe's room was twice the size of mine and spotless. A fluffy dark blue blanket covered his bed. An acoustic guitar sat in a metal stand next to the door. The walls were covered with posters of Christian bands. Witness, Doxology, Hedge, and Rockhouse stared at me, convicting me of the not-so-spiritual playlists on *My Precious* iPhone.

Gabe picked up his guitar and sat on his bed, strumming softly. "I'm starting a band. I asked Isabel to sing back-up, but she's too busy." He plucked out a tune on his guitar, staring across the room, eyes glassy behind his Buddy Holly frames. "We practically spent the whole summer singing together, but I hardly see her anymore. She's constantly with *Neek*."

I laughed at Gabe's impersonation of Isabel's accent. Maybe I should tell him Isabel was on a mission to follow Nick. Why was that mission still going, anyway? We'd found the traitor *and* caught Blaine and Tito. What else was Isabel supposed to be doing? I'd have to ask her.

Gabe set his guitar back in its stand. "Want to see my spy cam?"

"Sure."

Gabe went to his closet and pulled out a silver briefcase and a silver R/C car with black rubber wheels. The car looked like a boxy Volkswagen beetle with a web cam attached to the top. Mr. S had given us a special project. We had to pick one from a list he'd handed out. I'd picked hacking into Mr. S's home computer, which, sadly, had revealed no secret files about me or my parents. The remote controlled spy robot camera, the project Gabe had picked, was the most complicated one on the list.

Gabe handed me the remote control and set the car on the floor. "Try it."

I drove the car around the room and under Gabe's bed. I backed it out and picked it up. "It weighs a ton!"

"I welded it out of sheet metal. Has to be sturdy."

"You record anything yet?"

"Nah. Just watching my family." Gabe set the briefcase on his bed and opened it. "This took the longest to build."

Inside the case were a six-inch monitor and a set of controls. The screen flickered once, and then a black and white image of Gabe's floor appeared.

I squatted down and wiggled two fingers in front of the car's camera. My fingers appeared on the screen. "That's sweet!"

Gabe jumped up and flashed his wide, metal grin. "I've got an idea. Stay here."

He grabbed the car and left. I watched on the monitor as the hall floor jerked past. The picture twirled about, then stopped on another rug floor. Gabe's hands tilted the camera until it had a wide view of two twin beds at the far end of the room. A piece of fabric fell over the camera, dousing the picture, then shifted until the picture came back.

Gabe returned and shut his door behind him. "I hid the car under a shirt from their laundry basket, but it's peeking out just barely. Let's wait for them to come in."

I looked back at the empty room on the monitor. My gaze fell on a basketball under one of the beds. "Whose ball?"

"Mary's. I told you she was on the team."

Right. Point guard.

"Hey, my band needs a bass player," Gabe said. "Want to learn?"

"Uh, no." I had enough on my plate without getting talked into joining some band. I barely had enough rhythm to dance—no way could I make music.

Footsteps thumped in the hallway.

"Here we go." Gabe hit record just as Mary and Martha entered their room.

The camera's angle distorted their bodies. Big feet tapered into tiny heads. I crouched over the screen and grinned at how funny they looked.

One of the girls, wearing a hoodie and jeans, sat at a desk at the end of one bed and opened a book. The other, dressed in shorts and a tank top, leapt onto the second bed. She jumped up and down a few times, bounced into a sitting position, then bounced to her back. She propped her feet against the wall, her head hanging off the side of the bed, black sproingy Stopplecamp curls sweeping the floor.

"What do you think they're doing?" she asked, barely audible.

Gabe turned up the volume.

"I try not to think about what Gabe does in his room," the studying one said.

"I'd bet Gabe's showing off on his guitar, but I don't hear any music."

Gabe grinned at me and played the air guitar.

"Which one's which?" I whispered.

Gabe tapped the upside down girl. "Mary." Then he tapped the studying girl. "Martha."

"How old are they again?"

"Thirteen. Seventh grade."

Mary let her arms fall over her head until they touched the floor. She kicked off the wall, doing a backbend of sorts, and landed sitting on the other bed.

I raised my eyebrows. "She'd pick up LCT in no time."

Gabe stuck out his tongue and gagged. "Don't encourage her. She already thinks she's an agent-in-training, and she's not even supposed to know the Mission League exists."

Mary stretched out on her stomach on Martha's bed and propped her chin on her hands. "Think I should tell him?"

Martha continued to stare at her book. "Think I should tell Mom you're wearing makeup?"

"It's just lip gloss. She won't care so long as I'm home."

"It's red."

"Dad says I'm gifted."

Martha looked up from her book. "Everyone is gifted in some way, Mary."

"Shouldn't he know I dreamed about him, though? You'd want to know if it was about you."

Martha turned in her chair. "*Did* you dream about me?"

Mary picked up her basketball and spun it in her hands. "No."

Martha spun back to face her homework. "I'd do what Dad says if I were you."

"I've dreamed about him lots, you know."

"Probably because you're obsessed."

"Only some dreams express hidden desires. Mine are prerogative"

"*Precognitive* You've been reading that book again. Dad told you not to."

"I haven't, I just remembered what it said." Mary sighed loud and dreamy-like. "I just couldn't stand it if anything happened to Spencer and I could've prevented it. He's so cute."

I bolted upright, frowning.

Gabe switched off the camera.

"Hey." I switched it back on.

"Spencer . . ." Gabe reached for the switch again, but I put my hand over it.

"Just a minute," I said.

"Watch me make this shot." Mary lifted the basketball over her head and shot it at the laundry basket. Straight at the camera.

The screams came first. Then faces staring into the camera. Then the pounding footsteps.

Gabe sucked in a sharp breath. "Uh, oh."

I raced out the door and collided with Mary in the hallway, causing her to drop the spy car.

"*Mary!*" Gabe crouched down to rescue the car and carried it back into his room.

Mary stared up at me, wild springy curls framing her face. I swear the girl had grown a head taller since last summer. She had to be five feet tall now. "I like your hat," she said.

"Thanks." I recalled the entry I'd seen in Prière's intercession journal about one of Mr. S's daughters being gifted in prophecy. "You had a dream about me?" I bent down and tried to look into her eyes, but she twisted away to avoid eye contact.

Martha pushed between us and into Gabe's room. "Gabriel Stopplecamp, I can't believe you spied on us with that stupid car. I'm telling Mom!" She ran back into the hall toward the living room. "*Mom!*"

"Martha, wait!" Gabe ducked between me and Mary to chase after Martha.

"Hey." I grabbed Mary's shoulder and pushed her against the wall so she'd look at me.

She stared at my hand. Her wide-eyed gaze traveled from my hand and up my arm until her eyes met mine.

"Sorry." I let go. "Did you really dream about me?"

She pursed her lips, slowly rubbing them together. They were indeed dark red. "Dad said not to tell you."

Her voice was soft, and I leaned closer to hear better. "Tell me what?"

Her eyes stared into mine, big and brown and never blinking. Her face was no longer flushed, and she leaned toward me until her lips were by my ear. She smelled like strawberry candy and her curls tickled my face.

"It's just . . . don't go to Japan," she whispered. "Please?" Then she planted a hard kiss on my cheek, fled into her room, and slammed the door.

What on earth?

I stood alone in the hallway. My gaze flicked to a family portrait on the wall. Mr. S smiled at me, sending a flash of guilt over my body. I shook my head at the man in the frame, as if to plead my innocence. I hadn't done anything wrong. *She* kissed *me*.

Gabe and Martha's raised voices drifted from the living

room. I couldn't make anything out, but they were yelling. I suddenly wanted to leave. Too much drama here.

I snagged my backpack from Gabe's room and made my way into the living room. A rich marinara and garlic smell floated from the kitchen. My stomach growled.

Gabe stood in front of the couch, spy car tucked under one arm, his other arm perched on his hip. Martha sat between Kerri and Mr. S on the couch, arms folded, tears streaking down her face.

"He's apologized, Martha. Can you forgive—" Mr. S looked at me and stopped talking.

I breathed in through my nose, savoring the spaghetti-lasagna smell. "I'm going to walk down to C Camp. Sorry about the spy car thing."

"No." Gabe set the car on the coffee table. "It wasn't your fault. It was my idea."

"Spencer, you're welcome to stay," Kerri said. "We're having manicotti for dinner."

Drool. "Thanks, but I've got LCT practice at six, so . . ." I readjusted my Lakers cap and started toward the front door.

Gabe called after me. "What'd she do?"

I paused but wasn't about to tell him his little sister had kissed me, not with his parents sitting there.

"She said something, I know she did." Gabe's footsteps pounded through the house. Distant banging and Gabe's voice. "Open up, Mary!"

I seized the moment of chaos and slipped away. Outside, I pulled on my backpack and sprinted down the street, past Kimbal's sedan. It didn't start right away, but I heard it peel out when I rounded the end of the block.

I had hoped that hanging with Gabe would keep me out of

trouble, but this Mary drama was a whole new kind of trouble for me. I felt like I was on an episode of *Tween Diaries*.

I sprinted all the way to C Camp, the nondescript office building on 95 Juniper where Boss Schwarz taught League Combat Training to juvenile agents. Russ, the guy who guarded the front, saw me coming and opened the door.

"Thanks, Russ," I said, not stopping as I ran inside the air conditioned building.

I went straight into the locker room and shut my backpack in a locker. Then I walked through the locker room doors, past the room with the hot tubs—where Mario, C Camp's physical therapist, helped people who got hurt—and into the main room. The place was pretty much an athletic club, but instead of stair climbers and exercise bikes, there was an open floor covered in mats. Punching bags and weight benches were all on the left wall.

I was early, so I headed for the weights to get my mind off things. My one-rep max was 235—my personal best was 190 for eight reps—but I was tired and didn't have a spotter, so I put on 180 pounds. I did twelve reps and set the bar in the catchers to rest.

My mind wouldn't shut up. Don't go to Japan? The trip was just over a couple of months away. What could Mary have possibly dreamed that would make her say such a thing?

I grabbed the bar again, planted my feet, and started lifting.

"Hey, Tiger. Been wanting to talk to you."

I jumped and almost dropped 180 pounds on my neck. Beth peeked over the bar from above me, her head upside down, her dimples digging in with her smirk. Her ponytail hung to one side of her face, the ends curling around her neck and chin.

Why'd she have to be so cute?

I focused on the ceiling and finished my twelve, just to show off, then set the bar in the catchers. Good thing I hadn't started at 190. If I'd gotten stuck and had to do the roll of shame in front of Beth . . . Or worse, had to ask her for last-minute spotting help? Oh, that would've stunk.

I sat up and swung one leg over the bench. "What's up?"

She walked around the bench and leaned close. Beth had a thing for tough-girl T-shirts. Today hers read: Self-Saving Princess. She rubbed her finger down my cheek. "Who you been kissing?"

My hand shot to the place where Mary had kissed me. I wiped my cheek and looked at my palm. A smear of red was streaked across it. Oh . . . figs and jam-o-rama. Had Mr. S seen that? Had Gabe?

Beth rolled her eyes. "Looks like I made the right choice with you, player."

Yeah, that was me, all right. Scoring with the middle school girls. "I'm *not* a player."

"Sure."

I didn't have to take this. I stood so I could look down on her, hoping my height was just a little bit intimidating. "What do you want?"

She backed up a step. "To apologize. I've been thinking about it and . . . Truth is, I got scared. At District. I was worried you'd beat me, so . . ." She shrugged. "I've never done that in a match before. I'd do it again, you know, to save my life, but in competition . . ." She shook her head. "You were right. It was a low blow."

"Thank you." It did nothing to repair my loss of dignity, but at least she'd admitted it. That was pretty cool.

"You want to partner up today?" she asked me.

Fight her again? "I don't know."

"Come on." She kicked the toe of my shoe. "You scared?"

"No." A little.

"Well then?"

"Fine." I was such a sucker.

"Why wait for class?" Beth said. "Let's spar now."

"Okay." I followed her to the mats, ignoring the nagging sensation that I'd regret this later. I put in a mouthpiece and took off my Lakers cap, but Beth didn't like to spar with pads or gloves outside of class. She said it made people lazy.

Beth bounced and circled me. I turned with her. She got in a few good strikes. So did I. But when she just missed my face and her arm grazed my cheek, the skin-to-skin contact sucked me away. A sudden dizziness spun the room. My arms dropped to my sides.

I scramble over a broken chair in a weird-looking house. The floors are made of straw mats. Beth and an Asian guy are going at it with arms, fists, and feet. The sound of every hit makes me flinch.

A fist cracked against my jaw. I sank to my knees, back at C Camp with Beth, apparently getting my butt kicked.

"Spencer!"

My face throbbed. I tasted blood. Beth gripped my wrists and pulled. I jerked away and scrambled backward on my hands and feet in a crab walk. I didn't want her touching me if it meant another glimpse.

Beth got up and came after me. "Hey. It's okay, Tiger. It's me, Beth." She snapped her fingers in front of my face, like I was having some kind of psychotic episode. "You there?"

34

"I'm fine." I spit out my mouth guard and licked blood from my lip.

"You saw something, didn't you? Like the dream you had in Russia? Tell me."

I shook my head. "Prière said—"

"It involved me, didn't it? I know they can be like that 'cause my dad gets them. Glimpses, right?"

She sat down beside me. Her eyes studied mine. My stomach lurched. I didn't want to like her anymore. I didn't. Why was I so pathetic?

"Come on, spill it," she said.

I swallowed, needed a drink. "A fight in . . . in Japan, I think." But I was only guessing because of the Asian guy and the straw mats and since Japan was where we were headed that summer.

"What kind of fight?" Beth asked. "Was I in it? Were you?"

"Karate, I think. Just you and some Asian guy." But I shouldn't have said that. Prière would flip out. Why couldn't I say no to Beth? It wasn't fair: The girl made me weak.

"Be right back." I cleaned myself up in the locker room, making sure to get off all Mary's lipstick too. By the time I came out again, people were starting to arrive for LCT. Time to step it up. If there was going to be karate trouble in Japan, I'd be ready.

League Combat Training was the Mission League's combined martial arts. It had two goals: Subdue without harm and/or protect yourself enough to escape. The biggest thing to remember was *the strike points*. The system taught us to number strikes based on where they came from. This could help us stay calm during an attack, remove the emotional factor.

Numbers one and two were high hits from the left or right. Threes and fours came from the sides. Five was anything in the middle from the face to the groin. Six was straight down on the head. Seven and eight were low hits from the ground. A nine, between the legs. Most attacks were one through five. Beth had taught all this to me with a stick-man drawing.

I fought like a machine for the rest of the hour. When it came time to pair up, Beth grabbed a pair of focus mitts, and I delivered my offensive strikes in the same mechanical rhythm, hitting so hard she stumbled back a few times.

She kept trying to talk about my glimpse, to get more information out of me, but I was done falling for the feminine charms of Beth Watkins. Hopefully.

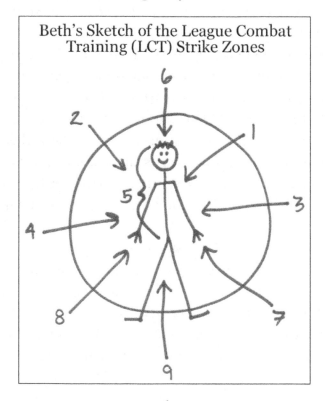

Beth's Sketch of the League Combat Training (LCT) Strike Zones

REPORT NUMBER: 3

REPORT TITLE: An NCAA College Coach Asks About Me
SUBMITTED BY: Agent-in-Training Spencer Garmond
LOCATION: Pilot Point Christian School Gym, Pilot Point,
California, USA
DATE AND TIME: Saturday, March 21, 7:00 p.m.

THE NEXT THREE WEEKS WERE INTENSE, despite one of them being spring break. First we won our quarterfinal game against Mission Prep, 59–56. Then on Tuesday night we beat Renaissance Academy 75–65. That put us up against Rock Academy at home. Winner would go to state.

The entire school and half the town showed up for the Regional Finals. By the end of the first quarter, Rock Academy had a three-point lead. They were scrappy as usual but on their best behavior. The point guard hadn't scratched me even once.

Their defense was tight, though, and so was ours. Neither team reached double figures until the second quarter. We took the lead for a while, but they took it back before halftime.

Adam Davis, their shooting guard, was on fire. In the end, he scored only fifteen points in the game, but he'd shot only three-pointers. Hit all five.

Sadly, they beat us, 42–38. We'd worked hard, but they'd always been a tough team. Won the So-Cal Regional Finals for the past five years. Won state twice. The cool thing? Their starting five were all seniors. Next year, I figured we'd take state. So I was okay that we hadn't won.

I was so full of it. I'd *really* wanted to go to the championship game.

When I came out of the locker room, a couple of reporters asked to talk to me, Desh, and Coach Van Buren. I'd talked to reporters before, so it wasn't all that surprising.

"Your team played well," the *L.A. Times* guy said to Coach.

"Thanks." Coach gripped my shoulder and squeezed. "Can't say enough about these young men, how much they've grown. Knew it was going to be a street fight with Rock. But we went to work and did our best."

We totally had. "Davis and those back-to-back threes," I said. "They've got some nice players." Players I wouldn't be missing next year. Buh-bye.

"Yeah." Desh chortled. "Davis hurt us out there. Not even Garmond could keep up."

True that.

The reporter turned to me. "Spencer, eighteen points, five rebounds, seven assists, and four steals. Are you disappointed in the outcome of the game?"

"Sure," I said. "But we gave it our all. I mean, this isn't Hollywood, so you can't always have that Disney ending."

Though that would have been nice.

We also talked to the reporter for the *Pilot Point Leader*. I saw some ESPN guy talking to Rock Academy, but he didn't come talk to us. Ah, well. There was always next year. In fact, I bet we'd take state back-to-back in my junior and senior years. I kept thinking about that so I wouldn't have to think about the fact that we'd lost.

I gathered my stuff and waited for Kip, then he and I headed for the exit together.

In the lobby, Coach was waiting by the trophy case. "Garmond!" He grabbed my shoulder. "I just talked to a guy named Mick Gilbert. He's a recruiting coach at Fresno State. And he wanted to talk about you." Coach shook my shoulder and slapped my chest with his other hand.

Don't faint, man. Act cool. I looked around the lobby. "Is he gone?"

"Yeah, I told him you'd be right out, but he said it was against NCAA recruiting rules for him to meet you right now. Just so happens that his nephew plays for Rock Academy. That's why he was here."

Coach's words rang in my head. "Wait. There are rules?"

"He said he liked what he's seen from you this year and that he looked forward to watching where you'd take the team next season. He asked if you were looking to play college ball."

Yes, yes, yes, I was! "What did you say?"

"I told him you were."

Oh-kay. I nodded, not knowing what else to do. A coach. An NCAA coach had asked about me. But Fresno? Play for the Mountain West Conference? Still, I could do far worse coming from such a Podunk school. "So what should I do? Nothing?"

"I'm going to look into this," Coach said. "I've never had a D1 player before. But I'm not going to let you down. I'll get this figured out."

"Thanks, Coach." I wanted to add that he should see about talking to some schools in power conferences, but right then some reporter started talking to him, and he waved goodbye.

NCAA basketball. Could my dreams really come true? Would I *really* get to play D1 ball? Please say yes.

Kip and I went outside and Kip punched my arm. "You dog!"

I punched him back and couldn't stop grinning.

I'd *really* wanted to make the state game. But as I zombied my way around school on Monday, I realized I was glad basketball was over for a while. I'd exerted too much energy over the past five months and hadn't gotten enough sleep. I was beat. And sick. I hated being sick. I felt weak, like I was going to puke. Everything ached. My head was warm. I wanted to sleep for a month.

I marked Sasquatch in the hallway before Biology class. I'd nicknamed him Sasquatch because he was the hairiest man I'd ever seen and because I didn't know his real name. Prière hadn't replaced his partner, Gardener, after the arrest last December. So Sasquatch, my lone protector, roamed the halls of Pilot Point Christian School posing as a security guard. I put up my hand to wave, but he wasn't looking at me. He was talking to a girl. I slammed my locker and headed his way, curious.

I recognized the fluffy long skirt before I saw Arianna's face. Sasquatch had his wallet out. He handed Arianna some money and she hugged him.

What the Kobe Bryant was going on there?

I slipped into Biology class to wait for Arianna, eager to ask about the loan from Sasquatch. She entered the room and went straight to the shelf to collect our frog, which I'd named Kermit. She set the pan on our table, and the smell of the formaldehyde-soaked amphibian and the wax in the pan made me wish I'd stayed in bed.

But then I'd dream. And I didn't want to dream anymore.

I'd had that same one a dozen more times. The one where I was hanging from the ceiling and Anya was holding the knife. I'd logged an official report each time, but it had been three months since I'd last met with Prière. Maybe I should email him. Ask if the whole reoccurring dream thing was normal. Not that I'd admit it out loud, but it was freaking me out. I mean, I just really wanted to avoid the whole thing coming to life, you know?

"We need to remove the stomach," Arianna said.

"Miss Piggy is going to be mad at us." I held back Kermit's rubbery flesh with the needle-like probe and pushed a pin into the wax to get a better look at his guts. "Hey! So that's what Nick looks like on the inside."

Arianna pursed her lips but didn't look at me. "Once we remove the stomach, we need to cut it open and describe the contents."

"I think he eats whatever *bugs* him." I poked his stomach with the probe.

Arianna took the probe from my hand and pulled the tray toward her. "Don't be juvenile."

"But I am a juvenile. I like being juvenile." I lifted the pan and held it upright so that Kermit's face was looking at Arianna "Look, Kermit's *croaking* up at my hilarity. See his

41

smile?"

"Spencer! He's going to fall out!" She grabbed the pan.

I let go and she set the pan back on the table. "Have you been getting enough rest?" she asked me. "You have circles under your eyes."

"I'm tired. Might be getting a cold." Or dying of some kind of athletic plague.

"Well, I'm not a bit surprised. You're exhausted. Between basketball and LCT, it's a wonder you can stand." She reached out and grabbed my fist, which I'd been mindlessly pounding on my forearm. "And stop banging yourself up. It drives me mad!"

"I'm just trying to get strong." Besides teaching me some LCT, Beth had taught me body conditioning. Arianna thought it was self-abuse.

"Look in the mirror, Spencer. You're an ox. Plenty strong for a sixteen-year-old."

Maybe an average sixteen-year-old, but not a guy who was looking to play NCAA basketball in a power conference.

"Well, if you can stay out of mischief this summer, you should have a nice, relaxing time. That's just a hunch, of course."

Arianna's dad was an agent, so she knew more than most about Mission League stuff, like Gabe and Mary and Martha did. Wait. Arianna had said they'd moved here for her dad's new assignment. Could his assignment be me? "Is Sasquatch your dad?"

Her unibrow sank over her eyes. "Excuse me?"

"The guy in the hall. The *new security guard?*" I gave her the air quotes.

She blew out a breath, her cheeks flushed. "I don't know

what you—"

"It's okay." I couldn't believe this. I was right. No way, no way! "I won't tell anyone that he was assigned to guard me."

"Really, Spencer. You're making no sense at all." Her eyes fluttered and she tucked her hair behind her knobby ears.

I'd had enough lie detection lectures from Mr. S to know that Arianna was a big fat liar. "I saw him give you money in the hallway. And you *hugged* him."

She turned her gaze on me, eyes glossy, chin trembling. "You call him a sasquatch?"

I chuckled. "Just 'cause I didn't know his real name and he's a hairy dude." Which totally explained Arianna's unibrow. "I didn't mean it as an insult. Your dad is amazing, Arianna. You should have seen him take down this guy who was built like a sumo wrestler. I've never seen anything like that. Ever."

Her eyes widened. "Something happened?"

I waved it off. "Last fall, after homecoming. It was no big deal. Not with your dad there." I couldn't believe Sasquatch was Arianna's dad. Man!

Arianna lifted her chin and glanced at me. "Dad is really strong."

"That's an understatement." The dude was a beast.

"It's been hard for me, knowing my dad was in Moscow, knowing he'll be in Japan, and not being able to say anything if I see him."

"Wait. Your dad was in Moscow? I never saw him, even after . . ." I stabbed Kermit. "Hold on. That's why you know where we're going in Japan."

"Dad didn't say anything. But from what I've overheard, I think it will be tropical."

In Japan? "I thought it snowed there."

43

"In some places. But not in the summer. I think we're going somewhere more akin to Hawaii."

I wanted to mock her use of the word "akin," but Hawaii trumped it. "You're serious?"

"Please, keep your voice down, Spencer. If you say anything to anyone, I'll only deny it. And I'll never tell you any of my *theories* again."

"I won't tell. I promise." I was going to Japan-Hawaii. Sahweet. I fought a sudden urge to stand up and rock the Gangnam Style dance.

"Yes, well, let's get back to the stomach, shall we?" Arianna said.

"Oh, yes, of course." Had to keep this girl on my good side now that I knew who her padre was. I cleared my throat and sat up straight, but one look at Kermit and I couldn't help it. "You know . . . Kermit looks a little big to fit in someone's throat, don't you think?"

• • •

After lunch, Kip, Megan, and I all had Algebra II. We went to their lockers first, then mine. I kept my locker about as tidy as my bedroom, so of course I couldn't find squat. While I searched for my textbook, Kip and Megan started making out against my neighbor's locker.

"Room for the Bible, Kip," Coach Van Buren said from behind me.

Kip and Megan peeled themselves apart like two strips of Velcro.

"Garmond." Coach's familiar grip pressed down on my left shoulder. "Been looking for you all day. Can I talk to you for a minute?"

"Yeah, we'll see you in class." Kip took Megan's hand, and they walked away.

I pushed up to my feet but left my locker open. Still needed to find that book.

"I've been reading up on the NCAA rules," Coach said. "We need to get you registered for the NCAA Clearinghouse. It's the program that gets you eligible to be recruited by schools. I'll wait until the school year is over to get your transcripts sent in. But you're going to need to take your SATs early."

"Now?"

"Sometime this fall is fine. That way, if you do poorly, you'll have time to retake them."

"Okay, I can do that." Ugh. Those tests did *not* sound fun.

Coach slapped my back. "Good. So we'll see you at conditioning and summer camp, right?"

"Uh . . ." Time to face the music. "When I'm back, sure. But I'm going to Japan on a mission trip, remember?" As if Coach could remember something I never told him . . .

Coach's face flushed. "Garmond, you want to play college ball. You need to get your priorities straight."

Hold up. "My priorities are fine."

"Really? Well, coaches can't see you play if you're not on the team."

Whoa. "Why wouldn't I be on the team, Coach?"

He looked down the hall and sighed. "I didn't mean that. You'll be on the team, sure. But if you miss camp, you'll be behind."

"I'll practice every chance I get. I promise."

"Not good enough. Most of the top NCAA prospects play AAU ball."

"But you hate AAU." Plus it cost a fortune that my Grandma didn't have.

"I'm trying to help you, kid. I believe you've got the talent to play Division 1 ball, but you've got to work with me here."

I set my jaw. What if he was right? What if going to Japan messed up my chances of getting a scholarship? It was only eight weeks, though. "Coach, I'm sorry, but . . . This mission trip. This is something I have to do." I couldn't very well add that I kept having prophecies about swimming with an Asian girl. So I left it at that.

"Okay, you do what you have to do. But you haven't left the country yet. There's still time to make the right choice." Coach walked away just as the bell rang, leaving me alone in the hallway with no pass to class.

I blew out a long breath. That was *so* unfair. There would still be lots of time to talk to coaches when I got back from Japan. And I still had my junior and senior year. Coach had to be messing with me. Bluffing.

I hoped.

• • •

Days and weeks rolled by, and it was suddenly the end of April. One month until we left for our mysterious tropical adventure, and time for new recruits to join The Mission League. Friday morning, Mr. S told us he'd have the names of the new recruits written on the whiteboard when we got to Room 401 that afternoon. We were supposed to pray for them and Prière and whoever else was involved in the whole recruitment thing.

I was late getting to class that afternoon because Coach

cornered me outside the gym and took me on another guilt trip—this one so big I almost had jet lag by the time he walked away.

When I walked through the door to Room 401, no one was praying. Everyone was talking. No sign of Mr. S, either. Maybe he was off riding in Kimbal's squad car like last year. I glanced at the whiteboard and read the three names.

Alpha—Wally Parks
Alpha—Grace Thomas
Diakonos—Lukas Rodriguez

"We get *two* noobs on Alpha?" I said. "Sweet!" That would finally even things up. Bummer about Lukas being on Diakonos, though. I'd met Isabel's little brother only twice, but the kid was fearless. Took down the Incredible Tattooed Hulk with a can of hairspray.

I sat at the Alpha table between Gabe and Jensina. I put my backpack on the chair beside me and dug out my Lakers cap. We weren't allowed to wear hats in school, so I always put it on the first chance I got after school.

Jensina, as a senior at the public high school, was Alpha team's leader this year. She was a small, shapeless bookworm who changed her hair more than Isabel, whose mom ran a hair salon. Right now, Jensina's short hair was oranger than mine. She had it in a ponytail today, which made her look like Misty from Pokémon.

"Do they all go to school here?" I asked Jensina. Lukas did, but I didn't recognize the other two names.

"Grace goes to Pilot Point High," Jensina said.

"Wally is homeschooled," Arianna said.

"My brother goes here." Isabel, the goddess, looked like Demi Lovato. Nuff said.

"Lukas and I are starting a band," Gabe said to me, but he was staring at Isabel like she might overhear and ask to sign on. "He's a drummer."

Of course he was. Lukas was too cool for his own good. I really hoped I wouldn't have to start hating him.

"I've never met Lukas," Beth said. She was wearing a pink T-shirt that said: Pretty tough. "What's he like?"

"He's a pain," Isabel said.

"He dresses punk," I said. "And he's got a faux-hawk. A tall one."

"*That* guy is your brother?" Jake grinned, his teeth bright against his dark skin. With dreads and a bowtie, Jake was his own version of cool, a black Matt Smith. And he wrote science fiction stories—so, yeah. "He had a part in the school play, right?" Jake asked Isabel. "I didn't catch his accent."

"Lukas is big into drama," Isabel said. "He can do any accent."

"Excellent. Looks like Diakonos caught the big fish this year," Jake said to Jensina.

"*Jake!*" Arianna said. "You'd rather have Spencer on your team? Truly?"

"I'd trade Spencer for Arianna," Jensina said.

"Deal!" Jake said.

Now it was my turn to protest. "Hey, I'm sitting right here."

"You know Mr. S doesn't allow trades," Arianna said.

"I'm just messing with you, girl," Jake said to Arianna. "I'd never trade that brain of yours."

"Thank you," Arianna said.

"Maybe Lukas can give me some insight about his sister,"

Gabe whispered to me.

I breathed a laugh. "Could you give a guy insight about *your* sisters?"

Gabe ran his tongue over his braces. "No guy better even look at my sisters."

"I rest my case." And Gabe had his work cut out for him too. I'd told him about Mary kissing me, and apparently it hadn't been the first time Mary had macked on one of Gabe's friends.

Glad the girl wasn't my responsibility.

REPORT NUMBER: 4

REPORT TITLE: A Demon Masquerades as a Hot Blond and
Tortures Me
SUBMITTED BY: Agent-in-Training Spencer Garmond
LOCATION: Harris Hall, Pilot Point Christian School, Pilot
Point, California, USA
DATE AND TIME: Monday, April 27, 5:52 a.m.

I HADN'T BEEN ABLE TO SLEEP because of that stupid Anya dream. So I arrived early to morning League, which was *so* not normal. I was the only one there. I even beat Mr. S. The room had twelve desks in three rows of four, a teacher's desk, and two round tables in the back. I sat in the center back of Harris Hall in my usual seat, took off my Lakers cap, and put my forehead on the desk. The basement room was chilly this early, and I stuck my hands between my knees to warm them.

The door yawned open. I let my head roll until my cheek rested on the desk, allowing me to see who'd come in.

Mr. S. crossed the room and set his briefcase on his desk.

He always came in before his wife and son showed. Something about him and Kerri working in different parts of town after class, I think Gabe once said.

Mr. S was bald and stocky with a pudgy gut that he always wrapped in one-size-too-small polo shirts. Today's shirt was salmon and grey stripes, which didn't help the gut look any smaller. He had glasses like his son, but unlike Gabe's cool Buddy Hollys, these looked like two circles of bulletproof glass. "Good morning, Agent Garmond," Mr. S said. "You're early today."

"Yeah." My voice came out in a raspy whisper.

"Is something bothering you?"

The dream. But I'd finally emailed Prière about all that craziness, and he'd told me it was normal. "Nah."

"Coach Van Buren came to speak to me last Friday," Mr. S said.

I grunted. The man was relentless.

"I must admit. I was surprised that you'd picked Japan over basketball camp."

"I didn't last year."

"Yes, but last year you didn't have a college basketball coach interested in you."

I grunted again. It wasn't *that* big of deal. It wasn't like the coach had offered to sign me.

"Don't worry about Coach Van Buren," Mr. S. said. "I'll keep working on him. And so will Principal McKaffey. Our school cares as much about missions as it does sports."

Another grunt. But maybe Mr. S. *could* help. I wasn't getting my hopes up. I mean, I'd never once gotten my way over a teacher. But . . . maybe.

"Would you mind assisting me today, Spencer?" Mr. S said.

51

"I never know how the initiates will react to their first day. It's always nice to have a backup plan."

No, I didn't want to help. I wanted to sit in my chair in the back of class and be left alone. But for some idiotic reason, I grunted a fourth time.

The door opened. Gabe and his mom, Kerri, wife to Mr. S, came in, followed by Beth, Jensina, and Nick—sans Isabel. Maybe her mission was over and she and Nick were finally on the outs. Gabe must be thrilled. He came and sat in the seat next to mine.

"No new recruits yet?" Beth was wearing her "Just walk away" T-shirt today. One of the perks of being homeschooled: No school uniforms. "Then I'm going back up."

But the door opened before she could. Jake entered with Isabel and Lukas-the faux-hawk-Rodriguez. Beth took a seat, her gaze locked on the feather duster in Lukas's hand.

I gave Isabel's brother the once over. Lukas stood a head taller than his sister and was thin and wiry. His bleached white faux-hawk was spiked a good five inches above his skull and ran down the middle of his head. He had earrings, diamond-looking ones. His black slacks looked painted on, his studded leather belt had a skull buckle, and the sleeves of his blazer were rolled up to his elbows. He'd slung his navy and red striped uniform necktie over one shoulder like a scarf. And he was wearing bright red Chucks.

I'd look like a moron if I tried dressing like that, but Lukas pulled it off. He carried the feather duster over to Mr. S's desk and held it out, frozen, like he couldn't decide what to do.

I sat up straight and put my hat back on.

Lukas and Mr. S stared at each other like Old West cowboys about to duel. Lukas jerked his hand closer to the desk then stopped. A little closer. Stop. Closer. Stop. The feather duster hung a centimeter from the fake wood laminate of the desk. The overhead lights gleamed off Mr. S's shiny, hairless scalp and one of four pewter rings on Lukas's hand.

Lukas grinned then, a crooked, sneaky grin that said so much without his saying a word. He tossed the duster onto Mr. S's desk. "Hey, Mr. S. How's it going?"

"Good, Agent Rodriguez. Is this feather duster a gift?"

"Izzy said she'd give me five bucks if I dusted your desk."

"*Ay!*" Isabel yelled. "*¡Arruinaste todo*, Lukas!"

"What did I ruin?" He looked back to Mr. S and shrugged. "I already work two jobs. What do I need five bucks for?"

Isabel slapped Lukas's arm. "*Que tonto eres.*"

"I'm not dumb. *¡Esta bien, Izzy! ¡Santo cielo!*"

The door opened, Isabel and Lukas shut up, and all heads turned toward the entrance.

A girl entered. Alone. Long, blond ponytail. Tan. Short. Wide blue eyes. Dark eye makeup. Empty-handed in the cleaning tools department. How'd she get in by herself?

This had to be Grace. And I'd seen her before. At homecoming. Lukas's date. She'd looked really good in the dark at the dance, but—great Caesar's ghost—the girl was go-go-gorgeous under regular lights.

"*Hola, Graciela*," Lukas said, his voice low and taunting.

She blinked slowly, but her stone-cold expression looked past Lukas to Mr. S as if Lukas wasn't even there.

Ouch. I guess things hadn't worked out with Faux-Hawk despite his Derek Hough dance moves. Excellent.

"Welcome to the Mission League, Agent Thomas," Mr. S said. "Please take a seat wherever you'd like."

"Thank you," Grace said, her voice girly and soft.

Everyone stared as she pranced down the aisle and slid into the seat in front of mine. A plume of coconut fragrance engulfed me. It felt like someone was stirring the contents of my stomach with a spoon. Her ponytail swayed slightly, the curling ends of her hair inches from my fingertips. Hypnotic. A familiar déjà vu flooded over me, but I didn't know why.

I couldn't help myself. I reached out and tugged a lock of silky golden strands.

Grace whipped around, her dainty features pushed into a scowl. She had perfect white teeth and large blue eyes that looked dark under her glare. "*Don't* touch me," she said, as if I were some leprous creep and she was afraid of catching something. The condescension in that sweet voice was like a kick to the groin.

Nick snickered.

Oh, come on! Would I never catch a break with a pretty girl? Like, just once?

Before I could think of anything to say, she spun forward again, her ponytail mocking me as it swayed and bobbed against the soft, tan skin of her neck.

I slouched down in my seat, and my knees bumped into the back of her chair. She turned her head to the side, eyes downcast, but didn't bother speaking to me again.

Whatever.

"Well, it's time to start." Mr. S stood and walked to the front of the room. "I must admit I'm disappointed with today's events. Missing students, and no successful *janitors*."

I couldn't see past that antagonizing ponytail, so I scooted my desk back and to the side a couple of feet, putting me in the aisle in the back middle of the classroom. The metal scraped on the concrete floor, and every head turned at the hideous

54

sound. "Sorry," I mumbled.

"There are four types of interrogation an enemy might use on a captive." Mr. S walked toward Lukas's desk. "Agent Rodriguez, do you think you can name one?"

"Bribes," Isabel said.

Mr. S looked from Lukas to Isabel. "Um . . . yes, Agent *Isabel*, that's correct. Agent Lukas. Do *you* have a guess?"

"Pull off a guy's toenails one by one?"

"Eww, Lukas," Isabel said.

"Torture, yes. But torture is often unnecessary. Sometimes simply pointing a gun at a captive might be enough to coerce them to speak. What might that be called, Agent Thomas?"

"Scaring them?" Grace said.

I grinned. Involuntarily, I might add.

"Close. We call that a threat, Agent Thomas. The fourth method is drugs, though this is rare, as most transgressors don't have access to such pharmaceuticals."

Yeah, right. A few months ago I'd been held at gunpoint *and* drugged. I guess I was just lucky that way.

Mr. S smirked at me, as if reading the look on my face. "Agent Garmond, would you care to come to the front of the class?"

I stiffened in my seat. "Now?"

"If you don't mind."

I trudged forward and grabbed the empty chair in the corner. I pulled it in front of the chalkboard, flipped it around backward, and straddled it, resting one arm on the back.

"Spencer is an average student at PPCS. Agent Lukas, if he were to be abducted, what methods do you think might be used to coerce information from him?"

If? Sometimes I hated the whole confidential side of the

Mission League. I'd love for Mr. S to tell everyone what had happened to me, what I'd survived—mostly on my own. Don't get me wrong, being alive and still getting to live in Pilot Point was good enough for me, but it would be nice to see these people look at me with a little respect. I think I'd earned it.

Instead, Lukas looked at me like I was a frog in a wax pan, his bleached hair almost white next to his dark, Cuban skin. He suddenly reminded me of Chaz. "Threaten his mom or sister?"

"That's the right idea . . ." Mr. S said. "Why won't that work, Agent Watkins?"

"Because Spencer doesn't have a sister, and his mom died when he was little," Beth said.

"Correct. Your captors will make it their business to know everything they can about you. Agent Thomas, what might you suggest as a tactic to coerce information from Agent Garmond?"

"Threaten to bash in his kneecaps," Grace said with a little too much enthusiasm, "or cut off the fingers on his right hand."

What the . . . ? Yikes!

"You believe physical threats would make him talk?" Mr. S asked.

"Not the pain," Grace said, flashing the "dark eyes" my way. "I'm sure he's tough enough to live through that. But he's a jock. So losing the ability to play basketball would be like death to someone like him."

Mr. S chuckled. He actually thought that was funny?

"Yes, I think that would be a logical assumption for an enemy of Agent Garmond. But we're the good guys, right, Agent Garmond?"

"Right, sir." I raised my eyebrows at Grace. *See, chickadee?*

We're on the same team. So, why can't we be friends?

"And for us, as agents," Mr. S said, "interrogation isn't about torture, beating information out of people, or shining bright lights in their eyes. For us, interrogation is the strategy of asking questions." He paused in front of Isabel's desk in the front row and turned to face me. "Know your subject. Desire. Ambition. Pride. Basketball *is* important to Agent Garmond. And when your subject is passionate about something, you can use that against him."

It took all of my effort to keep from looking at Grace. "Maybe. But assumptions are dangerous too. What Agent Thomas doesn't know is that I'm equally talented with my left hand."

Jake hooted.

"Well said, Agent Garmond." Mr. S turned to the class. "In this program you'll learn to be a quick thinker, to look beyond your first impressions, to observe and dig deep as you study potential targets. Hopefully for Agents Garmond and Thomas, first impressions aren't everything."

Amen to that.

The door swung open, and Arianna and a guy entered. The guy was carrying a broom.

Wait a second. This guy had been Arianna's homecoming date. Seriously? The chubby chess club guy was going to be a spy? Come on.

Wally began to air sweep, his broom not touching the floor. He had big lips and a bowl cut of thick brown hair. He was wearing Levi's, the high-waisted farmer kind, and a short-sleeved dress shirt that was tucked in, like he worked at the Office Depot. And this was not a school uniform, either. He *chose* to look like that.

"Thank you, Agent Parks," Mr. S said, taking the broom from Wally.

Wally's posture relaxed and he nodded.

"Twenty points to Diakonos for getting us a real janitor down here." Mr. S smiled at Arianna. "And twenty points to Alpha for Agent Garmond's willingness to sit in the hot seat. Now that we're all here, let's split into groups. Wally and Grace, join Alpha group. Lukas, you're in Diakonos."

I returned the chair to the corner, then walked to the Alpha table in the back of the room, passing Grace on the way. Her head came up to my chest—she was shorter than Isabel. But where Isabel had lots of curves, Grace had a small muscular frame. I remembered her nice legs from the dance and glanced down, but she was wearing jeans. Shame. Guys didn't forget legs like those. At least not this guy.

Jensina was already sitting at the Alpha table, Wally beside her. I sat across from them. Wally had his eyes closed and was mumbling. Praying, it sounded like. Grace sat primly beside Wally and avoided eye contact with me. Gabe sat next to me. It felt nice to have a full table again. All year there had been only three of us on Alpha team. Now we had five. I glanced over at the Diakonos table and did a quick count. They had six! Still unfair. But Jake, Beth, and Jensina would be graduating soon, and then things would be even Stephen.

"Hey," Gabe said. "Now that basketball's over, want to try the bass guitar?"

"I'm not joining your band," I said.

"Bass is easy. All you really have to do is count to four."

"Yeah? Well, I can only count to three."

"I'm not surprised," Grace mumbled.

I raised my eyebrows at Grace, who was looking at her

notebook. No way was I going to let that comment slide. "I'm sorry, did you just step out of my nightmare?"

"So we meet here in the mornings?" Grace said to Jensina, her girly voice louder than need be. "Then in room 401 in the afternoons?"

"That's right," Jensina said.

"Real nice," I mumbled, then said to Gabe, "Did you see that?"

Gabe scrawled on his notebook: Grace is a grouch. Don't take it personal.

I took Gabe's pen and wrote: Why?

Gabe: Don't know. Bass guitar? Please?

I pushed his notebook aside and gave him a dirty look. Thank you, no. I was not joining Gabe's rock band.

"Wally? Did you get that?" Jensina said.

"There's only one exit in this room," Wally said. "It's not up to fire code. We should find a new location in which to meet in the mornings. This one is unsafe."

"Oh." Jensina tucked a wisp of bright orange bangs behind her ear. "So, I'm supposed to tell the new recruits about how things work. But first let's all introduce ourselves so we can get to know each other. I'm Jensina Hicks. I'm a senior at Pilot Point High. I'm adopted. And I'd like to—"

"I never knew you were adopted," I said.

"You never asked," Jensina said, as if I was an idiot.

That wasn't fair. "Seriously? Who goes around asking people if they were adopted? Hey, Gabe? Were you adopted?"

"No."

"'Kay. Just checking." I grinned at Jensina.

"*Spencer* . . ." She held up her finger like she was about the shake it at me. Instead she said, "Wally, why don't you go next?"

"My name is Wally Parks. My credits currently have me at a junior, but Prière told me that I had to be a freshman for this organization. I'm an only child." He glanced at me. "I live with my birth mother *and* father."

"Thanks," I said. "I appreciate knowing that about you." I winked at Jensina.

"My mother schools me at home," Wally continued. "And it's best if you all know now that I suffer from obsessive compulsive disorder and multiple phobias."

That didn't sound good. "What kinds of phobias?" I asked.

"Germs and dirt bother me the most. But I also dislike vomit or sweat . . . saliva . . . Any sort of bodily fluid, actually."

Wowzer. "Do you have a shrink?"

Gabe elbowed me.

"Yes, of course. His name is Dr. Russell Judd," Wally said. "He's quite good, if you need someone to talk to. He takes Fridays off, though, so you couldn't meet with him on Fridays. If I have an emergency on Fridays I have to meet with Dr. Peter Sherman. I dislike Dr. Sherman. He leaves the window open during our sessions, and the exhaust bothers me."

A moment of silence settled over Alpha table as we absorbed this new information about Wally. I wanted to ask if he was related to Mr. Monk, but I held my tongue.

"Um . . . Spencer, why don't you go next?" Jensina said.

"Yeah, sure. I'm Spencer Garmond. I'm a sophomore at PPCS. We already established that I live with my grandma and play basketball. I'm sixteen, a Pisces, born on February 29. I also enjoy playing *Planet of Peril* and eating—

"That makes you four years old," Grace said.

She never let up, did she? "I *also* enjoy eating peanut

butter sandwiches, practicing League Combat Training, and riding bicycles built for two. And I *should* be getting my driver's license at the end of the month." Unless Grandma refused to drive me to take the test, which was always a poosibility.

"Thank you, Spencer. Your words make me miss Isaac." Jensina rolled her eyes. "Gabe?"

"Wait," Grace said. "Beth said your mom died, but what about your dad?"

Her tone was kind this time, but I wasn't buying her Girl Scout cookies. I narrowed my eyes. "My dad is a dangerous criminal."

"Oh." She looked away and flipped her ponytail over her shoulder. "That explains a lot."

I'd been *joking*, sort of. "Do I look like a punching bag to you?"

Her head whipped back to face me. "More like the Eiffel Tower."

"Oh, you wanna do tall jokes now, Goldilocks? 'Cause I can go all day." I leaned across the table. "Girl, you're so short, you could base jump off a curb."

She cocked an eyebrow. "I'm not short, I'm space efficient."

"Well, look on the bright side, Sunshine. When it rains, you're the last one to get wet."

"Spencer and Grace." Jensina slapped the tabletop. "This is my year to be team captain. I want to do a good job, but you're making that difficult."

"Sorry," I mumbled, wanting to add that Grace had started it, but that wouldn't help me look more mature in any way, shape, or form.

"I apologize," Grace said, flipping her ponytail again.

61

"Egotistical maniacs bring out the worst in me."

I lifted my hands out to the side and looked around the table, but no one was offering any sympathy. Fine. Little Miss Personality could have round one, but next time, I'd choose the location. Girl was going down.

"Gabe? Your turn," Jensina said.

"Yeah, I'm Gabe. I also go to Pilot Point Christian. I'm a junior. My parents are in this room. I have twin sisters. And I'm starting a band. If you know a bass player, let me know."

Before Jensina could explain about how the Mission League worked, Mr. S announced the exact location of our summer trip. Arianna had nailed it. We'd be going to Naha, Okinawa, a tropical island at the south of Japan. White sandy beaches, teal blue oceans, warm climate . . . I closed my eyes and grinned. Sounded good to me.

● ● ●

That afternoon, I got to Room 401 at the same time as Grace, so I held the door so she could go first. See? I was a gentleman. My grandma raised me right.

But Grace stopped in the doorway and looked up at me. "I'm glad you're tall, Spencer. It gives me more of you to dislike."

"I'm sorry, what?" I cupped my hand behind my ear. "You'll have to talk louder. I can't hear you *all the way* up here."

Grace went inside. I took a deep breath of coconut scented air and followed.

Room 401 was a regular classroom, but instead of a ton of student desks, it had two round tables and a bunch of chairs.

Mr. S had a teacher's desk in the front corner, and the walls were covered in posters featuring countries like Swaziland, Germany, Puerto Rico, Moscow, and now Japan.

Everyone was talking about the paradise we were about to visit. I just hoped Grace would keep her noxious self away from me so I could enjoy my upcoming vacay.

"Beth is passing out a worksheet," Mr. S said from his desk. "It's a list of phrases that will help you in Japan. Please start memorizing them. Then pair up and work on some of the conversations at the bottom."

At the Alpha table, unfortunately, the only empty chair was between Grace and Wally. Wally, who had a package of baby wipes sitting beside his notebook. Whee.

I pulled out the chair and stood there, trying to decide where to put my backpack. On my left, I smelled coconuts. On my right, antiseptic. Beth circled our table passing out papers. I settled onto the chair and shoved my pack between my feet. Most furniture wasn't designed for guys my size.

"How tall are you, anyway, Beanstalker?" Grace asked me.

"My *name* is Spencer." Jonas, really, but . . . yeah.

"Or Tiger," Beth said, slapping a sheet of paper on the table in front of me. She handed a paper to Grace. "Nice black eye, girl."

Grace folded her arms and looked away.

"Feisty little thing. Just your type, ay, Tiger?" Beth had the nerve to wink.

I glowered at Beth's braids as she returned to the Diakonos table. A sharp breath accompanied revelation. That was the first time Beth hadn't evoked pathetic longing in my gut. Had I gotten over her, finally? Please say yes.

I faced forward and caught Grace watching me. I leaned

closer and looked at her face. A bruise had yellowed the skin under her left eye. How had I not noticed that before? "So, what happened, Lemondrop?"

Her gaze snapped forward. "Got in a fight."

"You? Who'd you take on? A kindergartener?"

"Like you can talk, Spencer," Jensina said.

"I got in *one fight* last year." I lowered my voice and glanced at Nick.

"Two," Gabe said. "One here and one in Moscow."

"Thank you for clarifying, Gabe," I said. "But what happened in Moscow wasn't much of a fight. Isaac broke it up before I could end it right."

"Spencer has a violent streak," Jensina said.

I looked across the table to Gabe. "I have a violent streak?"

Gabe shrugged.

"Oh, thanks a lot." I threw my spiral notebook at Gabe.

"See?" Jensina said, laughing.

"I have to agree with Jensina's assessment." Wally pulled out a baby wipe and handed it to me. "Your sarcasm is an indication of a short fuse."

I scowled at the wipe. "I've only known you for a day."

"Take the wipe," Wally said pointing to a black smudge on my hand. "Public playgrounds are terribly unsanitary."

"I wasn't on a playground. I was playing ball out back."

"There are 971 students currently enrolled at Pilot Point Christian Schools: 332 in the elementary, 228 in the middle school, and 411 in the high school. Please?" Wally nudged the dangling wipe my way.

Wasn't Wally homeschooled? "How do you even know that?" I took the wipe and rubbed the black from my hands. Wally's posture eased. I turned back to Grace. "So what was the fight about? Did you win?"

Her gaze turned dark again, tempting me to shiver. "I always win." She flicked her ponytail over her shoulder and repositioned her body away from me, facing Gabe. I swear the ponytail laughed at me.

What did I ever do to her?

Gabe Frisbeed back my notebook. I slouched down in my chair and scribbled on it. I flipped over the paper that Beth had passed out and looked it over. It was filled with phrases, most of which we'd already learned this year. I read the first few.

How are you? • *Ogenki desu ka?*
I'm fine, thanks! • *Watashi wa genki desu. Arigato!*
And you? • *Anatawa?*
Good. • *Genki desu.*
Where is the bathroom? • *Toire wa doko desu ka?*
How old are you? • *Toshi wa ikutsu desu ka?*
I don't understand! • *Wakarimasen.*

Wakarimasen. I'd have to be sure and memorize that one.

Are you going to discard that?" Wally asked, pointing at my used wipe.

I looked at the wadded wipe on the table and shrugged. "Eventually."

"Do you mind? I could easily . . ."

"Be my guest."

Wally pulled out another wipe and used it to pick up my dirty one. He carried both to the trash next to Mr. S's desk. Not exaggerating. The dude was nuts.

"Before we work on the conversations," Jensina said, "Spencer, can you explain the handout to Grace? I think it will help if they learn pronunciations first. I'm going to help Wally."

Me? She wanted me to speak to Princess Snot? I glanced at her papers and saw that she had the packet that we'd all gotten at the beginning of the school year.

"Are you going to teach me something or what?" Grace asked.

"Simmer, short stuff." I straightened in my seat and grabbed her packet. I flipped to the Japanese alphabet page and set it on the table between us. "So . . . there's five vowel sounds in Japanese." I pointed at each *hiragana* symbol as I said it. "The 'a' sounds like, 'ah.' The 'i' sounds like, 'ee.' The 'u,' goes 'oo.' The 'e' sounds like, 'eh.' And the 'o' makes an 'oh' sound. Those are the only vowel sounds, so it's pretty easy to pronounce things. Um, there's a *hiragana* symbol for each vowel, and a different symbol for each consonant-vowel combo." I continued to point as I read each. "Ka, ki, ku, ke, ko. Sa, shi, su, se, so. Ta ,chi, tsu, te, to. Na, ni—"

Grace snatched the paper from me. "I get it."

Meow! "Well, memorize the alphabet and all the hiragana symbols first. Then I'll show you how to make words."

She tapped her Japanese textbook. "I can read. I'm sure I'll figure it out."

I felt weak. The mean girl was like a *Planet of Peril* mad scientist. She'd siphoned all my strength to use in her lab experiments. Game over.

I glanced at Arianna. She was talking up a storm to Lukas, who looked riveted. Even Wally was listening to Jensina. Why was Grace such a witch?

After ten minutes of blessed silence, Grace asked, "How can I write my name, then? There's no G or R or C."

"I'll show you." I flipped to a blank sheet in my notebook. I drew what I thought said Grace—gu-re-i-su, actually—and tossed the notebook in front of her.

She studied it for a long while. "None of those symbols are on this chart."

"That's because your chart is *hiragana*. I wrote your name in *katakana*."

"Why?"

"*Katakana* symbols are used for foreign words," I said. "Since your name is American, it would be written in *katakana*," I said.

She ripped the page out of my notebook and stuck it in her binder.

"Help yourself, Marigold," I said.

Up went her flagpole posture, and she turned away and began copying the *hiragana* alphabet with a pink ink pen. I ignored the ponytail dancing in my face and went back to the list of phrases Mr. S wanted us to memorize.

I *so* wished Grace was in Diakonos group so we could nab her for the initiation abduction. How much fun would it be to stick some duct tape over that little smirk and a pillowcase over that blasted ponytail? So fun. That's how.

Jake and company had better get her good.

REPORT NUMBER: 5

REPORT TITLE: I Adopt a Kid Sister
SUBMITTED BY: Agent-in-Training Spencer Garmond
LOCATION: Room 401, Pilot Point Christian School, Pilot
Point, California, USA
DATE AND TIME: Monday, April 27, 4:47 p.m.

AFTER CLASS, WE VETERAN AGENTS-IN-TRAINING hung
around to talk specifics about the initiation abduction that
would happen on Saturday, two weeks away. It was tradition to
have each team abduct the other's new recruits. Alpha team
would grab Lukas, and Diakonos had to get both Wally and
Grace. For once, things were in Alpha team's favor.

"Wally shouldn't be too difficult," Jake said. "But that
Skipper doll . . . She's a little spitfire."

"She's insane," I said. "Make sure to scar her for life."

"Spencer's afraid of girls," Nick said.

I didn't bother shooting Nick a glare. It wasn't worth the
effort.

"But she's so small, Spencer," Beth said. "How bad can she be?"

"Don't let the blond ponytail fool you," I told Beth. "It's pure evil."

Jake cackled. "Evil ponytails? You need to get some sleep, my man. Don't worry. Diakonos will bag the big bad ponytail for you."

Egg-cellent. I could hardly wait.

Jake and his team went elsewhere so we wouldn't be able to overhear their dastardly plans. That left Jensina, Gabe, and me alone in room 401.

"Isabel's family never locks the door," Gabe said. "Like, twenty people live at that house. We could probably walk right in the front door and no one would suspect a thing."

"But we're supposed to scare him a little, right?" I asked. "Beth and Nick scared the sweat out of me last year."

"I'm driving the van and doing lookout," Jensina said. "You two have to grab him."

"No problem," I said. "I can take Faux-Hawk any day. So long as he is nowhere near a can of hairspray."

"Hairspray?" Jensina rolled her eyes. "I need you guys to be serious, please. We've only got two weeks to learn his routine, and only one Saturday. Watch him at school, get to know him better. Find out what he does on weekends. You two track him Saturday morning, say from five until noon. I'll bring you some lunch and we'll all watch until five. Then you guys can get me some dinner and I'll cover until midnight. That should give us a pretty good idea of his routine. We'll meet here every day after class to report our findings, okay?"

"Aye-aye, boss," I said. "We're on it."

• • •

Isabel and Lukas lived in an old stucco house with a red mission tile roof three blocks from my place. The lawn was covered in broken-down vehicles and car parts. Gabe had been right: All sorts of random people frequented the place.

When Lukas was home, he stayed inside or worked on a rusty Impala in the yard. When he went out, it was almost always to his mother's salon, *Peluqueria Rodriguez*. Lukas worked there almost every day—the dude did manicures and pedicures, I'd seen it. He rode home with his mom after she closed up—except on Mondays and Thursdays, when he closed up by himself. Lukas also worked a lifeguard shift at the Pilot Point Athletic Center pool on Saturdays from two to six.

Gabe wanted to nab him at the salon. I vetoed. First: the hairspray. Last fall, Lukas had taken out the Incredible Tattooed Hulk with one spritz. I wasn't going down like that. Second: If I did manage to dodge the hairspray, I didn't want to risk messing up his mom's store with a fight.

Our best option was grabbing him on his way home from the pool, which, sadly, meant I'd miss the Lakers playoff game that was on at the same time.

What can I say? Such is the life of a spy.

When we were done scoping out Lukas's house, Jensina asked, "Where am I dropping you off, Spencer?"

"Can I come hang at your place?" I asked Gabe. Grandma was having quilt club tonight, and I was too old to help the ladies tie knots.

"Mary has a game at six thirty. I told her I'd go," Gabe said. "You want to come?"

I hesitated. I had wondered if Mary was any good at

basketball, and I'd also like to find out if she'd had any more dreams about me. But I didn't want to encourage her little crush. I left it up to Gabe. "Think it will be okay?"

"Mom talked to her. She won't be kissing you again."

"Excuse me?" Jensina said, looking in the rearview mirror.

"Hey, it's difficult for the ladies to control themselves around my awesomeness," I said, earning a hearty laugh from Jensina and Gabe.

But really? I'd had one girlfriend for six days in eighth grade. The closest I'd come to getting a girl since was when Katie Lindley had kissed me at Nick's party after Homecoming. But she'd been paid five hundred bucks to keep me in the house and steal my iPhone, so . . . yeah.

Casanova, I was not.

An hour and a half later Gabe and I sat on the bleachers behind Mr. S and Kerri in the middle school gym. Mary was indeed the point guard for her team. She looked so cute in her red and white uniform with a black knee brace and her bushy brown curls trapped in a wild ponytail on the back on her head. I noted the big two-four on her back as she dribbled down the court.

"She has my number."

"She picked it on purpose," Gabe said, a scowl in his voice.

"Because of Kobe," I said, totally understanding. His number was on the back of my Lakers cap. "That's why I picked it."

Gabe snorted and shook his head. "She picked it because of you."

"Really?" I had a fangirl. It was actually kind of endearing.

Mary yelled, "Let's run five!" and passed the ball to the right. She jogged through the key with her hand in the air. The gangly guard lobbed a pass to her, but it was too short. A stick of a girl from Glendale Middle School intercepted and took off for the other end. But the stick was slow. Mary caught up and swiped the ball back.

"Way to go, Mary!" I yelled.

Mary sped back to her end, dribbling through the disoriented players who still thought the stick had the ball. She went all the way to the hoop and scored. The scattered fans cheered, myself included.

Hey, she *was* pretty good.

By halftime, Mary had scored twelve points, had five assists—would have had ten if her teammates could make their shots. She also had four rebounds, two fouls, and three steals. At least that's what I'd tallied in my head.

I was smitten and ready to adopt her as my kid sister.

"Thanks for coming, Spencer," Kerri said. "She's good at basketball, don't you think?"

"She's awesome! She'll play varsity in high school for sure—I mean, if she wants."

Kerri giggled. "Oh, I think she'll want."

"Mom! Do you have my other kneepad?" Mary was suddenly standing on the bleachers one row down from Kerri, her cheeks flushed from the exercise. The rest of her team was out on the court warming up for the second half.

"Oh, honey. You had it in your bag, didn't you?"

"I gave *you* my bag to . . ." Mary spotted me and her eyes went wide.

I smiled, not wanting to ruin her game by existing. "Hey, Mary," I said. "You're doing great out there." She looked like she might pass out, so I kept talking. "Watch number 43, the chick with the skunk hair. She can't go left. Force her that way and you can steal."

"Oh." Her voice was nearly a whisper. "Okay."

"Here it is, sweetie. Your kneepad?" Kerri held out a black kneepad to Mary, who snatched it and fled back to the bench.

I looked at Gabe and winced. "Should I go? I don't want to mess up her game." I'd had trouble playing when Beth had been watching me, and I was practically an expert.

"It will be worse if you leave now," a voice said from behind me.

I turned around. Martha was sitting against the wall on the top row of the bleachers. She held a book—*The Grapes of Wrath*—in her hand. "She'll think you left on purpose. Like maybe you got bored with a middle school game, or maybe you thought she stinks, or maybe you thought her hair looked bad and couldn't stand to look at it."

I wrinkled my nose and glanced at Gabe.

He rolled his eyes. "It's fine."

The second half started, but when Mary fumbled the ball out of bounds, then accidentally threw the ball to skunk hair, I felt responsible.

"Let's go, Mair Bear," Mr. S hollered.

Mair Bear? "Come on, Mary!" I yelled, hoping the girl could get her head in the game.

The next time skunk girl brought down the ball, Mary rocked the defense, forcing her to dribble to the left side of the court. Skunk girl used her right hand, of course, and Mary swiped the ball and scored on the fast break.

"Whoo!" She'd taken my advice. How cool was that? Maybe I *could* coach basketball someday.

After the game, Martha rode home with her dad. Since Gabe was driving the minivan, his mom sat in the passenger's seat, so I sat next to Mary in the middle row of the van. No way was I going to ask her about her prophetic dreams with her mom right there. I hoped to get a chance later.

"My outside shot isn't very good, huh?" Mary said to me.

"It's a little flat. But it goes in, and that's what counts. Work to get a little more arc in your shot. Shoot up, not straight. Make it pretty. Make a rainbow."

"A rainbow? *Really?*" Gabe said, his voice monotone.

"Yeah." I tried to show Mary, but my hand hit the roof of the van.

"You're almost too tall for the van," she said, giggling. "Hey, do you think Myra is good?"

I slouched and leaned closer to Mary, trying to hear over the sound of the van's engine. "Which one is Myra?"

"The tall blonde with the pink glasses. She doesn't like to run, and I told her she has to."

"A lot of forwards are slow, but if she wants to be good, she's got to run. At least she makes her lay-ups, though. My coach would make you guys run for all the missed shots in that game."

Mary sighed and took out her ponytail. Her frizzy black hair exploded out and framed her face. "Most of the girls are just playing for fun or whatever, not to win. I know it's important to have fun and everything, and I do have fun, but I really want to win. I can't wait until I'm in high school. Will I get to go on the same basketball trips as you?"

The mere idea of Mary in the same vicinity as guys like Desh and Chaz made me sick. "You think you'll make varsity your freshman year?"

She crossed her arms. "I know I will."

I raised my eyebrows. The girl was confident, I'd give her

that. "It's hard to make varsity as a freshman. Not many people do."

"I will, and I'll get game time too."

"If you want it bad enough, work hard, and don't give up."

"So *that's* how you got so good. I just know you'll get a basketball scholarship."

"Thanks." How could Gabe find this annoying? I'd love to have a little sister like Mary who played basketball and hung on my every word. But then I caught Gabe glaring at me in the rearview mirror, and I recalled one of his Prude Patrol lectures about playing with a girl's heart.

Was it wrong for me to be nice to Mary? Because I really didn't want to hurt her. Ever.

When I got home it was 9:37 p.m. Grandma Alice fed me sandwiches, then I went to my room and crashed on my bed with my MacBook. I was so tired, but I needed a social media fix.

Kip had sent me three messages trying to get me on *Planet of Peril*. I shot off a quick apology email about Mary's game. I should really make some time for him before I left for Japan, but I couldn't stomach him and Megan together. And if by some miracle she wasn't there, she'd be texting him constantly. It stunk hanging out with someone who was only half paying attention to you.

I had a friend request and a message from Mary Stopplecamp. Aww. I accepted and clicked open her message.

Hi, Spencer!

I'm not supposed to talk about it, but I had another dream about you. My dreams are always of three guys with sunglasses beating you up. If you have to tell this to Prière or my dad or whatever, I understand. I don't mind getting in trouble for you. But all I know is that you get hurt in my dream and you're in Japan.

So please, please, please, please, please, don't go on the trip this summer. Stay home and do basketball conditioning and then show me what you learned when I get back because I have to go to Japan since both my parents are going and I don't have a choice.

Your friend, Mair

PS. If you insist on going, which you probably will since you're so brave, I have a sub-warning. This will probably sound stupid, but I don't know how else to say it, so here goes: Beware of foreign girls. Beauty can be misleading.

Yeah. Sounds crazy, right? Like there wouldn't be any foreign girls in Japan . . . Sorry.

I read her message twice. Three guys beating me up, huh? I knew how it felt to have intense dreams about people. And it was nice that she wanted to warn me. But if her dad knew, he'd probably told Prière. So it couldn't be that bad, right?

I could still back out of the trip. Stay home, do basketball conditioning, make Coach happy. But this summer I'd get my first test mission, though it would probably be something lame like helping Gabe run VBS or following Grace around.

Grace. Now there was a reason to stay home. If she and I

got paired up, things could get ugly fast. But if I stayed home, I'd be forced to play third wheel to Kip and Megan all summer or sit alone in my room. Both options sounded pretty miserable.

The second part of Mary's message, the PS . . . I scratched the back of my neck. *Girls*, she'd said. Plural. Wow. If that was a real prophesy, it was too much of a temptation to pass up.

Sweet. I was going to meet me some foreign girls in Okinawa.

I'd better make up some homemade field ops kits, just in case.

REPORT NUMBER: 6

REPORT TITLE: Change of Plans
SUBMITTED BY: Agent-in-Training Jun Uehara
LOCATION: Mission League Safe House, 2-11-10
Tsuboya, Naha, Okinawa, Japan
DATE AND TIME: Thursday, May 28, 8:08 p.m.

"THERE HAS BEEN A CHANGE IN your assignment," Toda-san said.

"Again?" Jun studied the somber face of his Mission League instructor. His assignment had already changed once due to the information in his reports. When his superiors had discovered Jun had made a connection with Bushi Kogawa, they'd wanted him to get as deep into the Abaku-kai gang as possible. What did International want now?

"Your parents have signed up to host some of the American agents-in-training," Toda-san said.

Jun knew this. He had been worried that it might interfere with his assignment.

"One of the young men we placed in your home is of special interest to International." Toda-san slid a photo across the table.

A pale, freckled boy with orange hair stared back at Jun. He wondered how someone with such hair could ever be inconspicuous—unless he was permanently stationed in Scotland or something. "What must I do?"

"He's important. International is sending an adult agent to monitor him, but there will be times when the adult agent can't see him. Do your best to keep an eye on him. Watch who pays attention to him."

"He is good, then?" Jun had been working with delinquents for so long, it would be a nice to spend time with a good guy.

"Hai. But we have reason to believe the Abaku-kai may take an interest in him."

"If that happens, should I reveal myself?" Jun asked. "Blow my cover?"

"I realize that this isn't an ideal situation," Toda-san said. "Your connection to the Abaku-kai is important. If at all possible, do not blow your cover. Simply report."

"And if I cannot?"

"This boy's life, and your life, is the priority."

"I understand." Jun looked back to the picture of the American with the smug expression and blue eyes. "I will do my best, sensei."

REPORT NUMBER: 7

REPORT TITLE: I Go to Japan and Meet an Asian Princess
Times Two
SUBMITTED BY: Agent-in-Training Spencer Garmond
LOCATION: Somewhere over the Pacific Ocean
DATE AND TIME: Monday or Tuesday, June 1 or 2. Who knew
what time?

THE NEXT FEW WEEKS FLEW BY. We'd tied with Diakonos, points-wise, on the initiation abduction. Lukas had given us plenty of trouble, and we were late getting him to Mr. S's house. But Grace saved us by being the one to guess it was a test.

Mary and I had become buddies. I'd gone to her last few games, and she was always asking me questions about what she should work on to improve as an athlete.

Grace still hated me, and I still didn't know why.

When we all showed up at LAX for the trip to Japan, one of us was missing. Nick. His dad had yanked him out of the trip at the last minute. Shocked the tar out of me.

Now to his credit, Nick hadn't bothered me much lately. I attributed this to two things: 1) I'd been too busy to even hear any sarcastic insults he might have thrown my way, and 2) Isabel might have turned him sorta-nice during their time "dating."

I really hoped to get a chance to ask Isabel about her assignment and if she had any clue what Nick had done to miss out on the summer mission. But Mr. S had warned us that things would be different this year. We weren't staying in the same place. They'd divvied us up into host families. Boys with boys, girls with girls. So I wouldn't be in the same house as Isabel.

I had one more bit of excitement before getting on the plane. When we were going through security, the guards pulled me aside and confiscated the homemade field ops kits I'd put in my backpack and wallet. All of them. The kits consisted of a flat razor blade and a paperclip hidden in a little box of gum. They might look a little pathetic, but I'd used the razor blade to get free when Blaine and Tito had guy-napped me last year. Ever since, I've had one on me at all times.

But yes, packing two razor blades in my backpack to get on an airplane had been dumb.

The flight from Los Angeles to Tokyo was a half hour longer than the trip to Moscow had taken last year. And Tokyo wasn't even our final destination. After a quick layover, we took another two-and-a-half-hour flight to Okinawa. Total flight time: twelve hours fifty-three minutes. And we'd soared into the future too. It was 6:41 p.m. when we landed in Okinawa, but back home in LA it was 1:41 a.m. last night.

I was a time lord. I was Doctor Who.

As we stood in the aisle waiting for the flight attendant to open the door, I found myself behind Lukas and in front of Gabe. Being so tall, I could see over everyone's heads. A few rows up, Grace and Isabel were laughing at something Arianna had said. This struck me as odd. I couldn't remember Arianna ever saying anything funny. Not intentionally, anyway.

"You should go for her this summer, Spencer," Lukas said. "Grace."

Excuse me? I choked out a laugh. "Yeah . . . she hates me."

"It's a game." Lukas jutted his chin my way. "She said she likes gingers."

"When?" I fought the urge to look at Grace but could still hear her laughter.

"Don't encourage him," Gabe said. "He'll have a much better trip if he stays away from girls."

That got a rise out of me. "So you're going to stay away from Isabel, then?"

Gabe looked down at his loafers.

"Yeah, that's what I thought." I nudged Lukas. "When did Grace say that about gingers?"

"Last night. Before we left. She texted me."

Sure. "She just randomly texted you, 'I like gingers.'"

"No. I texted her to see if we could try and work things out this summer. And she texted back that I'm not her type. So I asked, 'What's your type, Graciela?' and she says 'I like gingers.' Three words." Lukas raised one eyebrow. "I only know one ginger, man."

I shook my head. "You're lying."

"Why would I lie?" Lukas said.

"Well, then *she's* lying." She had to be. "She probably means some guy with orange hair from Pilot Point High.

Someone from her own school." Right?

Lukas smoothed up his faux-hawk. "If you say so."

The line started to move. Slowly. Lukas pulled his carry-on from the overhead bin.

"Is her name really Graciela?" I asked.

"Nah," Lukas said. "Graciela is a Spanish version of the name Grace. She used to like me calling her that. Funny how girls change."

Psychotic fit better for my experiences with girls. We reached the front of the line, and I stepped out of the airplane door and into a sauna. I was standing at the top of a portable metal staircase that led down to the tarmac. It was still light out, even thought it was almost seven at night. Above me, the sky was cloudy, but bits of turquoise poked through. On the horizon, the blue turned to purple and grey and yellow and orange. Almost sunset. I'd seen the ocean from the plane just before we landed, but I couldn't see it from here. The other passengers ahead of me were snaking their way to a one-story section of the terminal.

This was what outside felt like here? I'd never imagined the weather could feel so . . . thick. I followed the crowd, and when I stepped into the terminal, I was hit with a gust of air conditioning. Big difference.

A cheer went up from a crowd of Japanese teenagers holding necklaces made of fresh flowers. They were all wearing school uniforms with white shirts and navy blue pants or skirts. The boys had navy neckties. The girls had little navy blue bows at their necks.

A Japanese guy with black flat-topped hair tried to put a lei over my head. I leaned down to help him out. The purple petals were cool against my neck and smelled sweet. "Am named Jun Uehara," the guy said, patting his chest. "Am your host brother." He grinned, flashing a smile that revealed a chipped front tooth. Owzers.

Jun also put flowers over Gabe's and Wally's heads and claimed them as host bros. I frowned as a different Japanese guy put flowers over Lukas's head. Bummer.

An itch twinged my scalp. I scratched my head and felt someone's finger. I spun around and caught two Japanese girls with their hands in the air. They slapped their hands over their mouths and giggled.

The one with a bad case of acne—like I could talk—reached back toward my hair. "*Sugoi ne?*"

Her friend batted her eyelashes at me. I took a small step backward, a little freaked out. Someone elbowed me in the side. Mary.

"I told you," she said, flashing her teal green smile. "It's your hair."

"What about my hair?"

"There are no natural redheads or blonds in Japan," Mary said. "Look at Grace."

I glanced around the gate and found Grace surrounded by a mob of students. At least three people were touching her hair. "Dude. That's messed up." I dug out my Lakers cap from my backpack and put it on.

Another thing that was messed up: I was like a lighthouse in this place. I didn't see one guy over six feet tall. I knew my height was above average, but in LA and even Moscow there had been enough men who were close enough to my height that I didn't feel like a freak. But here? Grace would never quit with the tall jokes.

I followed Jun to the luggage area. While we waited for our suitcases, I ran into the bathroom and was dismayed to discover a toilet in the floor of the stall. An actual porcelain hole right there in the tile with a handle to flush and everything.

What the Kobe Bryant was I supposed to do here?

I went back out and hauled Gabe in to see the bizarre toilet. "Is it a floor urinal?" Because that was the best I could figure. "Where are the toilets?" I needed a toilet. I couldn't use those airplane toilets, and it had been a very loong flight.

"I think you're supposed to squat," Gabe said. "They had outhouses like this in Swaziland."

Squat? Come on.

Wally's eyes widened with horror. "I can't . . . Is this all they have?"

"I hear you, man," I said. "This is messed up." But I took a picture with *My Precious* and sent it to Kip.

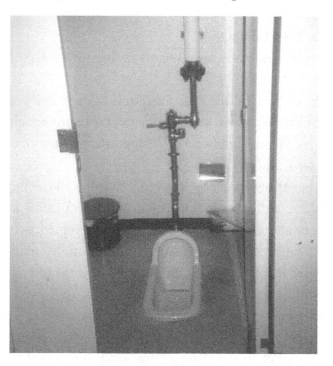

Gabe and I left Wally staring at the hole and drifted back out to the luggage area. Gabe told Lukas about the toilet and they ran off, leaving me alone at the carousel. I glanced to my left and made eye contact with Grace, who glared at me and twirled her finger in her ponytail.

Yeah . . . she was obviously in love with me. Stupid Lukas.

Grace was standing with three Japanese girls. One of them took out a camera, and the other two pulled Grace in between them and posed, their fingers twisted into peace signs.

"*Hai chizu!*" the girl with the camera said.

I spied Gabe, Lukas, and Wally outside the bathroom. They were looking at Arianna, whose mouth was moving so much it looked like she was lecturing a college class on some mega-boring topic. I went over to see why the guys were still listening.

"It's a traditional *washiki toire*," Arianna was saying. "A squat toilet. It's actually more sanitary than a Western toilet, though there's not always toilet paper available. Most homes have a Western toilet, though, which are called *yoshiki toire*."

"I shouldn't have come," Wally said. "I knew it would be difficult enough with my food allergies, but this I don't think I can tolerate."

The luggage carousel began to rotate, so I made myself useful before I had to listen to Wally break down. I pulled off any familiar luggage. My antique turtle of a suitcase came wobbling down the metal chute on its hard shell. I launched for it and knocked into someone in the process. "Sorry," I said.

"*Daijoubu.*"

The voice was a low purr. I looked down into big, brown anime eyes that belonged to a slender girl who was no taller than Grace. She had long black hair and thick bangs.

I frowned and cocked my head to the side, staring. This was my dream girl. I mean, not the girl of my dreams, but the girl from my reoccurring dream, the one who was swimming in the ocean.

"Daijobu *ka?*" she asked me.

I snapped out of my trance. Was I all right? I didn't have a clue. Because here was one very beautiful foreign girl. A girl I'd dreamed about already. And Mary had warned me about beautiful girls. So, what now?

"Supensa-san." Jun appeared beside me and wrenched my suitcase out of my hand. "Is time to go." He nodded at the Asian princess and walked away.

I trailed after him but looked back to the girl, who was now standing by Grace and Isabel. "Who was that girl?" I asked Jun.

"Keiko," Jun said.

Cake-o? I could remember that.

Jun led me and Gabe and Wally over to a bench where his parents were sitting. He introduced them as his *otosan* (father) and *okasan* (mother). They were both short and brown and full of smiles.

"*Sugoi . . .*" Jun's mother said, staring up at me. "*Kare wa se ga takai, ne?*" She slapped Jun's arm. "*Totemo* takai, ne? Ne, Jun. *Shinjirarenai, yo!*"

Sheen gee say what? I'd caught the word "takai," but that was it. Takai meant tall. Jun's father also stared up at me, though he didn't answer.

I offered Jun's mom a smile, and she kept on talking. "*Wa tashi wa akai kami o aishi te.*" She slapped Jun's arm. "Speak-u English. *Eigo.*"

"She says she loves red hair," Jun said.

Then she took off again, chattering incoherently. I recognized a familiar word here and there—tall, very, wow, cute, and of course, American—but my brain couldn't translate everything fast enough. Jun's father appeared to be mute. His wife spoke enough for both of them.

It was dark when Jun led us outside into the sticky heat. Shouldn't it have cooled off by now? I'd thought LA summers were hot, but this muggy tropical heat had clamped onto my skin like it was trying to suck the life out of me. We traipsed through an outdoor parking lot lit with streetlamps and up to a minivan that was so mini it looked like a toy. Jun's mom motioned me and Gabe to get in first, so I crammed into the third row with Gabe. I had to wedge my knees against the middle seat, and my head pressed against the ceiling. I really hoped I wouldn't have to ride in this thing much this summer.

Jun and his mother sat in the middle row. And for some reason Wally was in the passenger's seat.

"What's he doing up there?" I asked Gabe.

"Wally has to ride shotgun or he gets anxiety," Gabe said. "My dad explained it to Jun in the airport."

Yeah, right. "Well, tell Jun's mom that I can only eat at five-star restaurants."

Gabe chuckled.

Jun's mom turned and looked over the back of her seat. "Okasan speak-u English. So very very stew-rongu boee-zu, ne?" She giggled and reached over the seat to slap my knee. "*Watashi wa koun desu.* Okasan very very lucky. *San hansamu na otokonoko.* Three handu-some boee-zu. Ne? *Okasan no A-me-ri-kan* boee-zu."

That was Gabe and me. A couple of handsome boyzu.

Jun's father started the van and took off, peeling around

89

corners NASCAR-style. I gripped the seat in front of me. People drove on the left side of the road in Japan, and it was scary. I focused on the colorful electric signs, looking for kanji I recognized. Almost every sign seemed to be animated like we were in Vegas. The people on the sidewalks were all black-haired. No wonder I stood out. Maybe that was all Mary's dream meant: that Japanese girls would want to yank out my freakish orange hair. Of course that didn't explain the sunglasses guys. Maybe they'd want to kick my butt because all their girlfriends would be hitting on me.

There were palm trees everywhere. We passed endless businesses and lots of tiled sloping roofs. The drive lasted about twenty minutes before the minivan veered down a narrow alley with brick walls on both sides and jerked to a stop. Otosan climbed out and came around back to unload the luggage.

I was the last to climb out, sprawling out onto the sidewalk like some kind of a snake popping out of a can. I grabbed my suitcase from Jun's dad and approached the front door.

The house was a small one-story with a flat roof. Didn't look all that different from a house in the Neighborhood back home. It was painted beige and had bright turquoise trim and black iron window boxes. Bamboo mats covered the windows and flapped in the breeze. Tropical plants with huge leaves shaded the exterior walls. Two little stone dog monsters stared at me from a flowerbox beside the door, their eyes scowling. A ten-inch green striped lizard scuttled out of the flowers and up the wall. I jumped, then hefted my suitcase so it would look like I hadn't. Jun opened the door, and I followed him in.

The place wasn't much cooler inside. We entered a one-room living room/kitchen that was filled with more clutter than Mrs. Daggett's place. Bookshelves were filled with books, more stone dog monster statues in a variety of sizes, and a few glass boxes with fancy dolls inside. A couple of straw fans hung on the wall. The floor was grey-checked linoleum. There were two normal looking couches in front of an entertainment console with a TV/DVD player. A grand piano claimed half the room. The top was down, and stacks of books and papers covered most of it. A metal table with six chairs sat in the crook of an L-shaped kitchen. I saw a refrigerator but no oven. All the clutter made the place look smaller than it was.

Jun led us down a short hallway and pointed through a doorway on the left. "My parents' room."

I peeked in and saw a full-sized mattress and box springs made up into a bed on the floor. No frame.

Jun kept moving. "Bathroom is here." He gestured to an open door on the right. "When ready to take bath, am show you how."

I was relieved to see that it had a western toilet, but it also had a giant rubber trash can sitting next to the tub.

"I don't need assistance bathing," Wally said.

Jun snickered, and his smile lit up his face. "For the water. Must not waste."

There was only one other door. It was at the very end of the hallway.

"This room share with my brother. You sleep here also." Jun walked into the bedroom at the end of the hall. It was a little bigger than his parents' room, but there were no beds. Just a few shelves with books, a stereo, a closed laptop. A lamp dangled from a chain in the center of the room, and I knew I'd be hitting my head on that thing all summer. The same grey linoleum covered the floor as in the rest of the house.

Seriously? Five dudes on the floor of this room? I might as well be on a basketball trip. But for eight weeks?

I dropped the turtle suitcase and stretched, hitting my hand on the lamp chain. I was going to get so stiff on this floor. I'd need to find some way to keep in shape. I couldn't risk letting Coach be right about my deciding to come to Japan over his camp.

First stop, though? Bathroom with a real toilet.

When I finished in the bathroom, I found the others in the living room watching TV. Okasan stood in the kitchen, cooking up something that smelled like an ashtray. I sat on the sofa beside Gabe and checked out the show. Some dude in a clown costume was running around dumping buckets of cooked noodles over people's heads. Bizarre.

Okasan served up some hot, bitter tea. Mr. S had told us to be polite and at least try everything we were fed, so I held my breath and gulped down the tea. I wasn't much of a tea guy. Sadly, my enthusiasm thrilled Okasan, who brought me a second cup, which I sipped *very, very* slowly.

A half hour later, we all piled back into the sardine-can van. I had no idea where they were taking us at 8:45 at night. The trip was so short, I didn't know why we hadn't walked.

When I got out, I couldn't help but notice our surroundings had improved. Even in the dark, I could tell that this was the Snob Hill area of town. The gates and streetlamps were fancier. I could smell the flowers even if I couldn't see them. I stood on a spacious sidewalk that ran along a narrow street with an eight-foot-high brick wall on both sides. I could see the tile roofs of multi-story homes looming above, as if to brag about how big they were. And the crickets seemed to be yelling. Tons of them, even in the city.

I followed Jun to an opening in the brick wall and up a set of mosaic steps hedged in exotic shrubs. Stone dog statues as high as my knees were spaced here and there along the steps.

"What's with the monster dogs everywhere?" I asked.

"They are shisa," Jun said, holding open an iron gate for us. "A lion dog from Okinawan mythology. Ancients believed they warded off evil spirits. They usually come in pairs, one with an open mouth, one with a closed mouth."

"Why?" Gabe asked.

Jun let the gate close behind him, and we kept climbing the mosaic stairs. "The open mouth spreads good tidings. The closed mouth does not spread evil gossip."

"Creepy," I said.

At the top of the stairs, we came to an oversized wooden door that was carved with scrolls and flowers and reminded me of something out of *Lord of the Rings*. Whoever lived here had way more money than Jun's parents did.

Jun rang the bell. The door opened, revealing Keiko, the pretty girl from the airport—and my dreams. She wore a dark red blouse and a flippy black skirt that was so short Arianna would probably start protesting if she saw it.

"*Konbanwa*," Keiko said in that low, sexy voice.

I wanted to say it back, to tell her "Good evening, you gorgeous creature." But I didn't say anything. I always had a hard time breaking the ice with pretty girls. I usually did something dumb, like pulling Grace's ponytail. And last fall, I'd tried things the slow way with Beth, and that had backfired too. What was it going to take to get that exotic face to smile at me?

Keiko held the door wide, and we entered an air conditioned palace that was nicer than Sammy's mansion in LA. Fancy wall lights cast dim light over the front room. Tatami mats covered the floor. Dark wood shoji screens separated this room from the next. Shoji screens were little wooden window frames filled with white paper. Mr. S had taught us about them in class.

What little furniture existed was rich wood and of simple design. Everything was brown or beige. No clutter in this place. A flat stone hearth sat in the middle of the room and was built right into the floor like some kind of indoor campfire.

I would *so* live here. All it was missing was a big screen TV.

Several adults sat on their knees around the stone hearth, sipping tea. With everyone sitting and staring up at me, I felt like Gulliver walking through Lilliput. No, I'm not a fan of the book, but we'd had to read it in eighth grade.

Jun started across the room, shoes off. Gabe, Wally, and I kicked off our shoes and followed. I scanned the room for the lovely lady in red, but Keiko must have slipped away.

Someone grabbed my hand. I turned around, pleased to see that Keiko had never left. But she was now wearing a purple dress. And her hair was different. Curly, where I could have sworn it had just been straight. That was weird. What was up with the quick-change act? I felt my temperature rise at her touch—she was touching me! Holding my hand! Not glaring at me, like Grace always did.

She pulled me across the room—in the direction Jun and the others had gone. I would have followed her anywhere. We stepped past an open shoji screen and walked down a long, plain hallway, passed a dozen closed shoji screen doors.

The farther we traipsed into this mansion, the louder the sounds of laughter and Japanese chatter became. Keiko let go of my hand and pulled open a screen, which revealed a girls' bedroom packed with bodies. Arianna, Isabel, and Grace sat on a bed covered in a purple blanket. Three Japanese girls sat on a second, identical bed.

My host brother, Jun, sat on the floor in front of the second bed with his arm draped around Keiko—the girl in the red blouse who had answered the door.

Wait . . . what? I looked at the girl holding back the screen door.

Two Asian princesses? No way, no way!

Jun burst into laughter and clapped his hands, hysterical at my reaction. I looked from one girl to the other. They were identical—more so than Mary and Martha. I guess when God makes something that perfect, one just isn't enough.

"Keiko and Kozue are identical twins, Spencer," Arianna said.

Ko-say? I coughed up an airy laugh, trying to be cool. "You think?"

"They're our host sisters, high-tower, so we already knew."

Grace's hostility instantly chilled me. "Yeah, well, congratulations, Butterscotch. I'm sure you were confused at first, but don't blame yourself: Blondes are born dumb."

"*Spencer!*" Gabe said from behind me.

I winced. Yeah . . . I'd gone too far with the blonde joke.

"What's black and blue and orange and lying in a ditch?" Grace asked me.

Uh-oh. I had a feeling I was about to get burned. "The Philadelphia Flyers after playing the Kings?"

"A ginger who's told too many blonde jokes."

"So, you want to take me on, is that it?" I said. "You do know that I could beat you with one hand behind my back, Tinkerbell."

"You probably beat up girls for fun."

"What's your prob—?"

"Spencer." Arianna scooted forward on the bed, blocking my view of Grace. "How is your house and your family? What's it like?"

Jun coughed and looked at the floor.

"It's great," I said, hoping to avoid having to compare the mansion to the shack and embarrassing my new host bro. "Jun's mom makes this awesome tea."

Jun wrinkled his nose. "You *like* her tea?"

"It was wonderful," Wally said, sitting on the edge of the bed next to Arianna. "Green tea contains polyphenol antioxidants, which fight against free radicals. It slows the aging process and promotes longevity."

The three Japanese girls on the other bed giggled, hands over their mouths as if showing one's teeth was bad form. I doubted they had a clue what Wally had just said. I didn't, and I spoke English.

I looked over the room. There was a computer, drawers draped with clothing that must not have made the cut for tonight, and posters on the wall. I did a double take at one with an American girl dressed in black lingerie with a beast hunting belt slung around her hips. Big, bloody Japanese katakana symbols stretched across the top. It was a poster for *Jolt III: Return of the Daysman*. I *so* needed to get me one of those.

"Dude!" I pointed. "You guys like Brittany Holmes?"

Every Japanese girl in the room squealed.

The twin who was standing beside me, the one wearing purple, looked up, her eyes sleepy. "Light Goddess. We love."

I nodded, impressed at how Brittany's popularity stretched from Moscow to Okinawa. The girl was all over the planet.

"I've seen all but the new movie." *Jolt III* had hit theaters the day before we'd left, and Grandma had made me stay home and pack. So unfair.

"We'll take you," Jun said. "Is playing in Naha."

"Seriously?" Because that would be amazing.

"We go," Jun said. "Soon."

I'm going to see Br-it-tany. I'm going to see Br-it-tany.

But what if the movie was in Japanese?

Keiko pulled me inside the room and closed the shoji screen. The Japanese girls moved over so Gabe and I could sit on the bed. I sat between Gabe and the acne girl from the airport. Wally sat across from us, between Arianna and Isabel. Keiko sat on Isabel's other side.

I looked from Keiko to Kozue and back and forth. Which twin had I seen in my dreams? Were both visions the same girl? One of each? Could I ever know for certain?

"You have girlfriend?" a Japanese girl in a Keroppi Frog shirt asked Gabe.

"No," Gabe said with a shy glance at Isabel.

The girls shrieked. One with pigtails reached over the acne girl's arm and nudged me. "You have? Girlfriend?"

I shook my head. The girls squealed and leaned against one another, hysterical. I looked at Gabe and laughed. Crazy.

The evening passed in a blur of shrieks and giggles from the Japanese girls on the bed. Keiko talked quietly to Isabel. Kozue, the twin in red sitting with Jun on the floor between the beds, spent most of the night kissing Jun. I hoped they weren't going to make a habit of that. I'd been glad to leave the Kip-Megan creature back in LA and had no desire to spend time with its Okinawan counterpart.

Keiko, however, according to the acne girl, was single. Oh, yeah.

Keroppi Frog Girl, Pigtails, and Acne—I didn't catch their names—asked me and Gabe hundreds of questions. Pigtail girl asked me about KitKats and my favorite Brittany Holmes movie—*Jolt II*, of course. Keroppi Frog Girl kept asking about *Star Trek*. She really liked the re-launch movies and squealed at the mention of Chris Pine. Acne girl asked if she could touch my hair, so I let her. Hey, at least she'd asked. She said it was soft too. So there.

Wally went on and on to Arianna about which Japanese foods were healthiest. She must have been practicing her word of the year—listen—because she was letting the guy prattle on like Jun's mom. And Grace stayed in her corner of the bed, silent and glaring at me like a Goomba from Super Mario Brothers.

I ignored her. What else could I do? I wasn't going to let her spoil my trip. I had big plans for this summer and all the foreign girls that Mary had warned me about. As if Princess Keiko could be dangerous.

Grace, however . . . I had a feeling *that* girl could cause me plenty of trouble.

REPORT NUMBER: 8

REPORT TITLE: I Get My First Real Spy Mission and a Spicy Lunch
SUBMITTED BY: Agent-in-Training Spencer Garmond
LOCATION: Oroku High School, 1-5-3 Kanagusuku, Naha,
Okinawa, Japan
DATE AND TIME: Wednesday, June 3, 7:49 a.m.

HIGH SCHOOL WENT YEAR-ROUND for Okinawans, the poor saps. Jun had given us guys navy slacks, white polo shirts, and neckties: the school's uniform. Whee. I looked like a moron with pants three inches too short. And can I just say, long pants in this heat? Really? You'd think some Asian Arianna would have protested for shorter garments to keep everyone from suffering heat strokes. Because it was hot here. Not hot like, "Oh, let me find some shade." But humid hot, like a sauna, like Satan's lair. The heat clung to me like sweat and smoked down my throat with every breath.

When we left the house that morning, a cheer of children's voices went up. Across the alley road a dozen Japanese children pressed up against a long black gate, their arms and legs flailing between the bars.

"A-me-ri-kan! A-me-ri-kan!"

"My parents' preschool," Jun said.

I waved at the kids, which made them scream and laugh. Crazy.

We walked to school, which wasn't far—maybe five minutes, but that just made the heat worse. Oroku High School was four wings of four stories of stone with one wall of each classroom open to the hallway and the outdoor courtyard on the first floor of each wing. It must feel strange to see people walking by your desk during class. And what if it rained? Water probably wouldn't get into the classrooms with the overhang in the hallways, but wouldn't it be distracting?

Jun showed us a map of the school painted on a sign. He said we should meet him by the gym after our last class of the day. I snapped a picture on *My Precious* in case I got lost.

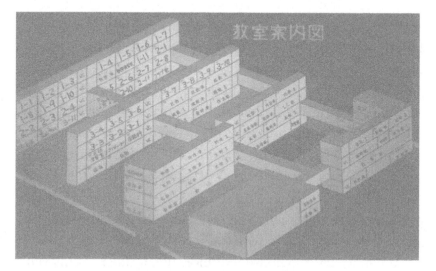

Jun led us up some concrete stairs. Japanese guys stared and said things I didn't understand. Japanese girls gawked and giggled. Clearly I was a freak here. But at least I was a cool freak.

Just as my eyes crested the floor of level three, I saw Mary Stopplecamp dressed in a school uniform, walking away from us. Those curls in that ponytail were unmistakable.

I pointed. "Gabe, isn't that—"

"Mary!" Gabe yelled, running ahead of us. He grabbed Mary's arm and pulled her around.

It wasn't Mary. It was Keiko. Or Kozue. I'd never know which.

"Sorry," Gabe said, backing away.

"*Ohayo*, Keiko," Jun said as the rest of us reached them.

Now that I was standing beside her, Keiko wasn't quite as short as Mary, but she was close. I couldn't believe both Gabe and I had thought she was his sister. Weird.

"What happened to your hair?" Gabe asked.

Keiko turned her head from side to side. "Imomoko hair sponge. Isabel did our hair today. Was too bushy so I put ponytail. Is cute, you think?"

Very. But not because it resembled Mary's hair. Because Mary was thirteen.

I'm just making that clear.

"Well, I go to class. *Ja ne*." And she turned and jogged away, curls bouncing.

"How can you tell them apart?" I asked Jun. Such intel might help me figure out which one was in my dream. And which one I could hit on without making Jun mad.

"Keiko has little mole," Jun said, tapping his left cheek. "But also, Kozue doesn't go to school here."

Convenient for me. "Where does Kozue go to school?"

"Shogaku. Is private school. Kozue wants study in America, so Shogaku is better. *Ikuzo.*"

We followed Jun to his homeroom class. I smiled politely when the teacher introduced us. Couldn't understand a word she said except for our names. Then, she went on with her teaching—whatever subject it was—and ignored us.

I sat in back with Gabe and Wally.

Guys and girls were fanning themselves with sheets of plastic covered in Anime, Hello Kitty, Keroppi Frog, or Japanese rock stars. I needed to get me one of those.

I wrote a note to Gabe on my schedule.

Me: Where are the others?

Gabe: ?

So we sat, doing nothing, until class ended. Then we followed Jun to another class. Another awkward introduction. And we sat in the back again. At least I could tell that this was a math class. Even I could recognize the writing on the whiteboard. It looked harder than any math I'd taken so far, though. Glad I didn't live here.

During third period, Jun dropped us off in the school library, which just about made my day.

Because the library was air conditioned.

The librarian sent us to a private study room in the back. It had four skinny tables with three chairs each. The girls had already taken over the front row: Jensina and Beth at one table—Isabel, Grace, and Arianna at the other. Jake and Lukas sat at the table behind Jensina and Beth. So Gabe, Wally, and I claimed the only empty one, me on the end, right behind Grace.

Great. I was looking at that blasted ponytail again.

Mr. S was standing up front with Prière, who must get massive frequent flyer miles as much as that guy traveled. He reminded me of the Where's Waldo guy, only he also had a thick, black moustache.

I draped my arms over the cool Formica and moaned. It felt *so* good. "How do people live in this heat?" I laid one cheek against the tabletop. My eyes drooped. I wondered how much time I had before Mr. S got this party started, because sleep would be perfect right now.

"Live in it?" Beth's voice came from my left. "How do they work out in it? We're supposed to practice LCT here, right?"

"The dojo is likely air conditioned," Mr. S said. "But if you all crack under a little heat, I'm not sure how I can recommend you for adult posts."

This was more than a little heat. I opened my eyes and looked to Mr. S, who was holding a stack of blue cards. Prière had a stack of red cards. My stomach did a back flip at the thought of getting a real assignment.

"You're going to pass out assignments, Mr. S?" I asked.

"'Time brings roses,' Agent Garmond."

Whatever. "Mr. S, are we really going to spend all day, every day in school here? The teachers talk so fast I can't understand what they're saying." Seemed like a big waste of time.

"You will each have four classes a day. The other two class periods and lunch will be spent in here. Some of the classes, like calligraphy, sewing, and cooking, should be fun for you. The others, you are meant to learn the language, so do your best to follow along."

Calligraphy? Sewing? Was he serious?

I turned my head, putting my other cheek on the cool

surface, and looked out the floor-to-ceiling window beside the door. I could see the rows of bookshelves. A Japanese man was walking this way. I expected him to turn when he reached the back wall. Instead, the door opened, and he came inside. I recognized him from the airport.

"Good Wednesday to you," the man said, nodding to us as he walked around to the front of the room. He was slender with thin black hair and patchy eyebrows and was wearing a rumpled beige suit.

I flipped my head on the table to see where he went. He greeted Prière with a nod and stood beside Mr. S. They mumbled to each other, then Mr. S cleared his throat.

"This is Hiroshi Toda-san," Mr. S said. "He is the League instructor for Oroku High School and all of Naha. My family is staying with his while we're here."

"*Hajimemashite, Toda-san*," Arianna said.

Toda-san nodded to her. All this nodding made me glad I had my head down.

"Toda-san would like to tell you a little about Okinawa," Mr. S said.

"*Hai, so desu.* Okinawa Prefecture is made up of the Ryukyu Islands. Long ago these islands were separate from Japan, but in 1879, Japan took control of Ryukyu Kingdom and this land became Okinawa Prefecture. Because Okinawa was a separate nation for so long, many people speak languages different from traditional Japanese. If your host family speaks words you cannot understand, could be they are speaking Okinawan.

"Okinawan people are independent and embrace a distinct culture. This shows in music and foods and language and even our mindsets. We are considered to be the healthiest people in the world. We have a low fat diet of fish, pork, seaweed, and vegetables. Our diet and good attitude of not worrying or getting angry, this is the medicine for a long life.

"Since World War II, the United States have had a military presence in Okinawa. There is an ongoing struggle between Okinawans and the Japanese government about the US bases. Okinawans frequently feel they are not cared for by the Japanese government. There is often much protesting, though it is always peaceful. Okinawa is a peaceful nation. Many don't mind the US bases here, but they would like the land back. I've found this is more an issue for the older generations. Okinawan youth have never known life on Okinawa without the US bases.

"It is the poorest region in Japan. Okinawa buildings are made of concrete with cement roof tiles and covered windows. This is because of frequency of tropical storms and typhoons. Okinawa relies on tourism and is famous for tropical beaches. Many come here to vacation.

"Okinawa is to Japan what Hawaii is to United States," Mr. S added.

"Hai, so desu," Toda-san nodded to Mr. S. "As to faith, Okinawa's indigenous religion is animistic, and there are also aspects of Shinto and Buddhism. While most don't practice any religion, they still believe in sacred spirits and that pleasing these spirits will ward off misfortune and bring blessings. Many also believe that spirits of their ancestors are always near, observing the life of their descendants."

"What about Christianity?" Jensina asked.

"Less than one percent of the Okinawan population is Christian. Please pray for the people of Okinawa to come to know of God's love and grace."

"What are the differences for students?" Arianna asked. "I noticed that students don't ask many questions of the teacher."

"Students are used to the teacher always being the master," Toda-san said. "And politeness and respect are very important in our culture. Most classes are lecture-oriented. Students in Japan face incredible pressure for academic success. They take very difficult tests to determine what high school and college they can enter. Because of this, they study very much after school and on weekends. Because of this pressure to succeed in school and later in life, suicide rates are very high."

"Is crime bad here?" Jake asked.

"We sometimes have problems with American soldiers," Toda-san said. "Also, there are four organized crime groups in Naha. Yamaguchi-gumi, Sumiyoshi-kai, and Inagawa-kai operate throughout Japan. But the Abaku-kai is the group which causes the most difficulty for Naha. Many teenagers are recruited to join. Even some students here at Oroku High School are members of Abaku-kai."

Organized crime. I wondered how C-Rok would do if we had a mob in LA. Scary.

"You will be volunteering at two places where we suspect Abaku-kai's involvement," Toda-san said. "Kimura Fitness and Kimura Bank of Naha. Please be very careful." He nodded to Mr. S then, and I gathered he was done.

"Thank you, Toda-san," Mr. S said. "We appreciate your time."

"*Kite kurete arigato*," Arianna said. All I caught of that mouthful was *thanks*.

"*Iie.*" Toda-san nodded again, like some kind of bobble head that couldn't help it. "I must go to my classroom now. Enjoy the lunch."

"*Ja mata ne*," Arianna called after him. Show off.

Mr. S took Toda-san's place up front and tapped his little stack of blue cards on the surface of Arianna's desk. "I want you to observe this summer. Try and understand what it's like to live here. Look for the things Toda san mentioned so that we can talk about it when we get together."

"Which is when?" Jake asked.

"We'll meet weekdays in this room during the third hour class period and through lunch," Mr. S said.

Excellent. I would relish my daily dose of air conditioning. And the food too. My stomach had that hollow ache going on. I needed sustenance. Hopefully I'd get more of it here than at Jun's place.

"Before we eat, we're going to hand out assignments," Mr. S said. "Prière will pass out red cards, and I'll pass out blue cards. You may talk *quietly* until your name is called."

I eyed the much smaller stack of red cards Prière was holding, wishing they weren't for seniors only. How sweet would it be to get a real assignment?

"Elizabeth Watkins," Prière said.

Of course Beth would get a coolio assignment. I flipped my head and put my first cheek on the table, but the surface was no longer cool. I scooted to the left and found a fresh cold patch of desk and moaned again.

Arianna turned around in her seat. "How was breakfast at your place?"

I was facing away from her, so I finally sat up. Arianna must have brought her collection of floor-length skirts to Japan, because she was wearing a floofy one instead of the pleated skirts the other girls had on. "We had some nasty soup that smelled like dirty towels. I chugged it but almost hurled.

Hopefully my host mom will make something else tomorrow."

"Most Japanese homes have miso soup as part of their breakfast each day," Arianna said. "Didn't you have anything with it?"

"Tea," I said. "Jun's mom serves mostly a liquid diet. I think our host family might be poor."

"She served rice too," Gabe said.

I leaned back so I could see Gabe around Wally. "Yeah, but I can't use the stupid chopsticks," I said. "Can't I use my fingers?"

"That's India, Spencer," Arianna said. "Please don't eat rice with your fingers here."

"And don't pass food with your chopsticks, either," Wally said. "It reminds people of the ancient ritual of passing bones."

Eww. "I can't even use them to feed myself, why would I try to pass food?"

Gabe slapped the tabletop. "Oh, and don't stick your chopsticks upright in your bowl of rice."

"Stop telling me what *not* to do. What *can* I do?"

"Miso soup is very healthy," Wally said. "I'm thankful it will be served daily. Seaweed is high in essential amino acids and a valuable source of vegetable protein. Plus it contains virtually no fat."

I was well aware that Japanese people ate seaweed, but all I could think of was that green stuff that washed up on the beaches in LA, tangled around trash. Disgusting. "Look at me!" I said to Wally. "You think I can maintain this awesome physique on nothing but seaweed, water, and rice? I *need* my fat."

"Spencer?" Mr. S called.

I jumped, ready to apologize for talking too loudly, but Mr.

S waved me over. Right. Time for the phony quest that would likely take me all summer to complete. I joined Mr. S in the corner adjacent to Prière and sat on the empty chair next to him. He handed me a blue card.

SOLO

FIELD: PROFILING: FACILITY SKETCH

Measure and draw the structure at 3-18-57 Jinan, Naha, Okinawa

I looked at Mr. S. "Where is this?"

He shrugged, a guilty grin on his face. "It's *your* assignment, Agent Garmond. You've got to find it."

Oh-kay. I stood up and tucked the card into my back pocket. "No problem." My eyes met Grace's at the table in front of me, looking up like I was the US Bank Tower. I hurried back to my seat before she could start another skirmish.

I'd barely sat down at the table beside Wally when Prière said, "Spence?"

A little thrill ran through me. "Seriously? A red card?" Sah-weet. I jogged to the empty chair beside Prière.

The Frenchman's dark eyes studied me, and his moustache twitched. "How have you been, Spence? Getting sleep enough?"

"Sure," I lied. Why did he always have to ask important stuff when other people were around? I wasn't going to complain about my widdle baby nightmares with Beth and Grace within earshot.

"You have not yet had a red card, is this correct?" Prière asked.

"Yeah." I eyed the little red business card in Prière's hand.

"I thought they were only for seniors."

"God will do what He thinks best, Spence. Now, you must understand that red cards are *confidentiel* between us unless I say otherwise. It this clear?"

I nodded. Gimme gimme.

Prière handed me the red card.

Partner: Grace Thomas
SERVICE: HELPS: COMMUNITY: FAMILY SERVICES
Run after-school recreation program
at Kimura Fitness Center.

"Grace?" I said. She looked at me, so I lowered my voice. "Are you nuts?"

"You, in particular, will be in charge of the gymnasium," Prière said. "Miss Thomas will assist you. This will be Monday to Friday after school from 4:30 to 5:30. You will begin this coming Monday, so have a plan for leading activities *à la* gym."

Fabulous. "Since when are partner assignments on red cards?"

"Since International decided it was to be so last month."

"But I thought . . ." Whatever. The whole thing had felt like a nasty trick, making me think I was getting a real assignment . . . Grumble, grumble.

"I am hoping this is not *une* error." Prière held up a second red card, his eyes twinkling like a grandpa who'd just pulled a coin out from behind my ear. "You were hoping for a solo assignment like this one?"

"Yes!" I snatched the card from Prière and read it.

SOLO

FIELD: PROFILING: WORLD
Track and report all movements and conversations
of Keiko Kimura.

Yes, yes, yes! I pumped my fist over my lap. Now, this was more like it. And it fit with the prophecies I'd been having about Keiko. Or Kozue. Or both. I glanced at Prière, fighting back a smile.

The Frenchman regarded me with raised brows. "I will tell you now that *Monsieur* Stopplecamp is already aware of both your red card assignments. You will report to him every Monday. A weekly written report is required on all assignments along with any intercession reports. Do you *comprends?*"

"Yeah, sure." Whatever you want, man. I was a real spy!

"Do you accept these assignments?"

"Yeah, yes. I do." I had difficulty maintaining calm. I wanted to stand up and whoop.

Prière scribbled something down on his clipboard. "Destroy the cards the first chance you get. Burn or shred— only do not throw them away. God be with you, Spence. At this time you may return to your chair."

"Okay, but did you get my intercession reports? I don't know what I should be doing about all that."

"I did get the reports, and they have been distributed through the correct channels. There is no reason for you to do anything."

"Well, what about—?" I glanced at Mr. S and lowered my voice. "What about the dreams that Mary Stopplecamp had about me? And those twins, Keiko or Kozue. One of them is the girl from my prophecies, so . . . ?"

"Agents are here to protect you, Spence. Do not worry about your safety, and—"

"I'm not *worried*. I can take care of myself."

Prière raised one eyebrow, as if unsure whether I was done interrupting. "Continue to write intercession reports and hand them in to Monsieur Stopplecamp. They will be distributed as usual but also to the agents that are protecting you. All will be well."

Easy for him to say. I strode back to my seat, lost in thought. Last year, Nick had been assigned to watch Pasha. Isaac to watch me. Isaac's had been a red card assignment. I hadn't really thought about Nick's assignment until now, but I bet his had been a red card too because both Pasha and I had been in serious trouble. So, did that mean that Keiko was in danger? She'd seemed so quiet. Like a China doll—er . . . a Japanese doll. Close enough.

And now that I thought about it . . . there'd been two girls in that restaurant booth in my dream. Could it be Keiko *and* Kozue? If so, one looked hurt. I had to make sure that my vision remained a warning so that nothing bad happened to either of them.

Wally was speaking with Mr. S, and Gabe with Prière, so I read my solo assignment again, then tucked them both in my back pocket with the blue card. I'd burn them later somehow.

Grace slid into Wally's empty chair beside me, the pleasant smell of coconuts with her as always. She set a little origami bird in front of me. "It's a crane. I made it for you. Cute, huh?"

"Adorable." And it was, actually. She'd made it out of white paper with little cartoon leaves on it.

"You got two red cards?"

My spine stiffened, and I looked at her out of the corner of my eye without moving my head. I was Jason Bourne, baby. I had no time for pixie games. "We're not supposed to talk about them, so don't ask."

"Can't I even look at them?" She smiled at me like we were buds.

I turned to face her and leaned close, hoping my height would be intimidating. "Nope," I said, popping the P.

Her left eyebrow twitched, but she held her smile steady. Her hair was down now, curling like wild Christmas ribbon to her elbows. I noticed she'd put the elastic band on her wrist. It wasn't fair. It hurt to look at someone so pretty and know she was a beast inside. Such a waste of hotness.

"You like living with Jun?" Grace asked me, which reminded me that I'd been staring.

I looked at my notebook. "Yeah, Jun's cool." Though the bedroom floor was like sleeping on the sidewalk. But it wasn't Jun's fault that his parents weren't rolling in dough like Keiko's and Kozue's fam.

"Jun and Kozue have been dating for five months," Grace informed me. "Do you think that's a long time?"

I shrugged. "I guess." Not as long as the Kip-Megan. They'd started dating when I was in Moscow last summer. Thankfully I'd be here when their nauseating one-year anniversary rolled around. Gag.

"Hmm." Grace's humming pulled my eyes back to her. She twirled a strand of curls around her finger and batted her eyes at me. "What's the longest *you've* ever had a girlfriend?"

My face flooded with heat, but I fought against it like Beth had taught me. I had nothing to hide. "Six days."

Grace's face lit up, her lips fighting a smile. "That's it?"

"Yeah, Sunflower, that's it." And thanks for rubbing it in."

JILL WILLIAMSON

"Well, I'm sure you'll get a girlfriend soon. Guys like you always do."

Why was she even talking to me? I glanced over my shoulder to make sure she hadn't found an accomplice to put a "kick me" sign on my back. "I'm not looking for a girlfriend, thanks." I was *such* a liar. I even felt my eye twitch.

"Any girl would be lucky to go out with a guy like you," Grace said.

I narrowed my eyes at the she-devil. "What's that supposed to mean?"

"Nothing." She looked down at her lap, then glanced back at me, then away again. "I'm saying you're cute." Another glance. "And nice."

Whaaat-ev-er.

The thing was, I'd learned a few things about girls over this last year. They were psycho. Allow me to review.

Anya: Beautiful women could try and kill you. And steal your best Lakers cap.

Isabel: Sometimes pretty meant not too smart and fingernails that prohibited the use of hands.

Beth: If a girl was nice, she probably only wanted to be friends or use her hotness on the LCT competition mat to make your brain go all stupid so she could kick your butt.

Trella: If a girl insulted you, she might actually like you, but what guy wants to go out with someone who calls him ape arms? Not I, said the fly.

Katie: And if a girl was all over you, she was probably being paid to steal your iPhone and help you get kidnapped by maniacs.

I rest my case.

And now Grace? Well, origami crane aside, I solemnly

swore that Little Miss Sunshine was up to no good. First it was all insults, but now she was coming onto me? Something was not right.

Mr. S's voice jolted me from my confusion with Grace. He went over the school schedule. He reminded us not to approach field agents we recognized who may be working undercover, which reminded me that Arianna's dad was around here somewhere, following me. Then Mr. S explained the passcode that was currently in use for agents to identify other agents.

"I want you to learn it in English and Japanese," Mr. S said. "If you need to use it on a Japanese person, use Japanese. Otherwise, use English. The passcode works like this." Mr. S turned to face Prière. "*Donata desu ka?*"

"*Kaeru no ko wa kaeru,*" Prière said.

I didn't know what Prière's words meant, but hearing the Frenchman speak Japanese made me snort a laugh.

"Now, in English," Mr. S said. "Who is it?"

"Like father like son," Prière answered.

Wacko. Passcodes never made any sense. Wouldn't we call attention to ourselves saying something so dumb? I wanted to ask, but the door opened. A round Japanese woman pushed a cart inside that was stacked with takeout containers. I looked longingly at them, wishing they were filled with fried chicken, and not rice and miso soup.

The woman fixed one tray at a time from the takeout totes and passed them out. It was filled with fancy little circles of rice wrapped in seaweed. Sushi rolls? Aw, this wasn't going to fill my stomach. I was going to starve in Japan. I wanted meat, and lots of it.

Grace stroked my arm with her index finger, and I twitched

at the thrill it sent through me. "Are you going to eat your guacamole?" she asked.

Guacamole? I examined my lunch. Ah. A quarter-sized glob of the green paste sat on the corner of my tray. They ate guac in Japan? Who knew? "Yes. Yes I am." At least I'd have a taste of something good to wash the raw stuff down with. Wasn't there any rice? I looked around and saw the woman place a bowl of rice in front of Jake.

Praise You, Lord in heaven. And I meant it.

Now if I could just get the stuff in my mouth . . . I'd have to find me a fork somewhere and keep it in a holster. I waited for Mr. S to bless the food, then I ripped my sticks apart and tried to balance the thin wisps of balsa wood between my fingers. How did people eat with these Pick-Up Sticks?

"Do you want mine?" Grace asked pointing to the guacamole. "I don't like avocados."

"Yes." I scooted my tray beside hers like we were little girls playing house. Grace used her chopsticks to scrape her guac onto my tray with ease, like she ate with chopsticks every day.

"Don't pass food with your chopsticks!" Wally said.

"Calm down," I said to Wally. "There is no one here to be offended."

Grace used her chopsticks to pick up a sushi roll, dip it in the soy sauce, and put the whole thing in her mouth. She glanced at me, eyes wide and blue, chewing, cheeks ballooned like a chipmunk.

I shuddered, conflicted by how cute and confident Grace looked eating something so nasty.

I went back to "eating" little bites of rice, two to three grains at a time on the wretched Pick-Up Sticks.

"Use them more like a shovel." Grace scooped up a heaping

pile of rice on her chopsticks and put the whole bite, successfully, in her mouth without losing a granule or messing up her pink lipstick.

I hated her more than ever.

The food woman came over and poured me, Grace, and Wally some tea.

"Do you have any water?" I asked her. "Iie, tea only."

What was so great about tea, anyway? I mean, let's face it. I was never going to become a tea drinker. And if I did, I'd get me a big ol' 7-11 refill mug instead of drinking out of dainty doll bowls.

I jabbed at my rice like I was stirring water. Shoveling it in worked if I kept my mouth touching the bowl, sort of like drinking it. After getting down a good-sized bite, I scooped up the guacamole on my chopsticks. I grinned and nudged Grace with my elbow. "Check it," I said. "Got the whole glob at once."

"I'm so proud," she said in a flat voice.

Whatever. Afraid I'd lose the guac, I brought my mouth to the chopsticks, stuck out my tongue, and sucked off the glob.

Fire incinerated my senses. I spit the green goop onto my tray, but it didn't help. "Arrrrggggppppthhhh!" I couldn't talk. My tongue singed. Acid. Someone had put acid in the guac. I picked up my tea and dunked my tongue into the tiny bowl. The hot liquid brought no satisfaction or relief.

Grace giggled hysterically, clutching her sides, her curls vibrating around her face. Wally just stared at me.

"What wrong with him?" Jake asked Grace.

"He ate the wasabi," Wally said. "Wasabi is helpful in preventing cancer, ulcers, and fighting tooth decay. It also prevents food poisoning, which is why it's often served with raw fish, like sushi."

I wanted to say, "Thank you, Encyclopedia Britannica," but I couldn't speak.

Jake snorted a delighted laugh, his eyes filled with joy at my expense. "You're not supposed to eat it all at once, fool. You're supposed to mix it in your soy sauce."

"Fankth," I managed, my eyes blurry with tears, my nose stinging.

"Haven't you seen *Cars 2*?" Jake asked. "That ain't no pistachio ice cream, Mater."

Nor was it guacamole. I refused to look at Grace—the evil little wench—and went back to eating my rice, one granule at a time.

By the end of lunch, my mouth was back to normal, but my temper was still smoking.

REPORT NUMBER: 9

REPORT TITLE: I Get into Karate Trouble
SUBMITTED BY: Agent-in-Training Spencer Garmond
LOCATION: Kimura Fitness Center, 3-18-57 Jinan, Naha,
Okinawa, Japan
DATE AND TIME: Wednesday, June 3, 4:12 p.m.

WHEN JUN LED ME, GABE, AND Wally to Kimura Fitness after school, I was thrilled to see that the address was the same as the one on my blue card assignment. Nothing like a little help on my homework to lighten my step. My excitement was short-lived, however, because the building was massive. How was I supposed to sketch this puppy in two months? I mean, come on.

Mr. S met us in the lobby, and once the rest of the Americans showed, he introduced a tall Japanese man I recognized from the get-together at Kozue and Keiko's house. For a Japanese dude, he was tall. Close to six foot. He wore a white karate gi top, flowing black hakama pants, and a red belt. He was barefoot.

"This is Kimura-san," Mr. S said, "who is Kozue and Keiko's father. He is the owner of Kimura Fitness and Kimura Bank of Naha. He is also Judan, the highest rank available in Okinawan Karate." Which Mr. S pronounced kah-rah-tay. "Kimura-san?"

Kimura-san bowed to us. "Arigato. For fifteen years I run Ten Ai Ko Dojo, where I teach the Budo—Japanese martial arts. Over years, dojo grow to include weight training and gym. Today we also have dance room. We are now called Kimura Fitness."

Kimura-san gave a tour of the facility. I sketched out what I could on the back of my school schedule, but I'd have to snoop around later if I was going to do this right.

I had yet to decide whether or not I was going to do this right, by the way. It wasn't like I was being graded. And I was way more interested on starting my track-and-report mission on Keiko.

When we got back to the dojo, a dozen students—dressed in white *kah-rah-tay* gis—were sparring, their reflections gleaming off the polished wood floor. No mats. Yowzers.

"Some of you are trained in karate, is correct?" Kimura-san asked.

"Hai," Mr. S said.

Hai, my foot. League Combat Training had *elements* of many different martial arts, jujitsu more than any other, but we'd been training to subdue without harm, not to break boards.

Kimura-san yelled, *"Hai! Seiretsu!"* and the students scrambled toward him, forming a line like soldiers. "These *Amerikan* students are from *Kariforunia*. Many train in karate also."

I saw Jun at the end of the row of students and wondered when he'd left us to get changed. I smiled at my host bro, but he didn't smile back. He stared straight ahead, glassy eyed like some kind of zombified soldier. Maybe it wasn't Jun, after all. These guys all kind of looked the same with their crew cut hairstyles and their white karate gis. Maybe it was a dress code.

One of the students stepped forward and bowed to the American group. "*Onegai shimasu.*"

Kimura-san gave the guy a small smile then surveyed us Americans. "Which Amerikan will fight? One round *jiu kumite.*"

"Garmond will," Jake said pushing me forward.

I stumbled to a stop and lunged back into the crowd. "I don't think so. Why don't you go out there and get pummeled?"

"You made District, not me," Jake said. "So get out there and show some American spirit, man."

I smirked at Jake. "Make Beth do it. She got closer to wining than I did." By using her feminine wiles to cheat, I might add. But I wasn't bitter. Much.

"But I cheated, remember?" Beth said from behind me, surprising me with her honesty. "You probably would've won otherwise."

"Nice." I wished Beth *would* fight this guy. It would be nice to see her lose for once.

Movement at the end of the room caught my eye. Keiko and Kozue had arrived, looking doubly gorgeous. I wondered which one was Keiko. They were too far away to see any moles. A stupid idea surfaced in my boy brain. Maybe I could impress her by taking down one of her daddy's students.

But karate? I never could remember the rules. To win I had to score more points—eight, I thought—and try not to get hit. Simple enough, right?

"Okay." I stepped forward and slipped off my sneakers, then crouched and peeled off my socks.

"Atta boy, Tiger," Beth said, giving me a shrill wolf-whistle.

Yeah, yeah. I just hoped I wouldn't die a humiliating death. I handed Gabe my Lakers cap and walked out to the center of the mat and bowed to my opponent. The guy wasn't so big. Looked to weigh about 150. He was wearing a sleeveless kimono that showed off his huge arms, though. Dude could probably do 200 chin-ups without breaking a sweat.

"We will use pads for this because Americans are used to it," Kimura-san said.

What? I looked at Beth and whispered, "What's *that* supposed to mean?"

"Pads are an American thing to keep insurance costs down for karate schools," Beth said. "It's like I said before: Pads allow you to fight lazy. These guys do 'hard style' martial arts. I've trained you well, Tiger, but you don't know this guy. I say, put on the pads."

"I trained you well . . ." What a nut. I'd learned more from Boss Schwarz than Beth. But she made a good point. For all I knew, this guy was a killing machine. I strapped on the sparring gear Kimura-san offered me: padded headgear, gloves, and boots. Mine were red. My opponent's were blue. I didn't bring my mouth guard to Japan, so I'd better not let myself get hit in the face.

I recited Beth's words. *It isn't the size of the muscles—it's the size of the brain. If you fight smart, you'll fight best.* Plus this guy had a smug look on his face that hinted: small brain, big ego.

Kimura-san backed away from the mat and called, "*Hajime!*"

Ego Boy started bouncing on his feet. Up down, up down, like the mat was on fire. I stayed back, gauging my foe, as Boss Schwartz liked us to call our opponents. Who knew what this guy was capable of? He sprung forward and jabbed a fist at my mid-section. I tucked my arms against my chest to block, then darted in with my own snap punch.

He blocked me.

I slid back a few steps, not liking the way these uniform pants felt. I'd probably rip out the crotch if I tried a side kick. Ego Boy came closer, bounce, bounce, bouncing the whole time. He launched forward and thrust a few punches. I blocked but stumbled back a bit. Ego Boy leapt into the air with a powerful roundhouse kick that nailed me in the chest.

Ugh. Just my luck. Ego Boy's skill matched his ego. Dude must do some serious body conditioning too—his limbs were like tire irons, even through the gloves.

"*Yame!*" Kimura-san yelled.

Ego Boy strutted back to his side of the mat. I did the same, trying to pretend that his kick wasn't stinging worse than one of Beth's.

"*Mawashi geri, nihon.*" Kimura-san pointed at Ego Boy.

The Japanese students cheered. The Americans clapped, as well.

"Come on, Spencer!" Gabe yelled.

Nihon was two. I didn't have a clue what the rest of Kimura-san's words had meant. All I knew for sure was that so far, I was losing in front of the pretty girls.

Kimura-san yelled, "Hajime!" and Ego Boy started bouncing.

I watched the guy, looking for a weakness. He kept on hopping, probably looking for the same in me. He wouldn't get close enough for another kick, though. A slightly more powerful one of those might crack my sternum. I circled slowly to the right. Ego Boy bounced with me. With each counterclockwise step, I inched closer. I suddenly lunged at him, sent three punches to his stomach, then a quick jab to his chin.

Contact.

Ego Boy staggered back, and the Americans cheered.

"Well done, Spencer!" Arianna called.

"Yame!" Kimura-san pointed at me. *Chodan, sita tzuki, ippon.*"

"Ippon?" I looked at Kimura-san. That was it? One point? I sighed and readied myself for another bout. At this pace, it was going to be a *long* match. And Ego Boy looked peeved. He paced back and forth on his side of the mat like a caged bull.

I furrowed my brows and waited for, "Hajime!"

Ego Boy came at me hard. I jumped back and curved in a circle, blocking a series of blows. I'd never seen anyone hit this fast, not even Beth. I could barely keep up.

Crack!

"Ahh!" Pain shot like a bullet through my jaw. My feet left the ground, and my back hit the floor hard. The air shattered in my lungs.

"Yame!" Kimura-san said.

No kidding. I rolled onto my side, forced a breath, then rolled to my front and heaved my aching form onto my knees.

Kimura-san was pointing at Ego Boy. Big shock there.

"*Jodan, ura uchi,* ippon. *Kani waza, sanbon.*"

Sanbon? He got three points for the sweep and another point for the strike? What was it now? Six to one? I stood and saw Beth out of the corner of my eye. Great. Six to one with Beth and Isabel and Grace and the twins watching. Why had I even bothered? Sweat trickled down my chin, and I wiped it away.

It was blood, not sweat. Perfect. I was losing six to one *and* bleeding—in front of everyone. I ran my tongue over my teeth just in case, but everything seemed to be accounted for.

"Hajime!"

I jumped to my feet and sank into a defensive stance. Ego Boy bounced forward, clearly no longer threatened by his pathetic, bleeding American opponent. I waited, jabbed a few meaningless hits and kicks his way, but bided my time for the right moment. I couldn't afford a dumb move. The crowd's gaze burned into me. I had to take this guy down. At least once. This was supposed to be my chance to impress Keiko, not star in the *Spencer Is A Loser* show.

Then it happened. Ego Boy lowered his hands and paced for three steps instead of bouncing. I darted forward and kicked him in the ribs, then punched a follow up to his gut.

"Yame!"

Yes! I skipped to my side of the floor and waited to hear my score.

"*Chudan, yoki geri,* nihon. *Jodan, shita tzuki,* ippon."

Isabel and Arianna cheered, and I grinned at them. Four to six. At least I didn't totally suck anymore.

"Hajime!"

Ego Boy was steamed. He darted around the mat and jabbed at me, but I was in the zone now, baby. For a long time we simply moved, neither of us getting in a hit. Then Ego Boy grinned and sent a hand strike to my throat. Not hard enough to do anything but sting, but mother pus bucket, it scared me.

The crowd gasped.

"Yame!" Kimura-san pointed at Ego Boy and spoke in Japanese. I massaged my throat and swallowed a few times, shocked by the smirk on my opponent's face. That lunatic was toying with me.

The Americans clapped. I looked around. What had I missed?

"Hajime!"

Whoa! I jumped back into position as Ego Boy flew at me, punching and kicking like I was a sparring bag. This went on until the guy landed a powerful punch to my solar plexus, knocking the wind out of me. Then he tapped my neck again, which made me jump. What the Kobe Bryant was this guy's problem?

"Yame!"

Jake booed.

I wanted to take this guy to the floor and get him in an arm bar. Forget the rules. It wasn't like he was following them. I wondered how the jumping bean would handle a little jujitsu. Because of my size, I was strongest on the floor. But Ego Boy was probably good at that too.

". . . ippon."

The Americans cheered. I hadn't been paying attention and wasn't sure what had happened. I think I got a penalty point. Maybe one before that too. If that was true—

"Hajime!"

—I just needed a sweep to win.

Ego Boy ran at me, sending a combination of moves my

way. I dodged or blocked all of them, waiting for the right moment. Ego Boy's eyes flashed. He stepped forward and faked a front snap punch, then sent a sidekick to my waist. I blocked the kick with my forearm, grabbed Ego Boy's arm and kicked out the leg he was standing on. Dude went down like a snowman in Okinawa. Whoosh.

"Yeah!" Beth yelled. "Way to go, Tiger!"

I grinned at the twins and wanted to say, *That's me. I'm a tiger.*

"Yame!" Kimura-san pointed at me. "*Ashi harai,* sanbon. *Shiro no kachi.*"

Applause and cheers rang out around me. I'd won!

Ego Boy stepped forward, his face slack as if someone had flipped the switch on his emotions. Creepy. He bowed slightly. "Arigato Gozaimashita."

Sure, *now* he was going to be polite. I bowed back. "Arigato Gozaimashita."

Ego Boy left, striding away like he was late, late for a very important date.

I smiled at the twins again—mission accomplished—then turned to my friends, grinning wide, and pumped my fist in the air, though my throat still felt like I'd swallowed a gumball that had gotten stuck halfway down.

Jun came over to congratulate me as well. "Supensa-san, you very good karate," Jun said, the gap from his chipped tooth showing in his wide smile.

"Thanks." I wondered if Jun had broken his tooth at this dojo. Maybe Ego Boy had done it.

Kimura-san directed his students in a few drills, so I sat down to watch and traded the sparring gear for my hat and socks and shoes. When the demo ended, Kimura-san led us

Americans back to the front entrance and outside. There was a big grassy lawn between the fitness center and the parking lot. I eyed a black sedan that was parked in the emergency zone. The driver's side window slid down and Sasquatch—er, Mr. Sloan—gave me a little wave.

I waved back. Man, his job must be so boring.

We stood around, waiting for who knew what. Jun, maybe? The twins? Mr. S was still inside, so maybe we were waiting for him. I was starving. It had to be dinnertime. I grabbed my backpack and pulled out *My Precious*. It was 5:48 p.m.

Arianna came over and grabbed my chin. "Hold still." She wiped my tender jaw with a damp paper towel.

I jerked back. "Arianna. Don't." It was a battle scar now. It made me look tough.

"I just want to make sure you were okay."

"Ooh! Me too, Tiger. I love wounds." Beth stepped over and examined my face. I flushed with heat but no longer protested as Arianna swabbed my jaw. I caught sight of Grace glaring over Beth's shoulder. The pixie had probably been rooting for Ego Boy.

"How can a punch draw blood?" Arianna asked. "A bloody nose makes sense, but a punch elsewhere . . . ?"

"I didn't have my mouth guard." I said. "Plus his fists are like rocks. Even with the gloves, they break the skin."

"Sounded like it," Beth said. "He's a mean one, I think."

"Why do you say that?" Arianna asked. "It was just a sparring match, right?"

Beth glanced at Arianna then back to me. "Friendly matches don't tend to draw blood—or the same foul twice in a row. He was messing with you."

She had that right. I wondered what had bound Ego Boy's

britches.

"You know, in America, karate is a big racket," Beth said. "A six-year-old can earn a black belt in a year, and they've got forty-seven degrees so they can keep charging for tests. But things are different here. These guys are serious about this stuff." She slapped me on the back and walked to where Jake and Jensina were sitting.

I watched her go, annoyed at the longing pang that shot through my gut. I grabbed Arianna's wrist. "I think you've got it, now. Thanks."

"Iie!" She skipped off towards a trashcan.

I rolled my eyes and sat on the grass across from Wally and Gabe. It felt good to sit. I massaged my hands a bit. They were sore from all those strikes.

Lukas came and sat on my right. "Dude, you rocked it!" He held out his fist and I tapped it with mine. "I get to take LCT this fall, right?"

"As long as you don't screw up," I mumbled.

"No *problemo*. I'm a good boy," Lukas said.

"Ha!" Grace said behind him, then walked after Arianna.

I raised my brows at Lukas, and he flashed a guilty grin. "Graciela forgets all the good times we had."

I snorted a laugh.

"That last sweep *was* pretty awesome, Spencer," Gabe said. "And I don't even like—"

A shadow settled over my left side. "*Mo ichi do* onegai shimasu."

I turned and looked up behind me. Ego Boy stood there, blocking the sun. He bowed and repeated his request. "Mo ichi do onegai shimasu."

I chuckled. Was he kidding? "Uh . . . no thanks, man. Once

was enough for me." I turned back and made a face at Lukas. What a nut. Did he think I was going to fight him again in the parking lot?

I don't think so.

Ego Boy poked me in the back. "Mo ichi do onegai shimasu."

I turned back to him. "Dude. No, thank you. *Shiranai. Nai.*" Not going to happen. I caught Isabel's concerned frown from across the lawn. Arianna and Grace stood beside her. I smiled at Isabel, determined to show Grace that I was friends with the goddess Isa—

"Hah ya!"

A sharp throb split my left arm. I gasped and rolled onto my right side in the grass, clutching my arm. Mother pus bucket!

Ego Boy stood over me, leering.

"¡Ay!" Lukas jumped up and over me, pushing Ego Boy out of my line of sight. "Get back!"

Beth was next to leap over me. "Get out of here!" she yelled at Ego Boy. "Jensina, get Mr. S."

Suddenly voices were everywhere, shouting a confusing mess of English and Japanese, but I could focus on only the pain. That lunatic had tried to break my arm!

Arianna sank onto the lawn beside me. Her fingertips traced my arm. "Spencer, are you all right? Can I see?"

I looked at her and tried to swallow. Pain seared in my arm like it was on fire.

"Grace, give me your soda." Arianna squeezed my arm and I growled. Then she held a can of soda against it and the coldness distracted me.

A shrieking nasal voice rose over the din. I tipped back my

head and scanned the crowd. Between Lukas's and Gabe's legs, then Mr. S and Mr. Sloan's legs, I caught sight of Ego Boy cowering on his knees before Kimura-san on the sidewalk. Kimura-san's face was red, and he was screaming so fast in Japanese that I didn't have a clue what he was saying.

That was the last I saw of him before Mr. S stuffed me into Mr. Sloan's sedan, and we headed for the hospital. The pain lessened some on the ride, and when Grace's can of soda got too cold on my arm, I drank it. Mr. Sloan thought this was hysterical.

I was glad someone was laughing.

Ego Boy hadn't broken my arm. He'd "deeply bruised" it, whatever that meant. Probably surrounded by too much muscle to get a clean break. It hurt bad, though.

The doctor put ice on it and gave me an ugly blue sling to wear until the pain went away. I wasn't wearing a sling without a cast. I'd look like a wimp. But I left it on in Mr. S's presence. He sat with me in the hospital, never left my side, which I admit, was nice. Then Toda-san showed up and we drove away in his Mr. Bean-sized car that looked more like a white gumdrop than a vehicle. I'd had to cram myself in the back seat like a Jack-in-the-box. *My Precious* said it was after nine at night. I didn't know where we were, but it looked like Naha.

"What if Ego Boy comes back?" I asked Mr. S. "That guy is a maniac."

"*Ego Boy?*" Mr. S looked back at me and raised an eyebrow. "Bushi Kogawa has been banned from the dojo. And if you see him, I don't want you fighting him again."

Gee, if you insist. "Bushi? Doesn't that mean warrior?"

"Mr. Kimura is extremely apologetic," Ms. S said. "He's paying for your medical bills himself."

"I should hope so. It was his lunatic student who decided to play break-the-bricks with my arm. What kind of crazy karate is Kimura teaching, anyway?"

Mr. S turned his Coke bottle glasses on me. "'you will never live in the promised land with a bad attitude.' I'm sorry this happened, but blaming Mr. Kimura is not fair. Remember we're in a different culture."

I blew a raspberry. "Well, someone forgot to tell Ego Boy how to behave in his own country."

Mr. S continued to stare at me, eyebrows raised, lips pursed.

"I'm just venting."

"Venting is fine. Vent to me all you want. But when you return to the fitness center tomorrow, I expect you to show grace and forgiveness to Mr. Kimura. It's not his fault his student attacked you. Remember, 'Manners maketh the man.'"

I blew out a groaning sigh. Mr. S was right, though. It wasn't Kimura's fault. It was Bushi Kogawa's fault.

"Yeah, yeah. I'll be good." I was glad I hadn't needed a cast. How much would it have sucked to spend the summer in Okinawa and not be able to go in the ocean? "Wait. I can go in the ocean, right? This weekend?" We were going to a beach that Jun had said was "best in Okinawa."

"I'm not sure that's a good idea, Spencer. You should take it easy."

"But there's no cast! If there's no cast, I should be able to go in the water." I mean, I didn't want to swim or anything—

barely knew how—but I didn't want to sit on the hot sand and watch everyone else have a good time, either.

Mr. S stared at me, but I couldn't see his eyes, just the passing headlights reflecting off his glasses. "If you're *very* careful. I've seen my kids play in the ocean, Spencer. You'd better steer clear of the crowd."

"I will." Except for Keiko. I needed to get *very* close to the Asian princess. The sooner, the better.

REPORT NUMBER: 10

REPORT TITLE: I Get Grafittied by the Sun
SUBMITTED BY: Agent-in-Training Spencer Garmond
LOCATION: Manza Beach, Okinawa, Japan
DATE AND TIME: Saturday, June 6, 10:18 a.m.

THE REST OF OUR FIRST WEEK FLASHED by, and on Saturday morning, Jun's parents drove us an hour north to Manza Beach, which turned out to be the location of paradise. The sand was white. The sky, cloudless. The water, turquoise, and so clear that I could see fish swimming around.

Since Mr. S was here, I was wearing my ugly blue sling, playing some one-armed beach volleyball with Jun when Kimura-san's fancy black car pulled up. It looked like a Town Car but had a Toyota logo on the front. Jun took off for the parking lot. I followed, jogging with quick steps over the scalding sand, then the scalding pavement.

Arianna and Isabel got out of the car and headed toward me and the beach. Then Kozue and Keiko climbed out, both wearing tiny bikinis: one pink, one blue. Hello. I stopped and stood on the side of one foot to keep my feet from burning. What about Kerri's 'no bikini' rule? I scanned the beach for Gabe's mom but didn't see her. Maybe she had no authority over the Japanese girls.

Before Jun reached the car, the twins ran off toward the bathroom, their flip-flops smacking across the pavement. They hadn't seen Jun *or* me. I felt stupid watching them go, so I turned around and tried to act cool.

"Hi, Spencer," Arianna said as she and Isabel walked past.

"Hey."

These two appeared to have one-piece swimsuits on. Isabel's was red, and she was wearing a pair of jean shorts with it. Arianna's was black, and she had some kind of big tie-dye scarf tied around her waist.

I followed them with little hopping steps, trying to keep my feet off the scalding asphalt. I stopped when I reached the edge of the beach and dug my feet into cooler sand. I turned back to wait for Jun, but he was halfway to the bathrooms.

And then my eyes locked onto Grace, walking toward me in slow motion from the black car. She was wearing a red and white Hello Kitty bikini, a Miami Heat trucker's cap, and big black sunglasses. Her hair was perfectly straight and flapped out with each step.

She peeked over the top of her sunglasses as she strutted around me and gave me a coy smile. "Hey, Spencer."

I frowned. "Hey." The sun glinted off a gold necklace she was wearing. A cross. Which made me look away again.

But Grace reached out and grabbed my hand. "I need help with my sunscreen."

"Uh . . ."

She towed me across the hot sand. I stumbled dumbly after her, gritting my teeth as my feet burned. I lasted ten steps before I jerked free from her. I mean, what was I doing? Grace was evil. I wasn't going to let her boss me around, no matter how amazing she looked in that bikini.

Grace glanced back at me without stopping. "Are you coming?" She sauntered across the sand, her flip-flops smacking with each step. She found a clear spot beside Isabel, dropped her bag, and spread out a big red and white polka dot towel.

And I just stood there, staring and hating myself for it.

When she finished with her towel, she set her hand on her hips and struck a pose, looking at me, I think. It was hard to tell with the sunglasses. "Do you like my swimsuit, Spencer? Keiko loaned it to me."

Um . . . I scratched the back of my neck and glanced toward the bathrooms. Still no twins. "I don't like your hat."

"The Heat rocks."

"Nah . . . James rocks. But they got no point guard. Just James and Wade and Bosh. And they can't rebound."

"I was born in Miami."

"Oh. Well . . ." I shrugged and drifted over to her towel until I was standing at the back end of it with Grace opposite me. "If you've got to root for the home team, I guess The Heat ain't half bad."

"Spencer, did you put on sunblock?" Grace kicked off her flip-flops and walked across her towel like it was a red carpet. When she got to the end, she reached up and traced her finger down the bridge of my nose. "Your nose is already hot."

"I'll just keep my shirt on." I burned pretty bad, but I didn't like rubbing lotion all over myself. It felt slimy. Another reason why I always wore my Lakers cap.

Grace pursed her lips. "Spencer, it's like a sauna out here." She turned around and sat on the front end of her beach towel and patted behind her. "Sit down."

Another glance at the bathrooms and no sign of the twins. I looked down on Grace, annoyed that she was so pretty. *You hate her, remember?* But I ignored myself and knelt on the back half of her towel.

She held a plastic tube over her shoulder. "If you put some on me, I'll put some on you." She pulled her hair over to one side of her head and twisted it, holding on with one hand.

I really *did* want to be friends with Grace—who wouldn't?— but something about her made me edgy. I took the tube of lotion and stared at Grace's back, at the sharp angles of her shoulder blades and the way the red ties of the bikini dangled down against her tan skin. My imagination warred with my common sense. I should get up and walk away. That would be smart. Instead, it looked like I was going to let this pretty little thing whip me.

Good think Kip wasn't here to point that out.

Arianna shot me a narrowed glance and put a large straw hat on her head.

Yeah, yeah. I'm an idiot. I squirted a drop of the cool cream onto one finger and rubbed it in on Grace's right shoulder. It smelled like coconuts. "You like coconuts," I said. I know, my chick dialogue needed work, but I was touching her. My finger on her skin. It was hard to think straight.

"I have coconut everything. Lotion, sunscreen, shampoo and conditioner, body spray—Spencer, you're going to have to use your whole hand. One finger is going to take you all day, and I want to swim."

Right. I squirted a mound of the cream on my palm and slapped it on Grace's back.

"That's better!" she said, which made me smile.

But the lotion wouldn't rub in. Grace's back looked like butter spread over cold toast, and I'd gotten it all over her necklace so that the chain was all filled with cream. So I kept rubbing until no white showed. I mean, I had to do this right. If I messed it up, she might never let me do it again. Plus her skin was really—

My vision blurred, my head spun, and a glimpse claimed my sight.

Large hands hold Grace's wrists, shake her. Tears stream down her face as she tries to pull away. "Stop it!" she yells. "Let go!"

I coughed, took my hands off her back, and focused on a very pale bruise just under her left arm. Figs and jam, that had been Grace? What was I supposed to do with *that* information? Who was hurting her? Her dad? A boyfriend? Someone else? Uncle? Neighbor?

"Done," I croaked, not liking the pity welling inside me. But maybe that was why she was such a . . . grouch. She had problems.

"Thanks!" Grace jumped up and pranced to the side. "Scoot up and I'll do you."

I blame the vision for distracting me, because I did as I was told.

"Shirt, Spencer," Grace said.

"Oh, right." I pulled my T-shirt over my head. It tangled with my sling, so I pulled off the sling and my Lakers cap and held everything in my lap, feeling like I'd just sold my soul to the devil. I glanced over at Arianna, who was watching me over the top of a book. She raised an eyebrow. I looked away.

"You're so white you glow," Grace said.

"It's a curse that comes with red hair," I said.

"*Ginger* hair."

"Right." I felt my cheeks burn, thinking of what Lukas had said. But there was no way Grace liked me. Unless she was just as awkward around guys as I was around girls. Maybe saying rude things and playing pranks was her way of flirting, like a little boy who chased girls around the playground.

Her fingernails tickled the back of my neck, and my necklace shifted. Grace peered around my side. "*You* wear a necklace?"

"So?" But it wasn't like I'd picked it out or anything. My cross necklace was a Mission League tracking device, a way for Mr. Sloan and whoever else to keep tabs on me. It was a silver shield with a cross on a bead chain. The back was engraved with Joshua 1:9.

"It's nice." Grace squirted the cold liquid on my back in long lines. I twitched when she touched me, but she seemed as timid as I had been, using her fingertips and rubbing up and down, then a curve. Suddenly—

"Rats! I'm all out, Spencer. I hope that'll be enough. I'm sure it will be."

Oh-kay. I scrambled to my feet, happy to put some space between us. I mean, Keiko was here somewhere, and I should really be with her, anyway, assignment and all.

Grace stood and bent down to tuck the empty sunscreen into her bag in a slow and deliberate manner, lingering in that pose. Then she took off her hat and sunglasses, shook out her hair, flashed me a dazzling smile, and jogged toward the surf.

I turned toward Arianna and Isabel. "Did you see what she

just did?"

Arianna kept her eyes locked onto her book. "I did."

"Wasn't that a little . . ."

"Yes." Arianna dropped her book into her lap. "Be careful, Spencer. I don't know what she's up to, but it isn't normal behavior for Grace. She's usually a sweet, shy girl."

"Are you kidding me? Grace has never been sweet or shy. She's a beast."

Arianna sighed, as if exasperated with an unruly child. "I'm only trying to point out . . . If I were you, I'd put your shirt back on."

"Why?"

"Just a feeling I have."

But I didn't put my shirt back on. I thought about it, but the twins arrived then. And I'd spent all year lifting—I was proud of my muscles. And now that I was all lotioned up, I was happy to display my awesomeness for all to see.

The girls pulled me into another volleyball game. Jun, Gabe, and me vs. Keiko, Kozue, and Isabel. Guys won, of course. After the game, everyone went into the water. There were these foam docks anchored and bobbing on the waves. Jun and Gabe took turns diving off them. I had fun jumping the waves with the girls. The fish came right up to my legs sometimes, and I'd kick and scare them away. The girls swam farther out. I could only doggie paddle and float on my back. It was all I'd learned when Grandma had taken me to swim lessons when I was in fifth grade. But the doggie paddle looked pathetic. And floating on my back wasn't very social. When I tried it I couldn't see Keiko. So I popped back up to see where my target was.

Jun and Kozue were closest, splashing each other. Gabe,

Isabel, Beth, Jake, and Grace were playing Marco Polo on the other side of the floating foam boards. I scanned the beach for Keiko and saw her entering the bathrooms again. Well done, Agent Garmond.

Two little kids were standing on the closest floating dock, so I waded past them to the other one. The water came up to my chest out here. The sand was smooth under my feet. I hoisted myself onto the dock and sat, watching the bathrooms for Keiko's exit, dangling my legs into the warm water, amazed at how nice it felt. The LA Pacific was always cold.

A soft breeze hit me, meshing with the water drops on my skin, and creating the perfect feeling of coolness. I lay down on the dock on my stomach with a good view of the bathrooms, my bruised arm at my side, my other dangling into the turquoise water. I held it still, waiting to see if a fish would swim up to my hand.

Isabel giggled and yelled, "Polo!" as Gabe waded in the wrong direction. I was tempted to get down and join the fun, but I needed to watch for Keiko. My eyelids drooped, though, and eventually I let them close.

● ● ●

Movement on the dock jolted me awake. I pushed up to sitting as a little boy jumped off the foam and into the ocean. Two other boys swam in the water laughing at me.

"*Baka na otoko!*" one said.

The other laughed so hard his face turned red.

What time was it? I scanned the water, but didn't recognize anyone in the surf. They wouldn't have left me behind. Not when we were over an hour away from Naha. Right?

The little boys were still laughing at me. I turned to look for where I'd left my stuff on the beach, and their laughter increased. Yeah, yeah. Ginger American. Big deal. It took me a while, but I finally marked Arianna and her big hat. She was still sitting on her towel, reading. It looked like everyone else was over by the volleyball net, even the twins. Good.

I yawned and stretched my good arm up over my head, then froze, a whimper on my lips. I hurt! I straightened my back. Ahh! Sunburn. Figs. I should have listened to Arianna and put my shirt on.

I slid off the dock, bending my knees to submerge all but my head beneath the sea. My skin felt cool and safe, until I moved. My back and arms ached with each step. I settled on a slow walk.

When I got to shore, I went straight toward my stuff to find my shirt. People laughed and pointed at me as I made my way across the beach.

Something was wrong. Something more than just me being tall and having red hair.

I knelt in the sand by my towel and dug through my bag. Where had I put my shirt?

"Baka!" someone cackled.

I whipped around, scanning the crowd.

"Oh, Spencer!" Arianna's regretful tone made me wince.

I found my shirt under my bag and struggled to pull it over my wet torso.

Arianna jumped up beside me and helped me roll the back down my wet, tender skin. The brim of her huge hat scraped the back of my neck.

"Hey! Watch the hat."

"Sorry. I don't know how to say this, Spencer, but—"

Arianna stepped over to Grace's towel and dug through her bag. She pulled out the tube of sunscreen and tossed it to me. It was heavy.

"She didn't run out?"

"Nope. Leant me some after you'd gone. I think she used it to write something on your back."

The blood drained from my face. The laughter and the pointing. "What does it say?"

Arianna shrugged. "It was hiragana. I couldn't tell."

"Well, try!" I spun my back to her.

"Okay, calm down." Arianna lifted my shirt—the fabric's movement aggravated my sensitive skin. She gave a little gasp. "It says *baka*. I'm so sorry."

I clenched my jaw. So, I was a fool, was I? I turned in a circle, searching the sand for that Hello Kitty red bikini. "Where is she?"

"Spencer, you'll only make it worse. You've got your shirt on now. If you play dumb, it'll be less fulfilling for her. Think about it: you know I'm right."

I kicked my foot in the sand, breathing rapidly through my nose. Arianna was right. If I'd done this, I'd want to see Grace squirm and cry and be laughed at by everyone. I nodded several times, convincing myself. "You're right. You're totally right." I scanned the beach anyway, then backtracked when I saw her Miami Heat hat. She was with the Keiko and Kozue playing volleyball. And she was wearing a black T-shirt and shorts.

"She changed," I said.

Arianna came to stand beside me and folded her arms. "Kerri made her. She got a thorough tongue lashing, too. Notice the twins didn't have to change."

I totally noticed. I wanted to go over and try talking to Keiko, but going near Grace right now would be dumb. So I flopped down on Grace's towel and brushed the caked sand off my feet, smearing it into Grace's towel. Arianna sat as well.

"You must have some idea why she hates me," I said.

"I honestly don't. It's strange, though. I've never seen her do anything like this, ever. I'll try to find out why."

Yeah, well. Good luck with *all that*.

When we got home to Jun's house on Sunday, I tried to hide my sunburn, but Okasan saw my face and neck and made me take off my shirt so she could inspect the damage.

There was no saying no to Okasan.

She gasped and said, "*Byooin!*" and chattered on to Jun so quickly I didn't have a clue what she was saying.

"She wants to take you to the hospital," Jun said. "She's worried that the burn will give you sun sickness."

"I'm fine." Although I did have a splitting headache and my back was on fire. But I'd had enough of the Japanese hospital the first time I'd been there. I had no intention of going back.

Okasan made me sit at the table so she could rub aloe over my back. It was embarrassing at first, but the aloe felt so cool and soothing, I quickly forgot to care that Gabe and Jun were mocking me from the living room. That aloe must have been mixed up by a wizard or something, because it had magical healing properties.

Sunday night, sleeping on the hard tile floor of Jun's room, I had second thoughts about the hospital. I hadn't been able to get comfortable on the floor before, but now with the sunburn, it was torture. Every time I shifted on the hard floor I fought not to cry out. And I'm not being pathetic, either. I ended up sleeping on my stomach.

I so wanted to murder Grace Thomas.

I turned my head to Jun's pile of blankets, wishing he was awake so I could ask him where his mom had put the aloe, but his blankets were flat. I pushed myself up—which hurt like figs and jam—and scanned the room.

Jun was gone.

REPORT NUMBER: 11

REPORT TITLE: I Get Spoiled Rotten and a Private
Gymnastics Show
SUBMITTED BY: Agent-in-Training Spencer Garmond
LOCATION: Jun Uehara's house, 17-21 Matsuo Shobosho
Dori, Naha, Okinawa, Japan
DATE AND TIME: Monday, June 8, 07:13 a.m.

WHEN I CAME OUT TO THE KITCHEN Monday morning,
Jun was sitting at the table with his mom and Gabe and Wally
and his little brother Joji. Okasan jumped up to greet me.

"Ohayo, Supensa-san. Daijobu-ka?"

"I'm fine," I said, lowering myself into the chair beside Jun.
My skin seemed made of paper. Every bend made it crackle
and smart and itch. At least I had finally ditched the arm sling.
"Daijobu."

Okasan moaned in sympathy and stroked my hair, her dark
eyes studying me. Then she scurried into the kitchen and
started clanking dishes.

"Where were you last night?" I asked Jun.

His eyes widened, but he said, "Sleeping."

"Liar," I said, wishing I knew the Japanese word. But the look on Jun's face was proof he'd understood me just fine.

"Explain later," he whispered as his mom leaned between us and set a cup of sweat sock soup and a bowl of rice in front of me. Yummy.

"You no like," she said. "What you eat in Amerika, breakfast?"

I ate peanut butter sandwiches or cold cereal, but when Grandma cooked for me, she made: "Eggs and toast."

Jun's mom grunted and strode back to the kitchen.

Uh-oh. I'd hurt her feelings. "But this is great." I picked up my soup cup and took a sip—and fought the urge to gag. So horribly awful.

Joji laughed at pointed at me. He was maybe eight years old and never spoke any English. He did laugh at us a lot though, and point.

Okasan started banging around in the kitchen, and soon I could have sworn I smelled eggs frying. Gabe shot me his angry eyebrows. I shrugged. She'd asked.

"Is she mad?" I asked Jun.

"She wants only to serve you." He shoveled in a huge bite of rice.

Jun's mom returned with a plate holding a piece of toast with a slice of white cheese melted on the top. "You like, yes?" She nodded to the toast, then walked off down the hallway toward the bedrooms. I didn't see any eggs.

But, yes, I liked. I took a bite of the cheesy toast, whimpering with joy. Real food. So, so good. I downed the toast in three bites. It was gone by the time Okasan returned with the jar of aloe.

She glanced at my clean plate and grunted, set down the aloe jar, and went back to the kitchen.

I took another sip of the soup through gritted teeth. Holding my breath helped a lot. Okasan returned with two plates: one with cheesy toast—four pieces—and one with little eggy rectangles. She took the soup from my hands and said, "Eat, eat," then carried the soup to the sink.

Beautiful, amazing woman! I picked up one of the egg chunks and a slice of toast. Gabe reached for a slice of toast, but Okasan returned and slapped his hand. "For Supensa-san."

I fought back a laugh at the expression on Gabe's face. But seriously, that was just mean. I ate the egg. It tasted like an omelet without any filling and was a little bit sweet. I followed it up with a bite of toast. Oh, yes. This I could do.

Okasan stood at my side, watching me eat. "You like?" She gestured to the eggs.

I nodded and said, "Arigato" over a full mouth.

"Is tamagoyaki. Egg. Jun," she tapped his shoulder, "Eigo."

"Tamagoyaki is a Japanese omelet," Jun said. "Very popular."

"Arigato," I said again.

"I write down. You take recipe to American okasan."

"Okay, thanks," I said. "Arigato."

Okasan pulled out the chair at the end of the table and dragged it behind mine. "Supensa-san. Take off." She tugged at my polo shirt then tapped the aloe.

No way was I going to argue with the woman who'd made me cheesy toast. I unbuttoned the top and pulled it over my head. Okasan took it from there, muttering. I caught the word "baka" and hoped I'd get the chance to introduce Grace to

Jun's mom sometime. See what good ol' Okasan would do to the girl who messed with her Amerikan bo-ee.

Okasan rubbed aloe on my back and neck and arms. It felt so nice. I could have sat there all day.

Tamago-yaki recipe Jun's mom wrote up for Grandma Alice.

Jun and Gabe and Wally finished eating and waited in the living room while Joji watched TV. Jun reminded his mom of the time, but she was not to be stopped. By the time we got to school, we'd missed homeroom.

After second period, I made my way to the library, eager for my daily relief from the tropical heat. I walked through the blessed coolness, inhaling the smell of old books. I reached the room in the back and opened the door to—

"Spencer!" Grace ran to me and threw her arms around my neck. Her hands rubbed against the burns on my shoulders. I grimaced, grabbed her wrists, and pulled her off me. A sharp breath filled my senses with her coconut smell.

Her cheeks flushed as she drew her arms back to herself. "Kozue said they were taking you to the hospital." Her eyes looked remorseful, but I didn't buy it.

"I'd think that would make you happy. Weren't you trying to kill me?"

The standard mask of indifference crossed her face. "It was a joke, Spencer. You make jokes all the time—can't you take one?"

"Sure. Ha ha. Funny joke, Grace. But just so you know, my jokes don't involve premeditated assault."

"Right," she snapped. "Just mental or emotional assault."

"Excuse me?"

"Just forget it."

"No. I want you to tell me what I did to deserve you hating me."

But Grace walked away and sat in the corner by Isabel. She flipped her golden curls over her shoulder and said, "Can you believe Mrs. Kimura fed us eel for dinner last night? Wasn't that gross?"

Isabel shot me an apologetic glance before answering, "It was strange but didn't taste so bad."

"Our host mom made eggs and toast this morning," Gabe said, "but only for Spencer. Wally and I have been polite and eaten everything she's served us, but Spencer wrinkles his nose and suddenly she's making him omelets."

"She was just trying to make me feel better because of my sunburn," I said, though if I'd been forced to watch Gabe eat the eggs and toast when I was stuck with sweat sock soup, I'd have been ticked off too.

Gabe went and sat by Isabel, so I slouched into a chair beside Wally and put my cheek on the table. Grace might have problems in her life, but why'd she have to make problems for me?

"I just don't understand why they won't give us lunch money." Arianna sat down on my other side.

"I've been spending my souvenir money on lunch every day because no one is giving me anything," Isabel said.

"The family is supposed to provide your school lunch every day but Wednesday," Mr. S said. "Are they not doing that?"

"I asked Keiko," Arianna said. "She told me that we were rich Americans and could buy our own lunch."

"What?" I sat up straight. "That doesn't sound like Keiko."

"How would *you* know?" Arianna asked. "Have you ever had a conversation with her?"

"Once." But Keiko was nice. I just knew it. "It's probably a translation issue."

"I speak fluent Japanese, Spencer," Arianna said.

True. I itched my shoulder. The sunburn was already starting to peel, and I itched everywhere. "Did you ask your host mom?"

"She said she gave Keiko the money," Arianna said. "I don't think Keiko likes me. I can't think why. I've been nothing but friendly."

Yeah, but Arianna's version of friendly took some getting used to.

"Is not just you," Isabel said. "She's not giving any of us money."

"I'll talk with Kimura-san," Mr. S said. "We'll get this solved."

I nudged Arianna. "Did you find out anything about . . . ?" I nodded toward Grace.

Arianna whispered, "She *said* she likes you. Thinks you're cute."

"Oh, I don't believe this." I put my head back down on the table.

"I don't either," Arianna said. "I think she's lying."

I rolled back to my cheek so I could see Arianna's face. "Could I be her assignment? Cozy up to someone?"

"Freshmen don't get assignments."

"There's always an exception, isn't there?" Because last year I'd been told that only seniors got red cards, and now I had one. Two, if you counted the partner card for doing the after school rec program.

She shook her head. "Not on this. Mr. S would never ask a student to play with another student's emotions. It's unethical."

"*She's* unethical," I said, which sounded dumb but whatever.

"I'm going to pray about this," Arianna said. "Please tell me you've been praying about this too."

"What would be the point?" I said. "God never answers my

prayers." Not that I had a clue what an answer would look like if I got one.

"Spencer, that's ridiculous. What do you pray for?"

"I don't know. Stuff."

"When do you pray? How often?"

I shrugged. I did not want to give this girl opportunity to lecture me through lunch.

"*Spencer.*"

"What? I pray when I think to, okay? After a vision, usually. Or if I'm worried about something."

"I think you should pray more," Arianna said. "But God isn't a genie in a lamp. Prayers are requests. And a request may or may not be answered."

"How about may never be answered?" Because I'd added a column in my intercession journal for answered prayers, and there were no check marks.

"I suppose that's God's prerogative. But I don't think you're being fair or looking deep enough at your life. If you did, I think you'd find that a lot more of your prayers are being answered than you think. And I think you should pray about Grace too. Then kill her with kindness."

Pray about Grace . . . Be kind to Grace . . . "Once I start down the dark path, forever will it dominate my destiny. Consume me, it will," I said in my best Yoda voice.

She rolled her eyes, but I could tell she was fighting a smirk. "You're impossible."

"Impossibly awesome."

• • •

The kiddies had yet to arrive for their first day at the new rec center. Since I was in charge of the gym, I decided we should play basketball, and told Grace so.

"That's your whole plan?" she said, attitude thick as always. "Play basketball?"

"Why complicate things?" I scratched some dead skin off my neck and pulled a rack of basketballs out into the middle of the gym. I tried a few until I found one with good air, then dribbled toward the hoop.

I sank a few three pointers, then some baseline jump shots. Grace got a ball and started to dribble, slowly, awkwardly, looking at the ball the whole time. It was pretty pathetic. I missed my next shot on purpose so she wouldn't feel bad about being so terrible.

"Guess you're not as perfect as you think," she said.

And that's what I got for trying to be nice.

Grace dribbled past me, so I swiped the ball from her, dribbled around her, and tossed it back. She dribbled toward the hoop, so I jumped in front of her on defense, hoping to intimidate her in any way possible.

She turned and dribbled back to half court, looking like some blind grandma. I laughed. "That's over and back, you know."

But she kept on going, all the way to the opposite end. Her lay-up hit the bottom of the rim. I chuckled. So sad.

I shot around some more until Grace came dribbling my way again.

"Play defense," she said to me. "I think I got this figured out."

"If you insist." But it's no fun stealing from someone who's *that* bad. So I stood in front of her, pretending like I was actually going to try.

She faked left, then drove around me and sank a jump shot from ten feet.

What the Kobe Bryant? I gaped at her. "You play ball?"

"Nope." She shook her head, smiling. "Don't you know which girls play basketball for Pilot Point High? I thought jocks kept a list in their cell phones or a little black book or something." She retrieved the ball and whipped a chest pass to me.

I slapped the pass down into a dribble. "Coach doesn't like us wasting time watching the girls. We're supposed to be thinking about the coming game."

She made a face. "How lame."

"Are you on JV?"

"I'm a cheerleader."

I paused and straightened, feeling a twinge in my mending sunburn as I did. "You are?"

Grace swiped the ball from me and dribbled out to half court again, much less awkwardly this time, the big faker. "I suppose you don't watch the cheerleaders, either?"

Uh . . . "I can't be watching cheerleaders. I've got to focus on the game. Cheerleaders are a distraction."

"That what your coach told you?" She stopped and shot from the free throw line. Her ball bounced off the rim.

I chased it down. "No, it's a fact I learned the hard way last year." All pretty girls were a distraction, not just cheerleaders. Stupid Beth Watkins, anyway. "Besides, the crowd comes to watch us, not you."

"Is *that* a fact?" Her eyebrows sank, her lips pouted, and her hands went to her hips.

I dribbled toward her and bounced the ball between my legs, barely catching it on the other side. Whoops. Almost lost that one. I rest my case about pretty girls being a distraction.

Grace sighed. "Well, at least when you suck, the crowd can see some talent in us."

I tucked the ball up under my arm. "We *never* suck."

She raised her eyebrows.

"What? Don't *you* ever watch *us*?" I asked.

"I can't be watching basketball. I've got to focus on my cheers." Her sapphire eyes laughed at me. She slapped the ball from my hand and dribbled toward the hoop.

"But you've got a decent shot," I called after her. "There's no skill in cheerleading. You should play ball instead."

She sank her lay-up and turned to glare at me. "No skill?" She left the ball rolling along the wall and marched over to the baseline.

"Where are you going?" I asked, kind of pleased to have made her angry for a change.

She spun around and took off running in a sprint toward me. She blitzed by my left arm, jumped into a front handspring, and flipped and tumbled the entire length of the gymnasium, landing with a little hop to slow herself down at the end. Some Japanese kids in red and black uniforms stood in the doorway at the other end of the gym and clapped. I just stared, my mouth gaping open. A flashback from our first away game last fall came back to me. Pilot Point High cheerleaders dancing to the Black Eyed Peas. I finally realized where I'd seen Grace before.

"Wait, I do know you!" I yelled across the gym. "You're that flipping one."

"Sure. Now you recognize me." Her voice was quiet from the distance as she walked toward me.

"I recognize your flips," I murmured and turned to shoot a

baseline jump shot. "*That's* skill."

Grace laughed, soft and musical. The sound let pressure out of my gut. No no, Garmond. Must not crush on the hater. Focus on Keiko, the Asian princess.

The hour dragged by. Kids came in and started playing basketball. They wanted to yank out my hair more than play ball, though. I would never admit it out loud, but Grace was right: I should have planned something more structured to pass the time. I would for tomorrow. We could start with free shooting, then practice passing, then dribbling. We had enough people to do a scrimmage, so maybe we could end the hour with that.

Once the last kid got picked up for a ride home, I pulled out my facility sketch and took a walk around the building. Jun was in karate practice, so I had some time to kill. I'd looked up the place on Google Maps to get the shape of the building. And so far I'd sketched in the rooms I knew. My measurements weren't adding up perfectly, but I was close. I guessed the inside walls were six inches thick. I turned on my tape measure app and checked some things. The width of the hall, the bathrooms. I even snuck into the girls' bathroom since the fitness center was deserted, except for the guys in the dojo. And, in case you were wondering, the fitness center had regular toilets in both bathrooms. No holes in the floor.

But I still had a big hole in my sketch on the western wall between the offices, the weight room, and the dance room. I wandered around on that end of the building. Something reeked like chemicals. I must have just missed seeing the janitor come through.

I gave up on the interior and went outside to walk the perimeter, trying to match up all my exterior doors with the interior ones. There was one exterior door I didn't have marked on the inside. I tried it, but it was locked. It looked to be in the same area as my mystery hole. Maybe it was some outdoor utility closet or where they kept the hot water heater or something like that. I jotted down my ideas and decided to go wait for Jun by the dojo.

I didn't get Jun alone until late that night. His mom aloed me up while we all watched some Japanese drama show on TV. His parents went to bed before it was over. Shortly thereafter, Jun got up and wandered to his room. So I followed him, leaving Gabe, Wally, and Joji alone with the TV.

I walked into Jun's bedroom and saw him checking his cell phone. "So where were you last night?"

He jumped and spun to face me. "Supensa-san. *Odokasanai de yo!*"

"Yeah . . . yo." I put my hand up to keep my head from hitting the chain on the light fixture. "Were you with Kozue?" If so, maybe he'd take me with him next time so I could talk to Keiko. I hadn't seen her since the beach day.

"*Eto* . . . Not Kozue. I have task. Is secret. For *Mishion Ligu*. Please do not say . . . to tell anyone. Am being careful."

He had a real assignment? "Can I come?"

Jun's eyes ballooned. "No! Please. You must not follow." He rubbed his face and looked like I'd put him in a real fix. "Is berry dangerous. Promise me to not tell . . . eto . . . to follow."

"Hey, no biggie," I said. "I won't say anything. I promise." I hadn't meant to freak the guy out. It wasn't my business what he did, anyway.

Jun relaxed then. "Thank you berry much, Supensa-san." He bowed his head, like I'd done him some kind of favor. I really needed to figure out how the whole bowing thing worked here. "I will come back," he said, then walked past me and out into the hallway.

I followed him back to the living room and watched him slip out the front door, closing it silently behind him. No one even looked away from the TV. Not Gabe, Wally, or Joji.

The guy was good.

I watched him all week. Every night around 11:00, he snuck out. Sometimes he came back in a half hour. Sometimes he was gone much longer. I itched to follow him, but maybe that was just my peeling sunburn. Besides, I'd promised. And I was a man of my word.

JILL WILLIAMSON

REPORT NUMBER: 12

REPORT TITLE: Shoko Miyake Makes Me an Offer
SUBMITTED BY: Agent-in-Training Jun Uehara
LOCATION: 2-11-10 Tsuboya, Naha, Okinawa, Japan
DATE AND TIME: Friday, June 12, 11:28 p.m.

JUN LAUGHED AT GORO'S CRUDE JOKE, hoping he sounded genuine. He was walking to a party with Bushi, Akio, and Goro, the three guys known as the San Doubou, the guys who ran the teenage part of the Abaku-kai gang in Naha. Jun had spent the last eight months working his way into the gang, and this was the first time he'd been invited to meet one of the adult leaders. Toda-san believed that Kimura-san was a high-ranking member of the Abaku-kai, so Jun expected to be introduced to Kimura-san tonight.

Jun followed Bushi and the guys to an apartment about eight blocks from Kimura Fitness. They entered the front door on the bottom floor of the building. The place was dark and reeked of incense and smoke. Punk music blared, and Jun

160

recognized the music of the popular band Kakushi Ken. A few dozen people were dancing. Five guys played a video game in the living room. Many held a beer or cigarette or both in their hands.

Jun stayed close to Bushi as he led the way through the crowd, weaving between bodies like a snake. Many yelled greetings to the San Doubou.

A girl ran up and shoved Bushi. "*Doko ni itteta ka?*" It was one of the twins. Jun's gut twisted. It *had* to be Keiko. Kozue would never come to a party like this. But as long as he'd known the twins, he could tell them apart only by the little mole on Keiko's left cheek. And right now it was too dark for him to get a good look.

Bushi grabbed Keiko's elbow and pulled her over to the wall. Both were angry, that much Jun could tell, but he couldn't hear them over the earsplitting music. Bushi tried to kiss Keiko, but she pushed him away and stomped off.

Jun watched her go, praying that had been Keiko, but also wondering why she'd been here at all, since Kozue had told him that Keiko and Bushi had broken up for good.

"*Ikuzo!*"

Bushi waved to Jun and the others to follow, and they walked to the back of the apartment and up a narrow flight of stairs. There was a single door at the top. Bushi went inside without knocking.

They entered a restaurant of some kind. A bar ran along one wall, and the rest of the room was filled with round tables. Empty. The place was dark, lit by a blue light piped around the edge of the ceiling and candles on the tables. It was also deserted but for a lone figure sitting at a table in the very back.

They approached the figure, and Jun was surprised to see a

Japanese woman at the table, a laptop open before her. Not Kimura-san after all. She looked as old as Jun's mom, though she was dressed in a fancy suit as if she were very rich.

Bushi bowed to the woman, then introduced Jun. Her name was Shoko Miyake.

Shoko closed her laptop and ran her eyes up and down Jun. "You want to earn some money, yes?"

"*So desu ne.*" Jun's family was poor, and Bushi had offered him a job that would change that. Delivering drugs. Toda-san had authorized Jun to accept the job on a temporary basis, though Jun was supposed to turn in to Toda-san any money he made.

"Do you do drugs, Jun?" Shoko asked.

"Iie."

"Good. I can't have my delivery boys tempted by the merchandise. I find out you're stealing from me, you'll be sorry. Understand?"

"Hai, waka."

"You tell people you deliver flowers. Bushi will set you up with a motor scooter. You get a call. You make the pickup, you make the delivery, you bring the money back to Bushi. You have access to Oroku High School students?"

"Hai."

"Prove you are loyal and reliable, and I might give you the school."

Give him the school? Jun didn't like the idea of his classmates buying drugs. "Arigato."

Shoko waved her hand, signaling the end of the meeting. Bushi snapped his fingers and motioned for Jun to follow him out of the restaurant.

On the stairs, Bushi punched Jun in the arm. "She likes

you. If you can get the school, you'll never be poor again."

"*Subarashii!*" Jun said, more excited about getting a motor scooter to drive than he was about his new "job." And he couldn't wait to speak with Toda-san and find out what his sensei knew about Shoko Miyake.

JILL WILLIAMSON

REPORT NUMBER: 13

REPORT TITLE: I Go on a Date with an Asian Princess
SUBMITTED BY: Agent-in-Training Spencer Garmond
LOCATION: Kimura Fitness Center, 3-18-57 Jinan, Naha,
Okinawa, Japan
DATE AND TIME: Monday, June 15, 4:19 p.m.

I DITCHED GRACE AFTER MONDAY afternoon's rec time
and went for another spin around Kimura Fitness, trying to
figure out my sketch. Jun and the twins and I were going to go
see *Jolt III: Return of the Daysman* today after Jun's karate
practice, and I couldn't wait. When I gave up trying to figure
out the mystery section of the building and came back to the
dojo, Jun was still karate chopping with his boys. So I went
outside to wait.

I passed by Grace, who was sitting on the bench out front.
Why hadn't she gotten picked up yet? I plopped down on the
grass under the shade of a mangrove tree and hoped she'd
leave me alone. Unfortunately she came over and sat beside

me on the ground.

"What have you been doing?" she asked. "Flirting with Keiko?"

"None of your business," I said, wondering if Keiko was here somewhere.

"Hey, isn't that Beth?"

I followed Grace's gaze. Sure enough, Beth was standing with Bushi Kogawa by the side of the building, where one of the back doors to the dojo let out.

"Ego Boy," I murmured. A Brittany Holmes rhyme from *Jolt II* popped into my head. *"In my stomach coils of dread. I sense evil up ahead."* I grinned at the idea that Bushi was a demon. But what was Beth doing with him?

Grace looked from Bushi to me and back and forth. Then she poked my arm. "His arms are massive," Grace said. "You should lift if you want arms like his."

"I do lift, thank you very much. I could bench you." Okay, that had sounded stupid, but I made fists and flexed a little, wondering why I cared what Grace thought about anything.

"Well, I think he's cute," Grace said.

"Cute?" I glared at her. "That guy tried to break my arm! I thought he was banned from the dojo."

"Maybe hanging around outside doesn't count."

"But why is Beth talking to him?" I scowled further as Beth's hearty chuckle floated to my ears. Maybe she was on a mission. But why her? Why would Mr. S or Prière assign any of the girls to track that maniac? At least put Jake on him.

"She's flirting," Grace said.

"She is not!"

The volume of my voice caused Beth and Bushi too look over to our tree. Recognition crossed Bushi's face, and he clutched his arm as if it was hurt and staggered around. Nice. He took a step toward me, but Beth grabbed his hand and pulled him around the corner of the building out of sight.

I felt like I'd been hit again. I didn't like Beth hanging out with that animal. Touching him. Flirting? I suddenly realized that my breath sounded like a bull about to charge. I swallowed and looked away.

"You like her," Grace said, an evil grin growing on her face, like the Grinch when he got his wonderful, awful idea.

I clenched my teeth. "*Liked*, Miss Thang. Past tense." This trip just kept getting better and better. I certainly didn't need another reason for Grace to antagonize me.

Jun's honking laugh turned my head. He and the twins came out of the front entrance. Oh, man! If I'd known the girls had been inside, I never would have come out here. I scrambled to my feet and walked toward the building.

Grace got up and followed me. "I don't trust them," she said. "The twins."

Yeah, yeah. "Because of the lunch money thing?"

"That's part of it, but there are other things. Trust me: They're no good."

Trust her? I barked a laugh and met Jun out front. His hair was wet and flat—he must have showered after practice. I looked from one twin to the other, trying to guess which was Keiko. Jun wasn't touching either of them.

But one had a small mole on her left cheek. I pointed at her. "Keiko?"

She grinned. "Sugoi! How you guess?"

I touched my cheek. "Your mole," I said.

"So smart, Pensa-san." She took hold of my arm. Her hands were warm, and I stiffened at her touch, scared I'd do something to make her let go. "You want to see Brittany Holmes, yo?"

"Yes, I do. *Totemo.*" I couldn't wait to see this movie.

"*Totemo . . .*" Keiko laughed. "*Gureisu-chan, ikuwayo.*" Keiko pulled me toward the street after Jun and Kozue.

I glanced over my shoulder at Grace, who was trailing along behind us. "Wait, Grace is coming too?"

"She is host sister to me and Kozue," Keiko said.

Great. But I wasn't going to let Tinkerbell ruin my date with the Asian princess. So I ignored her. I mean, I had a mission to accomplish, work to be done. I couldn't be bothered to worry about Grace and her "dark eyes."

We walked through the muggy streets of Naha, Jun and Kozue leading the way. I followed like a puppy, spending my time memorizing every millimeter of Keiko's face. Did I mention that she was gorgeous? She was wearing a tank top with skinny straps and jean shorts that left lots of skin out to the sun and my eyes. And she kept touching me. A shoulder nudge here, a hand on my elbow there. If Jun and Kozue had been bad guy spies, they could have led me right into the enemy camp, and I wouldn't have known until I was shackled to a chair.

It occurred to me then that I should pay attention to my surroundings. I *did* have to write this up in my weekly report. I glanced around me, ignored Grace's disparaging stare, and noticed that we were walking down a wide street in some sort of shopping district. There were people everywhere, as if there'd just been a parade. My guess was there were always this many people out and about in this part of Naha. Across the street, I noticed a huge sign that said OKINAWA with a 3-D white cat sticking out of the sign. On the street beside the entrance, a life-sized Buzz Lightyear stood guard. Good. Physical landmarks like those would help me map my route out later.

"What street are we on?" I asked Keiko.

"Kokusai Dori," she said.

Coke side Dori. Got it. I could remember that. Now back to more important things . . . I smiled at Keiko.

It was one thing to go on a date with a pretty girl, something I'd done only once in my life so far. But it was another thing to go with a friend whose date looked identical to yours. Every time I caught sight of Jun and Kozue holding hands or standing too close, I did a double take. My head knew there were two girls, but my instincts didn't seem to be getting the message.

Jun bought five movie tickets and we entered the theater. I wondered where he got the money to pay for us all. The theater wasn't that different from any other I'd been in, except for the katakana and kanji signage everywhere. We got good seats in the middle of the theater about ten seconds before the lights went down. We were sitting in one long line: Kozue, Jun, me, Keiko, and Grace. I felt good about the seating arrangement.

Two things instantly surprised me. First, the movie was in English with Japanese subtitles. Second, it seemed to be some kind of romantic comedy about a musician and his female manager. What happened to Brittany Holmes? I leaned over to Jun and pointed at the screen. "Brittany?"

Jun gave me the thumbs up and a wide grin that bared his chipped-tooth smile. "*Buritani Holumusu.* Much beautiful lady."

I glanced past Keiko to Grace, who just shrugged. Well, at least I wasn't the only one who was confused. I leaned back in my seat, bewildered. Much beautiful lady or not, the girl in this movie was *not* Brittany Holmes. It was that Amy Melinda chick who'd starred in that musical that had been nominated for an Oscar. I don't do musicals.

So I paid more attention to Keiko than the movie. Her wide-eyed expression was locked on the screen, and when she laughed, she leaned against me and touched my arm or leg.

I wanted to say something to her, make her laugh, but my mind was a void of static. I decided to stay quiet. I couldn't afford to mess this one up, assignment and all, so I focused back on the screen, where Amy Melinda was giving her guy the doe eyes.

Bo-ring. And sappy. Jun and Kozue must have thought so too, because they started making out, which put a lot of ideas into my head that I wasn't brave enough to act on, especially not with Grace here. So I slouched down in my seat and felt awkward and dumb. Yay.

Finally the credits rolled. I popped to my feet, eager to get out of here, find Arianna, and ask how my saying, "Let's go see Brittany Holmes in *Jolt III* " had gotten translated into "Let's go see an Amy Melinda chick flick." But Keiko tugged on my arm and said something.

I looked down on those Anime eyes and sort of forgot where I was. "Huh?"

"You want Brittany? Light Goddess?"

Music boomed in the theater. I twisted to see the screen just as the name Brittany Holmes flashed across the image of a high school football field.

Double feature? Apparently they still had those in the world. Who knew?

I plopped back into my seat as *Jolt III* started to roll. Keiko nestled close, so I put my arm around her. My gut clenched knowing that Grace would have seen that move and would say something nasty about it later.

Let her. I wasn't doing anything wrong.

The film opened with an attractive blond high school student—the very popular Shantell Mason, played by some chick I didn't recognize. She looked like a Playboy model more than a high school student. Naturally, her boyfriend was the star of the football team.

Figures. Football always got more attention than basketball. So unfair.

Enter the revving Harley and new guy at school, Bret, who'd just moved to town. He was Hollywood's typical twenty-five-year-old high schooler with a two-day beard and a couple of tattoos. In his first class he got sent to the office for talking back to a teacher. He even picked a fight with Shantell's football star boyfriend. Gutsy.

Shantell, of course, thought this was awesome. She followed Bret around and flirted with him, even with her football man standing beside her. The Harley made Shantell all weak in the knees. She said her boyfriend was boring and hopped on the back of Bret's hog for a ride.

I rolled my eyes. Puh-lease. The girl was hot and all, but where was my Brittany? Hadn't I suffered enough through the Amy Melinda chick flick?

Then things started to get weird. Shantell took Bret back to her place. She lived in a mansion of a house with no parents. They had died, and she had been raised by two butlers. Mr. Screem looked like a creepy doctor in a white suit. Mr. Keel was built like a heavyweight boxer with a black T-shirt that was two sizes too small.

Shantell and Bret made out for a bit, which must have inspired Jun and Kozue because they started sucking face again. I forced myself to concentrate on the movie and not my amorous neighbors, but Jun's elbow kept spearing my side. And here I thought I'd gotten away from Kip and Megan.

On screen, Shantell pulled away for some air and put her hand on Bret's bare and psychotically muscular chest, tracing one of his tattoos with her fingernail. "Did you know everyone has untapped power inside them?" she said in a breathy voice. "I can teach you to find it—to achieve connection."

I perked up. Power inside? Connection? Wasn't that pretty much the same words Dmitri Berkovich and his Bratva peeps had used when they offered me drugs in Moscow?

REPORT NUMBER: 14

REPORT TITLE: I Figure Out Some Berry Important Things
SUBMITTED BY: Agent-in-Training Spencer Garmond
LOCATION: Q Cinemas, Naha Main Place, Naha, Okinawa, Japan
DATE AND TIME: Monday, June 15, 8:04 p.m.

"SURE, BABY," BRET CHORTLED, PULLING in for another kiss. "Let's connect."

"It's not what you think." Shantell's hand slid down Bret's leg, along his leather pants, inching toward a knife holster that was strapped to his shin. "We need to harness the power inside you, and to do that we must ask for help."

Again a dopey laugh from Bret-the-moron, who was likely about to die. "You wanna call some friends?"

She chuckled, low and throaty, and pulled a knife from Bret's leg holster.

Keiko grabbed my arm.

It was Brittany's knife! The one that had been stolen in the last movie. How had this Bret guy gotten it? And he'd better

172

hop on his hog and hightail it out of there or he was shredded pork.

Shantell held the knife to Bret's throat. "In my stomach coils of dread. I sense evil in my bed."

No way! Only the Light Goddess spoke in sexy rhymes. Who was this chick? Was Shantell the Light Goddess in disguise?

"Please, don't kill me!" Bret pleaded. "It's not what you think!"

Shantell's creepster butlers appeared as if from nowhere and held Bret down. What? Had they been behind the curtains this whole time?

Shantell slid down Bret's body, off the foot of the bed, and backed across the room. "Oh, it's always exactly what I think. I'm a demon hunter. And you are the worst kind of evil scum."

She didn't kill Bret, though. The butlers carried him out to a huge stone table in the back yard, strapped him to it, and left him there. Shantell came outside wearing a gauzy red dress that was blowing around in a sudden hurricane force wind. Dozens of people followed her. I had no idea where they'd all come from. Maybe they'd been hiding in the curtains too.

Shantell climbed onto the table, lifted the knife above her head over Bret's body, and chanted some foreign words. She transformed then. Pale skin and blond hair darkening. Even the red dress morphed into that signature slinky black outfit the Light Goddess always wore.

Brittany Holmes, baby! Aww yeah. Some of the audience started clapping. I wolf-whistled. Take 'em down, girl.

Mr. Screem put a syringe to Bret's arm and injected him with something. I shuddered as the image of the kid shooting up in Moscow flitted through my memory.

Brittany walked along the stone table and stood over Bret's head. "One light. One mind. Darkness I will bind."

She chanted her rhymes and swayed in a rhythmic dance. Her spectators mimicked her, chanting and swaying. Bret seemed to pass out. Then his body started convulsing. His mouth opened way too wide in a bad special effect that still looked awesome. A demon flew out of his mouth. Bret pulled against the leather straps that held him. Brittany reached down and used her knife to cut the straps. Bret sat, spun around on the stone table, and looked up at Brittany and the black creature that hovered in the air above the table.

"Be gone, you fell beast." Brittany sprayed her can of holy water, which soaked the black demon. It screamed and wailed and disintegrated in the air. Lightning lit the sky over the scene.

My mouth was parched. It had been hanging open far too long.

"O Daysman, master of the light," Brittany said, "we present to you a new follower. Come into his life and unleash for him that which he seeks: the power within!"

Bret pushed to his knees on the table and bowed at her feet. "Goddess of Light, I pledge my service to you."

"Speak it, all of you," she said, waving the knife at the crowd.

Bret and the others spoke in unison. "Light, stream to my mind, descend down to earth, give power to my heart, and give my life worth. Light, guide my will. Goddess, show the way to harness power for myself and live the Daysman way."

"To the Daysman!" someone shouted.

"The Daysman!" the crowd echoed, going to their knees. Brittany took hold of Bret's hand and he rose. Then she kissed him, which made me blush for some reason. And when she pulled away, she said, "Let's go hunt some demons."

The opening titles came then. *Jolt III: Return of the Daysman*. Brittany and her new boy toy had some darkness to fight.

The movie was another ninety minutes of wild demon hunting. Pretty sweet, actually. Bret didn't make it—Brittany's men never did—but he'd been working for the demons, anyway, and she had to take him out.

After all, a demon hunter's got to do what a demon hunter's got to do.

On the walk home, Jun found a store selling *Jolt III* posters, just like the one Keiko and Kozue had in their room. He insisted on buying one for me, which was awesome. I just hoped I could get it home to the States without ruining it. He bought one for himself too.

After that, Jun, Kozue, and Keiko blathered on non-stop about the movie. In Japanese. Leaving me to walk beside Grace. I only knew they were talking about the movie because I kept hearing "*Buritani*" and "*Laitu Godesu*" every few seconds.

The language barrier convinced me that the Mission League could pay for a few texts home, so I texted Kip about the movie. He didn't text back. How long did it take a text to travel around the world, anyway? Wasn't this supposed to be a super spy phone? But maybe it was three a.m. back in Cali or something. I wasn't sure.

"That movie was so dumb," Grace said out of the blue. "Who acts like that?"

"Sexy demon hunters," I said. "Duh."

"That's *not* how you fight demons."

"How would you know?" I asked.

175

"How would *you?*"

"Look, if you can't say anything nice about the movie, just don't speak," I said.

"Fine."

With nothing left to occupy my thoughts, they returned to the film. That whole bit about connecting to the untapped power inside was almost word-for-word what Dmitri Berkovich, the Russian mobster and Bratva cult leader, had said to me last summer. I shivered just thinking about it. Could the *Jolt* scriptwriters have something to do with Bratva?

Seemed like a stretch.

Still.

Last fall, Tito and Blaine had stuck a needle in my arm that had made me pass out. Maybe they knew the real Brittany. Maybe they'd been going to take me to the real Light Goddess, but Kimbal and Sasquatch had arrived just in time to save my hide.

Or maybe I'd been watching one too many scary movies.

The house was dark, old, and smelled of mildew. Beer cans cluttered the floor around a tattered recliner with foam poking out of one armrest. A scream pierced the small home.

A clump. A crash. Broken glass. Another scream.

A blond girl raced from a room at the end of the hall and entered another, her ponytail sailing behind. Grace. She slammed the door. Locked it.

A crash shook the windows and I sat up, heart racing. It was dark. I was sitting on my blankets on the hard tile floor of

Jun's bedroom. Rain pounded on the roof and poured off the eaves. A flash lit the room, and I stared out the window at the dark branches swaying in the storm, scratching at the window.

A loud boom shook the house again, and I jumped as it carried on, long and loud and menacing. I'd never heard anything like it.

"Supensa-san? Daijobu ka?"

I turned and saw Jun sitting up next to me. "It's loud."

"*Taifuu.*"

"Typhoon?" I blurted out. "Aren't those dangerous?"

Jun shook his head. "Happen often in Okinawa."

I lay back on the floor. Another flash lit the bedroom, illuminating Jun's belongings. When the thunder came, I trembled along with the rest of the house.

Jun had hung his new *Jolt III* poster on the wall of his room, and, as hot as Brittany Holmes was, the thing was giving me the creeps in this weather. Especially when I started thinking about the Bratva-like phrases from the movie.

When I got back to Cali, I'd have to rent the movies with Kip so I could look for any other Bratva similarities, because those sayings were way too alike to be a coincidence. The thought brought my memory to the times I'd met Dmitri, which reminded me of Anya, which made me think of the torture dream and then the one I'd just had of Grace.

I should write it down. Someone was hurting her. Or already had. Or was going to in the future. She'd had that black eye when we'd met and that faded bruise under her arm on the beach . . .

My eyelids grew heavy. I closed them. Another flash of lightning flamed red though my closed eyelids. Later. I could log the Grace dream in the morning.

But the thunder shook my eyes open. I sat up and reached for my backpack.

Okay! I'll do it now!

The next afternoon a bunch of us walked home from school together. Jun, Gabe, Wally, Keiko, Arianna, Isabel, Grace, and me. I started out walking with the guys, but by the end of the first block, I was at Keiko's side. The heat wasn't so bad when I had a pretty face to distract me from it.

"So, do you know karate too?" I asked her.

"Some. My mother believe girl should be able to protect herself. But my father say karate is for boy."

"What do you think?" I asked.

"I would rather have peace."

"*Heiwa*," I said, holding up two fingers in the peace sign.

Keiko giggled and flashed me the peace sign back.

"Why do Japanese people always hold up the peace sign when they get their pictures taken?" I asked.

"It doesn't mean anything, I don't think. Is just cute photo pose."

We approached the little shop on the corner where we turn left. Arianna, Isabel, and Grace ran inside, followed by Jun, Gabe, and Wally, so Keiko and I went in too.

I loved this store. I loved Japanese candy and snacks, especially their ice cream stuff. There was this melon slushy thing that was so good. Today I bought two lemon ice cups and handed one to Keiko then rubbed my cup against my forehead before I opened it. She giggled. We went outside, leaving everyone else in the shop.

"How can you stand this heat?" I asked.

"Does not bother me." She spooned some of the icy lemon into her mouth and her lips puckered. "Pensa-san? You can keep secret?"

I slurped a dripping glob of lemon off the side of my cup. "Sure."

"Last night I had strange dream. A man covered in tattoo chase me." She paused. "I'm afraid it will happen for really, you know? In other words, do you think is crazy?"

Red light. Keiko dreamed about Tito in Okinawa? Nah. It had to be some other tattooed guy. "People have weird dreams all the time."

"No me. My dream are special, okay?" Keiko looked down at her lemon ice and closed her eyes. "Many times," she whispered, "my dream come to real life. I'm afraid tattoo man will come to Naha."

Man, I sure hoped not. Tito was supposed to be in jail. "I don't know." But what if Keiko was gifted in prophecy like me? Maybe that was why I'd been assigned to track her. To help her deal with her visions and glimpses and everything. The idea excited me. I was on to something here. I was sure of it. Could even be God's way of answering one of my prayers.

"You not think is evil, Pensa? My father says such dream come from evil spirits."

"What? No. Keiko, I get strange dreams too sometimes. They're from God. He's sending you messages. You should tell your League instructor. That Mr. Toda, right? Toda-san?"

Her eyes were wide with wonder. "You have dream too?"

I grinned. "Yeah. I've only met one other kid besides me who does." Mary's warning about beautiful foreign girls came to mind suddenly, but I pushed it away.

"Who else dreams?"

"Oh." Doubtful that Mr. S would like me telling people about Mary. "It doesn't matter. Is this the first time you dreamed about the tattoo guy?"

She nodded and grabbed my arm. "Please, you will tell me if this is bad, okay?"

"It's not bad, Keiko. Your dad's wrong." I was sure of it now. Prière had assigned me to keep an eye on Keiko because, like me, she had prophetic dreams. And her dad told her the dreams were evil. How sick. I'd do everything I could to assure her God had gifted her for a reason.

Gabe and Arianna would be so proud. And maybe God too.

I caught sight of Grace standing in the doorway to the shop, watching us, the disapproval plain on her face. I put my back to her and drank another mouthful of lemon slush.

Once everyone had bought their junk food, we all continued toward Jun's house. Keiko took hold of my hand, and I felt seven feet tall. My life was awesome right now.

Gabe came up beside me, shot me a Prude Patrol raised eyebrow, then opened a box of strawberry Pocki. "Jun paid for everyone," he said.

"Not me and Keiko." I spun around and found Jun walking with the girls. A bad feeling rumbled in the pit of my stomach. Where was Jun getting all the cash?

But maybe it wasn't really Jun that was bothering me, but Kimura-san. How could he think such garbage about his own daughter? But he was letting a guy like Bushi into his dojo, so clearly some of his bolts were loose.

Maybe I should tutor Keiko in intercession like Prière had done for me. Teach her how to make her own dream journal.

Prière had said that he never showed his journal to anyone, except for training purposes. But if I was training Keiko, that was pretty much the same thing, right?

That night, Jun, Joji, and I stayed up late playing video games. After I brushed my teeth, I came into Jun's room to pull up my piece of floor. Gabe and Wally were already sleeping. Joji slipped out and into the bathroom. Jun was standing at his desk, flipping through a leather book.

I walked over and stood beside him. "What's that?"

"Shizuka. Is book on meditation."

Meditation? "It's thick."

"Is cult. My task from Toda-san." He tapped the book. "This part of it."

Maybe this was how he was getting all the extra cash. "What's the assignment—I mean, 'task'?"

Jun pursed his lips, as if weighing whether or not to tell me. "I don't want to say too much, but something is happen at dojo. I think Kimura-san is involved. I have joined Abaku-kai to learn more. Bushi, he give this book to me, invite me to pray like Shizuka."

Ego Boy? "You joined the Japanese mafia?" Not surprising that Bushi was in it, but dang. Jun was pretty gutsy to go undercover to track that guy.

"Hai. Is berry dangerous."

No doubt. "Is that where you're getting all the money?"

Jun paled. "Hai. I have job helping to make deliveries. I am supposed to turn in money I make to Toda-san, but I have been keeping the tips. Is nice to have some to spend. Please keep secret?"

"Hey, I won't say anything." It wasn't my business. "Kimura-san and Bushi, huh? What about Kimura-san's daughters? They're not involved, are they?" Please say no.

"I don't think so. Kozue is good daughter. She studies hard. Keiko, she was berry wild. But she is getting better now at Oroku High. She used to go Shogaku as well. But she was failing her classes and get into trouble. But she was girlfriend to Bushi then also."

Keiko and Bushi? "No way!"

"Kozue said it was bad relationship. She said Bushi strike Keiko many times."

I might have to kill him.

"Is okay now. Kozue said that Keiko is no girlfriend to Bushi anymore. I don't think the girls know what their father is doing, but is berry bad."

Berry bad, indeed. My mission was clear. I had me a damsel in distress to save.

REPORT NUMBER: 15

REPORT TITLE: I Ride a Banana in the Ocean and a
Motor Scooter through a Mall
SUBMITTED BY: Agent-in-Training Spencer Garmond
LOCATION: Naha Beach Side Hotel, Naha, Okinawa, Japan
DATE AND TIME: Saturday, June 20, 10:48 a.m.

SATURDAY WAS SUPPOSED TO BE banana boat day, which sounded so silly that I'd been looking forward to it. But as Jun's dad drove us across Naha, it started to pour. He didn't turn around though. He pulled up in front of the Naminoue Driving School and we all piled out into the rain. Then he drove away.

"Hayakushite!" Jun said.

Jun ran through the parking lot. I put my beach towel over my head, and Gabe and I chased him, Wally trudging along behind. We crossed a narrow road, then a small parking lot that was at the top of a tiny beach. This was Naha, so even though we'd found the ocean, we were surrounded by buildings, including a freeway overpass. The roar of a jet taking off reminded me that we were also close to the airport.

Jun headed for a building on the left that looked like a warehouse.

I caught up to him and yelled, "Where are we going?"

He pointed at the warehouse. "Wait for typhoon to pass."

Another typhoon? At least there wasn't any thunder and lightning this time.

The warehouse had a huge garage door on one end, which was opened to the sandy beach. We ran inside. Jake and Lukas were already here, as were Jensina and Beth, all of their host siblings, and Mr. S, Kerri, Mary, and Martha. The warehouse was filled with little boats and jet skis and these inflatable hotdog-looking things that I guessed were banana boats. Life vests, throw rings, and buoys hung on the walls.

The rain hammered the metal roof above. I stood just inside the door and watched the rain pound the sand outside. In the sky, dark clouds sailed past like a low-flying airplanes. I'd never seen clouds move so fast. It kind of freaked me out.

But then the rain stopped and the sun came out. So weird.

Kimura-san and the girls hadn't arrived yet, but Toda-san gathered us together and started to pass out life preservers.

"Hi, Spencer," Mary said.

I looked down and saw her standing beside me, Martha on her other side. "Hey, Mair. How you been? Hi, Martha."

Martha raised one eyebrow and looked away. Whatever.

"You staying out of trouble, Spencer?" Mary asked me.

I'd normally find such a question obnoxious, but Mary meant well. "Yes, ma'am." Though speaking of foreign women, why weren't the twins here yet? I glanced out the garage door and could see only the edge of the parking lot.

Toda-san handed me a blue and white life vest. "You need extra-large, Supensa-san."

True that.

I strapped the vest over my T-shirt—I wasn't taking any chances with another sunburn. I followed Jun and Gabe out the garage door and toward the ocean. The temperature felt cooler than usual, though maybe it was because of the soft breeze.

Three Jet Skis were parked on the sand with banana boats hooked to the backs of each. Only one of the inflatable tubes was yellow. The others were red. I passed Wally, who was standing back from the surf, fully dressed, no life vest.

"You don't like Jet Skis, Wally?" I asked.

"The term Jet Ski is a misnomer," Wally said. "Jet Ski is a registered trademark of a specific line of personal water craft manufactured by Kawasaki. Over 90 percent of personal water craft accidents are caused by operator error. If I was allowed to drive a PWC myself in empty waters, I might be willing to try. As is, there is far too much risk involved."

"Suit yourself, man."

Movement up in the parking lot pulled my attention away from Wally. Kimura-san's luxury car drove into a parking space. The doors all opened at once. Kimura-san got out of the driver's side. Arianna, Grace, and Isabel climbed out of the back. Keiko and Kozue got out of the front—they were wearing bikinis again.

"Oh, those girls," Kerri mumbled.

I fought back a smile as the girls walked toward us. One of the twins stayed back, though, standing with Kimura-san beside the car. They were yelling at each other. I wandered that way in hopes of figuring out what was going on. Jun ran past me and met the twin who was with Arianna, Grace, and Isabel. She kissed him and took hold of his hand, then they continued toward the beach with the American girls.

Which meant Keiko was the one fighting with her dad.

Arianna reached me first and grabbed my arm. "Spencer, stay out of it."

As if I'd been planning to go stand between Keiko and her dad or something. "Stay out of what?"

Jun and Kozue walked past us, chattering to each other in Japanese. Isabel and Grace stopped with Arianna.

"Kimura-san confronted Keiko about the lunch money she'd been supposed to give us," Arianna said. "They've been fighting all day."

"She didn't take it, did she?" I said, knowing my Asian princess was no thief.

"Oh, yes, she did," Grace said. No Hello Kitty bikini today. Grace was in her black one-piece. And she'd left her Miami Heat hat behind. "Keiko said Americans are rich enough to pay our own way."

"That's what she told her dad," Arianna said. "She doesn't think he should pay for our lunch. And that's why she's been keeping the money."

"Come on," I said, but Arianna took Isabel's arm and walked past me toward the surf.

"You're still taking her side?" Grace asked. "Even after what Arianna said?"

I didn't answer. Didn't want to believe Keiko would do something so ghetto. It must be a misunderstanding. Had to be.

"You know, Keiko has a picture of you on her phone," Grace said.

"Really?" Though I tried to fight it, I grinned.

"A picture of your back." Grace folded her arms and smirked, like she'd just insulted my mother. "What I did to you at Manza Beach. She and Kozue were laughing at it."

Anger rushed through me. Grace was lying. Messing with me again. "Just shut up." I turned and walked back to the surf.

Four people could ride the banana boat at once, and Toda-san had started three lines. Jake, Lukas, Gabe, and Tetsu were already sitting on the yellow boat. Beth, Jensina, Acne Face, and Keroppi Frog Girl were getting on one of the red ones. Arianna, Grace, Isabel were standing in front of the third one.

I wanted to ride with Keiko, so I went and put my towel next to Jun's and Kozue's, hoping that she would get over here by the time the first three boatloads returned. I also kicked off my flip-flops and left them on my towel with my wallet.

Toda-san walked the first Jet Ski—I'm sorry, personal water craft—into the surf and started it up. Jake, Lukas, Gabe, and Tetsu held onto the banana boat as it slid over the waves, and Toda-san towed it out into the deep blue sea.

"Why don't you put on this T-shirt, hon?"

Kerri's voice, so near, made me turn and look behind me. She was walking beside Keiko, whose bikini was neon orange. Nothing like the bright color to call attention to how little of it there was.

"No, thank you." Keiko had her hair in pigtails, which looked so cute.

I looked back to the ocean and grinned.

"Hai hai, Pensa-chan." Keiko stopped beside me and slid her hand along my waist, reaching up under the back of my T-shirt until her fingers reached the life vest.

I froze as if a bird had landed on me and I was afraid that any movement might send it flying away. "Hey," I managed to

187

say, then dug for deeper words. "Nani kata?"

She shot me an amused glance. "Nanika *atta*. I am fine." She moved her hand from my back and held up a red and black life vest. "Can you help?"

Yes. Yes I could. I took the vest from her and unzipped it, then helped her put it on. I caught sight of Mary scowling at me. Grace, thankfully, had her back to me, getting towed out on the third banana boat.

Girls, anyway.

"My dad has houseboat," Keiko said. "You wanna see?"

"Where?"

"Another day. Is good place to be alone."

The words made me all hot inside.

We watched the banana boats get towed around and the riders get dumped into the ocean. It was making me nervous. I didn't want my head to go under the water. But I didn't want to look like I was afraid, either. Somehow, Tetsu managed to stay on every time. I couldn't figure out how he was doing it.

Finally Toda-san steered the banana boat back to land and Gabe, Lukas, Tetsu, and Jake climbed off, laughing. All but Tetsu were soaked.

"Supensa-san, Keiko, *ikou!*" Jun waved us over to the boat.

"Did you see Tetsu stay on?" Lukas asked.

"Tetsu is a ninja," Jake said.

Instead of striking a ninja pose, Tetsu started doing the running man, staring at Beth as if she might be impressed with his 90s dance moves.

Yeah, nice try, buddy.

Kozue climbed on the front of the banana boat, then Jun. I offered to let Keiko go next, but she shooed me on first. I climbed onto the squishy, wet rubber boat behind Jun. There were plastic handles on the sides, so I grabbed those rather than Jun. Keiko got on behind me. And when she slid her arms around my waist and snuggled up against my back, I decided she'd made the right choice in regard to seating arrangements.

Toda-san started the Jet Ski and revved the engine. The banana boat pulled away from the sand and bounced over the ocean waves.

We rode for a long while before Toda-san made his first attempt to tip us. He sped up, then took a sharp turn. When he didn't knock us off, he kept at it. One time, the banana boat went up on one side. The girls shrieked. My stomach slid around inside me. Keiko squeezed tight. But the boat slapped back down against the waves. I couldn't stop laughing.

The next time we tipped precariously, Toda-san gunned the motor and pulled us over.

I tried to go ninja like Tetsu and hold onto the handles, but the banana boat flipped upside down. My body plunged into the shockingly warm water, Keiko still gripping my waist. I panicked, I admit. Terror rose in my chest, convincing me I was going to drown. I kicked and flailed my arms, slapping at the inflated clump of rubber overhead, trying to find the surface.

The life vests did good work, though, and pulled me and Keiko to the surface. When my face broke through and I sucked in that blessed air, I also swallowed a half gallon of salty water. This left me coughing and hacking and probably looking like an idiot, again, but Keiko was laughing so hard she didn't seem to notice.

Life vests were an amazing invention.

Keiko swam toward the banana boat then, and I realized that this was the moment I'd dreamed about again and again. It usually felt good when one of my visions came to pass. But this time I was just confused. Why would I dream about this particular moment? What was God trying to tell me?

After all my research on how God had used prophecies in the Bible, I still had no clue how to interpret my own. Arianna had said to pray about it, and while I still wasn't convinced that God was even listening, I gave it yet another try.

Okay, God, I'm listening. Keiko in the ocean. Prière said my prophecies are usually warnings. So . . . is she going to drown? Are there sharks in the water? Should I not go swimming with her? Am I going to drown if I go swimming with her?

But the life jackets were doing a great job, so it couldn't be that. At least not now. In fact, once I'd figured out that I wasn't going to drown, I got the hang of the falling into the ocean thing. We all took turns riding the banana boats for the next few hours until that short woman who brought us lunch on Wednesdays showed up with a bunch of bags. We all sat on our beach towels while she passed out little box lunches.

Keiko put her towel so close to mine that they overlapped. She leaned against me and whispered in my ear. "Meet me behind boathouse, five minutes." Then she jumped up, said, "*Toire!*" and ran off toward the warehouse.

Uhm . . . oh-kay. Like me getting up in five minutes and heading off after her wouldn't be noticed by anyone. I watched her until she disappeared into the warehouse. Then I kept staring at the open garage door. By "boathouse" had she meant the warehouse? And she had said *behind* not *inside,* right?

The woman came over to where me and Jun and Gabe had our stuff, blocking my view of the warehouse. "*O-noriben ga tabetai desuka o-tori bento desuka?*" she asked me.

"Wakarimasen," I said, peeking around her side to get

another look at the warehouse.

She pulled out two boxes from a paper sack, one in each hand. She shook the one in her right hand. "This-su one . . . chicken." She shook the left one. "This-su one . . . seaweed."

"Chicken," I said, snatching the box out of her right hand.

"Is tori bento," she said.

I pulled off the lid. "Tori bento."

She nodded and moved to Gabe, who also took a tori bento. Jun took a seaweed one.

"Tori means chicken in Japanese," Jun said, once the woman was gone.

Now, that was something I wasn't going to forget. If we ever ended up at a restaurant, I was ordering the tori.

The little box had four containers filled with chicken, rice, some kind of coleslaw, a square of Japanese omelet, and orange slices. The chicken was cold, but really good. As usual, there wasn't nearly enough food. Before I started nibbling grains of rice, I decided that five minutes must have passed. I got my feet under me to stand, then froze when the idea crossed my mind that Keiko might kiss me.

Nah.

But what if she did? I'd just eaten a bunch of chicken. I faked a cough and put my hand over my mouth, trying to smell my breath. Couldn't tell. I inspected my lunch tray. No mint. Then I remembered that I had the remains of a homemade field ops kits in my wallet, collected from things I had in my suitcase. I grabbed my wallet and found the stick of Big Red. I shoved it in my mouth. It was as hard as rock, but there was still some good flavor in it.

"I've got to go to the bathroom." I jogged away. I heard Gabe yell something, but I didn't look back, hoping he'd think I hadn't heard him.

Sadly, Gabe ran up beside me. "I'm coming with you."

Oh, great. I gnawed on the gum and didn't answer.

We reached the warehouse. Gabe headed straight for the garage door. I slowed my steps, uncertain how I was going to lose him or which way Keiko had gone.

Before I had to make a choice, someone yelled, "*Ne, Gojira!*"

I looked out at the parking lot. Two Japanese teenagers were standing beside a pair of motor scooters. They both had the flat-topped hairstyles of Kimura-san's karate students.

Gabe came back out of the warehouse to stand beside me. "He called you Godzilla."

"No, he didn't."

"Yes, he did. Gojira is how Japanese people say—"

A girl's scream made us both jump. Keiko!

I ran around the back of the warehouse. At the opposite corner, some guy was holding Keiko up against the wall.

"Hey! Get your hands off her!" I ran toward them. The guy looked at me.

Bushi Kogawa.

He dragged Keiko toward a motorcycle. She shook her head and tried to pull away, but Bushi forced her to get on the bike. Just before I reached him, he started the bike and drove in a wide U-turn, spraying sand in an arc, laughing and taunting me. "Come and catch me, Amerikan," he yelled, coasting to a stop. I reached out, and my fingertips swiped the back of his T-shirt just as the motorcycle shot forward again. I sprinted after him, but he kept just out of my reach.

He drove up onto the asphalt of the parking lot and stopped again. I could hear Keiko sobbing and spouting

Japanese, and I poured on the speed. "You want her? Come on!" Bushi shot off toward the end of the lot. I chased him, then slowed and cut through the middle to head him off. The asphalt was smoother than wet sand under my bare feet.

"Spencer!" Gabe ran up beside me, panting. "What are you doing?"

"We have to help her."

"So let's go tell my dad."

"Good idea," I said. "Go tell him."

Bushi drove around the end of the lot and circled back toward me. The engine revved to full throttle.

"He's going to run you over!" Gabe said.

I didn't think he would because then he'd crash. But if he swerved at the last second, Keiko might get hurt. I heard Bushi's friends laughing and ran toward them. I pushed the first guy into the second guy's scooter. All three went down like Dominoes. I straddled the first guy's scooter, kicked back the stand with my heel, and flipped switches until I managed to start it.

Gabe ran up beside me. "What are you doing?"

"Tell Mr. S what's happened."

Bushi sailed by, and I accelerated the scooter after him. It was small and black and had a flat area in the middle for me to put my feet on. The whole thing felt small beneath me, but it kept up with Bushi's just fine.

Bushi glanced over his shoulder, saw that I was behind him, and increased his speed.

I cranked the throttle on my bike, and the motor trilled higher.

Bushi turned left on the narrow road between the beach and the driving school parking lots. Long swaths of green grass, tropical bushes, and sand filled the ditches beside the road. It ran straight ahead for a long shot, and Bushi stretched the distance between us. There was no way my scooter could keep up with his motorcycle, but for some reason, Bushi slowed down until I caught up. He was toying with me. What was this guy's problem?

I got close enough to almost ram my front wheel into his back one. Keiko screamed again. Then Bushi sped on ahead.

I cussed him out, knowing no one was here to report me.

We passed what looked like some apartment buildings. A freeway rose suddenly on our left. We sped beside it for a while, then Bushi turned right down a narrow, curvy street with hedges and palm trees on both sides.

I followed, but it occurred to me now that I was in trouble. If the police decided to grab me, I had no passport or wallet. Sure, Mr. S would find me eventually, but he'd be ticked. And for all I knew, Bushi was leading me into a trap.

Duh. Of course he was. But I couldn't leave Keiko with him.

The road T'd off at an intersection. Keiko yelled and slapped at Bushi, but before I could stop to get off my scooter, he rolled out into the main road and jetted across the busy street. Horns honked, and one pedestrian yelled after him.

Figs and jam. What now? I inched out into the intersection and almost got hit by a bus. I squeezed the brakes so hard I swallowed my gum. Gross. So much for kissing Keiko.

The bus stopped for me, though, and I was able to cross. I chased Bushi down another side street and into a busy street with two lanes of cars going each direction. I had to slow down behind a car, which was more like a ladybug on wheels. Bushi was three cars ahead, and as I watched, he surged around another. Though it freaked me out, I steered out from behind the ladybug and accelerated between the two rows of cars.

I recognized the Okinawa store with the 3D cat and Buzz Lightyear. We were in the shopping area near the movie theater. A few blocks later, Bushi took a sharp left into an alley. When I reached it, I saw that it wasn't an alley, but that covered Heiwa Street with all the shops. I stopped and turned slowly into the shopping area. People yelled at me, and I caught sight of a black sedan on the street behind me.

Mr. Sloan. Of course he'd be following me as always. Good. At least I'd be safe if Bushi was leading me to his mafia pals. But Mr. Sloan couldn't drive the car in here like I could the scooter. I hoped he could keep up on foot.

I moved easily down the wake Bushi had parted in the crowd. I passed shops and kiosks and vending machines, racks of clothing, hat and shoe stands, ladies pushing strollers, and all kinds of people.

Bushi slowed to swerve though a large mob of shoppers, then sped to the right where the street divided. It took me a bit to get through the mob—I heard Keiko scream—and when I turned to the right, I saw that Bushi had crashed into a flower stand. Fresh flowers covered the street. The motorcycle lay on its side, and Bushi was picking it up. Keiko lay a few yards from him in a pile of reddish orange flowers that matched the color of her bikini. She wasn't moving.

I accelerated down the street and stopped at Keiko's side. Bushi took off down the street. I let him go.

I put down the kickstand and climbed off the bike. "Keiko?" I crouched at her side.

A woman came at me with a broom, pointing after Bushi. "*Kare wa kanojo wo nagutta!*"

"Wakarimasen," I said, hoping I sounded polite. "I'm

American." I tapped my chest. "Amerika."

"Oh, si. That-o boeeu." She pointed after Bushi. "He . . . how you say, nagutta! Panchi." She tapped her fist to her cheek.

He punched her? I tipped Keiko's face toward mine. The skin around her left eye was bluish and had already puffed up so much that her left eye was merely a black slash of eyelashes. That mother pus . . .

I shook her shoulder. "Keiko?"

She groaned then and opened her eyes, though the left one barely cracked a quarter of an inch. She cried out and pushed herself up, touched her eye. Tears dripped down her cheeks. "Bushi?" She looked over my shoulder, down the street.

"He's gone," I said.

She started bawling then, pushed up onto her knees, and hugged my neck. I pulled her close and held her, not knowing what else to do. I was very aware that my hands were flat against her bare back. An idea came to me then. I closed my eyes and willed a vision to come, hoping I could see something that would help me help her.

But nothing happened.

I tried it again, this time praying for God to show me. But He didn't.

I really wasn't surprised. I did *not* understand how this stuff worked. I wondered if I understood God at all.

"Spencer!" Mr. Sloan crouched beside us. "You're okay?"

His European accent seemed stronger than usual, but I never had heard the guy talk all that much. "Bushi hit her."

The police arrived then. I explained as best I could, but Keiko and the florist took over and did most of the talking. Mr. Sloan spoke fluent Japanese too, and he got involved, showed one of the officers his badge. I wondered what kind of a badge it was. Probably an INTERPOL one, since they funded the Mission League.

Some medical people showed up to check out Keiko. Mr. Sloan was still talking with the police. So I gathered up the flowers on the street and set them in a pile inside the door of the woman's flower shop. She seemed like a nice lady. I felt bad that Bushi had messed up her place.

A cop drove away the scooter I'd stolen. Another cop escorted Keiko out of the shopping area. Mr. Sloan and I followed them.

"What's going to happen?" I asked him.

"They're going to take her to the hospital to make sure she's okay. Then they'll question her."

"And me?"

"I took care of it. You're coming with me."

Oh-kay. I wasn't sure if that was good or bad, but I'd much rather be with Mr. Sloan than hauled off to some Japanese jail. But when we got out of the shopping area, Toda-san's little white gumdrop was parked behind Mr. Sloan's black sedan, and Mr. S was standing beside it.

Yeah . . . I was definitely in trouble.

● ● ●

"But Mr. S," I said, "he would have gotten away if I hadn't chased him."

"Can you prove that, Spencer?"

I was riding in the back of Toda-san's car. Mr. S was in the passenger's seat and Toda-san was driving. Mr. S had put me on probation. That meant if I got in trouble again, he'd send me home. I'd asked him to define *trouble,* but he'd just glared

197

at me.

"I didn't have time to think," I said. "I just had to get her away from him. He's beat her up before, Jun said. I think God wants me to track her so that she can get into the Mission League where her prophecies can do some good."

"Kimura-san's daughters rejected Mishion Ligu," Toda-san said. "And Keiko . . . she tells many lie."

"Oh, come on," I said. "You didn't see what he did to her eye. And don't forget he tried to break my arm. Why won't someone arrest *him?*"

"The police are looking for him," Mr. S said. "They told me he's one of the leaders of a dangerous gang and that they've been after him for a while. Leave it to them, please."

"I wasn't going after him." I looked out the car window. It was nighttime now. Bright lights everywhere. "I was just trying to help Keiko."

"You could have helped Keiko by telling me and Toda-san. Not by stealing a motor scooter."

"I *borrowed* it."

"Do I need to send you home to Kimbal now?" Mr. S asked. "This kind of recklessness is what got you in trouble last year."

"No. I'm sorry, okay? Next time some guys abducts a girl and beats her up, I'll just stand by and watch."

Mr. S groaned and rubbed his head. I didn't mean to be difficult, but it was *my* red card to track Keiko, no one else's. And I wasn't going to just stand there and let anything happen to her on my watch.

REPORT NUMBER: 16

REPORT TITLE: More Visions Lead to More Lectures . . . Whee
SUBMITTED BY: Agent-in-Training Spencer Garmond
LOCATION: Kimura Fitness Center, 3-18-57 Jinan, Naha,
Okinawa, Japan
DATE AND TIME: Monday, June 22, 4:15 p.m.

MONDAY AFTERNOON WHEN I GOT TO the rec center,
Grace was already there playing ball with Mary Stopplecamp. I
scanned the gym for Mr. S, not in the mood for any more *You
disappoint me* lectures. No sign. He must be off talking to
Kimura-san. Maybe about Keiko. I hadn't seen her at school
today, and I was dying to know how she was doing.

I crossed the gym. As Grace went up for a lay-up, I snuck
up behind her, stole the ball, and dunked it, one handed. I
hung from the hoop a minute, then dropped to the floor in
front of Mary. "Hey, Mair."

"I didn't know you could dunk!" Mary said. "And with one
arm too? Wow."

"Since eighth grade," I said with a glance at Grace, who was standing there with her arms folded across her chest, shooting me the "dark eyes." *Yeah, yeah, you hate me.* Whatev. "It's actually easier to dunk with one arm than two."

Mary hugged me around the waist. "Spencer, I'm glad you're okay. Gabe said you went after Keiko. I should have known you wouldn't listen to me." She scowled at me as if she were scolding a puppy.

With her hugging me, my arm automatically fell around her, so I turned her away and walked along the baseline, not wanting Grace to overhear us. "I couldn't let that guy hurt Keiko." But that was dumb because Bushi had hurt her any way. Maybe Mary was better at interpreting prophecies than I was. "Is that what you meant by me staying away from pretty Asian girls? That I would try and rescue one?"

"I don't know. Just that you'd get into trouble with them. I'm more worried about those three guys."

Right. Mary's dream about the three Asian guys pounding me. "Well, yesterday had nothing to do with a bunch of guys beating me up."

"How do you know? That crazy guy already almost broke your arm. Now you chased after him. Why wouldn't he gather up his friends to kick your butt?"

The girl had a point. "Who told you all that? I thought you're not supposed to know what's going on in the Mission League?"

She lit up with a smile. "I'm observant. I heard Dad talking to Mom about it last night."

"Well, stop observing things that don't concern you," I told her, looking at Grace, who had come toward us chasing a conveniently loose ball. Eavesdrop much?

A kid squealed, pulling my gaze to the gym's entrance. Three kids had arrived for the after school program. Two were standing by the door. The third was sprinting toward the rack of basketballs.

"Spencer, you believe I had dreams about you, don't you?" Mary asked.

I turned my back to Grace and lowered my voice. "Why wouldn't I?"

"Gabe said I'm making it up."

I huffed. "Gabe doesn't know what it's like. I do."

"So if you see the three guys with sunglasses . . . ?" Mary wrinkled her nose.

"I'm out of there."

She beamed at my answer, her teal braces a bright contrast to her peachy cheeks. "And what about the girls? You'll stay away from Keiko too?"

Not a chance. "You know you're the only girl for me, Mair."

She grinned bigger. "So how about taking me on a date, then?"

Uh-oh. I glanced at the clock. Five minutes before we needed to get started. "How about I walk you out?" I headed for the exit.

Mary's footsteps plodded after me until she caught up and walked beside me. "Spencer, have you ever seen the movie *Little Women* or read the book?"

I flubbed my lips. "What do you think?"

"Well, Amy is the youngest sister in the book. And when Beth gets scarlet fever, Laurie takes Amy to her aunt's house. And she's worried she'll die before she ever gets kissed. So Laurie promises to kiss her before she dies."

I wasn't following. "Which sister is Laurie?"

She pushed my arm. "Laurie's a boy! He's the neighbor, and he's in love with Amy's sister Jo."

"So Laurie is a boy, but Joe is a girl?"

She pushed me again. "The point is, I don't want to die before I get kissed by a boy, either. So will you promise to kiss me before I die?"

This was one persistent girl. "It's not cancer, is it?"

"*Spencer!* You're missing the point."

"Seems like the point to me. Amy's sister had the beaver fever, so she was worried she had it too, right?"

"Stop being difficult. Will you promise?"

I narrowed my eyes. "From what Gabe said, you've already kissed plenty of guys. Including me."

She opened her mouth, staring at me. "He has no right to say those things to people! And I only kissed your cheek. It's *not* the same."

"Yeah, well, how about I promise we talk about this again when you're on your deathbed?"

Mary grabbed my hand and pulled on it. "Spencer, be serious."

The skin-on-skin touch caused a vision to flood my mind.

Mary sits in a restaurant booth, hands tied, face pale, Keiko sitting beside her. Or maybe it was Kozue.

I wheezed, sucking in air like I just remembered how to breathe.

"Spencer?"

I blinked until Mary's face came into focus, her big brown eyes looking up into mine, her eyebrows furrowed with worry.

"Spencer, what did you see?"

I shook my head. "Just dizzy. I haven't been eating enough with all the bird food they serve around here." I glanced at

Grace and saw her gathering the kids at the center of the gym. "I've got to go, Mair. See you around?"

She nodded and gave me another waist hug. I held her tight, worried about the glimpse I'd just had. All along it had been Mary at the table, not Keiko and Kozue. So why was Mary with one of the Asian princesses? Why was she tied up? And what could I do to stop it?

Grace had the kids in a circle with one kid in the center. The kids in the circle were bounce passing by aiming the ball near the middle kid's feet. Pretty clever.

I took a quick drink from a water fountain and jogged out to the circle of kids. They parted to make a place for me.

"*Konnichiwa,* Supensa-san!" several chimed.

"Konnichiwa," I said, avoiding looking at Grace.

"Mo ichi do," Grace said, bouncing the ball past the kid's feet to me. It came low, at my knees, and I fumbled to catch it. I passed it off quickly, and on it went.

Thoughts of the Japanese twins and Mary occupied my mind for the hour. I couldn't wait to get out of there. Then I got to thinking that maybe Mr. S was still here and I could tell him that the girl in the vision had turned out to be Mary. I didn't want to, but I wasn't going to mess around where Mary was concerned.

When the last kid got picked up, I slipped out of the gym. But there was no sign of Mr. S, and as I neared the dojo, I could hear Jun's class calling their punches.

"*Ichi, ni, san, shi, go, roku, shichi, hachi. Ichi, ni, san, shi . . .*"

It seemed like an opportune time to solve the mystery of the outside door for my facility sketch. But I scoured the building, and there was no way into it. I had a hole in my floor plan that was about twenty feet by thirty feet, way too big for a water heater. My only guess was that there was a meeting room or something that came out from Mr. Kimura's office. But the offices were locked, so I gave up and went out front to wait for Jun.

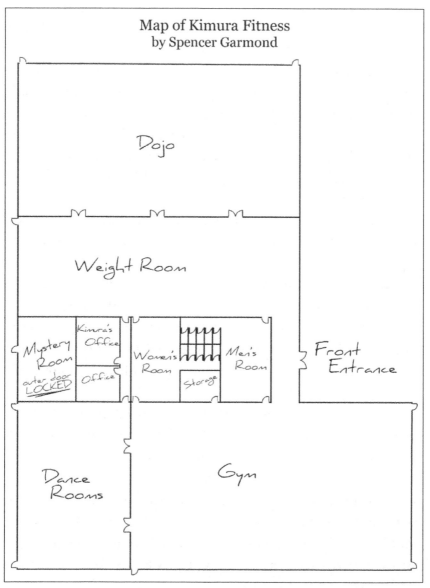

Map of Kimura Fitness
by Spencer Garmond

• • •

Reports were due to Mr. S every Friday. For my intercession reports, I just copied everything out of my journal. But this time I was making an amendment to an earlier report. An amendment involving my teacher's daughter. A few times this week I'd looked for moments to tell Mr. S about Mary's appearance in my glimpse, but it had never seemed to work out. So today I'd submit it on paper where I wouldn't have to look the man in the eye until it was all out in the open.

The report for the incident with Bushi and Keiko took a lot more work—real reports always did. Keiko's life might depend on any clues I'd picked up, so I took my time and did it right. I also wrote a quick report about my theory of Kimura-san treating Keiko badly because of her prophetic gift. I hoped Mr. S would think it was a better theory than my report last week on a possible connection between Bratva and *Jolt III*, which, in retrospect, did seem like a stretch.

So that Friday, in our air-conditioned meeting room in the back of the library, I handed in everything to Mr. S and sat down at the table where Wally was telling Gabe about the disinfectant spray our host mom had bought for him.

We *so* didn't deserve her.

I hadn't seen Keiko since they'd taken her away in the ambulance. All week she'd been gone from school. This annoyed me because I liked her, which I knew was dumb. But it also worried me. What if something had happened to her? Jun told me that Kozue said she was fine, but that wasn't good enough for me. I wanted to see her with my own eyes.

The door to our meeting room banged open, and Beth entered. She took the only empty chair, which happened to be at the desk beside mine. Both of us were sitting on the outside of the inside row. I hadn't seen much of Beth this summer—or anyone in Diakonos group, for that matter. But the last few times I'd seen Beth, she'd been with Bushi Kogawa.

"Why are you hanging out with Bushi?" I asked.

"Really?" She rolled her eyes. "You're smarter than that, Tiger. What happened to your brain? I know you *had* one—wait, don't tell me. It vanished when you met Thing 1 and Thing 2."

Grace giggled behind us. I glared at her, but a rush of understanding softened my anger. "He's really your assignment?" I whispered to Beth so *Graciela* couldn't hear.

"Duh, lover boy," Beth said without looking at me.

Her tone hurt. "You don't have to be so condescending." I forgot to whisper.

"Ooh, that's a big word for you, Spencer," Grace said from behind me. "I didn't know jocks had such vocabulary."

I glared over my shoulder, and when Beth chuckled and knocked knuckles with Grace, I glared at her too. What was with the mean vulture girls circling around me, anyway?

"Spencer? Could you come here, please?" Mr. S said.

Gladly. I joined Mr. S in the front corner of the room, happy to get away from the she devils, but I didn't feel all that much better knowing that once he saw my report, he was going to want to talk about my vision of Mary.

"First of all," Mr. S said, which made me think he probably had ten lectures on his list, "I received a call from Toda-san regarding Keiko. I'm telling you this because of your track and report assignment. At the time of the accident, Keiko had traces of iVitrax in her system."

Hold up. "Wasn't that the stuff Blaine and Tito doped me

with in Pilot Point?"

"It was."

"What does that mean? What is iVitrax anyway?"

"iVitrax is the brand name for solyflexlyn, an anesthetic that numbs the body. It was originally manufactured in Russia by a private lab."

"Bratva?"

"Could be. iVitrax has never been approved for use in the United States but is legally prescribed for medical use in over fifty foreign countries as a pre-anesthetic."

"In Japan?"

"It's legal here for anesthesia. However, the dry form is illegal here, as is use of the drug without a prescription. Street names for iVitrax are rose, rose water, or petals."

"So, Bushi drugged Keiko?"

"According to Toda-san, Keiko doesn't know how the drug got into her system. I just thought you should know." He tapped the stack of papers in his lap. "Now, this report is not like your others, Spencer."

I glanced down expecting to see the intercession report about Mary, but my Keiko report was on top.

"Reports are meant to be just the facts. Insight is fine, but I don't see any interaction with Mr. Kimura in this report. What is your basis for accusing him?"

"Well, Keiko said—"

"Besides what Keiko said."

"Oh, well . . . that's it."

"'You see but you do not observe,'" Mr. S said. "First assignments can be hard, Spencer, especially when you're assigned to track someone of the opposite sex. Be very careful. Everything Keiko says should be suspect. She might not be guilty of anything, yet she might not be the victim you perceive her to be, either. Remember Ryan Matheson's experience with Anya? She showed up at the field office covered in bruises. Ryan trusted her but you didn't. And *you* were right. Don't let your feelings blind your judgment of this situation."

Mr. S comparing me to Ryan was about as low as he could go. "Mr. S, that flower shop lady saw Bushi hit Keiko. That really happened. Anya, Ryan couldn't see that she was psycho."

"Because he thought she was a victim. It's instinctual for a man to want to save a woman in distress, but you're assigned to *observe* this girl. If you allow yourself to get emotionally attached, she could blind you."

"You think I like her?" Had my report somehow made that obvious? Because I'd tried *really* hard to hide it.

"I can tell you like her. From what you put in this report and what I see with my own eyes."

"And you think she's into something bad?"

Mr. S shook his head. "I don't know what she's into. That's what you need to find out. I'm simply advising you to be smart. Investigate her the way you learned in class." He held up my report. "This is biased. It tells me nothing about Keiko Kimura except that she has a mean ex-boyfriend, argues with her father, and that Spencer Garmond thinks she's swell."

"*Swell?*"

"I hope you're right, but remember Ryan. I was there for his debriefing. He thought Anya was swell too. He was very wrong."

Awkward. "Okay. I get you. I'll be careful."

"Thank you." Mr. S dropped my report into the stack on the floor by his chair. "And give me something more concrete next week, okay?"

"Okay." I itched the back of my neck. A fluff of dead skin came back with my fingers. Nasty.

Mr. S cleared his throat. "Now, about your intercession report . . ." I looked beyond those thick glasses and into Mr. S's watering eyes. "You couldn't tell what kind of restaurant? If it was here in Japan or back home?"

"I'm sorry, Mr. S. All I remember is the booth. Maybe if I spent more time with her I'd see it again."

"That's usually not the case."

I looked at my hands, recalling how I'd tried to force a vision with Keiko. "I know."

"I've asked Mary to stay away from you. No offense, but you're the most high-risk student I've ever had. If anything happens, odds are it would have something to do with you."

"Gee, thanks a lot."

"I don't mean to blame you. Mary keeps going on about her dreams regarding you, and I'm afraid she'll seek you out, despite my insistence that she not. Men aren't the only ones with heroic tendencies, you know."

Great. So on top of finishing my gigantor sketch of the rec center, platonic spying on Keiko—so unfair—teaching kids basketball, avoiding another head-to-head with Bushi, and volleying insults with Grace, I needed to make sure I didn't accidentally lure Mary to her ultimate demise. Piece of cake.

"If she comes to see you again, send her away, and don't be nice about it," Mr. S said.

"She's just a kid. I hate to hurt her feelings." Plus it was nice to have a girl worry about me, even if she was only thirteen.

"Her life could be at stake, Spencer," Mr. S said. "Let me worry about her feelings."

"Sure, Mr. S. No problem." No problem at all.

REPORT NUMBER: 17

REPORT TITLE: My Last Delivery of Rose Petals
SUBMITTED BY: Agent-in-Training Jun Uehara
LOCATION: 2-51 Izumizaki, Naha, Okinawa, Japan
DATE AND TIME: Friday, June 26, 9:42 p.m.

JUN KNOCKED ON THE DOOR AND WAITED. It was his last delivery. Once he got the money, he'd take it to Bushi then go home and try and get some sleep before he had to go to the Okinawa Prefecture Peace Park with the Americans in the morning.

The door opened. A middle-aged man stood there. Jun had been surprised at how many older people bought drugs from the Abaku-kai. He had expected them all to be teenagers, but he supposed it made sense that adults would have more money that kids.

"I have a delivery," Jun said.

The man nodded and pulled out his wallet. A small child ran up to him at the door and hugged his leg. The child couldn't have been more than three years old.

"To-chan," the kid said around the thumb in his mouth. Jun couldn't tell if it was a boy or girl.

The man handed Jun two 5000 yen bills. Jun handed the man the package.

And Jun left.

This assignment was starting to bother him. Sure, his position with the Abaku-kai had been able to get him into places that adult agents couldn't go. But that didn't mean he had to like it. And he felt worse when he saw things like that. The little kid. His report would bring the cops here to investigate. And maybe the man would go to jail. Then who would pay the bills for the kid? Who would take care of him?

Then again, drug addicts probably weren't the best fathers. And it was late, well past a little kid's bedtime.

Jun had a ton of money in his pocket right now—50,000 yen. Bushi would let him keep 10 percent, which he'd turn in to Toda-san. Everything else Bushi had given Jun, Jun had kept, including the motor scooter. Toda-san had only said Jun couldn't keep the drug money. It was a technicality, he knew, but he was hoping Toda-san wouldn't find out.

Jun drove the scooter to the Abaku-kai's apartment complex. Inside, he found Bushi playing video games with a crowd of teenagers.

Akio, Bushi's second in command, handed Jun a beer. Jun accepted the can but didn't open it. Bushi saw Jun and passed the controller to Goro. Bushi stood and walked down the hallway. Jun followed.

Goro snatched the can of beer from Jun as he passed the couch.

"Are!" Jun smacked Goro on the back of the head and

snatched the beer back. "*Taco.*"

Bushi laughed, and Jun felt he'd played that well. He pulled out all the money he'd collected after his deliveries today and handed it to Bushi.

Bushi flipped through the money, counting it, then peeled off 5000 yen and handed it back to Jun. Bushi pocketed the money and handed Jun a tiny paper envelope.

"Another delivery?" Jun asked.

"A bonus. For you."

The floor seemed to sway under Jun's feet. This was a package of rose petals. "But I thought Shoko—"

"It's yours," Bushi said. "Take it yourself, sell it, give it to your girlfriend. Whatever you want. Or you can bring it with you when you come to Shizuka tomorrow night."

"When I come?" Bushi had given Jun the Shizuka book and urged him to read the prayers, but he'd never mentioned that there were any meetings.

"The address is in the package." Bushi walked past Jun, returning to his place on the couch. He swiped the game controller from Goro and snapped his fingers. "Akio! Biiru."

Akio jumped up and fetched Bushi a beer.

Jun stayed as long as he felt he had to, then walked outside. He stopped under a streetlight that was beside a driveway and opened the package. There were five petals of rose inside, which was worth another 5000 yen. There was also an address.

A tip? Or something more.

He could try a petal, see what it was like. He might not get home, though. What if he tried one at home, when he was lying in bed, safe? No one would know. Then he could give the rest to Toda-san in the morning along with the money.

Iie. He couldn't do that. He knew better.

But he did wonder what was so great about a petal. He'd seen people doing them at the Abaku-kai apartment. They always made it sound so great.

No. Doing drugs was stupid.

"Nani o shiteru no?"

Jun jumped and looked toward the voice, which had come from a car parked in the driveway. The door opened and a Japanese man got out. His hair was short and his face was covered in the scruff that comes from missing a few days of shaving. He was wearing black jeans and a black T-shirt.

Jun shoved the petals into his pocket and crossed the driveway, putting the car between them. He didn't need some user trying to rob him. His scooter was across the street.

"Donata desu ka?" the man asked.

The code phrase. This man was an agent? *"Kaeru no ko wa kaeru,"* Jun said.

The man nodded to the passenger's side of the car. "Get in."

Jun moved toward the car, still unsure if it was wise to obey this man, agent or not. "Where are we going?"

"Toda-san wants to talk to you."

"Oh." Jun got inside, wondering what his instructor wanted so late at night. The agent started the car and headed north, toward the safe house.

"How did you find me?" Jun asked.

"I always know where you are," the agent said.

Jun's head tingled at this confession. He thought over the things he'd done in public with the Abaku-kai. Nothing terribly embarrassing, he supposed. Yet the idea of this man following him without his consent bothered him.

The agent said nothing for the entire ride. Jun sat silently, feeling as if the petals in his pocket were glowing. They both knew they were there. He was so glad he hadn't taken one. He could hardly believe he'd even considered it.

At this time of night they were able to reach the safe house quickly. Jun followed the agent upstairs and through the front door of the apartment. Toda-san was sitting on a couch watching TV. His instructor stood to greet them.

"Why didn't you tell me I was being followed?" Jun asked.

"Turn out your pockets," Toda-san said.

The gruff tone of Toda-san's voice earned instant obedience from Jun. He reached into his pockets and put his keys, the 5000 yen, a few coins of his own, and the package of petals on the table next to a clear plastic cup.

Toda-san picked up the cup and thrust it against Jun's chest. "Bathroom, *now*."

Jun stumbled back a step and took hold of the cup. "But I didn't do anything."

"I'll be happy to put that in my report once I have proof. Go."

Jun's urine sample was clean, of course. He hadn't even drunk any alcohol that night. But he'd come very close to taking a petal.

Toda-san sat him down at the table and introduced field agent Michito Itou. "You've done well, Jun," Toda-san said. "I'm sorry about the test, but it's protocol to do sporadic testing on agents who are working undercover when drugs are involved."

What if Jun had taken a petal? A little curiosity would have ruined everything. He was glad Toda-san would never know how close he'd come to blowing it.

"We're interested in this invitation to Shizuka, to know who will attend. But it's much too dangerous for you to go. Itou-san will watch the address that night, see if he can identify whoever shows up. If Bushi asks you about it, give him whatever excuse you like."

"Why can't I go?" Jun had earned his invitation to the Shizuka meeting, and he wondered what went on there.

"Participation would require you to take the drugs," Toda-san said. "It's part of their ritual. One you won't be participating in. But we would like to talk about something else. Itou-san?"

"The Abaku-kai is getting ready to make a shipment of rose to Shanghai," the field agent said. "We know where the shipment is leaving from, but we don't know where the drugs are made. Find out as much as you can. Ask Bushi if you could learn to make it yourself. Something that might get him to show you where they cook it."

Bushi wouldn't find such a question suspicious, especially considering how little money Jun's family had. He simply needed to make it look like he wanted a way to earn even more money. "I can do that," Jun said.

"Good," Toda-san said. "Now let's talk about the amount of time you spend with Kozue Kimura."

Jun had wondered when Toda-san might bring up Kozue, seeing as her father was the Toda-san's number one suspect. "She's my girlfriend."

"She's not to be trusted, Jun," Toda-san said. "Not with her father's involvement in the Abaku-kai."

"*Suspected* involvement," Jun said, truly hoping that Kimura-san's name would be cleared, for Kozue's sake. "I've never seen Kozue in the Abaku-kai apartment. Ever."

"But you saw Keiko there," Toda-san said.

"Once, yes. But she was yelling at Bushi."

"We have no proof that his daughters are involved in any of this," Itou-san said. "But your behavior has not been cautious."

Jun was furious that the agent had been spying on him and Kozue. "You must know something or you wouldn't be telling me this."

"You told me Kozue attends Shogaku High School," Toda-san said.

"Hai. Keiko used to go there too, but three months ago—"

"I read your report, Jun," Toda-san said. "And Itou-san checked it out. Kozue lied to you. She dropped out of Shogaku at the same time as Keiko did. Keiko is attending Oroku, but Kozue is not attending school at all."

REPORT NUMBER: 18

REPORT TITLE: An Asian Princess Kisses Me for her Birthday
SUBMITTED BY: Agent-in-Training Spencer Garmond
LOCATION: The Kimura's house, 1021-3 Tomishiro-aza, Naha,
Okinawa, Japan
DATE AND TIME: Sunday, June 28, 7:03 p.m.

KEIKO AND KOZUE TURNED SIXTEEN ON June twenty-eighth. Kimura-san was throwing them a party despite it being a school night. It would be the first time I'd seen Keiko since chasing Bushi through the streets of Naha. I could hardly wait.

Jun and I went shopping for birthday presents for the party. I had no idea what to give Kozue, so I bought her a CD that Jun said she'd like. Jun had already bought her a silver necklace with a jade bead on it. He bought Keiko some Anime novel. I bought Keiko a journal with a lacy purple cover that she could make into an intercession journal. I hoped to give it to her in private where I could explain what it was for. If I could get her to talk more about her dreams, maybe I could find out something good for my next report and prove to Mr. S that I wasn't a moron.

The girls' party was even bigger than the welcome party Kimura-san had thrown for us when we'd arrived. The place was packed with people. Jun found Kozue right away, leaving me to weave through the crammed house looking for Keiko.

"Hi, Spencer." Arianna's voice distracted me. She was standing by a table filled with food, wearing a hideous rainbow striped skirt.

"Where'd you get that skirt?" I asked.

"Heiwa-dori. Our host mom took us shopping. I think she's trying to make up for the lunch money thing."

That skirt looked more like the woman was trying to punish Arianna. I scanned the crowd and easily caught sight of Grace. With all the dark hair in the room, her blond mane stood out.

"Are you looking for Keiko?" Arianna asked me.

My eyes settled on Keiko's sweet face then, standing in the corner of the room, talking to Isabel. "I just found her." I nodded toward the corner.

Arianna tapped the package under my arm. "Is that for Keiko? What'd you get her?"

I looked at the package, then back to the corner.

Keiko's gaze met mine, and a smile lit her face. "Pensa!" She pushed her way across the room and walked right up to me, so close her shoes bumped up against mine. The skin around her left eye was yellowish now. The swelling was gone.

"Hi," I said.

"*Kisu shi-te.*" She fisted the front of my shirt and pulled it down. Her other hand slid around the back of my neck and she stretched up on her toes.

I wasn't going to argue.

Our lips met, and I could feel myself trembling against her. She was kissing me! Asian Princess was kissing me! Someone in the crowd wolf-whistled, which inspired scattered applause and some more whistles. I put my arms around her and pulled her close. She was small but solid and warm. I could have stayed there forever. But she started the kiss and she ended it, looking up at me, slightly dazed, cheeks flushed.

I did that. I made her glow. I wanted to text Kip and brag.

"You saved my life," she said.

Now it was my turn to flush. Everyone was looking at us, so I held out my gift. "Happy birthday." But when she tried to take it, I held tight. "I need to give it to you somewhere . . . private."

She raised one eyebrow and gave me a sly grin, then took my hand and led me through the house, down the hall toward her bedroom. But we didn't go in there. Instead she opened a shoji screen across the hall from her room, and we went inside.

It was an office. A big wooden desk stood in the middle of the room. Bookshelves lined the wall behind it. A sofa filled the opposite wall.

"My father's office," Keiko said, sliding the screen closed behind us. She pulled me to the sofa and we sat.

I handed her the package. She tore off the paper, and when she saw the journal, she frowned at me. "Is for school?"

My heart trilled as I took the journal from her hands and flipped it open. "It's a dream journal. You keep track of your dreams so that you can report them to Toda-san or whoever."

"Report?"

"Yeah. I write a report for every dream I have. The reports go to the . . ." I stopped myself before telling her about the

International Office and the Mission League server. I wanted to help her and impress her too, but I had to be careful, like Mr. S said. "If you log your dreams, you'll have a reference for yourself."

"You do this for your dreams?"

"Yeah."

"Can I see your dream book?"

I shifted uncomfortably. "You shouldn't show your journal to anyone."

"But, Pensa, I could learn much from yours, I am certain."

I loved it when she called me Pensa. I stared at her for a few seconds, my gaze trailing the curve of one sculpted eyebrow to those deep brown Anime eyes to her glossy pink lips. Then I caught myself and cleared my throat. "See? Look." I turned the pages to the sample entry I'd written. "I wrote in the dream you told me about. It's really easy."

"I will learn this." She took hold of my hand and pulled it into her lap. "But I'm still afraid."

I stared at our hands as she laced her fingers between mine. "Keiko, why did you refuse to join the Mission League?"

"What it is?"

"Um . . . Mishion Ligu? Toda-san, he could help you with your dreams."

"Ah, my father said we cannot join Toda-san."

"But why?"

"Shiranai." She released my hand and hugged the journal to her chest. "I love this, anyway. Arigato."

"You're welcome. Happy birthday."

She tossed the journal on the floor, and the thump startled me. Then she crawled onto my lap and kissed me again—also startling. I felt like a popsicle that had suddenly melted all over the leather upholstery.

For the next . . . oh, let's just say an indeterminate period of time, I admit, that I voluntarily, enthusiastically, kissed a girl, and I liked it.

The following Saturday I found myself sitting in a kabuki theater between Gabe and Jun. Besides Tetsu's skill at performing the running man dance, Jake's and Lukas's host brother also did kabuki, which was sort of like a traditional Japanese form of Broadway. Tetsu had a part in a big show and invited us Americans to come and watch. Seemed like a lame way to spend the Fourth of July, but, hey, this wasn't America.

The show was called *Kanadehon Chushingura*, whatever that meant, and was about forty-seven samurai who tracked down their lord's killer to administer revenge. At least that's what the program said in an English translation added for our benefit.

I couldn't follow the production at all. When I wasn't eyeing Jun and Kozue and lamenting the fact that Keiko hadn't come, I caught myself nodding off. Maybe I'd already missed Tetsu's big moment. All the actors were dressed in colorful kimonos and had white painted faces or wore sculpted masks. For all I knew he'd been up there all along.

But suddenly Jun elbowed me. "Tetsu," he whispered, pointing to the stage.

A figure clad in a black hooded kimono slid across the stage one step at a time. His face was completely obscured by the hood. He wore white slippers and held a samurai sword out in front of him.

All right! Some action.

But it was slow coming. A turtle could have crossed the stage faster than Tetsu wearing those white slipper socks.

He finally reached the far side of the stage, where a man in a red kimono and black mask lay sleeping on a mat on the floor. Tetsu raised the sword above his head then swung it down, stopping inches from the figure. The lights went out and the audience applauded.

Jun whistled and clapped.

Wait. That was it? I leaned close to Gabe. "Did he kill that guy?"

"I think so," Gabe said.

How very dramatic. A minute later, the lights came back on and the set had changed.

Come on, it still wasn't over? I sighed and sent Gabe a pleading "make it stop" look. He only smiled.

When the performance ended—*finally!*—we spent another hour posing for pictures with Tetsu in his costume. I had no idea why. After that, Keroppi Frog Girl, whose name had turned out to be Yumiko, left with Jensina and Beth. But us? Nooo. Tetsu offered to let us try on some of the costumes. Gabe was at the front of the line.

Behind me I heard Jun offer to walk Kozue home. Dude was going to ditch me with the kabuki wannabes while he made out with his Asian princess? How was that fair? I wanted *my* Asian princess.

"I'm coming too," Grace said, following them out the door.

I glared after them for half a second. But if Grace was getting out of here, so was I. "Wait up!" I ran after them.

"Anyone else?" Jun asked? When no one answered, he told his dad that he had me and Grace, and we left.

The night was sticky with humidity but cooler than the day. A bunch of crickets were singing at once. I walked with Grace behind Jun and Kozue, who were clinging to each other as usual.

"Where is Keiko tonight?" I asked Kozue. I'd already asked Jun and he'd had no answer for me.

Kozue glanced over her shoulder. "I don't know where she goes sometimes."

Great. *Thank you for being so helpful.* I just hoped she was okay. Probably at a friend's house. But not knowing made me worry. Why hadn't I asked Keiko for her cell phone number? Would International be upset with my phone bill if I started texting a Japanese girl? Was long distance texting more expensive than the roaming charges I'd probably already incurred for texting Kip from here? Either way, I hoped Prière wouldn't be mad.

Up ahead, Jun and Kozue stopped in the middle of the sidewalk to start kissing. Unfortunately, Grace and I quickly caught up, so I put one hand on Jun's shoulder and the other on Kozue's and pushed them forward. "Keep moving, dementors. We can't get home without our guides."

Jun pulled away from Kozue and looked at me. "What it means: demmenor?"

"They're those hooded creatures in Harry Potter that suck off your face," I said.

Grace giggled, actually laughed at something I'd said. Jun still looked confused, but he took Kozue's hand and continued walking.

"Weird play, huh?" Grace said. "That kabuki thing?"

"Yee-ah." The crickets rang out around us, mocking the fact that I couldn't think of a thing to say to Grace that was halfway interesting.

I looked at her flawless, tan skin. No bruises. I thought back to that first day in class when she'd said she'd been in a fight. It had never occurred to me that the fight might have been with a family member or some jerk wad ex-boyfriend like Bushi. I didn't like all this pretty-girls-getting-beat-up stuff that was going on with Keiko and Grace. Life had been so much easier when I'd assumed everyone lived in descent homes.

"You've been good here, huh?" I said. "Except for bugging me all the time. No fights."

Grace tensed beside me. "I *bug* you?"

"Puh-lease. I know you do it on purpose, I just don't know why. So who's this person you fight with back in Cali?"

She shrugged but didn't answer.

I shouldn't bother. I mean, what had Grace ever done for me that I should go out on a limb to connect with her? That's right: nothing. Zippo. Nada. Still, I said, "Is it someone you're close with? A friend or someone in your family?"

She sucked in a sharp breath, held it, then burst into laughter.

My eyebrows furrowed, confused with her response to such a personal question. "What?"

"You're *so* stupid. You think you know me? You think you can figure out my life so you can trick me into hooking up with you? It ain't gonna happen, Spencer. I'm not the dumb blonde you think I am, okay?"

I shrank back slightly, looking down on her. Her pupils had dilated and she was blinking like there was something in her eyes. She shoved my stomach with both hands. I barely swayed and just stood there, shocked, waiting to see what she'd do next.

She continued to glare for a second or two, then turned and stomped after Jun and Kozue.

All righty then. So much for the whole "love your neighbor" thing. Last time I try reaching out to that girl. But it hadn't been a total waste. Agent Grace Thomas had totally exhibited the symptoms of being a big fat liar, which meant that someone in her life was *messed up*.

I kept my distance from Grace the rest of the walk. We were like a caravan in the desert. Jun and Kozue led the way, stopping every three yards to give mouth-to-mouth to each other. Then came Grace, arms folded, scowling. And finally me, strolling along by myself.

I was so relieved when I recognized the concrete walls of Kozue's street. She and Jun turned up the stairs at the Kimura mansion. A few seconds later, I heard the gate clang on the other side of the wall. Grace stopped at the bottom of the stairs and turned back, not looking at me, thank goodness, but staring blankly out across the street. I reached her in time to catch her major sigh.

"What's wrong?" I asked.

She rolled her eyes. "Jun and Kozue. They're up on the porch. And I'm sick of standing there like an idiot while they make out. She never opens the door for me. And I don't have a key."

"Ask her to open the door."

"It's rude to interrupt."

"They're being rude, so you might as well too."

"If that's your philosophy on life, it explains a lot."

I didn't respond. A sudden chill came over me in the muggy heat. I folded my arms and drew into myself for warmth, wondering how long I was going to have to wait for Jun to say goodbye to his girl. Maybe I should have stayed at the kabuki house and tried on a kimono. At the rate we were moving, I was beginning to think that Gabe and Wally would beat me to Jun's place.

Grace gasped, staring over my shoulder, her eyes bulging like she'd swallowed a mosquito. I turned around. Three guys dressed in black were walking toward us. And despite the dark night, all three were wearing black sunglasses.

It was Mary's vision, come to life.

REPORT NUMBER: 19

REPORT TITLE: I Take on Three Karate Experts and Lose
SUBMITTED BY: Agent-in-Training Spencer Garmond
LOCATION: The Kimura's house, 1021-3 Tomishiro-aza, Naha,
Okinawa, Japan
DATE AND TIME: Saturday, July 4, 9:37 p.m.

MOTHER PUS BUCKET!

Without looking away from the guys, I flailed my hands at
Grace, pushing her toward the steps. "Go, go, go."

"What are you doing?" She elbowed my side. "Get your
hands off me."

"I've got a bad feeling." This was it. The vision Mary had
warned me about. I could still avoid it, though. I pushed Grace
up the first step, my heart pounding. "Go! Now! Hurry!"

She pushed back. "Stop touching me! I told you to—"

"Just until they pass, Grace, please!" I grabbed her waist
and carried her up two steps.

She screamed like I was attacking her, kneed me in the

thigh—missing where I *know* she'd been aiming for. So I dropped her and made to throw her over my shoulder, but she slipped past me and ran back down the stairs.

She stopped on the bottom step and glared at me like I was some kind of demon dog. "I told you I don't want to go up there!" She folded her arms and leaned against the inside wall.

I was trembling with anger at Grace and . . . honestly, I was terrified. But Jun must have heard Grace scream, right? I looked between the black iron bars of the gate, but the walkway twisted out of sight and I couldn't see the front door, just sculpted hedges and flowers.

"Jun?" I yelled.

No answer. Mr. Sloan had to be out there in his fancy black car, right? Ready to sweep in and save my hide?

I could do nothing but stare out the opening the stairs cut in the concrete, watching the street, knowing they were coming, hoping Mr. Sloan was watching.

The men appeared, passed by the opening, their backs to me now. And then they were gone. They'd walked right by. It was going to be fine. Just a coincidence. I released a pent-up breath and relaxed, rubbed my face.

Grace screamed. I looked up in time to see some guy drag her to the street. I ran down the steps, reached the sidewalk, and someone seized the neck of my shirt, flung me backwards. I stumbled to a stop in the center of the street.

One of the guys had pinned Grace against the wall and was holding her there. The other two stood side-by-side, facing me. The one on my right was Bushi Kogawa.

Bushi crouched into a martial arts position. *"Tatakawa seru, Gojira."*

The other two guys laughed at that.

Oh, Lord, help me. What was I supposed to do now? They were going to kill me. I scanned the narrow road, which was too narrow for cars to park on the street. No black sedan. No Mr. Sloan. Where was that Sasquatch, anyway?

Stall. I had to stall. I raised my hands. "I don't want to fight."

The guys chittered in Japanese, hysterical over my actions. I held my ground, determined to keep the peace as long as I could—or at least until Jun showed up to help. I shook my head and kept my hands held out, palms away from me. "Heiwa."

The guy holding Grace cackled. I scowled in his direction, distracted by his menacing laugh. Did Kimura-san give classes on evil laughs at the dojo?

Then Bushi attacked. He punched my stomach dead center, delivered a blow to my temple, then one to the other temple, his hands chopping and slicing at Cuisinart speed.

I cowered, my mind completely blank. What had I been learning all year? Strike points, you moron!

I tried to get into defense position, but Bushi was all over me, swirling around like a cloud of smoke. I backpedaled, stunned by his speed. Bushi climaxed by kicking me in the chest. The force sent me flying back like I'd been hit by a car. I landed on my butt and skidded back two yards on the asphalt.

Grace shrieked a desperate cry. The guy who'd pinned her against the wall was getting handsy.

I popped to my feet and sprinted toward the guy holding Grace. I jabbed two quick punches into his thigh and back-fisted his temple. The guy crumpled, releasing Grace.

One of the other guys grabbed my arm and dragged me back. Jun and Kozue must have gone inside or they would have heard Grace's screams. "Run, Grace. Get Jun!"

This time Grace ran up the steps. The clang of the gate was

a small consolation to my pending demise. At least Grace wouldn't be hurt. And Jun would come and help me soon. I just had to hold my own until then.

I could do that.

But I'd be happier if Mr. Sloan came driving up this road right about now.

I twisted free from my captor's grip and had barely crouched into position before Bushi came at me again. I blocked a one, five, a three to my arm, another three, then took a hard five to my gut. I stumbled back, my stomach burning. Someone grabbed my left arm behind my back, and Bushi delivered a series of fives to my face.

Where was Jun? I couldn't win this fight alone. And if help wasn't coming, I needed to get away. I rocked backward and twisted, yanking my right arm up and over the arms of the guy behind me, which forced him to let go. I snapped a back kick to Bushi's face, hoping to get him far enough away from me that I could run.

But Bushi dodged my kick and stayed close. My instinct was to clinch against him and take him to the ground, but with three against one, I needed to stay on my feet. Grace's former captor was trying to stand, so I kicked him in the back of the knees, and he went down again.

I bolted for the stairs, but Bushi intercepted, arms swinging. I gasped, my arms too slow to keep up my blocks. A fist snuck through and blitzed my eye. The right side of my face seared with blinding fire. Something wet trickled down my cheek.

They were killing me. Where was Jun?

I managed a decent five to Bushi's face, and his sunglasses went flying. He sent a low five to my stomach, then another five to my chest. I sagged as he pounded the air from my body, my ears begging to hear the sound of the gate and Jun coming to my rescue or the sound of a car motor and Mr. Sloan's funny accent.

I tried to back out of Bushi's reach, but my knees had turned to sponges. Bushi sprang forward, grabbed my arm, and threw me. I landed on my side and slid across the street, scraping up my arm.

I had to move, to get up. But I could hardly draw breath as I lay there, staring at the street lamp above and the moths that fluttered around it. My body throbbed. Bile burned the back of my throat.

And then my life got worse. All three attacked, kicking and punching at once, egging each other on in Japanese. Shoes dug into my back, my stomach, and my face. I curled into a ball and tried to protect myself, but my hands weren't shield enough for the onslaught.

A car skidded to a stop. Mr. Sloan! *Thank You, God!*

But instead of a funny European accent, some guy said, "*Isoginasai.*"

I was lifted off the ground by the back of my jeans and my arms. The tips of my sneakers dragged across the street as they moved me face down, inches from the ground. I opened my eyes and saw an open car door. They were going to toss me in.

I groaned, a pathetic protest. A mixture of saliva and blood bubbled from my mouth and stretched down to the concrete, where it pooled underneath me.

Someone grabbed my ankles, and my body jerked to a stop. For a moment I was suspended, pulled in both directions, a rope in a tug-o-war.

"Drop him, man!" Jake's voice.

Why was Jake here?

A meld of anxious voices spoke at once. Someone yelled my name. Bushi and his friends released me, and I fell to the street. Car doors slammed and tires peeled away.

I lay on my face, happy they were gone and that I was still here. I'd stay here. It was nice here. Quiet in the sweet darkness. Safe. The asphalt was cool on my face. The crickets were still singing.

A hand on my back. "Spencer? You there, man?" Lukas.

"Get his feet," Jake said. "On three. One, two, three."

My body was lifted off the street. I moaned and managed a "No" through another bloody gurgle, afraid my body was going to fall apart like a house of cards.

"It's okay, Spencer. We've got you." Jake. "Tetsu, get the gate."

Pain flooded back as Jake and Lukas moved me. My face stung, warm and wet. My whole body throbbed with a deep ache as they jostled me up the stairs, past the gate, and inside Kimura-san's air conditioned house. They laid me on something soft, all but my shins, which were on something hard. I blinked one eye, fully awake now, and fully aware of the pain. A sofa. In someone's living room. My legs were too long and were resting on the wooden arm.

I gasped as the liquid in my throat threatened to choke me.

"Easy." Jake lifted my head and tucked a square pillow underneath. "Jun, call Mr. S."

"Hai." Jun vanished.

Jun. Where had Jun been when I'd needed an extra set of hands? And still no Mr. Sloan? Had they gotten to him?

I looked down at my shirt. It was covered in blood spatter that had to have come from me. I reached a finger up to feel my face. It felt numb and swollen, but so did my hands. I turned them over and saw that my knuckles were cut up and blistered.

Jake was standing over me, Lukas beside him. I spied Grace hovering in the corner, staring at me in horror. Did I really look that bad? Maybe she'd start being nice to me now.

I tried to swallow. A bitter salty taste flooded my throat and I gagged. My chest heaved, overcome with emotion and pain and my effort to try and suck in a clean breath.

I heard Grace's voice. "Can I do something to help?"

"Yeah," Jake said. "Get a washrag and a bowl of water. Some for him to drink too." Footsteps over the wooden floor. "Spencer, anything broken?"

"Dunno."

"Got all your teeth?"

I dragged my tongue through my aching mouth. "Yah."

"Lucky man," Jake said.

Lucky? Really? Grace returned with a bowl and towel. Kozue appeared behind her with a glass of water.

Jake took the water, held up my head, and put the glass to my lips. "Drink."

I sucked the water down. I could breathe again, but that hurt too.

"I cannot find Mr. S," Jun said.

Jake set the glass on the floor and stood. "I'll be right back. Grace, can you start on his face?" Jake left the room without waiting for her to answer.

Grace knelt beside the sofa. I had to admit that, despite the horrible pain, it was a pretty nice moment. After all of her hating on me, I'd saved her from those guys.

Grace wrung out the cloth and water trickled into the bowl.

The fabric came at me, brushed my swollen lip, and I winced, my face on fire. "Spencer, I'm sorry," she said, her voice cracking. "I should have gone past the gate."

"Nah yer fall." I sucked in a deep breath that hurt my chest. "Did I lose?"

She didn't laugh. "There were three of them. It wasn't a fair fight."

"But you should have seen what you did to *them*, Spencer," Lukas said.

I tried to laugh, but it sent a stabbing pain through my gut. "Didn't get a hit in. Did I?"

"There were stretchers," Lukas said. "An ambulance hauled those jerks away."

I wanted to laugh about it, but I couldn't. "Bushi."

Grace nodded and rinsed her rag out. "I saw him. Jun and Kozue had gone inside the house. It took me a while to find them. I'm sorry I wasn't faster."

Images flashed through my mind. Bushi and his guys had been trying to stuff me in a car. Why? "I need Mr. S."

"Jake went to call him."

"Someone's after me." I closed my eyes and sucked in a ragged breath. I wanted more water.

"Who?" Grace asked.

I didn't know who. If I did, I wouldn't be nearly as freaked out. "More water?"

Thankfully at that moment Jake returned with Mr. S and Kerri.

"Oh! Spencer! My heavens!" Kerri ran to me and took the washcloth from Grace. "Grace dear, you go and sit with the others."

Grace frowned and sat by the fireplace in the middle of the

floor.

Mr. S stood behind the couch, looking down at me. "What happened?"

I opened my mouth but gurgled a slur of nonsense. Something was definitely bleeding in there. Maybe I'd bit my tongue? I licked my lips and pronounced carefully, "Bushi."

Mr. S's eyebrows rose.

"There were three of them, Mr. S," Grace said. "Spencer told me to come inside, but I didn't listen. It was all my fault." She choked down a sob, then told the story of what happened outside and her search for help inside. She embellished a bit when she told them I'd rescued her—a huge kindness, considering the source. I *had* saved her hide, but I just wish I could learn to rescue myself.

"I saw three guys beating the tar out of someone and thought, dang!" Jake said. "Then I saw that orange hair, the car pulled up, and I jumped to it. They were gonna nab him."

I accepted a sip of water from Kerri. "We should get him to a hospital," she said.

"They could be looking for him there," Mr. S said.

They? Who was this "they" that Mr. S seemed to know all about?

"Don't be ridiculous, Pat," Kerri said. "He needs x-rays."

But Mr. S was never ridiculous. He knew something. And once I got him alone, I was going to make him tell me.

I lay on the sofa for the next hour while Kerri and Mr. S discussed what to do with me between phone calls Mr. S made on his cell. I drifted in and out of consciousness. At one point, I overheard Mr. S talking to a man with a European accent.

"Someone needs to contact me if plans are changed," the man said. "I saw you all enter the theater, but he never came out."

Mr. Sloan? I lifted my head to get a good look, but I couldn't see them.

"Turns out some of them decided to walk home early," Mr. S said. "Jun told his parents and Kimura-san, but he didn't think to tell me."

"Nor did Kimura-san think to tell you," the man I thought was Mr. Sloan whispered, which explained why Sasquatch didn't save my hide. Kimura-san had made sure of that. Or was I just being paranoid?

"He needs to see a doctor," Mr. S said. "He could have broken ribs. But I hate taking him back to Oroku Hospital. I'm sure there's an informant there."

"Dr. Maki can't perform x-rays. We could take him up to Camp Foster."

Broken ribs? My heart rate quickened as worry grew in my mind. It hurt to breathe fast, though, and I fought to calm myself to keep the pain at bay.

"Will you stay with him when I can't?" Mr. S asked.

"Absolutely," said the accent man. "He'll never be out of our sight or Itou's."

Mr. S sighed long and wearily. "Thank you, Christophe."

Wait, who? Arianna's dad was named Jean, like the guy in *Les Misérables*. Again I tried to crane my neck to see who Mr. S was talking to, but when I finally managed to look up over the back of the couch, the men had left.

I let myself fall back to the couch. It looked like I'd be spending some more time in a Japanese hospital. Whee.

REPORT NUMBER: 20

REPORT TITLE: I Get Stuck in the Hospital . . . Again
SUBMITTED BY: Agent-in-Training Spencer Garmond
LOCATION: US Naval Hospital, Camp Foster, Okinawa, Japan
DATE AND TIME: Saturday, July 5, 12:34 a.m.

MR. S HAD BROUGHT ME TO A US NAVAL base hospital
fifteen miles north of Naha, in hopes of throwing off whoever it
was that he was worried about. I didn't get x-rays—I got a CT
scan and an MRI and an IV. And a catheter. Yeah . . . I wasn't
happy about *that*. And, frankly, if I had to choose between
reliving the beating or the examination, I would have taken the
beating again, hands down. Talk about humiliating.

They dressed me in blue and white striped hospital
pajamas and put me in a room next to some Japanese guy with
a broken leg. It looked like a regular hospital room to me
except that my pillow had a huge white kanji symbol on it. I
didn't notice much else before falling asleep.

Saturday morning, I found out that I didn't have any

broken ribs, only a whole lot of broken blood vessels and massive bruises, which had turned purple over the last day. According to Mr. S, I also had a nasty one on my right eye. My torso was spidery with purple and red lines. It was awesomely gross. I felt like an x-Man starting to mutate.

Mr. S told me there was still some internal bleeding, but it wasn't bad enough for surgery. And since I had good blood pressure and my spleen and liver were okay, the doctor decided to observe me, waiting to see if the bleeding would stop on its own.

That first full day in the hospital, I did little but sleep and talk to Mr. S when he came in to say hi. He didn't know how long they planned to keep me. I asked him who he thought had sent Bushi to abduct me and why, but he'd only hint that it was connected to the whole profile match thing. Seemed like a crock to me that anyone had the time, money, and desire to chase some teenage kid around the world. I wished the Mission League would just bring me up to speed on everything in the profile match case so I would know what to watch out for.

The second day I felt a lot stronger, but I was soooo booooored. I hadn't seen anyone I knew except Mr. S, who paced around the place, paranoid that someone would find my room and try to swipe me. I suspected that Mr. Sloan was nearby as well, along with the mystery agent with the European accent.

I was sick of lying on my back, so I tried to sit up. Pain stabbed my gut, and I fell back against the pillows. It felt pathetic not to be able to sit. My roommate's mattress was bent like a squiggly line, propping him up so he could watch the TV. It took me a while to figure out how to work the controls on my bed, but when I did, a small thrill of independence shuddered through me.

Day three, Keiko poked her head through the open doorway and ended my loneliness. "Hai hai, Pensa-chan!" She walked toward my bed, her face growing more pale with each step. "*Aremaa!*"

My heart swelled at the sight of her. "I'm okay." I probably reeked. It had been a few days since I'd showered, and I didn't have any deodorant. I hoped my hair wasn't too messy.

She grazed her finger over my right cheek and wrinkled her nose. "*Ge.*"

I wondered if it looked as gross as it felt. But a beautiful girl was touching me, so I wasn't going to complain.

She sat on the edge of my bed. "My father said Bushi . . . Is my fault, Pensa. I should stay away from you."

"No!" That was the last thing I wanted.

"But is my fault." Keiko looked down at the floor.

"No, it's not." I took hold of her hand and tugged on it until she looked at me. "Keiko, hey. It's not your fault."

Tears welled in her eyes, and I looked so deeply into them that I could see myself reflected there. I pulled back with a deep breath before I got totally lost, and I examined her injury. But her black eye was gone now. I couldn't see any hint of it. I hoped I'd heal as fast. I didn't think Grandma would be very happy to find me black and blue at the airport.

"It's Bushi's fault," I said.

"Bushi is tako."

I huffed a laugh at her outrage, but it hurt, so I made myself stop. Tako was a term for "jerk," but it literally meant octopus. The image of Bushi with eight tentacles made me smile. But so did the image of Bushi looking like a *taco*.

"Pensa, my otosan, he does not know I come to byooin."

Her eyes flickered to the door and back as if her dad might be out in the hallway. "But I had to see you are okay. And I had to tell you something."

"What?" But I already knew. She loved me. Wanted to marry me. Bear my children and all that. I had expected as much, of course, just not this soon.

"I dreamed about a Russian woman," Keiko said, her voice laced with tears. "She was hurting you." And then Keiko started crying.

I just started at her. She couldn't mean Anya, could she? I mean, it was a big world. But seriously, *could* Keiko have dreamed about Anya? "Where were we, in the dream? How was she hurting me? What did she look like?"

"She had yellow hair. Very pretty face. I don't know where you were or why you were hurt. It was just her face and your face. Nobody said anything."

"Weird." That wasn't how prophecies happened for me. Why wouldn't she have—?

"Pensa, do you have your journal here? I tried to write my dream down, but I need help." Keiko glanced around the hospital room as if my journal might be lying open for anyone's perusal. I followed her gaze, suddenly dismayed that I might have come at this from the wrong side. Could Keiko have made up all that dream stuff ? Why? Someone would have had to tell her that mentioning Anya would get a rise out of me. But who? Her dad?

"Pensa? Your journal?"

I looked back at those pretty brown eyes. She wanted my journal. Figs and jam. And here I thought *I'd* been tracking *her*. So did that mean that her dad was working with Anya? That didn't make sense. What would connect Anya to Japan?

"I don't have any of my stuff here, Keiko."

"Wakatta." She jumped to her feet. "*Oitoma,* Pensa-chan. *Faito.*"

Uh, oh-kay . . . I blinked, surprised that she'd traveled so far for such a short visit. She'd said her dad didn't know she was here, but if she was doing someone's bidding, it had to be his, right?

Before I got a chance to ask who'd driven her here, she gave me a quick peck on the lips. "*Mata ne!*" And she left.

I pondered her visit as I watched some anime cartoon on the TV. If my hunch was correct, someone had sent her after my journal.

But what if I was wrong? Maybe Keiko really had had a dream of Anya and me. Maybe she'd come here to warn me because she liked me. And if she was innocent, the poor girl blamed herself for what Bushi had done to me.

I still felt like my first theory was the most logical: God was giving Keiko visions about me so I could help her know what to do with her gift. That way, when I went back to Cali, she'd have some guidance.

Unless she was a big fat liar.

All these thoughts made me drowsy. I watched the Japanese cartoon until the credits rolled and its oriental theme song lulled me to sleep.

I awoke to a familiar chuckle. Beth had sprawled out in the guest chair, her back against one arm, her feet propped up on the other. She was laughing at the television.

I turned to see what was so funny. A Japanese man wearing a smiley face mask was dumping a massive bowl of rice onto another man's head. The man, already knee-deep in rice, pretended he couldn't walk. Someone in a frog suit danced in the background. Bizarre.

"Hey," I said.

Beth jerked her head toward me and smiled her dimply smile. "Hey, Tiger. I saw your girlfriend leave a while back. You two have a nice time?"

I tensed and looked back to the TV where the ridiculous man was now up to his neck in rice. "Go away, Beth. I don't need a lecture right now." Or ever.

She twisted on the chair until she was sitting normally then scooted to the edge and propped her elbows on her knees. "I think you do. Because I was sitting out in the lobby when I saw one half of double trouble come out of your room. You're in the field, Tiger, *training*. This is not the time to play lovey dovey."

"Like you can talk. I saw you flirting with Bushi."

"I was not flirting. I was being nice to him to try and get information. Do you seriously think that every girl who is nice to you actually likes you?"

Was that a trick question?

"What do you possibly hope to accomplish with this little girlfriend of yours?" Beth asked. "We'll be home in a month and you'll never see her again."

I didn't really consider Keiko my girlfriend, but that was none of Beth's business. "James Bond had lots of girlfriends."

Beth snorted. "Okay, one, James Bond is a fictional character. Two, you are *not* James Bond. You're more like that cartoon skunk that scares the cats away. Three, is James Bond the kind of man you really want to be?"

I didn't like this topic. Beth had seen one too many shrinks in her day and was trying to act like one. So I said the only thing I thought might get her to shut up. "Keiko is my assignment. I got a red card."

She raised one eyebrow. "Seriously?"

"Why would I make that up?"

"Good grief." She rolled her eyes. "Then stop kissing her and start paying attention. Track and report isn't a dating service. Look at you! You could've been killed. Didn't I teach you better than this? I know Boss Schwarz did."

I stared over her head at the TV. "There were *three* of them."

"And you should have run. I told you. There are no rules on the street. There are no fair fights. You've gotta be ready to face lunatics like Bushi."

"Which has nothing to do with Keiko. I'm just saying. You've got two lectures going at once, Beth. I can't keep up."

"Track and report, Spencer. Have you been? Have you investigated her past?"

"I already know she used to date Bushi." I frowned. "You know something else?"

Beth shook her head and laughed. "Oh, no. I ain't gonna do your work for you. If you won't do it, you'll learn the hard way." She blew out a dramatic breath. "But at least you'll learn."

"Is this really the only reason you're here? To yell at me? No flowers?"

"Don't go reading more into this than there is, Romeo. Everyone's here." She hopped to her feet and strode toward the door. "Now that you're up, I'll let Mr. S know. Awesome bruise, by the way." She smacked her fist against her cheek twice—*bap, bap*—and left the room.

REPORT NUMBER: 21

REPORT TITLE: Following Kozue Leads to More Questions
SUBMITTED BY: Agent-in-Training Jun Uehara
LOCATION: US Naval Hospital, Camp Foster, Okinawa, Japan
DATE AND TIME: Monday, July 6, 2:38 p.m.

JUN SAT ON HIS MOTO SCOOTER AND watched Keiko exit the Navy Base where the hospital was. She walked across the street to the shopping center and to the place where Kimura-san's Toyota Crown sat parked. She climbed inside, and the vehicle sped away.

Jun hit the gas and followed the sedan, keeping a safe distance back. It *had* to be Keiko, right? He'd been certain that only Kozue had gotten into the car with her father when they'd left Naha that morning, but Keiko must have been in the vehicle before Jun arrived. His only way to tell the girls apart was the mole on Keiko's cheek and now the necklace he'd given Kozue for her birthday, but he was too far away to be able to see either.

It made sense for Keiko to visit Supensa-san. But not Kozue. Jun wasn't certain how the girl had even gotten onto the military base.

Shame filled Jun at the thought of Supensa-san's attack. Jun had suspected an attack had been coming, but Toda-san had promised that the adult agents were watching Supensa-san. So when Jun had seen the San Doubou coming up his road, he'd taken Kozue into the house to protect his cover. The agents had not come to help, however, and Supensa-san had almost been taken. In this, Jun had lost honor for himself, Toda-san, and the Mishion Ligu.

What did the Abaku-kai want with Supensa-san, anyway? Jun was certain his host brother had never heard of the Abakukai or the San Doubou before coming to Naha. Jun had toyed with the idea of asking Bushi, but Bushi had already yelled at Jun for asking about the rose lab. He would only call suspicion to himself if he asked about Supensa-san too.

How would Supensa-san react when he found out that someone had ransacked Jun's house and Supensa-san's things? Jun was certain that the Abaku-kai was responsible, that they'd been looking for something specific. Jun didn't like putting his parents in danger and was counting the days until the Amerikans left to return home.

He only hoped he could help keep Supensa-san alive until then.

REPORT NUMBER: 22

REPORT TITLE: I Tour a Castle, a Boat, and Get Kicked in the Face
SUBMITTED BY: Agent-in-Training Spencer Garmond
LOCATION: Jun Uehara's house, 17-21 Matsuo Shobosho
Dori, Naha, Okinawa, Japan
DATE AND TIME: Monday, July 6, 7:16 p.m.

WHEN I FINALLY GOT BACK TO JUN'S HOUSE on Monday night, his mother had made a bed for me in the living room. She thought I needed to sleep on something softer than the floor. I have to admit, it was a relief. She'd left all my things in Jun's room though, but I figured I couldn't very well change my clothes in the living room, so I didn't bother dragging the turtle out to my new digs.

But when I did go looking for clean clothes and my toothbrush, my suitcase looked like someone had dumped it out, danced on my clothes, then crammed everything back in. I mean, I'm no Arianna or Wally, but I do fold.

"Jun? Did you go through my stuff?"

Jun's eyes widened. "Two nights ago someone broke into our house. Everything messed up. But we thought nothing was stolen. Are you missing things?"

"My journal."

I dug through my suitcase in a panic before remembering that I'd left my journal in the library classroom on Friday along with my facility sketch of Kimura Fitness. I breathed easier, hoping it would still be there tomorrow. "It's okay. I left it at the school."

"This journal is important to you?" Jun asked.

"Very," I said on a heavy sigh. "And I'm pretty sure Keiko was looking for it."

Jun's expression hardened. "They are helping their father after all, I think. The girls."

Hearing it from Jun cinched it. "Yeah." Mother figs and jam! Every time I liked a girl—*every time*—she turned out to be insane on some level. "So what are we going to do about it?"

"We can do nothing," Jun said.

"No. I can't sit back and let the Twinadoes cause mass destruction. Not on my watch."

"What can we do?" Jun asked.

"Catch them in the act. If we can get evidence of them doing something for their dad or saying something, then we can give that to Toda-san or Mr. S or whoever, and they'll bust them." I just hoped we'd have better luck than Candace trying to get the dirt on Phineas and Ferb.

"But it's only our word," Jun said. "How will we get evidence?"

I pulled out *My Precious* and waved it at Jun. "These babies can work magic. So be looking for times you could record her, eavesdrop. Do you know where to get some bugs?"

Jun wrinkled his nose. "What kind of bugs? To scare?"

"Never mind. But if you need me, text me. And I'll text you. Deal?"

"Hai hai, wakatta," Jun said.

But Jun's mom kept me home the rest of the week, which was, frankly, one of the most boring times of my life. Jun's mom was there, of course, feeding me cheesy toast and tea. But there was no computer, only Japanese TV shows and the couch. All day long. All week. I sat watching the clock until Jun, Gabe, and Wally got home from school.

I kept hoping Jun would bring Keiko to see me so I could try and get some dirt on that sneaky daddy's girl, but he never did. I asked him once, but he said he couldn't. I didn't push it. Maybe he was embarrassed about his house or something. But it killed me to miss four days of seeing Keiko when we were only here for three more weeks. As much as I wanted to bust her, I also wanted to be wrong. Sure, the odds were psychotically against me. But I really liked thinking about the "What if?" Or maybe I was just reliving our time together in her dad's office the night of her birthday. Like I said, I was bored.

Mr. S came by daily to check on me, which was pretty much the highlight of every day. That and the cheesy toast and Japanese omelet squares. Pretty sad, I know.

After three hours of sitting on the couch on Tuesday, I decided the best thing I could do was stay in shape. So I started stretching, which hurt like King Kong squeezing my waist, but I kept at it. Because if I just lay there all week, I'd be even more stiff, and that wouldn't help. So I kept at it, and by Friday, my bruises had mellowed. Instead of being purple and red, they were brown and yellow. Still gross. But at least I could stretch my arms over my head without whimpering like a girl. And my sunburn was totally gone. So I had that going for me. Which was nice.

Sunday Jun led me and Gabe and Wally into downtown to tour Shuri Castle, which was supposed to be one of Okinawa's biggest tourist attractions. We walked ten blocks to the Yuri Rail, rode that for a few stops, then walked the rest of the way. The day was cloudy and hot, and I was thankful to be in a T-shirt, shorts, and flip-flops instead of the school uniform and my sneakers.

When we arrived, the other Americans were already there, along with their host siblings, which meant I'd get my chance to spend some time with Keiko. Even Kerri and Mary and Martha had come along.

There wasn't much to see out front of this "castle." Just some sweet looking gray stone walls that had patches of fuzzy green moss growing all over them. I heard Arianna tell Wally that the castle was at the top of the hill.

"Check it out!" Lukas was standing at a kiosk, holding up a cartoon map.

They had them in several languages. I got an English one. It was a cartoon map of the park that said *Shuri Castle Stamp Rally* at the top. The map had a bunch of empty rectangles to stamp along the way to keep track of where you'd been.

I read the instructions out loud. "'Visitors can get a reward if they have completed either the red, blue, or yellow course, or have stamps twelve or more. This campaign is only for junior high school students or younger.' Oh, come on! So unfair."

"I'm doing it anyway," Lukas said.

"Me too," I said. "Which path are we taking? There's a 'See It All' path, an 'Express Course,' or a 'Take It Easy' course."

"'See It All,'" Mr. S said.

"I'm in junior high," Mary said to me, "so I can get the reward at the end."

"Share it with me?" I said.

"No way!" But she smiled like it wouldn't take much for me to twist her arm. And I would, if candy was involved.

Once we all had our stamp maps, we approached the stone walls and a fancy gate. An archway was cut through the wall. On top, there was a bright red painted house with one of those traditional sloping red tile roofs. There was a pair of huge shisa dogs on either side of the gate. I swung an imaginary katana sword at them, imagining I was taking out some ugly beasties.

"What are you doing?"

I turned around. Grace was standing behind me, arms crossed, slouched in that "I'm too cool for this world" pose she wore so well. She was wearing a white Miami Heat T-shirt today that made me cringe every time I saw it.

No reason to lie to the pixie. "Pretending I'm a samurai warrior, of course."

She rolled her eyes and slipped past me through the arch, which was practically a tunnel as thick as the walls were. On the other side, our group had found the first stamping station. It was a little desk with a roof on it. The stamp was at the bottom of a block of wood that was attached to the table with a ball chain. The ink was red. I stamped my little square for the gate, careful to make it all fit in the rectangle. Lukas stamped his upside down.

"This gate was rebuilt in 1974 after having been burned during World War II," Arianna said.

"People died here?" I asked.

"Part of the Battle of Okinawa took place here," Arianna said. "It was the fourth time Shuri Castle was burned to the ground."

"Did you forget that we visited the Cornerstone of Peace monument at the Okinawa Prefecture Peace Park?" Wally said, the look on his face . . . Well, the dude was ticked off. "It lists the names of those who died during the Battle of Okinawa. It said that 149,193 Okinawan civilians, 77,166 Japanese soldiers, 14,009 US soldiers lost their lives and—"

"Hey, man, sorry I don't have a brain like a computer. I forgot, okay?"

"Don't ever forget, Spencer." And he stalked ahead of us.

"His great grandfather died here, in Northern Okinawa," Arianna said, then ran after him.

Well, I felt like a jerk. I knew World War II had been bad. Plus, the man who'd given us the tour of the monument the other day had repeatedly apologized to us, as if the whole war had been his fault. I'd thought it was weird at the time, but I guess war affected people even generations later. I wondered what my grandparents and great grandparents had been doing during World War II. At the rate I was getting answers to my past, I'd likely never even know who they were.

And speaking of investigating mysteries . . . I marked Keiko's location over by Isabel and went back to work. Our group moved on. We walked up a bunch of stone stairs and toward another gate. There were all kinds of people walking around in traditional kimonos. There was even a place to rent them if you wanted to take the tour in costume.

Too hot for that. Though I wouldn't mind getting myself one of those pointy straw hats.

"I thought this was just a castle," Lukas said.

"True that," I said. The place just kept going: paths and gates and stairs and gardens and more paths and more stairs and more gates. In the distance before us and behind, the red tops of the gates popped out above the gray spider-webbing stone walls and green trees. Pretty cool.

"This was the largest castle in Okinawa," Arianna said. "It was the center of the Ryukyu government for centuries until the Japanese government took control. The actual palace is at the very top."

Which explained all the stairs. I still thought it was weird that this huge place was smack dab in the middle of a massive city. It was so peaceful up in here. Naha's version of Central Park, perhaps.

We found two more gates on the stamp map: what Arianna called the "Stone Gates of Sonohyan-utaki" and "Shurei no mon." Keiko found one of the stamping stations and ran over to it. When I caught up to her, she stamped her map, then pressed the wood block into the red ink pad again and offered to stamp my paper. Instead I pulled the sleeve of my T-shirt over my shoulder and tapped my bicep, flexing just enough to make myself look stronger. Keiko giggled and stamped my arm. We made a game of it, then, stamping each other in various places, which honestly didn't get inappropriate at all. I promise I was good. Though it didn't help me learn anything about her dad. It was a process, though, right? Get the girl to trust you, then use that trust to figure out what you needed to know?

That's what she'd been doing to me, right?

252

We found the Bridge of the Nations bell, which was big enough that Lukas was able to stand inside it. We all knocked on the bell while he was in there, and he came out laughing. Then everyone had to try standing inside. I was too tall, of course.

Finally, we got to the top, and the castle and courtyard came into view. The courtyard was as big as two basketball courts, side-by-side. The ground was striped—two-foot-wide red stripes had been painted across the courtyard, leaving the same size stripes of plain grey concrete in between. A perpendicular six-foot-wide stripe cut down the middle of the courtyard like the red carpet from the Oscars, leading up to the castle entrance.

The main castle structure itself was a sprawling red building with stacked tile roofs like something out of *Mulan*. There were two dragon heads on the crest of the topmost roof, but I thought the whole thing looked like the face of a big dragon staring straight at me: the door the mouth, the little dragons on top its ears. When we got closer, I noticed two stone shisa dogs on either side of the entrance guarding the place.

The girls oohed and ahhed and started taking pictures. I snapped a few on *My Precious* as well.

"The appearance of dragons in the architecture is a sign of how China was once a bigger influence on Okinawa than Japan was," I heard Wally tell Arianna.

Mr. S paid for everyone to go inside the castle. We had to take off our shoes and carry them. Inside, the pillars and walls were all painted red-brown. We looked at a bunch of exhibits that were behind glass: antique pots, old kimonos, fancy wooden shoes, things like that. There was a whole room filled with calligraphy, black ink on white paper on huge gold scrolls. It was pretty sweet looking, even if I didn't know what any of it said. There was a stamp station in that room, so we all got caught up on our stamp map. Keiko and I both got stamps on our noses.

We all headed for the stairs. I let the girls go first and ended up at the very back. Then, just as I started to climb, Mary showed up at my side.

"*Spencer*," she said in a tone like I should know what she was talking about. Then she poked my nose. "Nice stamps."

"For your information," I said in a low voice, "I don't trust Keiko, okay? She's up to something and I'm trying to figure out what. So don't start with me."

"Fine, I won't." And her accusatory tone vanished.

We climbed the stairs and found our group standing in a hallway that was lined with sweet black and white drawings of all the different kings sitting on their thrones. Even though the dates were different, they all looked like the same guy to me.

I found Keiko and we wove our way deeper into the building. It was cool in here, but I didn't think it was air conditioned. The floor was hardwood, natural looking—no red-brown paint—and there were lots of shoji screens. I really liked the look of the light colored wood and the cream shoji screens. I think I'd like them in my house someday.

The last place we went in the building was the throne room. It was painted in that red-brown color with gold and black accents.

The king's throne was a fancy chair painted in bright red and gold. It was sitting up on a shiny black platform with a pair of solid gold shisa dogs in front of it, one on each side. The wall and pillars around it were bright red and painted in blue and green and gold dragons and flowers and scrolls. Huge signs of gold kanji letters hung up behind the throne. There was even a sweet crown behind a glass wall, and the thing looked like it weighed fifty pounds.

After the castle, we went back outside and walked around a fancy Japanese garden. There was a little house in the middle of a pond, and tons of ducks swimming. I had a great view of Naha City from up there. Plus I could see the ocean, the airport, and ships down in the port.

We finally made it all the way through our stamp map. Mary and Martha were awarded sheets of stickers for completing it. Lukas and I tried to turn ours in, but the lady wouldn't give us any. Not even my red hair seemed to impress her. But Mary gave me a sticker of a cartoon shisa dog, which I put on my shirt.

From Shuri Castle we walked to a nearby restaurant for dinner. I hoped they had some Kentucky Fried Tori. In the foyer, there were several dozen pairs of shoes lined up along both walls, and we had to leave our shoes there. I was used to doing it at houses and castles, but at a restaurant? Weird.

The waitress led us to our table, which was only about two feet off the ground and surrounded by pillows. Apparently we were supposed to sit or kneel. There were three circular grills built into the table, each about three feet from the next. I parked myself right in front of one so I'd have easy access to whatever was cooking.

Mr. S ordered—I didn't even get a chance to ask for chicken. But I needn't have worried. Jun said this place served *yakiniku*: Japanese barbecue. When they brought the food, it was plates and plates of raw meat and vegetables and mushrooms. And we got to cook it ourselves with tongs on the smokeless barbecues on the table, then put the meat on top of our bowls of rice. Meat-wise, there was chicken, pork, beef, fish, shrimp, calamari, and sausage.

I was in heaven. Hog heaven. And I ate like it too.

I was sorry to leave that restaurant but so happy to be stuffed for the first time since I'd left California. From the BBQ place, we split up into host family groups and my group started our walk to the Yuri Rail. Since the twins were with us, so were Arianna, Isabel, and Grace. But there was some confusion outside the restaurant. Kozue said she forgot something and ran back inside. Maybe she'd accidently put on the wrong shoes. We started walking without her.

It was only six thirty—the sun would still be up for another hour. We walked one city block at a time, moving slowly, I guessed so Kozue would be able to catch up. I liked looking at all the shops we walked past. But I wasn't sure where we were until a plane took off, straight ahead of me. Then we turned a corner, and I recognized the Yuri Rail in the distance, passing over a street, and that helped me get my bearings. I didn't think I'd ever be able to find my own way around this city on my own, though.

"Pensa-chan." Keiko nudged my side.

I smiled at the red stamp smudge on the end of her nose and really hoped she wasn't pure evil. "Yes, Keiko-chan?"

"Remember you said you would come to see my father's boat. Want to see?"

"Now?"

"We are so close. Right over there is pier. It will only take a few minutes."

I frowned at that. It would be good to see this boat. Get some pictures of it for my report. But was this some kind of trick on her part? Or did she really want to show me the boat? Maybe she just wanted to be alone with me. My imagination instantly started blowing things out of proportion.

Was it worth the risk? That was the question.

But she smiled at me and tugged my hand, so I couldn't help but smile back. It was probably a good thing that I was going back to America soon. Keiko was a bad influence on me.

I glanced ahead at the others. We'd fallen behind. Jun, Arianna, and Isabel were a block ahead. Wally and Grace were closest. I texted Jun, keeping my phone out of Keiko's view: *Going with Keiko to see her dad's boat. I'll get pics. If I don't come back soon, send help.*

"What are you guys doing?" Grace asked.

I looked up and found Grace and Wally facing us. They must have walked back while I'd been texting.

"Keiko and I are going to run over to the port and see her dad's boat," I said. "We'll catch up to you guys in a minute."

"Trafficking poses a threat to maritime security on a daily basis," Wally said. "It's the most common type of maritime crime, be that in the form of drugs, humans, or exotic plants and animals. Trafficking starts and ends in ports."

"*Nande?*" Keiko asked.

I shook my head to shush her. "Thanks, Wally. We'll be careful." I urged Keiko to go before Wally said anything else. She took off running, pulling me along beside her.

Jun texted back: *Hai hai. Be careful.*

Good plan.

Two blocks later we turned onto a road I recognized. It was the road that led to the Naminoue Beach where we'd ridden banana boats and I'd chased Bushi on the motor scooter. This time we walked right past the beach and kept going. I stopped and pretended to take a picture of beach but really snapped a pic of the street sign. I couldn't read it, but Toda-san would be able to. I forwarded the picture to Jun.

As we neared the port, I could see the masts of boats in the sky, dark against the bright colors of the setting sun. "Does your dad's boat have a name like *The Black Pearl* or *Red October*?"

"Hai. Is called *Dragon Star*."

"Ooh. Sweet name." Not one I'd forget, either, but I should get a pic of that too.

The port wasn't at all what I'd expected. I'd been thinking of the marinas back home with wooden piers and booths to buy ice cream or cotton candy. This place was vacant concrete filled with commercial fishing boats. The *Dragon Star* was a fishing boat?

Keiko led me down the concrete pier. The place was deserted. We passed one rusty old tugboat after another. They were the size of four city busses parked two-by-two. Big and ugly. We passed by the sixth one and came upon something very different. There, sandwiched between two rusty tubs, bobbing on the teal water, sat the *Dragon Star*. It was sleek and clean, white with a bright green hull. It looked like a lime sitting next to a field of barnacled shoeboxes. I bet it was fast.

"Sweet," I said, taking a picture with my phone. I zoomed in and took a second picture of the boat's name and forwarded both to Jun.

A white roof covered the cockpit, and a navy blue canvas cover snapped over the back end. A swim platform hung off the very back, and two Jet Skis were tethered there. Sammy's dad had a boat like this. His was a Sea Ray Sundancer. I wondered what kind this was.

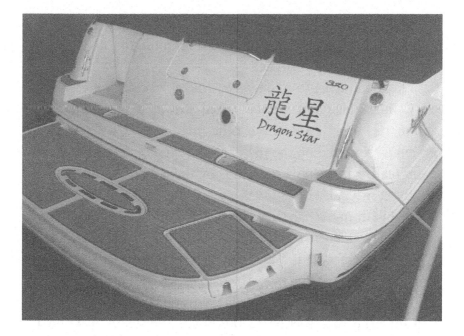

Keiko stepped off the pier and onto the swim platform. The boat bobbed a bit under her weight. She unsnapped one side of the canvas cover, stepped over into the back, and waved me to follow.

I didn't see anyone on the boat. But Sammy's dad's boat had a cabin downstairs, so there could be someone below. I'd already gotten my pictures of the boat, so there was probably nothing else in there that would help my case against Keiko or her dad.

Yet there was still the microscopic chance she was a victim in all this. I mean, even if her dad had told her to get my journal, her crush on me could be real. My journal was still in the high school library, so there was no danger of her getting that. And between Mr. Sloan, Jun, and my necklace, I had enough guardian angels to save my hide if things went bad.

Didn't I?

I mean, what if she really only brought me here so she could have her way with me?

I texted Jun: *Getting on the boat. Don't see anyone.*

I didn't like how the boat had moved when Keiko had gotten on, and I was three times her size. I pocketed *My Precious*, squatted on the pier, and reached one leg over to the swim platform, keeping my hands on the concrete. I shifted my weight slowly, and once I was certain the boat wasn't going to capsize with my weight, I pushed myself up and brought over my other leg. Then I grabbed the little half wall between the swim platform and the back and stepped over. I didn't like standing on a boat like this. At least not where I could fall off.

Once I got both legs in, I ducked under the sagging cover and into the rear section of the boat. There was a white L-shaped bench along the left and back side. Keiko was up in the cockpit, so I ducked my head and went further inside. The ceiling was low, six foot four, maybe. The button on the top of my Lakers cap dragged along the roof, so I hunched down.

The cockpit had a bench seat on the left side too. Keiko was sitting there, smiling at me. The driver's seat was a cushioned swivel chair that sat separately on the right in front of a panel of controls and a wooden steering wheel.

I pointed at the captain's chair. "Can I sit there?"

"Hai," she said.

I sat in the chair, turned it from side to side, gripped the wheel. I liked it. "The sea hates a coward, men. Buck up, says I, and haul those sheets taut!" I cranked the wheel. "Man overboard! Three points off the port bow. Heave to, men! Luff the sails! Back the jib!"

Keiko wrinkled her nose. "Do you know what you are

saying?"

"Sort of." From a combination of Sammy's dad and pirate movies.

"So you are Captain Supensa-san, then?"

"I'm Cap'n Redbeard. And this is my pirate ship, the *Dragon Star*."

She stood up and grabbed my chin. "You have no beard."

"Only true pirates can see it," I said. "You must be a landlubber."

"What it means, *landlerber*?" Keiko asked.

"Nothing," I said. "Can I drive it?"

"It is docked, Pensa."

"Oh, come on." I gave her what I hoped was my most charming grin. "Let's pull up the anchor and hoist the mainsails. Please?"

"Is not sailboat." Keiko took hold of my face and kissed me, major. I let go of the steering wheel and hugged her closer. But she pulled away. "Come and I will show you downstairs."

She didn't have to ask me twice. I mean, yes, the thought of this being a trap flitted in one ear and out the other along with Beth's warning to stop kissing her and pay attention, but what did Beth know about kissing? She was waiting until she got married. And I could still feel Keiko's lips on mine. If we were truly alone on this boat, I was sticking with the pretty girl and hoping for the best.

I followed her to the back of the boat and down a ladder. Sammy's dad's boat actually had steps, so this one must be older or cheaper or something.

I walked backward down three rungs, then held on to the edge of the hole and leapt the rest of the way. The boat rocked on my landing.

Empty. I released a long sigh. See? Nothing to worry about. Just me and an Asian princess and an empty boat. Maybe I'd finally have me a story worth telling Kip. I was sick of hearing about him and Megan and all the crazy things they'd done.

The main cabin wasn't all that different from Sammy's dad's. A little smaller. Reminded me of a motor home. The ceiling was a bit higher down here. Six-foot-seven at least. There was a bed on the far end, shaped into a point at the bow, following the contours of the boat. There was a kitchen on the left side of the boat, a booth and table on the right. The bathroom door was behind the ladder.

There were two skylights: one over the end of the bed and the other over the floor between the kitchen and the table. The cabin glowed from the skylights and the television sitting over the mini fridge, displaying a fuzzy salt and pepper image. Red letters spelled out MUTE across the bottom of the tiny screen.

Keiko took my hand and drew me forward, toward the bed. The bed! The bed! I bit my lip and trailed after her, keeping my other hand on the ceiling to help my balance as the waves rocked the boat.

Keiko climbed onto the bed, turned, and sat on the edge with her knees to my stomach. I was debating whether to follow her up or wait until she asked me to when something clunked behind me. Keiko's eyes shifted, focusing on something over my shoulder.

"*Privet, Spin-seer.*"

Blood drained from my cheeks at the sound of a fake Russian accent I instantly recognized.

Anya.

Mother figs and pus bucket jam.

Keiko squeaked, swung her legs up onto the bed, and

scooted back into a pile of pillows. I turned slowly.

Anya stood just outside the door to the shower, Bushi right behind her, his arms folded across his chest. Anya *and* Bushi? My mind spun, trying to put the pieces together, but nothing fit. Why was Anya with Bushi? Had they known each other before I'd come? Or had Anya known I was coming, made some calls, and found herself some Okinawan henchman in the Abaku-kai?

A bang turned my head back to the bed. Keiko had pushed out the skylight and was climbing though. You go, girl! Did that mean she was innocent or trying to ditch me with her ex?

Once she was out, her head poked back through. "Pensa, come!" she said. "Ikou!"

See? She did care! But there was no way I could fit through that little opening. "Get help!"

"Hai." Her head disappeared. I heard her footsteps above us and turned back to Anya and Bushi, but neither of them were moving to give chase.

"It will not make a difference, Spencer," Anya said.

"What do you want?" I asked. "You really have nothing better to do in life than chase me around the world?"

Anya hummed, a delighted sound like she'd just taken a bite of her favorite ice cream. "You are so naive."

True that. And I still wasn't positive if Keiko had led me here on purpose or if she was going for help.

Bushi slid into the booth and stretched both arms along the tabletop, drumming it with his hands.

Anya stepped toward me. "One year and look at you! You've grown so strong." She ran her long red fingernail from my shoulder to my elbow. I flinched back, then shoved past her and ran toward the ladder.

I was halfway up when someone seized the waistband of my shorts. Bushi's arm wrapped around my chest and pulled me down. My back hit the floor before my feet, rocking the boat and sending a pulse of pain through my bruised abs. Bushi sat on my chest and pressed his forearm against my neck, which made it really hard to breathe.

My head was wedged up against the booth's bench, my feet against the shower door. But my arms and legs were free. Maybe Bushi wasn't trained in jujitsu after all. I just needed a moment for the pain to fade and to straighten my spine, and I could get myself out of this mess.

"You've met Bushi, yes?" Anya said. I couldn't see her face with the table in the way. "He didn't like sharing his girlfriend with you, but it was necessary."

"*Ex*-girlfriend," I said, trying to decide what move would be best to get him off me. An elbow escape should do the trick.

Anya cackled and rattled off a command in Japanese. Seriously? The woman spoke Japanese *and* Russian *and* English? She crouched under the table, a syringe in her hand. Bushi shifted slightly, drawing his arm back until the side of his hand was against my throat, reminding me that he could karate chop me at any time. His other hand grabbed for my arm, like he was going to hold it down for Anya.

"I don't think so." I dug my left elbow under his leg and brought my left knee up to meet it. That freed up my leg enough so that I was able to hook my foot over the top of his leg.

"Hold him still," Anya said, then repeated herself in Japanese.

Bushi growled and moved his hands to my shoulders, like that was going to do any good. I twisted to the other side, slid back my hips, and hooked his right leg until I had him in my guard, which meant that Bushi was still on top of me but my legs were wrapped around his waist. Not a good place for him to be.

I used my legs to pull him toward me and wrapped his neck in an arm triangle. Bushi grunted, tried to slip out, hammered his free hand against my side, but I had him.

Anya held the needle up to my arm, and I put on the pressure. Bushi grunted again—I was hurting him. I rolled him into Anya's legs. Didn't know if she'd stuck him with the needle or not, but they both yelled. Anya tripped over Bushi and fell back. I released Bushi and scrambled up the ladder.

Before my head could pass to the top level, Keiko appeared above and stomped down on my face. Fire exploded against my left ear. I slipped down the rungs and slammed the bottom of my chin on one, biting my tongue. Salty blood filled my mouth.

I looked up the stairs, dazed. What the . . . ? Well, that answered that question.

My hesitation was more than enough to lose my window of escape. I barely saw Bushi's hand chop at my temple, then nothing.

REPORT NUMBER: 23

REPORT TITLE: I Get Tortured but Make a Date for the Future
SUBMITTED BY: Agent-in-Training Spencer Garmond
LOCATION: Aboard the *Dragon Star*, Okinawa, Japan
DATE AND TIME: Sunday night, July 12, time unknown

I AWOKE DANGLING FROM THE CEILING. My head and tongue throbbed. I felt like I was going to puke. I'd never been knocked out before, not by someone's fist, anyway. It wasn't a pleasant feeling. I squinted up at my hands. A white cotton rope was wrapped around my wrists and tied to the skylight in the kitchen. A black skylight. It was night now? How long had I been out?

My body swung and twisted as the boat rocked over waves. My right hip struck the edge of the table. I looked down. For some reason I wasn't wearing a shirt. Just my basketball shorts. My ankles were also tied together—my feet dragged on the floor behind me. I'd lost my flip-flops somewhere down here.

I tried to focus on my surroundings, and my eyelids fluttered at the pain in my head. Anya was standing at the counter, looking at the bed and talking to someone in Japanese. I couldn't understand her. The salt and pepper was still playing on the TV. The round ceiling lights were on too. The microwave clock blinked 00:00.

I planted my feet under me and stood. The movement made my skull scream. My hands touched the skylight. I fiddled with the rope, but the knot was tied above deck. I let my hands fall back until they were resting on top of my head. Where was my cap?

"Spencer, did you have a nice rest?" Anya asked.

I had to blink to focus on her and was glad to see her eyes were normal and not that creepy inky black that took over her sometimes. When we'd been in Moscow, Arianna had thought Anya was possessed by a demon. I used to think that was nuts. I wasn't so sure anymore.

Anya was wearing a white tank top and white slacks. I stared at the tattoo on her bicep, the labyrinth maze in red ink. A shiver flooded through me, knowing all it represented: A journey to power. Connection to the source.

I remembered Dmitri Berkovich and his offer to shoot me up with Bratva's "connection." I glanced at my arm, looking for signs that they'd injected me. I didn't see any. Perhaps Keiko's kick to the face and Bushi's karate chop had accomplished their objective.

Keiko.

I looked behind me and saw Keiko and Mary Stopplecamp sitting in the booth. Mary's hands were bound, and her eyes were all red and watery like she'd been crying.

What? How had she gotten here? Oh, my dream. Oh, no. It

had never been a restaurant booth in my dream—it had been a boat. This boat. And I'd gotten on it on purpose!

"Mair, why? How did *you* get here?"

A tear slid down her cheek. "I'm sorry, Spencer. I was trying to help."

I *was* a baka. I was the biggest baka there ever was. I was Ryan Matheson. I was every guy who died in a horror movie because he went off with the pretty girl, hoping to get lucky. I hated Keiko, but mostly, I hated myself. "Hey, don't cry. It'll be okay." I held eye contact until she gave me a smile, then I turned back to Anya, who was now holding a military boot knife. Aw, great. I hoped that Mr. Sloan was on the way and Jun was sending reinforcements, because this was not good. "Let her go, she's just a kid."

Anya clicked her tongue. "Aren't you *both* just kids?"

"Come on! You don't want her."

"She's obviously very fond of you to try to rescue you from us. Brave too."

The horror of this situation hurt my brain. I was desperate to get Mary out of this. "Let her go. Please? I'll do whatever you want."

"Just seeing how much you want this delights me," Anya said, smiling wide. "I think she will help us get information from you. Yes. I think she will be very helpful."

As my vision played out word for word, anger and hopelessness clashed inside me. I sat back on the table and kicked my feet at Anya, but my legs let me down by getting nowhere near her face. She was too far away.

Someone on my left giggled. Up in the very back corner of the bed, Keiko was nestled against Bushi, his arm around her. What? No, she was at the table beside Mary. I turned back to the table. Neither girl had on the pink tank top Keiko had been wearing at the castle. In fact, they were both wearing all black. Long sleeved shirts and pants. One of them was Kozue, obviously, but which? Both of them had a mole on her cheek. How did that happen?

Think, you moron.

My gaze fell to the silver chain Jun had given Kozue around the neck of the girl at the table. I whipped back to where Keiko sat with Bushi and spotted a smudge of red Shuri Castle stamp ink still on her nose.

"I love watching his eyes as he pieces the whole thing together," Anya said, her face lit up with a devious smile. "Are you there yet, darling? Have you got it all now? I think he's close, girls. His face is quite red. That's right, Spencer. Bushi. The girls. They work for me. Don't be upset. It was nothing personal. I'm sure the girls had a lovely time toying with you."

Bushi uttered a slur of angry Japanese. Keiko stopped his words with a kiss. I looked at the floor, sick. I couldn't believe this was happening. I'd walked right into Anya's trap, knowing it was very likely a trap, *and* I'd brought Mr. S's daughter with me. It couldn't get any worse.

But then Anya tapped the knife on the kitchen counter, reminding me that things could get far worse. "It's time to tell me what I want to know, Spencer."

I didn't like the looks of that knife and my lack of shirt. I spotted my shirt in a heap on the floor with my Lakers cap and flip-flops. Why remove my shirt? "I don't have a clue what you want from me."

"Come now, Spencer, let's not play games."

"I'm not the one playing games. Why don't you ask Keiko and Kozue? They're the experts at *games.*"

"Aww. Bitterness is not attractive, you know. Now tell me, who is the first twin?"

My eyebrows scrunched together. The first? "Uh, Jun said Kozue was born first, but they're both liars, so who really knows?"

"Not them!" Anya stepped back and sighed. "Let's start at the beginning. Who is heading the profile match case?"

"I don't know. No one tells me squat." And even if they did, I wasn't about to tell Anya.

"Are *you* the match?"

I shook my head. "I don't know." Which was true: I didn't. *Could* it be me?

"Keiko said you have a journal for your prophecies. Where is it?"

"I haven't seen it since your people searched Jun's house." Which was true. And I was proud at how I'd deflected that question.

"Do you know the story of the profile match?" Anya asked. "Do you know the prophecy?"

"A little." A very little. The ropes around my ankles pinched at my circulation—my arms had begun to tingle. I leaned back and tried to straighten my arms, but there wasn't enough room.

"What if I told you the prophecy says that the profile match will betray the Mission League?"

"Yeah, right." My dad had done that, and I wasn't about to follow in his footsteps. But I didn't know if I was the profile match, either, so . . .

"It's what your father tried to do. He thought if he could live out the qualifications in the prophecy, it would prove that he was the match."

"You're lying." But that did kind of make sense. Maybe my dad hadn't been a devious traitor. Maybe he had been trying to do the right thing and it backfired. If so, I'd certainly inherited that trait from him.

"You believe what they told you about your parents?" Anya said. "You also believed that Keiko liked you. Haven't you learned that you can't trust people?"

Okay, that ticked me off. "You don't know I'm the match, so why do you keep chasing me everywhere?"

"You're him." She waved the knife in front of me.

The blade was like a magnet to my eyes—I couldn't break my gaze from it. "What's the knife for, anyway?" I didn't want to get hurt again. I didn't want Mary to get hurt. *Please, God, help us.*

"One of the prophecies states that the profile match will bear the mark of his faith. But there are no marks on you, except those that Bushi left. Lovely bruises, by the way." She cocked one eyebrow. "We looked for the other mark while you were . . . sleeping."

That's why they'd taken off my shirt? "You're all freaks, you know that? Psychotic—"

Anya brought the blade up to my chest, which shut me up. "What if I marked you with a pentagram?" She circled the knife in the air, drawing the shape. "Or the Bratva labyrinth?" She turned so I could see her tattoo. "What would that say to your agent friends? That I declare you *not* to be the match?" She reached up and yanked off my cross necklace, snapping the chain. She dangled it in front of my face. "You've made your choice."

The mere sight of the necklace thrilled me. Mr. Sloan could find me. Help was coming.

Anya tossed the chain on the floor. "The cross is the mark of *your* faith. So, if I give you that mark, I force you to fulfill the prophecy. And since I've caught you, I also subvert the outcome of the prophecy long before it can take place."

She was crazy, that much was certain. "What's supposed to happen that's so—"

"That's a ridiculous idea," Mary said. "Real prophecies can't be forced."

Anya brought the knife to my chest and scratched it lightly back and forth. I sat back on the table again and curled my spine, every muscle tense, waiting for the pain. But it didn't come.

I looked into Anya's eyes. Inky black darkness flooded her pupils. I whimpered. Oh, Lord, help me. I needed a verse. One of those spiritual warfare ones Mr. S had taught us. Something about putting on armor or a belt. "The fight isn't against flesh and blood but . . ." Aww, nuts. "Stand firm with the belt of truth buckled and . . . um . . . keep your feet on a firm foundation of . . ." Seriously, I had the worst memory on the planet.

"'Truly I tell you,'" Mary yelled, "'that if two of you on earth agree about anything they ask for, it will be done for them by my Father in heaven. For where two or three gather in my name, there am I with them.'"

Oh, nice one. "Good girl, Mary," I said. "Say another one."

"'The Lord will grant that the enemies who rise up against you will be defeated before you. They will come at you from one direction but flee from you in seven.'"

Hatred gleamed in those black eyes, but Anya didn't scream or melt or anything like that. She merely chuckled. "Your Bible verses are cute, but I too have God's free will."

Pursing her lips, she pointed the blade over my heart and poked it gently into my skin. "Does that hurt?"

Uh, yeah? I thought about swinging away from her, but with my arms hooked, I'd likely just swing back and stab myself.

Mary was still at it, but her voice was getting weepy. "'I have given you authority to trample on snakes and scorpions and to overcome all the power of the enemy—nothing will harm you.'"

Something clumped overhead. The boat jerked violently to the side, as did Anya's blade, sending a searing sting across my chest. I yelled. Anya dropped the knife and grabbed the counter to steady herself. I looked down at my chest, adrenaline pulsing. Blood oozed from a six-inch-long gash. I yelled again, more in panic than in pain.

I'm gonna die. I'm totally gonna die.

Anya glared at the ceiling. "Bushi!" She jerked her head toward the stairs. Bushi scrambled down from the bed and up the ladder. Anya crouched to pick up the blade and slid it into the kitchen sink where it clattered against the stainless steel. "Who is the first twin, Spencer? I must know!"

Forget the first twin. Who was going to stop the bleeding? My fingers trembled above. My head whirred. I closed my eyes. Better. I needed Advil. And a big Band Aid. And sleep. I had to be sleeping now.

"Answer me! . . . want to know . . ."

Someone was talking. Anya was. She slapped my face, a numb sting.

". . . in shock." Mary sounded like she was speaking through a CB radio. "You . . . to help him before . . ."

"*Dōshite . . . shita no?*" One of the twins.

"I didn't mean . . ." Anya.

A thud echoed through the boat from above. ". . . is wrong to . . . watch them. Kozue, I want . . . with me."

The stairs creaked. The boat rocked. I was cold and sweaty. I opened my eyes and noticed I was hanging from my arms again and they were shaking. All of me was shaking. No Anya. Mary was inching toward the counter. I blinked to keep my eyes open, looked down at my chest and the wide stripe of blood dribbling down to my shorts. Shouldn't that hurt? My eyes lost focus.

Thuds came from above. The boat rocked from side to side. Keiko was kneeling on the bed, her head poking out through the open skylight. Something tickled my ankle. My feet sprang apart, tingling madly.

Mary was crouched at my feet. She stood up, holding the knife. Her eyes were brown. Pretty face. She bit one side of her lip, stepped behind me, and started to cut the ropes above my head. "You've got to stand up, Spencer," she whispered.

I did. But my feet were so dead I couldn't feel them. Just nubs at the end of my legs. I felt my arms break free from the skylight. Mary untwisted the rope from my wrists. I let my arms fall to my sides, took one step, and collapsed.

"*Nan desu ka?*" Keiko's voice, floating above me.

I rolled onto my side and curled into a ball. Another shaking fit seized me. I spied my T-shirt under the table and reached for it. Pulled it over my shoulder. Warm.

"You stay there, you . . . *girl!*" Mary yelled. "Spencer, put your feet up. You're in shock."

Shock?

I vaguely remembered something Mr. S had said about getting a shock victim to elevate his feet. I rolled onto my back and propped my feet on the bottom step that led to the bed. There wasn't much space where I'd fallen, and it looked like I was sitting on a chair on my back. Keiko was perched on a stair above mine, glaring at Mary, who stood on my other side, clutching the bloody knife. Mary looked like a maniac with her hair frizzing out wildly and her hands covered in blood.

My blood. I was bleeding.

I wadded my T-shirt and pressed it over the cut. Dull pain throbbed from the wound. As my head started to clear, the pain got worse.

An engine revved to life. Then another. The sound brought me back even more. The Jet Skis. What was happening up there? Maybe Mr. Sloan had finally tracked us down.

Keiko stepped over my torso and to the floor. "My boyfriend can beat Supensa-san," Keiko said. "Already has twice."

I groaned in my defense. Bushi didn't fight fair. None of them did.

"He left you," Mary said. "I think he ran away with Anya. She makes a better girlfriend. She's American, she's older, and she has a way better figure than you."

"*Damare!*"

Keiko lunged at Mary. But Mary held out the knife, and Keiko shrank back. Her feet knocked against my side, so I reached up, grabbed Keiko's waist, and pulled her down. She screamed as she fell.

Mary sat on top of her, but Mary weighed so little that Keiko bucked her off. Mary threw herself over Keiko again, trying to hold her down. I got to my knees, my head spinning, and nudged Mary off Keiko. I rolled the sneaky she-devil onto her stomach and straddled her back.

"Bushi!" Keiko screamed.

"Find something to tie her with," I said.

Mary tossed me the rope my ankles had been bound with. Then she opened drawers until she tossed me a potholder.

"What's this for?" I asked.

Mary pointed. "Her mouth."

I shoved the padded fabric through Keiko's lips and tied her hands behind her back. Mary handed me another piece of rope, and I tied her ankles.

I rolled her onto her side and wiped my thumb over the mole on her cheek. Pasty brown makeup came off, revealing plain skin.

So this was really Kozue. And because of the red stamp ink on her nose, I knew that Kozue been with me today at the castle. She'd been the one to lead me to the boat. But which one had kissed me at the birthday party? And which one had Bushi punched?

I clenched my jaw. Double, Double Toil and Trouble had totally outplayed Jun and me.

I stood then, a little too fast. I swayed and clutched the table until I felt steady again. My cut was still oozing blood, making me almost panic. The thing looked nasty. I reached into my pocket for my iPhone, but it wasn't there. Which almost sent me into shock again. "Where's my phone?"

"Anya took it," Mary said. "I think she put it on the counter."

I spun to face the counter and spotted *My Precious* on the back of the sink. She'd turned it off. I powered it back on. I'd missed a handful of texts from Jun that went from curious to freak-out mode. That made me feel better, actually. "No signal out here." I slipped the phone into my shorts pocket. "Help me move her to the shower."

Mary stepped in front of me. "Spencer, wait."

But I'd already lifted Kozue under the arms. I dragged her past Mary toward the stern and the shower.

"Spencer, Grace is in there."

What! Grace? I shook my head to try to think clearly. Was everybody tied up here?

Mary ran past me and pulled open the shower door. Grace was indeed sitting on the floor of the shower, bound and gagged, and glaring at me. Her eyes popped at the sight of the blood, though.

I dropped Kozue. "What's *she* doing here?"

Mary crouched in the shower and began sawing at Grace's ropes with Anya's knife. "She was following you, and I was following Kozue. I saw Kozue steal Mr. Sloan's keys, and I got suspicious. Then Bushi and Mr. Kimura trapped Mr. Sloan and the Japanese agent in their car, so I figured they were going to go after you next."

"I've suspected the twins from the start, but you wouldn't listen," Grace said, allowing Mary to help her stand. "When Wally told me where you were going, I came after you."

Kozue inch-wormed at my feet, heading toward the ladder. I put my foot on her back to hold her still. "Wait. How do you trap someone in a car?"

Mary came out of the shower and sat at the table. "Kozue stole Mr. Sloan's keys, and Bushi and some other guy parked cars on either side of their car so they couldn't get out."

"Why didn't you tell your dad?" I asked.

"I sent Martha to tell dad, and I followed Kozue. I wanted to be able to tell them where you were."

Which was exactly what I'd done to Gabe when Bushi had

taken off with Keiko on the motorcycle. I was a bad role model.

Grace stepped out of the shower. "I ran into Mary on the pier and tried to get her to go back."

"But I didn't listen and we were too loud and they caught us," Mary said. "But Grace put up such a fight that they shut her in the shower."

"You forgot when that guy hit me," Grace said. "I thought I was going to puke."

This back and forth was hurting my head. "Okay, fine. Let's put Kozue in the shower and get out of here."

"I thought that was Keiko," Mary said.

"The mole was fake. Makeup. I suspect they've been trading places on us all summer."

"Wow," Mary said. "I keep trying to get Martha to do that with me, but she won't. I wanted her to go to my math class the day of my final, but she said it was cheating."

That would *so* rock to have an identical twin. But I'd corrupted Mary enough for one day. "Martha's right. That would be cheating. And if you're serious about basketball, you'll push all those dumb thoughts way out of your head so you don't risk getting suspended."

"You're such a hypocrite," Grace said. "Like you've never broken the rules during basketball season."

True that.

"No, it's a good point," Mary said. "I didn't think about that."

"Just open the shower door, will you?" I said.

Grace helped me stuff Kozue in the shower, and I shut the door in the evil princess's face, which made me feel just a tiny bit better.

I crept up the ladder. At the top, I paused and peeked

through the hole, surprised there were no streetlamps at the pier. I heard Anya cursing in Russian up in the cabin. She looked to be alone and talking into a CB radio. The Jet Skis were gone. Bushi and Keiko must have taken them. I blinked and squinted out over the side. We weren't at the pier. We were out on the ocean, drifting. What the Kobe Bryant?

No wonder help hadn't arrived yet. Or maybe it had, and Bushi and Keiko went to chase it away. But why were we just sitting here? Was Anya waiting for something or someone? Another boat, perhaps?

I stood there for a moment, freaking out. I noticed a fat inner tube hanging off the back side of the boat, then caught sight of distant lights. The shore was a ways away, though.

I descended a few rungs and whispered, "Bushi and Kozue are gone, and we're out at sea. Anya's up there, but I don't know if I can fight her like this." I felt like a wimp to admit it, but my chest hurt bad. "Plus she might have a gun," I added, to ease my bruised ego. "But there's an inner tube. I think maybe we should get off."

"Are you crazy?" Grace scowled at me. "That's your plan? Float around in the middle of the ocean?"

"Don't you give me the 'dark eyes,' chickadee. You have a better idea?"

Believe it or not, her scowl actually deepened.

I didn't have time for drama. "At least I can see the shore from here. But Anya could drive us anywhere. Or she could be waiting for a bigger boat. I think we should get off now, while we can."

"I agree," Mary said, kicking off her flip-flops.

Grace growled like a cat, the sound deep in her chest. "Fine. But you own me eighty bucks, because that's how much

279

these shoes cost." She pointed to her teal and black Adidas.

"Take them off and tie them around your neck." I spotted my pile of stuff on the floor under the table and picked up my Lakers cap and shirt. I could live without my flip-flops.

My Precious, however. How was I going to keep it dry? I put on my cap and tucked my iPhone inside my T-shirt. I grabbed the corner of the hem and the top corner of the opposite sleeve and spun it until it was a long twist of fabric, which I tied around my head like a bandana, centering my iPhone right on top of the brim of my hat.

Mary opened a cupboard over the sink and pulled out a pink backpack and a black purse. She handed the purse to Grace. "Bushi put our stuff up here. You can put your phone in my pack."

"It will get wet," I said.

"Not if I put it in the top pocket."

"Will you put mine in there?" Grace asked her, removing a cell phone from her purse.

"Sure. I can take your shoes too."

While the girls packed, I crept back up the ladder, grabbed the inner tube, and stepped over the back wall onto the swim platform. I blew out a deep breath and lowered myself into the water, clinging to the edge of the swim platform. As the saltwater entered my cut, I squeezed the edge of the platform in a silent scream.

Mother of all pus buckets, that hurt!

Mary appeared next and slid into the water beside me, backpack bulging on her back. I would have traded my iPhone for a lifejacket right then. My heart felt like popping corn in my chest. How deep was the water here? How long could I float on my back, anyway? If I got tired, would the inner tube hold me?

Mary tugged at the inner tube. I didn't want to let go of it, so I kept my right arm hooked through the center. Grace climbed into the water then. Mary clung to the other side of the inner tube and swam away from the boat, pulling my arm out with her. I was going to have to let go of the swim platform.

I hated my life right then.

So I leaned onto my back, looking up at the starry sky. My shorts felt heavy on my legs. The moon was almost full, hanging in the sky like a fat balloon.

Grace pushed off the swim platform and grabbed the inner tube. It bobbed beneath the water for a moment, which freaked me out. I kicked and waved my free arm, splashing in the silent night, hoping to get away from the boat. Did I mention that the saltwater was killing my cut?

A cold, wet hand on my shoulder stopped me. I looked back at Mary.

"Stop," she whispered. "Just hold on and let me get us farther out."

"Why you?"

"Because you're hurt and you're a sucky swimmer, and I'd like to escape without you drowning. Plus, I can swim without making noise."

I wanted to protest, but the girl had, like, four good points.

We started gliding away from the boat, my back facing the shore. Grace must have been helping Mary because the two of them were facing me. My cut stung like figs and jam. I tried to hoist myself up a little, but I was too heavy and only made the inner tube go underwater.

Grace shot me the "dark eyes."

"Sorry," I said, panting a little at how bad that blasted cut hurt. I grit my teeth so Grace wouldn't think I was a wimp, but then something awful occurred to me. "You don't think sharks will come, do you?"

Grace snickered.

But Mary's eyes widened and she looked at my cut. "Is it still bleeding?"

"I think so." And even if it had stopped, wouldn't the water moisten any forming scabs? I should have tied some fabric around it. Ripped up the bed sheets or something smart like they always did in the movies. What if I bled to death before we got to shore?

"What happened to you anyway?" Grace said.

"Anya cut me with her knife."

"And all those bruises on your stomach and back? Are those from the day Bushi and his friends attacked you?"

"I have high hopes for you, Agent Thomas. A glittering career . . ."

"Shut up," Grace said.

Gladly. We were about ten yards away from the boat when a tiny light focused on us. A slur of Russian and English curses floated over the dark sea to our inner tube.

"Faster," I said.

The girls' legs must have turned into paddlewheels because we jerked forward. The boat engine sputtered but didn't start. Maybe something was wrong. Please let there be something wrong!

"We could go faster if you got on top," Grace said.

"Yeah, climb up on the inner tube, Spencer," Mary said, patting the black rubber.

"I'm not *dead*," I said. Plus, I couldn't let the girls rescue me. I had to maintain some form of masculine behavior.

"Don't be dumb," Grace said.

"Please, Spencer?" At least Mary's voice was kind. "You're dragging down the front like a rudder. It's like driving a car with the hand brake on."

"What do you know about driving a car?" I hated the idea of the girls doing all the work. "How am I supposed to get up there, anyway? In case you haven't noticed, I'm not graceful without a basketball in my hands."

"Climb up on your front and flip over," Grace said.

That sounded simple enough. The girls held the tube steady. I reached across with both arms, grabbed the other side of the tube between the girls, and pulled myself up, gasping as my cut slid over the rubber. I pulled a little more, then I flipped myself over. My rear sank into the hole, my back and legs resting on the sides of the tube like it was a pillow.

Huh.

Mary smiled. She put one hand on my shoulder and the other on the tube. Grace moved down and grabbed my right leg. Then they started kicking again. Anya still hadn't managed to start the boat. Could she really be alone on that thing? Maybe we actually stood a chance.

But the shore still seemed pretty far away. I could barely see lights flickering in the distance. "Is this the right way?"

"Unless you want to swim for China," Mary said.

I looked back to the boat, squinting to look past it for a shore on that side. But I couldn't see anything in that direction. For a while, the only sound was the splashing and glubbing of the girls kicking and breathing heavily.

"I'll catch up, you know," Mary said softly. "You're only four years older than me. Three and a half, really. Did you know my dad is seven years older than my mom?"

Eww.

"So three and a half years is nothing, really."

Grace and I made eye contact, and I looked away from her. "I think your dad would disagree, Mair."

"We've talked about it, Dad and I," she said, panting slightly. "I'm not allowed to date until I'm sixteen, and my dad says he has to know the boy too. But he said he won't consider letting me date you when I'm sixteen until I'm sixteen. He thinks I won't still like you then."

The idea of Mary talking to Mr. S about dating me weirded me out. "You probably *won't* like me then. You'll like some other basketball star who's—"

A roar of an engine shocked the night.

"The boat!" Mary kicked harder, but there was no way the girls could outswim the *Dragon Star*. The shore was still so far away. Were we going to get run down? Chopped up by the propeller blade?

As Anya powered the boat in a slow U-turn, another engine buzzed in the distance. I whipped my head around and saw a Jet Ski zooming up behind us. It curled around our inner tube, sending a spray of water out behind it. It was Mr. Sloan.

"Get on!" he yelled.

All of us?

"I thought it was illegal to drive a Jet Ski at night?" Grace said.

"It's also illegal to kidnap children," Mr. Sloan said. "Now get on!"

Mary swam over to the Jet Ski, and Mr. Sloan helped her get on in front of him. Then Grace scrambled up behind him. I rolled off the inner tube, keeping one arm hooked through the middle. As the saltwater attacked my cut, I fought back a string of swear words and paddled toward the Jet Ski.

Anya's boat cruised our way, a single headlight splitting the darkness. I climbed up on the Jet Ski and sat behind Grace.

"Hold on tight!" Mr. Sloan yelled. "This craft is only made for two."

A bar ran around the back edge of my seat, but the smell of coconuts prompted me to grab Grace's waist. She was even smaller around than Keiko. The Jet Ski darted forward, jerking me back so fast I had to move my hands to the bar to keep from falling off.

The Jet Ski bounced over the dark sea. Grace's ponytail whipped my face, and I turned my head to see the *Dragon Star*. Anya was still following, but the distance between us was growing quickly.

Just as I started to relax, another Jet Ski screamed out of the darkness. Mr. Sloan jerked our Jet Ski to the side, and we just missed colliding with Bushi. He whipped his craft around and quickly caught up, bouncing over our wake, just behind on our left. The waves slowed him slightly. I was thankful for that.

Until I heard the gunshot.

REPORT NUMBER: 24

REPORT TITLE: There Are Two of Too Many People
SUBMITTED BY: Agent-in-Training Spencer Garmond
LOCATION: Pacific Ocean near Okinawa, Japan
DATE AND TIME: Sunday night, July 12, time unknown

A SECOND JET SKI ZOOMED UP ON OUR right. Keiko. She swerved close and tried to knock her craft into ours. I punched her shoulder, and she veered away.

Another gunshot knotted my insides. I cowered over Grace's head. Who was shooting? I chanced another glance over my shoulder. Bushi and Keiko were still behind us. Way behind them, Anya followed in the boat, its headlight bobbing left and right. Did she even know how to drive that thing?

A third shot spat into the water beside me. Ahh. Anya had the gun, shooting and driving at the same time. Perfect. Hopefully she shot as well as she drove boats.

The dark shadow of land loomed on our right. There were

no lights, but I could make out the shapes of a craggy cliff. Jagged rocks loomed in the water near the shore like we were coming up on a tight zone defense. Mr. Sloan veered toward them, and I grabbed the bar tighter.

The Jet Ski slowed as Mr. Sloan navigated his way through the shafts of rock. The cliffs loomed above like some LA skyscraper. Grace and I jerked left, right, forward, and back in unison, our fate in the hands of Mr. Sloan's expert driving skills.

He stopped suddenly behind a pointed rock that looked like a tiny cruise ship jutting out of the sea. The air reeked like seaweed.

The Jet Ski idled softly, vibrating under my feet. I could hear the hums of the other Jet Ski engines reverberating off the rocks making it sound like they were everywhere at once.

A breeze sailed past. Grace shivered against my chest. A motor surged behind us, and I whipped around. No one was there. The sound faded, then revved and faded again. They must be driving around the rocks.

The sound rose again then burst as Keiko's Jet Ski appeared behind us.

"She's here!" I reached over Grace and tapped Mr. Sloan's shoulder, but Mr. Sloan had been watching. Our Jet Ski jerked forward. My body fell back, and I barely had time to grab the bar. I got my balance again as Mr. Sloan snaked around the dark boulders.

Between two large rocks, I saw Bushi closing in on our left. Mr. Sloan steered the Jet Ski to the right, and Bushi disappeared from view. We zigzagged around the rocks.

Suddenly, Keiko was speeding toward us in a horrifying round of chicken. Mr. Sloan slowed to a near stop and swerved hard between two rocks. Keiko's leg shot out and struck my waist. Already off balance from the abrupt change in direction, I fell off.

I plummeted beneath the dark surf. The sound of sloshing water was muffled in my ears. Salt water entered my mouth. I flailed my limbs, desperately searching for a rock to grab hold of or the ocean floor to push myself back up. But there was nothing. How could the water be so deep this close to land?

I flapped my arms and kicked and flapped and kicked. Before I realized I was even close, the muffled water sounds fell away as my right ear emerged above the surface.

I straightened myself to float on my back and gasped for air, choking on the gallon of seawater still trapped in my throat. I scanned my surroundings as best I could from my back. At first, I heard nothing but the ringing in my ears and my own gasping and coughing. Then the water leaked out of my ears, and the sound of the motors was there, buzzing nearby. I pointed my head toward the nearest rock and kicked. Thankfully, this particular rock was extra craggy and looked like I'd be able to climb onto it.

I kicked as hard as I could, but the surf pushed me to the right. So I flipped onto my stomach and doggie paddled toward the rock. I threw in a few wide arm strokes that I thought looked like a crawl stroke, and it seemed to move me faster. If I lived through today, I was *so* taking swimming lessons.

I finally managed to reach the rock. Before I had a chance to climb up, a wave slammed me against it. I hit my chin on the rock and got a mouthful of ocean water. It wasn't easy, but I clambered up the slimy thing. My shorts clung to my legs and water ran off me and down the rock like a stream. I squatted on top, careful to get my feet in a good position, then I slowly straightened my legs until I was standing.

The *Dragon Star* had stopped outside the rocky area, floating on the dark water like a killer whale. The field of jagged rocks were black against the shimmering water. Little black dots of the Jet Skis flickered past the spaces between the rocks. When they were in view, the engine sounds magnified. Out of sight, the engine sounds were muted. It sounded like three mechanical heartbeats: whaawww . . . whaa . . . whaawww . . . whaa . . . Didn't they realize I wasn't—

A wave exploded against the rock, showering me with water and almost knocking me off my perch. I crouched back down and sat.

I ran my hands over my head to squeeze the water out of my hair and realized that I'd lost my iPhone and my cap when I'd fallen in the water. Guys don't cry. But I wanted to. And I realized then that I'd forgotten to look for my cross necklace too. Anya had broken it and thrown it on the floor. And I'd been too busy obsessing over my iPhone to even think about it.

Now, here I was, sitting on a rock in the middle of the ocean in the middle of the night, no way of communicating, no trackers to bring help to me, and only my thoughts to keep me company. And my thoughts weren't very pleasant.

Another wave hit me then. I hung on and held my breath and managed to keep the water out of my mouth this time. When the ocean settled down, I squeegeed my hair again.

Okay, God. I'm an idiot. No one knows this more than You. Is this Your version of Jonah and the whale? Are You trying to tell me I'm an idiot? I get that. I do. I'm selfish and cocky and . . . Please just let Mary and Grace be okay. It's my fault they're in this mess. They were both doing what I should have been doing. I'm sorry, okay? I'm so—

A Jet Ski zoomed out of the darkness and stopped in front of my rock. I could see Grace's white T-shirt right away, and then Mr. Sloan and Mary came into focus too.

Oh, thanks, God. That's real big of You, man. My first answered prayer. Only I hadn't prayed for help. I'd prayed that Mary and Grace would be okay. Not that I was complaining, but could God not hear me or something?

"Garmond!" Another crashing wave nearly drowned out Mr. Sloan's voice and almost swept me off the rock. The Jet Ski knocked against the rock, and both girls screamed.

Once the water settled, I quickly slid down to the back of the Jet Ski and grabbed the bar behind me.

"We thought we'd lost you," Mr. Sloan said. "You okay?"

"I'm fine. They're both way over there." I motioned toward Anya's boat. "If we go the other way and keep inside the rocks, I don't think they'll see us."

"Excellent," Mr. Sloan said, steering the Jet Ski where I'd suggested.

The ride was slow and twisting. We finally exited the rocky area, and Mr. Sloan headed for a small section of beach. He pulled right up onto the sand and killed the engine. A man with a flashlight and a gas can ran toward us.

"Get off," Mr. Sloan commanded, taking the flashlight and handing it to me.

I hopped off onto the hard sand and held the flashlight on the nose of the craft where the man was unscrewing the fuel cap. The dude had long blond hair like an '80s rock star. It was tied back in a ponytail.

"Where are Jean and Doug?" Mr. Sloan asked.

"Right here."

I jumped at the familiar voice behind me. I turned around and stared in deep confusion at the two men standing there. One was Mr. Sloan, but Mr. Sloan was also standing next to the Jet Ski with Grace and Mary. I looked back and forth between the men. They were even wearing the same beige camouflage clothes, which were the standard battle dress uniform (BDU) for the Mission League.

"Are you kidding me right now?" I mean, what was up with all the twins?

The other man, Doug, was wiry with orange hair and a small pointed beard. He wasn't wearing a shirt. I turned back to the man filling the tank and noticed that he was wearing a white T-shirt and shorts like Grace.

"Are you guys supposed to be us?" I asked.

'80s rock star guy put down the gas can. "You don't think I can pass for a twelve-year-old girl?"

"I'm fifteen," Grace said.

"Oh, sorry," the guy said, capping the tank.

"Garmond, Grace, Mary, come with me." Our Mr. Sloan, the Jet Ski driver Mr. Sloan, walked off toward a rocky staircase and waved us to follow.

Mary and Grace jogged after Mr. Sloan, and I followed. I could still hear the occasional, distant revving of one of the other Jet Skis out on the ocean.

Mary slowed and waited for me to catch up, then ran alongside me. "You lost your phone?"

"Yee-aahh. When I fell off the Jet Ski. My hat too."

"I'm sorry."

"Thanks, but it's just a phone." A powerful, gorgeous multi-touch iPhone with all my songs, a camera, unlimited texting, access to an amazing app store, the Internet, GPS . . . And I'd had that cap since I was eleven. It had been one of the first caps made with Kobe's new number.

Where the sand turned dry, shards of something bit into my feet. Probably coral. I took quick steps, wincing. We got to the rocky stairs, and I let Mary and Grace go up first. The steps were steep, narrow, and thankfully, smooth. The back of Grace's tank top had a red stain in the center. She'd been hurt? But then I realized that it was my blood.

I glanced down at my cut. It wasn't bleeding anymore, just oozing pearls of blood. Between the cut and my bruises, my torso looked like something out of a Brittany Holmes movie. I was halfway up the stairs when I heard the roar of our Jet Ski's engine below. I peeked back down to the beach and saw the dark shape shooting back onto the ocean.

"Where are they going?" I asked.

"They're taking the Jet Ski out to pose as decoys," Mr. Sloan said. "It'll be dark for another few hours, so it should stall them for a while."

At the top of the stairs, Mr. Sloan led us down a grassy path. The moon was full and bright, and it lit the surrounding jungle in a silvery glow. A warm breeze was like velvet on my skin. The crickets sang to us. I felt peaceful suddenly. Safe. Give me a pillow and a blanket and I was done.

We walked about 200 yards and reached a Japanese house with the traditional sloping tile roof. Mr. Sloan stopped at the door and knocked three times.

"Donata desu ka?" a deep voice called.

"Kaeru no ko wa kaeru," Mr. Sloan said.

The door swung in, held open by a Japanese guy who was also dressed in Mission League BDU. Mr. Sloan ushered us into an open room, and the Japanese guy shut the door.

The place had white walls, shoji screen doors, and bamboo blinds over the windows. The floor was covered in tatami mats. There was one of those campfire hearths in the middle of the floor like Kimura-san had at his house. A porcelain tea set and a steel kettle sat on one edge of the hearth. There was a desk with a bamboo chair against one wall. A few fancy vases filled a shelf. And one of those oriental rugs lay on the floor between the desk and hearth. No couches or tables. The place was pretty bare.

Mr. Sloan pulled back the rug and opened a door in the floor. He started down a wooden staircase, then looked up at me and grinned. "Come on, then."

At the bottom of the stairs, at least thirty men and women occupied a cramped basement. Most were sitting on the floor, some were standing, and all were dressed in the standard BDUs and were hanging on the words of a gray-haired man who stood in the far corner and was pointing to a large map on the wall.

"Our intel says that Shoko is loading up the shipment and leaving before dawn. So we're going to apprehend her tonight. The Abaku-kai compound is about a half mile north of here, two hundred yards inland. Alpha squad, you'll come in from the south. Bravo squad, cover the back of the compound and watch for vehicles on this service road." The man pointed to a road on the map. "Charlie squad will come in from the north, and Delta squad, you'll cover the beach. We've got a few boats out there in case they get sea bound, but we don't want to let that happen."

A hand shot up from the middle of the crowd. "Sergeant Parish, sir, what about Anya Vseveloda?"

"The *Dragon Star* is still at sea," Parish said. "Don't get in the way of letting it dock. We want all our targets in the compound before we strike. Also, keep in mind that our map of the compound came from an agent-in-training. While everything looks correct, allow for error."

I wondered if Jun had made the map.

Mr. Sloan tapped my shoulder and waved me to a small bathroom across from the foot of the stairs. "Let's take a look at that cut. All that seawater likely kept it nice and sterile."

"I don't think a can of soda will help this time, huh?" I said.

Mr. Sloan's eyebrows sank in confusion. "We don't have anything to drink here but sink water."

Oh-kay. I guess he'd forgotten about how I drank Grace's soda on the drive to get my arm looked at. He wet a towel and wiped it gently over my cut. I winced as the fabric made contact.

"Ooh, sorry about that."

I strained to hear what Sergeant Parish was saying, but the running faucet drowned the man's voice.

Mr. Sloan cleaned around the wound and applied antibiotics but ignored the blood all over the rest me. He threw the towel to the floor and grabbed a piece of gauze and a roll of duct tape. "Arms up." He set the gauze against my cut. "Hold that for me."

I held the gauze over my cut with one finger and lifted my elbows out to the side. Mr. Sloan pulled out a length of duct tape, stuck down one end of the gauze, then wrapped it around my back to the other side. Then he ran the duct tape around my chest a second time. My cut throbbed, but it was likely going to hurt more when that tape came off.

"That ought to hold it for now." Mr. Sloan set the tape on the sink, grabbed a white shirt off the back of the toilet, and tossed it to me. "You'll live."

"Thanks," I said as Mr. Sloan slipped back out to the briefing. I set the shirt back on the toilet and snagged the towel off the floor. I wet a clean corner and washed the blood off my stomach.

I pulled on the T-shirt. It bunched under my armpits, and the hem barely reached my waist. I studied myself in the mirror. My left eye was purple where Keiko—Kozue? who knew, really?—had stomped on it. The shirt said, "I ♥ Okinawa," but it was so small on me it looked like I was trying to wear Mary's shirt. My hair felt crusty from saltwater, but it didn't look too bad.

When I came out of the bathroom, the agents were filing up the stairs.

Mary ran up to me. "Are you okay?" Then her eyes took in my appearance and she smirked. "Nice shirt."

"I'm fine. Where are they going?"

"They're moving into position," Mary said. "That's what that boss guy said, anyway."

Grace walked up to us and folded her arms. "I tried to warn you about the twins, Spencer."

Yeah . . . I didn't want to talk about the Beautiful Disasters just then. "So what are *we* supposed to do?"

"We have to stay down here until Mr. Sloan comes back," Grace said.

"By ourselves?"

"No one will know we're down here if they cover the trapdoor," Grace said. "At least that's what Mr. Sloan said."

"Hey, what was up with Mr. Sloan's look-alike?" I asked.

"Maybe he has a twin like me," Mary said. "And like Keiko and Kozue."

Too many twins for my brain to keep up with. "Or maybe he's a clone. Or maybe the Mission League has those sweet *Mission Impossible* facemasks."

"You're an idiot," Grace said.

"Beats being a big ol' meanie," I said, but it felt nice to argue with Grace. Normal.

Soon Mary, Grace, and I were alone in the basement, the trapdoor secured from above. I sat against the wall and looked down at the circle of blood that had filtered through the white cotton just above the red heart. The shirt now read, "I ♦ Okinawa." I peeked down the neck hole. The tape had come off on the bottom. Great. My skin was probably too wet.

Grace had gotten her cell phone and shoes from Mary's backpack, and sat beside me, playing with her phone, which I felt was rubbing it in. If I'd only given mine to Mary . . . "You have a signal?"

Grace shook her head. "Mary tried to call her dad, but Mr. Sloan said that those guys picked this place to ship out their drugs because it was deserted. We're in the middle of a park. Your iPhone might have gotten a signal, though, since they're so awesome. Too bad you lost it."

I gritted my teeth and closed my eyes. Must not kill the hater. Must not kill—

"You're going to sleep?" Mary asked.

I looked at her and shrugged one shoulder. "Might as well. We could be here for hours."

She nodded and curled up into a ball on the floor on my other side, her hands tucked flat under one ear.

I reached over and slapped Mary's knee. "Hey. You did really good tonight. Thanks for getting me free. You were like a real spy girl."

"You're welcome." She beamed, and it hit me that she was a very cute girl. Gabe was going to have his work cut out for him.

The three of us stayed put, silent. Mary fell asleep, breathing deeply. I got up to use the bathroom. When I came back, Grace shot me a loathing glare, so I purposely sat on Mary's other side.

"What's the matter, Spencer? Don't you like me anymore?" Grace said, glowering at me over Mary's sleeping form.

"Never did like you Grace," I said.

"How does it feel?" Grace asked. "To be the object of someone's cruel prank?"

"Are you confessing?"

"The twins, Spencer. How does it feel to be used?"

I shot her a dirty look, hoping it was my version of the "dark eyes." "Why are you doing this?"

"Doing what?"

"You know. Always being angry at me. Cutting me down. Writing 'fool' on my back. All that."

Her nose and forehead scrunched up in angry wrinkles. "Because you're a jock."

"Seriously? You hate all athletes then? What's your problem with sports, Grace? You *are* a cheerleader. And you said cheerleading was a sport."

"I'm a cheerleader because I like gymnastics, and that's the closest Pilot Point High has to the sport. And I have no problem with sports. It's the players who think they can do whatever they want, who think they own the school and everyone in it. It's the players I hate."

"I guess you'll just have to hate me then." I really didn't care anymore. I was tired of riding this weird emotional roller coaster with Grace. A roller coaster I never asked to ride on.

297

But she glared at me with tears in her eyes, which flashed my mind back to my vision of her hurt. I was such a sap. I sighed heavily, disgusted with the pity I had for her. "You're going to cry now? Because if anyone should cry it's me. You've been torturing me since I met you."

"Whatever." She rolled her eyes.

"I just don't get why you hate me so much just because I play basket—" I sucked in a sharp breath, furious that I hadn't thought of it until now. Kip and Desh and the guys.

Grace narrowed her eyes. "What?"

"You're *that* cheerleader! The one Desh messed with at the Rock Academy tournament?"

Grace's bottom lip trembled. Then she buried her face in her hands and a loud wail burst out of her.

Between us, Mary groaned and rolled onto her back.

Wowzers. How had I missed that one? "Grace, I'm sorry. I swear I didn't know."

"*Sure* you didn't. You were all there."

"*I* wasn't there! I was sleeping. They asked me to go but I said no. I didn't want to get in trouble." I got up and moved over to Grace, squatted in front of her. "Hey, I'm sorry that happened. I really am. Those guys are lousy. They're—"

"They're your best friends. Arianna told me."

"Yeah, but . . . I-I'm not like that." I mean, I might have been a total moron sometimes, but there were levels of moron. And I wasn't *that* low. "I wasn't even there that night. I was sleeping. I swear."

She glared at me.

"Look, I'll tell you my side of it, okay? I was beat. I'd sprained my fingers bad in the game, and we had another game the next morning. I wanted to make all-star for the tournament, so I went to bed. Kip woke me up and told me they were going to hang with the girls, but I went back to sleep. Next thing I knew, Coach was screaming at us to get up. We had to run lines for an hour in the middle of the night. And I didn't find out what happened until the next day. Ask Arianna. I told her all about it."

Grace looked at her hands, her dark lashes nearly closed. "He scared me." Her voice was barely a whisper. "What he did."

I grimaced. "Desh . . . He's a creep."

Her face hardened. "Why didn't you tell him so?"

"You think he listens to me?"

She punched me in the arm.

"Ow!" I cringed, overacting. "That's my bad arm, Grace!"

Her eyes went wide. "Oh, I'm sorry!"

I grinned. "Gocha."

She punched me again. "Jerk." She sat silent for a long moment, then sighed. "I just assumed you were with them."

"I wasn't."

She looked at her hands, and I wondered what she was thinking. I wanted to convince her that I was telling the truth, but I was afraid to say anything else.

She peeked at me, then, without lifting her head. "Can we start over?"

"Yes. That would be perfect."

Grace smiled then, a wide, beautiful smile that lit up her whole face. She extended her hand. "Hi. My name is Grace Thomas."

"I'm Spencer Garmond." I shook her hand, and she squeezed. "That's some grip you got there." I squeezed harder.

"There's one thing you should know about me if we're

going to be friends," Grace said, adding a second hand to the squeezing war she'd started.

"What's that?"

Her face turned red as she tried—and failed—to crush my fingers together. "I don't like to lose."

"What a coincidence." I squeezed so hard that Grace shrieked and rolled onto her side, giggling. "I don't either."

A crash jolted me awake. I looked around the basement, heart racing.

A thud upstairs. A man yelled. Silence.

I shook Grace awake and held my fingers to her lips. Footsteps overhead. I woke Mary in the same way and dragged both girls to the stairs and tucked them underneath, in case someone opened the trapdoor and looked down. There wasn't enough room for me to hide under the stairs too. "Stay there," I mouthed, then slipped across to the bathroom and watched through the crack behind the door.

At the top of the stairs, the trapdoor creaked open. A figure dressed in black crept down the stairs and out of my line of sight. I held my breath, hoping not to make a sound.

I shifted but still couldn't see the intruder. The bathroom door swung back a hair, and a silhouette darkened the wall above the toilet. I shrank back. A foot appeared. I grabbed the door and smashed it into the person on the other side. A heavy grunt. Stumbling.

I darted out of the bathroom and attacked my stunned opponent with an elbow to the gut. The figure crumpled, and I easily subdued him in a headlock on the floor. He was wearing black and a ski mask.

"Tiger . . ." a familiar voice croaked.

"Beth?" I released her and pulled off her mask. "What are you doing?"

She snatched back the mask and massaged her neck. She was wearing fingerless black leather gloves. "I came to warn you. They're coming . . ." She wheezed. "They followed you to base . . . Decoys didn't take."

"What do we—"

She grabbed my elbow and pulled me toward the stairs. "We have to go! Now!"

"Mr. Sloan said to wait for him."

Beth's eyes pleaded. "I've been following Bushi. Mr. Sloan doesn't know that the agent upstairs is on Bushi's side. Come on!" Beth sped up the stairs.

"Grace, Mair, let's go." I beckoned the girls out from under the stairs.

Beth froze halfway up the stairs as the girls came to stand beside me. "I thought it was just you."

"I thought you were in a hurry?" I said.

Beth shot me a nasty glare and disappeared through the trapdoor. We climbed back into the main room. Beth closed the trapdoor and covered it with the rug. The Japanese agent lay slumped on the kitchen floor.

I pointed at the guy. "Did you do that?"

Beth shrugged. "He's just knocked out."

Japanese voices drifted from outside. Footsteps thudded on the porch.

"Quick!" Beth urged us past the hearth and into the front corner of the room. We pressed up against the wall, Beth closest to the door, then me, then Grace, then Mary.

What looked like two masked ninjas crept inside and went straight for the trapdoor. The first pulled it open and went down. The second followed. Beth rushed up behind them, shut the trapdoor, and latched it. A moment later someone below started pounding on the trapdoor.

"Nice," I said to Beth.

"You okay?" She pointed to my blood-stained shorts.

I nodded, feeling suddenly like the smallest person in the room. "Hey, Beth. You were right about a lot of stuff. Keiko and Kozue were bad news."

"Keiko and Bushi have been dating for three years," Beth said. "He was jealous that she was cozying up to you—probably why he creamed you instead of grabbing you like he was supposed to. His dumb ego likely saved your hide." She put her hand on my shoulder. "Let's go."

I sandwiched Mary and Grace between us and followed Beth toward the door. But before we reached it, it swung open.

Bushi stood there holding a sheathed katana sword. He pulled it from its sheath, and the eerie sound of steel sliding against wood made me shiver. He held the long, gleaming blade in his grip, pointed right at me.

REPORT NUMBER: 25

REPORT TITLE: I Fight a Samurai Warrior and Live to Tell the Tale
SUBMITTED BY: Agent-in-Training Spencer Garmond
LOCATION: Japanese house near Suicide Cliffs, Okinawa, Japan
DATE AND TIME: Sunday night/Monday morning, July
12/13, time unknown

I PULLED GRACE AND MARY BEHIND ME and picked up
the kettle from the hearth. "Grace, take Mary and get in the
corner." I held the kettle out like a shield. The lid popped off,
and a gush of tepid water ran down my arm.

Bushi chuckled. "You all wet, Supensa-san. Where you put
Keiko and Kozue?"

Ah, so that's who those masked ninjas were. "Don't worry
about them," I said. "They'll be safe in prison."

"Ee-ah!" Bushi cut the blade toward me, and it clanged
against the kettle, jarring my teeth.

"Hey!" Beth kicked the back of Bushi's knee. "You're going

JILL WILLIAMSON

to kill someone with that thing."

Bushi's legs buckled, but he caught himself in a low crouch. "Not kill, *Besu-san*. Only let bleed." He jabbed the sword forward again, and I blocked it with the kettle. "Anya make bleed. Now Bushi make bleed. Hoo-ee!" He thrust the sword out, slashed it sideways. I jumped back.

Beth jumped forward and kicked Bushi's leg again. This time when Bushi caught himself, he sliced the sword at Beth, who pulled out the desk chair and used it as a shield. The sword cut deep into the bamboo.

I hurled the kettle at Bushi. It hit his head and clattered to the floor.

Bushi gave his head a quick shake. He wrenched his blade free from the chair and sidled back toward me, leering. "Nice trying, Supensa-san. I am karate expert. Body like steel."

I knew *that* from personal experience.

Beth came at Bushi from the back, using the chair as her sword/shield. Bushi swung the sword her way again, and she backed up. I pitched the saucers and teacups from the hearth at Bushi one at a time. Some hit my target, others Bushi shattered with the katana blade, uttering a cry with each swipe.

Those samurai cries made him twice as intimidating.

I ran out of tea cups and tossed a few cushions, which Bushi easily deflected. Beth got in another kick to his back that made him turn the sword on her for a few swipes, so I picked up the grill from the hearth and held the heavy iron out in front. Bushi wheeled back to me and dragged the tip over the metal grate. *Clack, clack, clack, clack, clack, clack, clack.* He smiled wide, then attacked.

The grill stopped all his blows until he slid the blade through the bars and pricked my shoulder. I leapt back and twisted the grill, wrenching the blade, and with it, Bushi. He twisted with his sword but lost his grip on the weapon and his footing.

Yes! Please fall.

But instead of falling, he spun around and kicked the grill. I fell on my rear, and the grill landed on my chest, sending a bolt of pain through my cut and smearing my white shirt with charcoal.

Beth kicked in the backs of Bushi's knees yet again. He buckled but turned it into a breakfall and bounced right back up like some kind of roly poly toy. Beth came at him, fast. And soon Bushi and Beth were dueling with arms, fists, and feet.

And that ended my visions about Japan.

I pushed the grill off me. Something moved on my left. Mary, out in the middle of the room, picking up the sword.

"Into the corner, Mair."

Mary took hold of the weapon and scurried back to Grace.

"Ee-ah!"

Snap! A strangled cry. I whipped around. Beth lay on the floor clutching her leg. Bushi stood over her in the pose of a guy who'd just broken some boards.

Maniac! I vaulted the fireplace and tackled Bushi. We rolled for a moment, grappling on the tatami floor. By some miracle, I landed on top. Bushi wrapped his legs around my waist. True, I was in his guard, but I had the leverage, the power, and I was ready to use it.

"Jujitsu for the streets, rule number one, Bushi. Don't ever get your back on the ground."

I grabbed Bushi's shoulders and slammed him into the floor. Bushi gasped for air. I picked him up and slammed him again. Bushi's eyes rolled back. I slammed him again, and he lay still. "Grace! Unlatch the trapdoor. Mary, be ready with that sword in case those other two try and come out." I dragged Bushi toward the trapdoor.

The moment Grace pulled it open, one of the twins tried to come up. But Mary held the sword over the hole, and I pushed Bushi's body down the stairs. Keiko/Kozue—whichever one it was—reached for him and—

Grace slammed the door and latched it.

I breathed out a long sigh, glad *that* was over.

"Tiger!" Beth's voice was tight with pain. I ran and crouched beside her. "I think he broke my leg. Can you carry me piggyback?"

"Of course." A fire burst in my chest knowing that Bushi had hurt Beth the same way he'd tried to hurt me. I helped her sit, then turned my back to her. "Grace, Mair, get outside."

Beth wrapped her arms around my neck. "I'm just going to let my left leg hang, okay? Don't try to grab it."

"Gocha." I stood and heaved Beth up onto my back. It was awkward to only hold her right leg, but I managed to get her settled.

I carried her outside and found the girls waiting on the porch. Grace had her cell phone out, as if the pale screen was any match for the moon. The thick tropical forest spread out before us, lit by the moonlight filtering through the trees and glistening off the tops of leaves.

Beautiful, amazing moon. I didn't want to think about how dark it would have been without it.

"Which way?" Mary asked, still holding Bushi's samurai sword.

"Back toward the water." I descended the porch to the left and started down the path Mr. Sloan had brought us up. The moonlight lit the path enough for me to see. I could do this.

"No, go the other way," Beth said. "There's a boat waiting at the bottom of Suicide Cliffs and gear to rappel."

Rappel? Down Suicide Cliffs? Talk about a foreboding destination. "How are we supposed to rappel with you hurt?"

"Worry about that when we get there," Beth said.

I would have liked to have worried about it then, or at least made some kind of a plan. Instead, I listened to Beth and turned around. We passed the house, and the jungle seemed thicker this way. Darker. Waist-high grass and ferns made the trail even harder to see.

The path curved through a cluster of mangrove trees, which completely blocked the moonlight. I slowed, squinting as I weaved around the trees.

Behind me, a girl screamed.

"Spencer!" Grace yelled. "Mary is gone."

I whirled around. Grace's face was lit with the bluish glow of her cell phone.

"Mair?" I yelled. "Look for her, Grace. Maybe she fell, twisted her ankle or—"

"Spencer! Again I have found your little friend." Anya's voice came from behind Grace, back toward the cabin.

"I'm sorry, Spencer!" Mary screamed from somewhere in the darkness.

Mother pus bucket!

"I know how much this one means to you," Anya said. Flashlights came on suddenly in the distance, maybe fifteen yards away, obscured by the jungle vegetation. "Come to me, and we will reunite you."

I ground my teeth. Beth's breath was hot in my ear. My chest stung. My legs, abs, and feet ached. So did my head. I wanted to go home—America home.

"This girl has found Bushi's lovely sword," Anya yelled. "But you've already seen it, haven't you?"

Mary screamed so loudly I could hear her pain.

"Okay!" I yelled. "I'm coming. Don't hurt her."

"Tiger, you can't!" Beth said.

"Well, I can't leave her." I crouched to let Beth off my back. "Stay here with Grace. Pray." Hopefully God answered Beth's prayers better than He answered mine.

I walked toward Grace, took hold of her shoulder. "Help Beth get off the path, into the grass where you guys won't be seen."

"What are you going to do?"

"I don't know. Get Mary back." I weaved my way back through the grove of trees and grass toward the flashlight beams.

It wasn't until I reached the cabin that Anya came into view. She was standing on the dirt at the bottom of the porch steps. She had Mary on her knees before her and was holding her by the hair, the katana sword resting on Mary's shoulder.

Two men rushed off the porch and pinned me to the ground.

Tears streamed down Mary's face. "I'm sorry, Spencer."

She was sorry? If Anya didn't kill me, Mr. S would.

REPORT NUMBER: 26

REPORT TITLE: Three of Us Rappel Down Suicide Cliffs with One Harness
SUBMITTED BY: Agent-in-Training Spencer Garmond
LOCATION: Jungle near Suicide Cliffs, Okinawa, Japan
DATE AND TIME: Sunday night/Monday morning, July 12/13, time unknown

THE MEN HAULED ME AND MARY TO A grove of bamboo. One guy handcuffed my left hand to a thick stalk, then handcuffed Mary's left hand to my right. We weren't there more than five minutes before the men returned, pushing Grace toward us. Two other men followed, carrying Beth between them.

Come on! "Didn't I tell you to help her hide?"

"I tried," Grace said, her bottom lip trembling.

"She did try." Beth's face was really pale. Could someone die from a broken leg?

The man handcuffed Grace's left hand to Mary's right so

that we were all in one big line. He and his partner mumbled to each other in Japanese, apparently out of handcuffs. They ended up tying Beth with a couple head scarves to a different grove of bamboo that was across from us.

"I guess they don't think you're much of a threat," I said to Beth.

"Their mistake."

I hoped she was right.

"Tell the men to bring the jeep!" Anya yelled in the distance.

I squinted through the bamboo and mangrove trees to a clearing lit up with several sets of headlights. A flurry of people dressed in black darted around Anya in the silvery night. In her white outfit, she glowed like a gray angel. I shuddered. *So not an angel.*

God? A little help here? Pretty please? If not for me, then for Mary. She's a nice kid. And Grace, well, she's had a rough time of it too. And Beth is hurt.

The way the guy had cuffed me to the tree, I was facing Beth. She was dressed in black. "Beth, did you pick those clothes or did they come from the Mission League people?"

"Sergeant Parish gave them to me for my assignment."

Awesome. "Do they have a kit in the pocket?"

She looked blank and very pale. She needed a doctor.

I jerked my elbow toward her pants. "A field ops kit, in the pants pocket. Check and see." The real field ops kits were 100 times better than mine. I wanted a paperclip, but the night vision contacts would be helpful too.

Beth frowned and reached into her left pants pocket. Then she tried the right. Her face softened, and she pulled out her hand.

I got up on my knees and stretched as close as I could toward her, but I still couldn't see. "What do you have?"

"A coin. A piece of candy. And I think this might be a contact lens case."

Good, good. "Check again for a paperclip. And if there's a stick of gum, don't chew it."

Beth shoved her hand back in her pocket. "How do you know about this stuff ?"

"Kimbal showed me once. And I used Ryan's kit in Moscow."

"What's a field ops kit?" Grace asked.

"It's a collection of gadgets that look like junk but can help get the agent out of a scrape," I said. "There's usually a coin, which is really a bionic ear. There's a pill or piece of candy, which is concentrated ipecac. And a set of night vision contact lenses. The gum is C4—"

"Got it." Beth held up the paperclip.

Yes! "Guys, can we stretch out and reach Beth? I need that paperclip."

"What's the paperclip do?" Grace asked.

"Holds papers together," I said. "But we can also use it to pick the locks on these handcuffs."

The girls stood. Grace walked toward Beth, and Mary's arms stretched out between us like a scarecrow. At our longest, our line just barely reached Beth, who dropped the goods into Grace's hand.

"You can't reach Beth to untie her?" I asked.

Mary pulled on my arm as Grace tried to reach Beth, and I stretched myself as far as I could, pulling against the bamboo.

"Not quite," Grace said.

"Okay, come back then."

The girls came back and sat beside me. Grace handed everything to me. "I wish you were on this side, Beth," I said. "I suck at locks."

"An agent is only as good as his biggest weakness," Beth said.

"That's why agents have partners." I tugged my hand that was cuffed to Mary's. "Give me some slack, Mair." She did, and I popped the night vision contacts into my eyes. At first they felt cold and foreign, but the more I blinked the more natural they became. The world around me lit up as if a green sun had risen. I saw now that we were sitting off to the side of a wide section of the path. To my left, flashes of light came from Anya's camp. Back the other way, a warm breeze made the ferns and tree leaves bounce. The trail toward the cabin was a pale green stripe. I shoved the other spy kit things in my pocket, just in case, then set to work on the handcuffs.

I think a year might have passed as I tried the locks.

Finally, Mary took the paperclip from my cramped hand. "Let me try," she said. "I've been playing with locks for years."

"Go for it," I said, imagining Mr. S giving his toddler twins a box of locks for Christmas.

Gunfire almost stopped my heart. Not because I got hit but because of the nearness of the sound. Something big was going on over in Anya's camp. A Jeep rolled up, headlights sweeping the forest for a moment. People were yelling in Japanese, and Anya was the loudest.

My right hand came free of the cuffs, which clattered against the bamboo. I stared at Mary. "You're amazing."

She beamed, then turned to the cuffs linking her to me.

"No." I grabbed her arm. "Let's get Beth free then get out of here. We don't have time to mess with the other cuffs."

Mary pocketed the paperclip, and the three of us made our way to Beth. Once we'd untied her and I'd gotten her on my back again, I padded back through the grass toward Suicide Cliffs. And this time, because of the night vision contacts, I moved faster.

The cuff on my left arm tugged behind me where Mary and Grace followed. I slid through the trees, taking a shortcut. Part of my head screamed that I was a fool to take a shortcut through the dark woods, but the night vision contacts lit up the forest. If the girls disagreed, they didn't mention it.

I came out in the place I'd told Beth and Grace to hide. Now on a solid path, I broke into a jog through the waist-high grass. Mary and Grace plodded behind, slaves to my pace and better vision. At least this time, with Mary cuffed to me, I wouldn't lose her.

By the time we reached the cliffs, my legs were cramped. I squatted to set Beth on the ground and panted. "What am I looking for?"

"There should be a black duffel bag somewhere close to that mangrove tree." Beth pointed at the green outline of a tree at the edge of the cliff surrounded by the vast blackness of the ocean. I walked toward it and scanned the ground. The bag was shoved under a bush at the base of the tree.

"Grace, Mair, help me pull this out."

We dragged the bag out of the nest of bushes and over to Beth, who unzipped it. A flashlight clicked on, and she held it in her mouth. I squinted away from the blinding beam. Light and night vision contacts didn't mix.

"Yame!" someone said. "*Anata dare?*"

Beth dropped the flashlight and put her hands in the air. I looked where the voice had come from. "Jun?"

"Supensa-san?"

"What are you doing here?" I asked.

"I have a task to be here. Why are you here?"

"Guys, we don't have time for twenty questions, okay?" Beth picked up the flashlight and went back to looking through the duffle bag.

"Is that Besu-san?" Jun asked, coming closer to us.

"Yes," Beth said. "I've got Spencer, Grace, and Mary with me. I need to get them down the cliff." Beth pulled out coils of rope and set them around her, then handed me a harness. "Put that on. Works like a pair of pants."

I stepped into the harness, Mary's hand bouncing awkwardly at my side. "Beth is hurt, Jun. Bushi broke her leg."

"I *think* he broke my leg," Beth said.

"Shinjirarenai! I can carry you to my motor scooter," Jun said. "That may be safer than going down the cliff."

"*Might be?*" I said.

"Yeah, thanks, Jun," Beth said. "That would be great. Help me get these guys down the cliff first, though." She zipped up the duffle bag and shoved it back into the bushes.

"There's only one harness?" I asked. "How are all three of us going to get down? We're handcuffed, remember?"

"I'm not big on heights," Grace said.

Beth looped three different thick ropes around the base of a tree. "You'll have to take turns with the harness. Spencer goes down first so he can catch you guys. Mary, get out the paperclip and start working on those other cuffs."

Voices drifted over the grass. Men, shouting in Japanese.

"Hurry," Jun said, "they are coming."

I crouched low and whispered, "We don't have time for messing with the cuffs. How much do you weigh, Grace?"

Her jaw dropped, and she flashed me the "dark eyes."

"I weigh one-sixty," I said, ignoring her drama. "Mary?"

"Sixty-three."

I grinned at Mary and did the math. "That's two twenty-three. Grace?"

"Ninety."

Beth grunted. "And you didn't want to tell us that, why?" She clipped two carabiners through the ropes on the tree, then looped another knotted rope into both carabiners.

"That's three-thirteen," I said. "Beth, how much weight can—"

"It's tech cord, Tiger. It'll hold," Beth said.

Oh-kay. I didn't know what tech cord was. "Now what?"

Beth buckled the harness snug at my waist. She clipped two more carabiners through a loop on my harness, then hooked a metal figure eight through them. The rope was already threaded through. She moved the huge coil of slack to my right and placed the ropes in my right hand. "Lift up to go. Pull down to brake. Try it."

I fiddled with the rope, stepping back and stopping myself. "I get the concept."

She pulled off her gloves. "Put these on."

The gloves were sweaty and way too small for my hands, but I crammed them on anyway, appreciative for the protection. The cord burns I'd gotten last summer in Moscow had taken a month to heal. I pulled the glove's Velcro strap around my wrist. It barely reached.

Beth pulled out the duffle bag and removed another rope. She tied it into three loops, two big ones with a small one in the middle. She waved me down and looped the small loop over my head and one shoulder. "Mary, get this rope loop around your waist. You're in front. You and Grace put your cuffs over Spencer's head. That's right." Mary was now standing on my right, her left hand behind my head, hooked to Grace's, who was standing behind me. Jun came forward and tightened the rope loop around Mary.

"Grace, you get in the other loop," Beth said. "You're riding piggyback. *Don't* let go of Spencer, either of you. And, Tiger, you keep a tight hold on that brake at all times unless you want to free fall, which I don't recommend." Jun came around me and tightened Grace's rope loop.

In the woods, someone yelled in Japanese—the voice was so close it sent a throb of panic to my heart.

"Quick!" I whispered.

"You ready for this, Tiger?"

"I was born ready." Then I met Beth's gaze—her eyes looked like pools of black through the goggles. "I don't know what I'm doing, Beth."

"You'll be fine. Stay in a sitting position and use your feet to walk and bounce down the rocks. The boat is directly below us. Keep your brake on, and you can't fall."

"But the girls could."

"Nope, they're tied onto you," Beth said. "So, unless you forget the brake . . ."

My head lolled back at the stars. "Fine. Let's do this." I crouched and picked up Mary, setting her over my right hip like a mother holding a small child. "Sixty-three, huh?"

She swatted the back of my head with the hand that was hooked to Grace's.

I crouched for Grace, and she jumped onto my back. I resituated her leg over Mary's on my right but could do nothing to hold Grace on my left as my left hand was attached to Mary's and holding the main ropes. This wasn't so bad. I had a pretty good grip on the ropes and Mary. If Grace could hold on—

"*Tiger*," Beth said. "Right hand. You're not holding the brake."

Figs and jam!

"Mary, you're going to have to hold on," I said. "Use your arms and legs." I let go of Mary and found the brake rope. "Got it." I was thankful for the handcuffs and ropes. Although I didn't relish the idea of either girl falling, at least they were sort of locked/tied on.

"Hold on tight, girls," Beth said.

They were. I felt like I was in a chokehold at the dojo. And both the girls' legs around my waist hurt my bruised abs. Too bad I couldn't tap out.

I hadn't bothered to look over the cliff. With a name like Suicide Cliffs, it couldn't have been an encouraging view. I crept back and felt my heels go off the edge. I kept the ropes braked and leaned back. My toes gripped the rock edge as I let out the rope an inch at a time. A bead of sweat trickled from my forehead down my nose.

Three lights flickered in the field beyond the mangrove tree. Flashlights. They were coming. I took a deep breath and let out another inch of rope. We eased farther back, but I didn't move my feet.

"Tiger," Beth's voice nagged. "Go already! You're gonna twist if you don't."

My toes clung to the rock, not wanting to let go. I released my left foot and felt the smooth rock that jetted straight down. I wondered how far.

I bent my right knee, pressed my left foot against the cliff wall below, then released. The ropes fell taught against the rock edge, and we were suddenly very heavy and swinging fast to the left.

Grace screamed as we hit. My left arm scraped against the rock wall.

"Get your feet on the rocks!" Beth yelled down to me. "Let out some slack! Sit! Sit with your feet against the cliff !"

My limbs were like a vise refusing to give in. I let out the brake enough that our knot of twisted bodies sank a couple inches. Grace's arms choked me as she hung off my back. At least her right leg was wedged between me and Mary.

"Let out more, Tiger!" Beth commanded. "Get yourself straight."

I let out more slack, and we slid down slowly, still dragging against the rocky cliff.

"Get your feet on the wall!" Beth called.

I kicked my legs, feeling for a foothold with my toes as we continued to inch down. I finally managed to straighten myself out into a sitting position and took baby steps down. Mary's hold on my neck diminished as her weight transferred to my lap. I looked up at Beth and Jun's green faces, peeking over the cliff above.

"Good!" Beth said. "You got it now, Tiger. Be careful! We've got to go." And their faces disappeared.

I kicked back and let out more slack. We fell several feet. As we swung back at the cliff, I bounced on my toes to catch us. I grinned. Except for the fact that Grace was choking me, this wasn't so bad.

I kicked out again and slid us down, a yard this time. How tall was this cliff anyway?

One of the three ropes in my upper hand went slack, fell

past me. What?

"Uh . . . Grace?" "Yeah?"

"Someone cut one of the ropes."

A scream shuddered Mary's body.

"Then, go!" Grace yelled. "Go!"

I kicked out hard and let out the brake. We plummeted a good six feet before my toes found the rock. I kicked out again and prayed the boat was near. On a third go, Grace's right leg slipped free, and she clamped onto my neck with all her strength.

"You're close, Spencer," Mary said, "but we're too far right. One more big one, maybe."

I kicked out and released the brake. We slid down and cut right into the water up to my waist. The girls screamed. And when my feet found the wall, it was slimy with algae.

"Okay, well, at least now, death by falling isn't an issue," I said.

"Yeah, just death by drowning because we're tied up like a big pretzel," Grace said.

I held the brake and turned to see where the boat was. A rubber dinghy bounced against the rock cliff two yards to my left.

"*That's* the boat?" I yelled, not believing this could be a professional escape plan. There wasn't even a motor.

"There's a bigger boat out there," Mary said. "I saw it from the top. They probably can't anchor this close to the rocks."

Good theory.

"We need to swing over," Mary said. "Can you swing?"

"Not in the water." I tried walking to the left, in the direction of the boat, but we were too heavy and my feet kept slipping on the algae. Then a wave smashed against the cliff, catching us in the middle of an eruption of saltwater. Both girls screamed again, and I blinked, trying to clear the water from my eyes and the night vision contacts.

Once my vision was somewhat back to normal, I gripped the upper ropes with my left hand as tightly as I could and let go of the slack. I brought my right hand up to join my left. Mary looked at me with big eyes as her hand lifted up over her head, attached to mine.

"Going up." I pulled and growled. My one-rep max was only 236. No way I could do 313. One hand up over the other. Pull, man! We inched up, but every time my gloves slipped back down. "Help me?" I panted.

Mary's cuffed hand and Grace's free one joined mine on the ropes. Together we made progress. I felt my body leave the water. Once we were about two feet above the surface, I planted my feet again. Held us steady. I got a good grip on the upper ropes with my left hand and quickly slipped my right hand back down for the brake. Once I had us steady, I stepped to the right on the rock cliff, then the left. Then right, then left. I bounced from foot to foot until we were swinging.

We swung over the boat, and Grace snagged it with her free foot. When we swung back, the boat trailed after us a ways, then stopped, like there was a rope on the other side, tethering it to something. That stopped our swinging.

"There must be an anchor," I said.

Another rope went slack in my left hand, then fell past me.

Mama. One left. "Grace?" I croaked. "Can you climb onto the boat?"

She looked down. "I think so, but I'm hooked to Mary. Just let go and we'll swim to it."

"How?" I said. "We're all tangled together."

"I don't want you to drop us," Mary said.

"Look, if you can get to the boat, you'll pull us over." I hoped. "On three, okay? One." I gripped the upper rope tight again and released the brake. "Two." I reached my right hand up to the main rope and let go with my left so my arm would be out of the way in case Grace pulled Mary with her. "Three."

Grace let go of my neck. Mary's head flew at mine, slipped past to my back, pulling my feet off the cliff and twisting me away from the boat. I couldn't see what was going on under me, but Mary and I were suspended between the rope and the boat.

"I'm on," Grace said, "but I can't sit down."

"Mary, climb to my back?"

Mary slid around to my back, which brought the rope up against my face and twisted me around so that my back was to the cliff. My handcuffed-to-Mary arm was now twisted over my rope arm. I stretched my arm across my front, toward her as far as I could. Mary got both feet in the boat. Grace was sitting on a little bench in the boat and holding Mary's legs.

"Good. Now pull me over or row this way. Something." I let myself slide down the rope, which heated my hand through the glove. I stretched my leg toward the boat. Not working. Gravity was stronger.

"Just let go," Grace said. "You're not that high over the water."

But my weight might pull Mary overboard or hurt her arm. I swung a leg, trying to get a foot in the boat, but the third rope gave way.

I fell.

321

REPORT NUMBER: 27

REPORT TITLE: I Get Eighteen Stiches and a Reality Check
SUBMITTED BY: Agent-in-Training Spencer Garmond
LOCATION: Suicide Cliffs, Okinawa, Japan
DATE AND TIME: Sunday night/Monday morning, July
12/13, time unknown

I WENT STRAIGHT INTO THE WATER, feet first. I gripped the rope tight, for no other reason than to do something. My head didn't go under, though. My left arm and side slapped against the rubber boat, my arm stretched up over the side where Mary and Grace were gripping my hand. Grace let go and reached over for my other hand, and the girls dragged me over the side of the inflatable dinghy.

I sat on the floor for a moment, lying against the rubber side, breathing, resting. Every bit of me hurt. And my chest stung. Rappelling down the cliff had killed any healing that had been going on with my cut.

A shot rang out, bringing a soft hiss from the rubber boat.

"Oh, no!" Mary said. "They shot a hole."

"Find it! Put your finger in it, Mair!" I yelled, scrambling to sit. I found two oars on the floor and dipped them into the water. "But get down in case they shoot again."

I rowed, first going the wrong way, then I stopped, remembering there was probably an anchor to pull up. Grace helped me with the anchor, and once we had it in the boat, I rowed away from the cliff. Yells echoed down from the top of the cliff, but no more bullets came. Maybe Anya had reprimanded the shooter since she wanted me alive. Or maybe they'd only been trying to slow us down.

When the dinghy rounded the cliff, I spotted the boat Mary had seen from the cliff top. *The Defender* sat about fifty yards out. With a name like that, it had to be on our side.

I rowed hard, knowing that rest was coming. I turned around every once in a while to make sure I was rowing the straightest course. By the time the dinghy bounced against the hull of *The Defender*, our raft was almost completely deflated and it was nearly dawn. I was thrilled to see men in Mission League BDUs running on the deck, scrambling to get us aboard.

Two agents helped us onto the boat. One ran into the cabin and returned instantly with a pair of bolt wire cutters. He snapped the handcuffs at the chain. I collapsed on the cold deck and closed my eyes.

● ● ●

I awoke to the low murmurs of men's voices. The sky was light grey, and I cringed at the brightness. I still had my night vision contacts in. I was lying on the deck, and there was a wool blanket on top of me. I wondered what time it was. My head told me it was still time to sleep.

I rolled onto my side and pried the contacts out of my eyes. I left them on the deck. They didn't recycle well. I threw off the blanket and stood. The boat had docked. The men's voices were coming from the cabin. My body was stiff, and I inched toward the voices, stretching with every step.

Inside the cabin of *The Defender*, Mr. Sloan was speaking with one of the men who'd rescued us. Grace and Mary sat huddled in wool blankets.

Mr. Sloan hurried to my side. "Good, you're up. We need to go. You feel okay?"

"Sure," I said. Liar, liar, pants on fire.

Mary walked over and hugged me, smiling, her teal braces muted in the dawn light. I smiled back, then gave Grace a smile too. Smiles for everyone. We were alive.

"Are Beth and Jun okay?" I asked.

"Yes. Jun drove her into Mubuni where he called Toda-san, who called an ambulance. She was taken to the Itomanseimei Hospital."

Good. We followed Mr. Sloan off the boat and down a long pier that looked different than the one Keiko and I had found the *Dragon Star* docked at. The air smelled strongly of seaweed. A host of barnacles clung to the edges of the dock.

Mr. Sloan led us through a deserted parking lot to a single black van that sat idling. A Japanese man I didn't recognize jumped out of the front and opened the side door. He was dressed all in black and had a scruffy face. Mr. Sloan waved us inside the van.

"Are you sure you can trust this guy?" I asked Mr. Sloan. "That Japanese agent back at the jungle house was working for Anya.

Mr. Sloan frowned. "Japanese agent at the jungle house? This is Agent Michito Itou. He's been helping me track you since we arrived."

Then Mr. S got out of the passenger's side door. "You can trust Itou-san, Spencer."

"Daddy!" Mary yelled, flying into her dad's arms like she hadn't seen him in three years.

"Get in the van, sweetheart," Mr. S said. "I'll join you in the back."

So Mary and Mr. S climbed into the back row of the van. I avoided eye contact, feeling responsible for his daughter's multiple near-death experiences tonight. I helped Grace in next, surprised that she let me. Maybe things would be different now that we'd cleared up the whole Desh-is-a-moron thing. I hoisted myself in, but I tripped and fell on my face between the front and middle seats. My left hand upended a box of bungee cords that was under the seat.

"Spencer!" Mary's voice.

A hand grabbed my arm. Grace. "Spencer, are you okay?"

"I'm fine," I said, feeling stupid. I managed to get myself settled in the middle row in the seat behind the driver and beside Grace.

The driver got back in front, Mr. Sloan took the passenger's seat, and the van lurched away.

"Are you all right, Mair Bear?" Mr. S asked.

"I'm fine, Daddy," Mary said.

"Garmond needs a doctor," Mr. Sloan said, looking back at

me. "I don't feel good about taking him to the hospital this time. I've already called Maki-san. We're picking him up on the way."

Maki-who? And on the way to where?

"What's wrong with Spencer?" Mr. S asked.

I looked down at my shirt, which now read more like, 'I was murdered in Okinawa.'

"He's cut," Mr. Sloan said.

"Why can't I go to the hospital?" I asked. "I should be on the frequent visitors plan by now."

"They'll be looking for you there," Mr. Sloan said. "Kozue found you last time."

Oh, right. "Wait. That was Kozue?"

"We've had a tracker on her for a few weeks now. That's how we found you tonight."

The necklace Jun had given Kozue for her birthday. I reached for my own necklace, then remembered that Anya had broken it. "I lost my necklace."

"No, I have it," Mary said. "I put it in my pocket before we snuck off the boat." She reached over the seat between me and Grace, my cross necklace hanging from her fist.

I took it from her. "Thanks, Mair." I wanted to say more but didn't know what.

"You're welcome," she said. "Thanks for saving my life."

"Yeah, but if it hadn't been for me, it wouldn't have been necessary."

"That horrible Anya did it!" Mary said. "She had a knife, like the kind you gave me to take fishing, Daddy, remember? I thought Spencer was gonna die, but I knew he wasn't because of my visions and everything, but he was bleeding, like, everywhere, but then Bushi didn't come back down . . . and then Anya and Kozue went up . . . or Keiko. I'm still confused about which one is which and—"

So was I.

"—then I got the knife from the counter and cut myself free, didn't I, Spencer? And then I cut Spencer free."

"She was amazing, Mr. Sloan," I said. "A total spy ninja warlord."

Mary giggled like I'd embarrassed her. "Well, one of the twins tried to stop us. So I tried to stall her or whatever while Spencer rested. He was in shock."

She kept on talking, but I tuned her out. Living through it once had been bad enough. I slouched down and watched the city pass by as we drove, shivering with the air conditioning in the van. My clothes were still damp.

"Mary, did you say Anya was trying to make a scar on Spencer?" Mr. S asked.

"Uh-huh. She said . . . Well, I didn't really understand what she said, but it was something about Spencer not having a scar, so she was going to give him one. Something about forcing a prophecy, which I told her wasn't possible. Is that right, Spencer?"

I opened my mouth to try and explain, and settled on: "Yeah, that sounds right, Mair."

The van stopped. Mr. Sloan jumped out and opened the side door.

A short, pudgy elderly Japanese man climbed in beside me. He was wearing a sweater that looked too tight, and he was holding a black briefcase. "Arigato," the man said.

We rode in silence for a while. Mr. Sloan spoke Japanese to the man with the briefcase, and I studied the mass of bungee cords on the floor by my feet, wondering who the pudgy stranger was. It must have been about twenty minutes before the van stopped again. Mr. Sloan got out and opened the side door.

"Mary, this is your stop, Mr. S said, climbing out of the van.

Mary followed her dad, then turned and grinned at me through the open door. "Well, see ya, Spencer. Bye, Grace."

"Bye," Grace said.

I looked back to the pile of bungee cords. "Bye, Mair."

Mr. S and Mary walked away. Mr. Sloan rested his arm on the top of the van and leaned in the open side door. "Take off your shirt, Spencer, and let's have the doctor take a look, all right?" Mr. Sloan said.

"Seriously?" I stared at the Japanese man. "We can't go to a clinic or something?"

"The League doesn't have a field office in Naha," Mr. Sloan said. "Maki-san helps out when needed."

I pulled off the Okinawa shirt, careful not to let the fabric rub against my cut. My whole chest seemed pink next to the duct tape. Had the cut swelled, or was it dried blood? I couldn't tell.

Maki-san pulled off the duct tape, which smarted like crazy. The cut looked awesomely gross. The duct tape had left a clean rectangle of skin in the dried blood on my chest. The skin around the slash had swollen a bit, leaving a dark red gash that looked deeper on one end than it was on the other. It wasn't bleeding anymore. Maki-san mumbled something in Japanese. Mr. Sloan answered. I couldn't understand a word.

"Was the knife new?" Mr. Sloan asked.

"I don't know. It was silver . . . Not rusty or anything like that." See? Words like knife, silver, rusty, stabbed, bleeding— these were words they didn't bother teaching us when we were learning a new language.

Mr. Sloan translated this to Maki-san, who pulled out a bottle of pills from his bag and handed me three, along with a bottle of water.

"What are they?" I asked.

"Painkillers," Mr. Sloan said. "They should kick in by the time he's ready to sew you up."

Wait. This guy was going to *sew* me? The idea both thrilled and terrified me.

Mr. S returned to the van and took his seat in the back. Mr. Sloan shut the side door and got back in the passenger's seat. The van pulled away. I opened the water and swallowed the pills. The water tasted so good that I downed the whole thing.

Shortly thereafter we stopped in front of an apartment building. We all got out, and Mr. Sloan led the way up a concrete staircase that split the building in two. It seemed to me like the driver and Maki-san had been here before, as they chattered on in Japanese, hardly looking where they were going.

I walked behind them with Grace and Mr. S, carrying my I ♥ Okinawa shirt. I might need stitches, but I had a guess why Grace was still here. If this safe house was the closest thing to the Mission League's field office in Naha, they were probably going to question us. I just hoped Goliath wouldn't be here this time. That guy made me want to suck my thumb.

We entered a tiny apartment. The main room had a round table with five chairs, three sofas, and a TV. Three doors led off the main room, two were open. One led to a bedroom, the second was a bathroom. I wondered what lay behind door number three.

"Spencer, with me," Mr. Sloan said. "Grace, you stay with

Mr. Stopplecamp and Itou-san."

I glanced at Grace as we parted ways, her sitting down at the table with Mr. S and the driver, me headed toward door number three, which turned out to be a medical room. There was a cot, a sink, some shelves packed with medical stuff, and a couple chairs.

"Lie down," Mr. Sloan said.

I obeyed, surprised to find the cot so stiff. The thick canvas scratched my back.

Maki-san pulled on a pair of rubber gloves, then dragged a chair over to the cot and examined my cut. He said something to Mr. Sloan in Japanese, and Mr. Sloan started rummaging through the shelves. The two men continued to talk to each other in Japanese. I was too tired to try and understand what they were saying. Mr. Sloan brought the doctor a couple of bottles of who-knew-what and several medical packets that looked like they had sterile wipes in them. Then he sat on the second chair and folded his arms to watch.

Maki-san washed my cut with one of the bottles, squirting the liquid into the wound. I braced myself for the sting, but it never came. Yet every time his gloved fingers touched me, it felt like he was reaching inside my chest.

He opened one of the little packets. I could smell the alcohol and braced myself as he swiped the cut. Yeah, it stung, but it wasn't as bad as the salt water had been. Then he used an eyedropper thingy to squeeze globs of liquid Benadryl into the gash. This stung at first but quickly numbed the area. Now that was a neat trick.

After that, Maki-san opened another little packet and pulled out a curved needle that looked like a fishhook that was already threaded with black thread.

"So, it really needs stitches?" I tried and failed to ask in a smooth voice.

"Absolutely." Mr. Sloan reached back to the shelf and grabbed a pack of chopsticks. He ripped them open and handed them to me without breaking them apart. "Maki-san did his best to numb the wound but you might want to bite down on these."

Mama. I took the chopsticks and shoved them in my mouth.

"*Junbi dekitayo,*" the doctor said.

"He's beginning, Spencer," Mr. Sloan said.

I tensed. I felt the needle prick my chest and sucked a sharp breath up my nose. It felt like . . . like someone had stuck a needle in my chest. It wasn't so bad, actually. The skin was pretty numb. But then Dr. Maki pulled the thread through. *That* was the weirdest feeling, that thread pulling through my skin. I quivered and bit down on the chopsticks to distract myself, but the pain really wasn't as horrible as I'd feared. The salt water in the fresh wound had hurt ten times more.

"Atta boy, Garmond," Mr. Sloan said. "You're a tough one, you are."

That's right, I am. Seconds after that cocky thought passed through my mind, one of the stitches surprised me with a sharper pain than the rest, and my whole body jerked in response.

"Easy, now," Mr. Sloan said. "Almost done."

I decided to start watching, in case I ever needed to sew someone else up—or to sew myself up. I caught Maki-san tying off a stitch. He was doing them one at a time. When he stuck the needle in me to make another one, I wimped out and looked away. So gross.

Finally, the doctor sat back and patted my shoulder. "*Jyuuhachi.*"

"Eighteen stitches?" I asked. Sweet!

The doc nodded, then rattled off a sentence to Mr. Sloan.

"He says it will probably leave a scar," Mr. Sloan said. "Hard not to, though, with a gash like that."

A scar . . . Just what Anya had wanted. But it wasn't a cross. So there, Anya.

Just when I thought I was done, Dr. Maki swabbed my shoulder where Bushi's katana blade had nicked me. I'd totally forgotten about that. I couldn't see it very well, but the doctor cleaned it and stuck two butterfly bandages over it. No more stitches. Yay.

"How do you feel?" Mr. Sloan asked me.

"Okay," I said automatically. What I really wanted was to roll on my side and sleep for a week.

Mr. Sloan grinned wide, and from my low angle I noticed that he had a gold filling on one of his molars. "You look like bangers and mash."

I had no response to such a comment.

"I'll check on the others," Mr. Sloan said. "If they're done, we'll come in here to get your statement. So you just relax for now, but don't fall asleep on me yet, okay?"

"Yeah, okay." Easier said than done, though.

Maki-san patted my arm and walked to the door with Mr. Sloan.

"Arigato," I said.

The doc bowed. Then Mr. Sloan opened the door and they left me alone.

Statements. Whee. All night I'd been pushing back the weight of what was happening in order to survive. But now all I could think of was Mr. S sitting here while I explained how I'd put his daughter into danger multiple times because she'd been trying to rescue me when I'd been off being an idiot. Again.

If something had happened to Mary because of my stupidity . . .

I lifted my head and inspected my stitches. They looked nasty. Black hash marks on my pink skin, tied off individually and pulling the gash on my skin neatly together. It was actually pretty sweet. The doc did nice work.

The door opened then, and three men entered: Mr. S, Mr. Sloan, and the Japanese van driver guy, who was holding a small black case. The driver sat on the doctor's chair. He set the case on his knees, opened it, and pulled out a digital recorder. Mr. S took the chair beside him, and Mr. Sloan set up a folding chair next to Mr. S. Three men sitting in a row at my bedside: Driver, Mr. S, and Mr. Sloan: one, two, three. Weird.

"We need to officially debrief you," Mr. S said. "But first I'd like to ask you, off the record, what you told Mary about the Mission League. Did you tell her anything specific?"

I shook my head. "I didn't tell her anything but to mind her own business. No offense, Mr. S. I know she's had visions about stuff, and I should have listened to her, but I . . ." I took a deep breath. "I didn't want to listen."

"What did she tell you?" Mr. S asked.

"She said she'd dreamed about three guys in dark sunglasses attacking me, which happened outside Kimura's place. I think she dreamed that one a few times. That's why she told me not to come to Japan. Then she must have had another vision, because she warned me not to trust Japanese girls when I was here."

"You think she meant Keiko and Kozue Kimura?" Mr. Sloan asked.

"I do now." Stupid Asian princesses, anyway.

Mr. S nodded to the van driver. "Go ahead."

The driver pushed a button on the recorder and spoke into it. "This is Field Agent Michito Itou of Naha debriefing juvenile agent-in-training Spencer Garmond, a resident of Pilot Point, California, USA." The guy spoke perfect English and had no accent. "SF Agent 2269 and Service Agent Pat Stopplecamp of Pilot Point, California are also present." Itou recorded the time and date and then looked at me. "Try to forget about the recorder. We're just having a nice chat. No one's in trouble, okay?"

I nodded, but I also knew better. I was in *big* trouble.

"Agent Garmond, tell us what happened tonight," Itou said.

So I told them how Keiko, who was really Kozue, had wanted to show me her dad's boat. "But it was a trap. Anya and Bushi were there, and Anya wanted me to tell her something about a twin, but I didn't know what she was talking about. I mean, there are so many twins around me right now, I don't even understand." I eyed Mr. Sloan. "And then I saw Mary, and Anya pulled the knife and—"

"Slow down." Mr. Sloan said. "Stay in order. Just give us the facts, then we'll go back and talk it out as much as you need, okay?"

I swallowed and started the story at the point when we were at the pier. "We walked to the pier and saw Kimura-san's boat, the *Dragon Star*. Kozue showed me around, and when we got downstairs, Anya and Bushi were there. I tried to get away, but Kozue—I think it was her—kicked me in the face, then Bushi knocked me out. When I came to, I was tied up, and Keiko . . . Well, both girls were there."

"Keiko and Kozue Kimura?" Mr. Sloan said.

"Right. And Mary too." I glanced at Mr. S. "So Anya wanted to talk about the profile match. She asked me a bunch of questions that I didn't know, and kept wanting to know something about a twin, but with all the twins around these days, I didn't know what she was talking about, and I was freaking out because of the knife. I asked her to let Mary go, but she just laughed."

Mr. Sloan asked me to be very detailed about the questions that Anya wanted to know. I did my best. Then I explained about how Anya's eyes had gone all black and how Mary had said the Bible verses. It seemed to take forever to tell the whole story, and after what seemed like hours, Itou-san finally clicked off the recorder and packed up the machine.

"So what happened out there?" I asked. "Did you catch Anya and Bushi? What about all those agents and their mission to catch that Shoko woman?

"We stopped the drug shipment," Itou-san said. "But Shoko Miyake wasn't there. And Anya got away. We did apprehend Bushi Kogawa and Keiko and Kozue Kimura, but we did not catch their father."

"Kimura-san's involved," I said. "He has to be."

"I agree," Itou-san said. "But without proof, there is nothing we can do."

At least they got Bushi this time. I was glad of that.

"This is not my investigation, but it seems to me you're missing a piece of this puzzle," Mr. Sloan said. "The drugs. iVitrax. This is what your investigation is ultimately about. Stopping the shipment was well and good, but without locating

JILL WILLIAMSON

the source, finding out where the drugs are made, this problem will start over again and you'll have a new shipment to stop."

"I know," Itou-san said. "But we haven't been able to figure it out where they're making it."

"Might you have any ideas, Spencer?" Mr. Sloan asked me. "Hear anything from Keiko or Kozue that hints at a place where the drug is made?"

"iVitrax, you mean? They make it?"

"Similar to how meth is made," Mr. S said. "They cook it."

Goosebumps broke out over my arms. "At the fitness center," I said. "There's this place at the fitness center that I haven't been able to map out. A big room. No doors on the inside, but there's one on the outside of the building. Locked."

"Spencer was assigned a facility sketch of Kimura Fitness," Mr. S explained.

"How big a room?" Mr. Sloan asked.

"Around twenty by thirty." My heart was thumping now. "And it smells funny in that part of the building too. Like science class." Like a meth lab. There was one near my friend Paco's house when we were in fifth grade. We used to pretend to be cops and spy on the drug dealers until his brother Carlos—a.k.a., C-Rok—yelled at us.

"Let's check it out," Itou said.

"Now?" Mr. S said.

"We stopped the shipment," Itou said. "My guess is they're going to be cleaning up shop for a while so they can lay low. We need to catch them before everything is gone."

"Where is your facility sketch?" Mr. S asked me.

"Uh . . . at the school. I forgot it there last week." With my dream journal. So glad the Twinadoes didn't get their hands on that.

336

Itou scrounged around the place and found me a new T-shirt. It was heather blue, had a huge picture of Mario on the front, and actually fit me. I still didn't have any shoes. We all piled into the van again. We drove to the school, which was already in session for Monday morning. Talk about a long night! I fetched my sketch and my dream journal, then we drove across town to Kimura Fitness to see if my theory might pan out.

REPORT NUMBER: 28

REPORT TITLE: I Fight a Dangerous Criminal Who Wears
Platform Heels
SUBMITTED BY: Agent-in-Training Spencer Garmond
LOCATION: Kimura Fitness Center, 3-18-57 Jinan, Naha,
Okinawa, Japan
DATE AND TIME: Monday, July 13, 9:21 a.m.

WHEN WE GOT TO KIMUR A FITNESS, Itou parked beside a
fancy gray car. Three guys got out of the car: our decoys from
the Jet Ski chase: the blond guy who'd pretended to be Grace,
the real Redbeard who'd played the part of me, and Mr. Sloan
II.

"Wait in the van," Mr. S said to me and Grace.

Itou, Mr. Sloan I, and Mr. S piled out of our van. The six
men circled up in the parking lot.

"What do you think they're talking about?" Grace asked.

"Oh, you know, Mr. Sloan is telling them how it's going to
go down. I've seen him work. He's amazing. I just don't know

why there are two of him."

"I got the impression Itou was in charge," Grace said. "This is his country."

I watched the men talk, their hand motions, their facial expressions. Itou *was* the one holding my map. "Maybe."

The men split up then. The decoys went around the side of the building where I knew the mystery door was. Itou and Mr. Sloan I headed for the front doors.

Mr. S came over and opened the driver's door. "You two stay in the van."

"Okay," Grace said.

But Mr. S was looking at me. "Spencer? I want your word that you will not leave this vehicle."

Like I had the energy to chase down any baddies after the night I'd had. "You got it, Mr. S. Can I take a nap?"

"Fine by me." Mr. S shut the door and jogged after Mr. Sloan I.

"He's going with them?" I said. "I didn't think he was allowed to do that."

"Why not?" Grace asked.

"Well, Mr. S is a special agent. Not a field agent." And he wasn't exactly in top shape, either.

"Maybe they want an extra set of eyes." Grace moved from her seat in the back to the driver's seat.

"What are you doing?" I asked.

"I just want to look. I love the cars in Japan. Everything fits me."

I snorted. "That's because you're a midget."

"When we get home, you and I can go to the Ford dealership and try out some big boy trucks, okay?"

That got a smile out of me. Were Grace and I were really

going to be friends now? I decided to give it a try and moved up into the passenger's seat, which wasn't easy. "I really thought there might be more legroom up here, but there's not."

She giggled, holding onto the steering wheel like a kid whose parents had gone into the store. "I'm really sorry for all the mean things I did to you this summer, Spencer. It was wrong. When I saw you in class that first morning and you didn't recognize me, I thought I'd finally have a chance at payback."

And she paid it back well too. "I get it, Grace. It's cool. You don't have to keep apologizing."

She looked at me, and her eyes seemed even brighter blue than usual. "You forgive me, then?"

Something twisted in my stomach, but I ignored that cute look on her face. I was done with girls. For now. Friends was the best—and safest—plan. "Yeah, sure. Bygones, and all that."

We both sat staring at the front doors of the fitness center.

"Do you think you're right? That there's a drug lab in there?" Grace asked.

"I don't know." I'd feel pretty stupid if they came out and said it was only a conference room.

A door opened on the far end of the building. The door that came out of the end of the gym.

"Check it out," I said, pointing.

A woman stepped out, dressed like some kind of businesswoman in a fancy red suit with skin-colored platform sandals. She scanned the parking lot, then stepped outside and held the door as it closed, like she was trying to keep it from making a lot of noise. She was holding a huge white purse over one arm.

When she turned and started trotting this way, I got a good look at her face. "It's her, Shoko Miyake," I said. "The Japanese bad guy boss. Give me your cell phone."

Grace gasped. "Anya's people have it. They took my purse and Mary's backpack too. That phone was brand new. My mom is going to kill me."

That statement gave me pause, considering the dreams I'd been having about Grace, but I was pretty sure Grace's attacker in the visions was male.

"How do you know it's the bad guy boss, anyway?" Grace asked.

"I saw her picture on the LOC list when I was in Moscow."

"What's a LOC list?"

Shoko was headed our way.

"Get down," I said.

We slouched in our seats, and I saw the keys dangling from the ignition. I opened the glove box. Nothing but papers. I turned and scanned the floor of the van and spotted the box of bungee cords under the middle row.

Those crazy sandals *clomp clomped* past us. Her shadow ran across the backs of our seats.

"We've got to stop her," I said.

"Are you nuts? Mr. S said we have to stay in the van."

"Yeah, but she's a notorious criminal, Grace. We can't just let her get away. Start the van. Quick!"

"I only have a permit, and it's in my purse!"

"We're not going to leave the parking lot."

"Which doesn't make it any less illegal."

"Grace, please?"

She growled at me. "If you get me kicked out of the Mission League, I'm going to be mad at you again." But she started the van and put it in drive.

The van jerked once, twice, as Grace steered it out of our parking spot and after Shoko. The woman turned to look over her shoulder at us, then started trotting faster.

"Go past her," I said. "Keep her on my side of the van so I can try and hit her with the door." I rolled down my window. Maybe I could do this thing without getting out of the van. How very Tarantino of me.

"That's not going to work," Grace said.

"Works on TV." I turned in my seat and unlatched the door, holding it so that it would still look closed. A bell started dinging.

"The van wants you to shut the door," Grace said.

We were going too slowly for the door to do much damage. "Faster, Grace!"

The van lurched forward. Shoko was headed for a white car. We were almost close enough. I secured my grip on the door. In three . . . two . . . I shoved it open.

I wish I could say the woman went flying like people always do in movies. But my door merely struck her elbow, which only made her stumble. Somehow her gigantor purse got stuck on the driver's side mirror. Then she was chasing us, plodding along on those dumb shoes, yelling in Japanese.

I pulled the purse in through my window and tossed it in the middle seat behind me. "Slow down," I said. "Let her catch us."

"Catch us? Why?"

"So I can catch her." Which sounded good in theory . . .

Grace slowed and circled the end of the lot. Shoko was standing between us and the fitness center now. And she looked ticked off. I guess she really wanted her purse. I wondered what was in it. Maybe I could use that. Get her close, pull her into the van somehow.

I moved back to the middle row of seats and opened the sliding door. I tossed Shoko's purse in the back row so she wouldn't be able to see it. I grabbed a handful of bungee cords from the box and held them up until I found the shortest one. I held a hook in each hand, then shoved the cord part between my legs where it wouldn't be obvious. "Now pull up beside her so I can talk to her."

"What if she isn't Shoko, Spencer?" Grace said. "What if she's just a woman who was working out? Or what if she has a weapon?"

That would be bad. "She's not holding anything. If she had one, it's probably in her purse."

Grace slowed the van beside Shoko so that the woman was standing by my open sliding door.

"Konnichiwa," I said. "Can we offer you a ride?"

Shoko clomped up to the open door. Her cheeks were flushed, and strands of her long black hair clung to her cheeks. "You the American boy," she said, a hint of disgust in her voice.

"*The?* Is there really only one?" I said.

"Give purse!"

"Sure. Hold on." I glanced around the floor like I was searching for the purse. Shoko leaned inside, looking for herself. Keeping my hold on the bungee cord, I grabbed her, wrapping the cord around her arms as I did and pulling her into the van, over my lap. "Go, Grace!"

The van rolled forward. Shoko screamed and squirmed on my lap, kicking her legs. I leaned out of the way of those heavy shoes and locked the hooks together behind her back. Then twisted my legs up onto the seat so I could push her onto the

343

floor. It wasn't easy. I have long legs and they aren't that flexible. But I got her down there, and as always in a Japanese vehicle, it was a tight squeeze.

Shoko was still screaming, but I didn't have any way of stopping that. I pushed her feet up and slid the side door shut. Hopefully, Mr. Sloan and the agents would come out here before anyone else came investigating the screaming woman. Shoko bucked and kicked, so I put my feet on her back to hold her down and decided to try and bind her ankles. She got me in the eye with one of her massive shoes before I managed to grab both her feet. I took another cord and twisted it around her ankles until it was tight.

Grace pulled back into the parking space Itou had originally chosen and shut off the van. Nice.

"Help me bind her hands better," I said, tossing a bungee cord to Grace.

She turned and stood between the two front seats. Once I got a good grip on Shoko's hands, Grace was able to wrap the cord around her wrists.

"What do we do now?" Grace asked.

Like I knew. "We wait for the agents to come out." I slid back on the middle bench, putting my back to the wall and stretching out my legs on the seat toward the door. Shoko was still struggling, rocking the van with her attempts to get free from the bungee cords. I'd wrapped them super tight, though.

"You might as well relax," I said to her. "The agents will be here in a minute."

She yelled at me in Japanese, and I was pretty sure she was swearing.

"Spencer . . ." Grace's eyebrows were all scrunched up. She was worried.

"It's fine," I said. "And if they're mad, I'll take the blame. It was my idea."

"What if there's a reward?" Grace asked.

"Then we split it, of course."

Grace grinned, which was something I hoped to see more of. I was glad she and I were getting along now.

"Here they come!" Grace pointed out the front windshield.

Sure enough, Redbeard held the door while one of the Mr. Sloans pushed Kimura-san out of the building. Cuffed. "Yes!" I pumped my fist. "They wouldn't have arrested him unless they'd found the mystery room."

Redbeard and Mystery Sloan took Kimura-san to the grey car and stuffed him in the back.

I opened the sliding door. "Hey, Mr. Sloan! We've got another one for you in here."

Redbeard shut the car door and came to look. "What'd you do? Who is that?"

"Shoko Miyake," I said, shrinking a bit at Redbeard's tone.

"What?" Redbeard glared at me, then leaned in to look at my catch. "How do you know?"

I looked at Grace, paling slightly. "Uh . . . it looked like her?"

"Are you kidding me? You abducted some woman because you *think* she looked like Shoko Miyake? Sloan, get over here!" Redbeard leaned inside the van and reached for Shoko's arm, I hoped it was Shoko, anyway. "Help me get her up, kid."

Get her up? It had been all I could do to get her down. I got on my knees and grabbed her waist. She started bucking again. Redbeard pulled her ankles out the door. I picked her up and fed her out the door until Redbeard had her on her feet. Her hair was a mess, all frizzy and sticking to her face. She yelled at him in Japanese.

"Looks like her," Redbeard said to Mystery Sloan.

"*Namae wa nan da?*" Mystery Sloan asked.

"*Hottoite kure!*" Shoko yelled.

"She probably has her license in her purse," Grace said.

Her purse! I reached over the back of the middle bench seat and grabbed it. I handed the purse out the door to Redbeard just as Mr. S and the second Mr. Sloan exited the building.

"What's this?" Mr. S asked, when they reached the van.

"Shoko Miyake," Redbeard said, holding up a red wallet and grinning wide. "Your boy caught her."

"That's what I'm talking about!" I offered Grace a fist.

She looked at it, then me. "Oh." She tapped her fist against mine.

"But how?" Mr. S asked.

"Grace and I saw her coming out of the end of the gym," I said.

"And we didn't even have to leave the van to catch her," Grace said. "But I did drive the van. I'm sorry."

"I made her," I said.

Mr. S took off his glasses and rubbed his eyes. "It's time to take you two . . . somewhere else."

Redbeard put Shoko into the grey car with Kimura-san. I'd have loved to have known what they said to each other in there. Grace came and sat beside me on the middle bench, and Mr. S and one of the Mr. Sloans got into the van. Itou stayed with the grey car. The Mystery Sloan started driving back toward the safe house.

"You're taking us back to get our statements again?" I asked.

"We have to," Mr. S said. "Do you even know . . . ? Do you understand that Shoko Miyake is the Japanese equivalent of Dmitri Berkovich?"

Jeepers. "Dmitri was a lot more intimidating," I said.

"It is early," Mystery Sloan said. "And I suppose you did catch her off guard."

"I would have called you if I hadn't lost my cell phone," I said. "And those shoes. If women criminals wore better shoes, they'd have a better chance of running away."

Mr. S laughed at this, which gave me hope that the guy wasn't going to kick me out of the Mission League.

Mystery Sloan pulled the van into a parking lot.

"You're a twin, aren't you?" I asked him.

He looked in the rearview mirror and raised his Sasquatch eyebrows at me. "Hold that thought just one minute more and I'll explain." Then he hopped out and went inside.

I took a deep breath and sighed. As if this night into morning hadn't been long enough, now I had to wait. Again.

"Tired?" Mr. S said.

So very. But I couldn't complain to Mr. S when all this was my fault. "I'm really, totally sorry, Mr. S. About everything that happened tonight. And this morning. And any time I might be forgetting right now."

"Are you upset with me, Spencer?" Mr. S asked.

"Me? At you? No."

"Then why do you look at me like you are upset?"

"I don't know. You just have that angry dad look on your face. It's my fault your daughter almost got killed tonight, and I feel like I'm at your mercy. You could take it all away."

"Take what away?"

"Gabe . . . the Mission League . . . any chance of figuring

out what really happened to my mom. Plus I'm afraid to talk to Mary now because I don't want you to think I'm trying to corrupt her. I really have been trying to be good. But I know I was dumb about Keiko . . ." I glanced at Grace. "I should have listened to you. No girls ever really like me. Every time they act like they do, it's because they're up to no good."

"Mary likes you," Mr. S said.

I barked out a laugh. "Yeah. That's true." If nothing else, at least I had me a fangirl.

"Mary may be young," Mr. S said, "but she's an excellent judge of character. I don't blame you for her part in tonight's events. She is very persistent. And I'm sorry if I've intimidated you, Spencer, but that's my job. As for Keiko, well, we all make mistakes. Learn from it and don't be so hard on yourself. Someday, if you like, I'll tell you some stories of my goof-ups when I was younger, and you can have a good laugh."

Mr. S mess up? I doubted I'd be impressed.

The door opened and Mystery Sloan climbed in with two paper sacks. "I don't know about you, but I'm famished," he said.

The greasy smell of fried food filled the van, and I swear my stomach screamed. I was so hungry I could drink three bowls of sweat sock soup. I might even eat sushi.

He drove us back to the safe house. We went inside and sat around the kitchen table. I sat between Mr. S and Grace, hoping Grace would give me a buffer. Mr. S was being nice now, but I knew my lecture was coming.

Mystery Sloan set his bags down and passed out chopsticks and bottled water. Mr. S got some paper plates from a cupboard in the kitchen. He even found me a fork in one of the kitchen drawers. Then Mystery Sloan pulled out four

Styrofoam containers and set them in the middle of the table. He took the seat across the table from me.

Mr. S prayed for our food and thanked God that Grace and I were safe. I had to admit that God had answered my prayer there. Then we all dug in. Tempura and rice had never tasted so good. I would've stuck my face into it if I'd had to, but the fork was nice to have.

Once we'd eaten, Mr. S cleaned off the table while Mystery Sloan recorded our statements, which didn't take long this time around. Grace folded her napkin into an origami crane.

"So, you want to know about me, eh?" he said as he put away the digital recorder. "It's confidential, so if I tell you two, you must not tell the other students. Mr. S only found out about it a month back."

"I won't tell," I said, sitting back in my chair.

Grace leaned forward. "Me either."

"Very well. I am, in fact, Christophe Sloan, Jean Sloan's brother. Officially, though, I don't exist."

Sasquatch's brother? "But how can you—?"

"The Mission League trains a special class of agents in a program called Project Gemini," Christophe said. "They look for twins—sometimes siblings who could pass for twins—and recruit them for the program.

"When I was seventeen, I was approached by a man who invited Jean and me to a preliminary meeting. There we got a basic understanding of Project Gemini and what it would mean for us personally. At first we were both against it."

"Why?" I couldn't imagine not wanting to be a part of something so selective.

"Because the program has one major flaw. You both assume one identity. One of you ceases to exist forever."

JILL WILLIAMSON

"You don't exist?" Grace asked.

"That's right. Try and look me up. Christophe Sloan has been erased from history."

"And you didn't want to be erased?" I asked.

"Would you?" Christophe snorted an airy laugh and continued. "Jean had more of a life than I had. He was more visible, had made a bigger splash. So I knew I should be the one to disappear. But in Project Gemini, no one really disappears: We become one.

"There are times when we go on assignment together, but mostly it's one or the other. The one who stays home keeps up the home life, work life, the appearance that everything is normal, the alibi. We've moved a lot over the years. France, Spain, Japan, England. We moved to America when we were assigned to your case."

That got my attention. "*My* case?"

"A young man set to be recruited into the Mission League," Christophe said. "A possible profile match involving a major prophecy, a potential target. Our family dynamics matched the case well. Arianna was your age. We were fairly certain she would be recruited, so we knew it was a good time to move before she settled into a training program."

"So you've been following me since you got there? Before Moscow, I mean?"

Christophe nodded.

"Does Kimbal know there are two of you?"

"He does not. And you must not tell him."

Wow. "So, the night of homecoming . . . ?"

"You had Jean terrified that night. Running across town in the dark. He thought he was going to lose you."

"So Jean was following me that night?"

350

"Yes," he chuckled. "I was following a different lead when Jean called me. He'd lost you. So I tracked your necklace and went to the club."

"Oh. Then it was you at the club." So it was this person, this Christophe, who'd batted Tito aside like a shower curtain. "And one of you was with me when Bushi almost broke my arm. And a different one of you patched up my cut, because I made a joke about the soda can, and whichever of you didn't get it."

"Ah, that is correct. Jean drove you to Oroku Hospital to have your arm looked at. I attended your cut last night. And here you have the most challenging aspect of Project Gemini: What happens to one of us must happen to both of us. It's important that we tell each other everything. Apparently Jean didn't think the soda can worth mentioning. Nor did I understand your comment about the Japanese agent in the, uh, jungle house."

"It sounds like a terrible sacrifice," Mr. S said.

"Some days are worse than others, but yes, I had to give up living a normal life. I can't just go to the store or a movie. Jean and I must run everything we want to do past each other. I can't have a family of my own, a wife, or even a girlfriend. It can be lonely, but Jean and Virginie and Arianna, they make it easier. I chose this sacrifice because I believed it was God's call for my life. And I've never regretted that."

Man. It sounded rough. Christophe Sloan was my new hero. "Is that what Keiko and Kozue were doing? Project Gemini?"

"Of a sort, it seems. Clearly the girls were not so far removed from their aunt as their father claimed."

"Aunt?"

"Shoko Miyake. She was the local mission target for

tonight—Anya would have been a nice bonus. But Shoko is the leader of the Abaku-kai."

"And we caught her," Grace said, grinning at me.

"That you did," Christophe said.

"You didn't know that the girls were part of it?" I asked. "Because I got a red card and . . ." I didn't know if I should finish that in front of Grace.

"The entire family was being watched, yes. You were supposed to bring us any suspicious information you noticed about her, but no one considered they might use the girls against you." Christophe turned to Mr. S. "Perhaps you will now have to instruct your protégés on how to track and report members of the opposite sex, no?"

Mr. S hummed his agreement. "We've been over it." His eyebrows crept away from his piercing brown eyes as he focused on me. "But a review might be necessary."

I examined a grain of rice on the table that Mr. S had missed when he'd cleaned up, thinking that it was going to be a loooong time before I lived this one down.

REPORT NUMBER: 29

REPORT TITLE: I Get a Letter from a Long Lost Relative
SUBMITTED BY: Agent-in-Training Spencer Garmond
LOCATION: Library, Oroku High School, 1-5-3
Kanagusuku, Naha, Okinawa, Japan
DATE AND TIME: Tuesday, July 14, 11:22 a.m.

THE NEXT MORNING AT JUN'S HOUSE we all sat in silence at the kitchen table, eating cheesy toast, tamagoyaki, and rice and drinking tea. Okasan had tried to start a conversation about school, but no one had answered. I was too tired. I'd gotten to stay home yesterday and sleep all day. But today I had to go back to school. We were still here for two more weeks. Jun said Kimura Fitness had been temporarily closed, and I felt bad for the kiddies who went there to play.

With Kimura-san and his daughters in custody, Arianna, Isabel, and Grace were moved to another house, so Jun, Gabe, Wally, and I walked to school alone.

"Come on, Spencer," Gabe said once we were finally out the

front door, "tell me what happened. I'm dying here. Plus, I heard Dad tell Toda-san something about Mary being involved. And Mom was going on about her having a concussion."

I hadn't gotten to hear Mary or Grace give their full stories, so I couldn't help Gabe out there, but I did tell them what had happened. I left out the parts about the Misters Sloan and Project Gemini, of course, and Jun filled in some of what I didn't know.

When Keiko, Grace, and I never showed at the Yuri Rail, Jun called Toda-san and told him who was missing. Once Gabe and Wally were safe at his house, Jun went to Toda-san's office. When he couldn't find his instructor, he tracked Kozue's necklace on Toda-san's computer, then drove his motor scooter out to Mabuni, which was the town closest to Peace Memorial Park and Suicide Cliffs. In Mabuni, he called Toda-san again, and this time got ahold of him. Toda-san told him to stay in the jungle and make sure that the rappelling bag was there for whoever needed to use it. And that's where we'd found him.

"Mary holding a samurai sword," Gabe mumbled. "That girl is nuts."

"The steel for katana swords is made from a rare type of iron sand," Wally said. "It's the ultimate slicing machine."

Oh-kay. "It's too bad Anya took it from Mary," I said. "It would have been an awesome souvenir."

Gabe snorted. "That's all we need, Bushi coming to America once he gets out of jail, searching for his sword."

I shuddered at the idea of Bushi out of jail. "Yeah, I don't ever want to see that guy again. Sayonara, muchacho."

Jun wrinkled his eyebrows my way. "What it means,

muchacho?"

"I think he means, *"Sayonara, shonen,"* Wally said.

This made Jun burst out laughing.

"What?" Wally said. "Is my translation incorrect?"

"Is okay, *Wori.*" Jun rolled his eyes at Wally. "Supensa-san, I should have warned you when I found out Kozue had lied to me about where she went to school. I did not want to believe it, though."

"Yeah, me either. Lesson learned, though. Girls are evil."

"Not all of them," Gabe said. "Isabel's not evil."

"*All* of them," I said. "Especially Isabel."

"Shut up," Gabe said.

"Make me."

Gabe tried to whack me in the arm, but I darted out of the way and almost got run over by a miniature Coke truck. The driver honked at me and shook his fist out the window as he passed.

We walked the next block in silence. I'd had my fill of near-death experiences this summer. Anya had almost won. She'd messed with me, threatened me, hurt me, but she'd also given me something: Another clue to my past.

She'd been sincere when she'd mentioned my dad thinking he was the profile match. I didn't exactly know what to do with this information. I still didn't have the whole story about what really happened when my mom died, but what if it had been an accident? Not that that made it okay, but what if? I much preferred the idea that my dad had intended to do something good and messed up, over the thought that he'd intended to do something bad.

But that made me wonder what he might have been trying to do. Had he been trying to prove he was the profile match in some strange way like Anya had been trying to give me "the mark of my faith"?

Some faith. After Moscow I'd intended to read the Bible and pray more, but then school got going, then basketball, then LCT. I was always too busy. I always forgot. I hadn't even been able to come up with one spiritual warfare verse when Anya's eyes had gone all dark. Mary kept thanking me for saving her life, but if it hadn't been for her . . .

Forget this. I didn't like my depressing thoughts. "Hey, you guys want to see my stitches?"

A week later, in Jun's second period math class, Mr. S showed up and pulled me out of class.

"What's up?" I asked as I followed him to the staircase.

"After what happened last week, with all the official statements and with Grace there, you and I didn't have a chance to talk in private," Mr. S said. "So I thought we could take this hour to do that."

Oh, goody. And here I'd thought Mr. S was going to let me off the hook. I should have known better.

We walked into the gloriously air conditioned library and to our meeting room in the back. Mr. S motioned to one of the front tables, set down a notebook, and said, "Have a seat."

I sat, and Mr. S pulled a chair to the other side of the table and sat across from me.

"I've listened to the mp3s of your debriefings," he said, "and I've read your official report of the events of July 12. In fact, I've gone over them several times in painstaking detail.

And while I don't think it was the best plan for you to go to the port alone with a girl you suspected might be luring you into a trap, it *was* your track and report mission, and you did stay in contact with Jun. I can't fault you for those choices. They were yours to make."

"Seriously?" I wasn't in trouble?

"Seriously. But there is one discrepancy between your verbal statement and your written report. Something that concerns me."

Uh-oh. I swallowed and shifted in my seat.

"You said that once you'd taken the pictures of the boat, there was nothing else there that would help your investigation. Why, then, did you get on the boat? You told me in your verbal statement it was to see what it looked like and if Keiko might let you drive it."

"Yeah, so?"

"In your written report, you also mentioned the hope that Keiko might be innocent, that she might like you, and that she might be taking you aboard to"—he glanced at his notebook—"'have her way with you.'"

"Geez, Mr. S, I was joking."

He raised an eyebrow. "Curiosity killed the cat, Agent Garmond. You didn't know it then, but your curiosity would put Mary and Grace's lives at risk, as well as your own."

I looked at one of the scabs on my knuckles and hoped he wouldn't go where I was thinking he might go.

"It occurred to me that you might lack a male role model in your life. Has your basketball coach or Mr. Kimbal spoken to you about girls, Spencer?"

Oh, please no. "Mr. S . . . you don't have to—"

"Have they?"

"No, but—"

"Did your grandmother have a talk with you, then? On this subject?"

"Uh . . . she . . . not . . ." I scratched the back of my neck.

"Because I'd be willing to talk with you about these things."

This was *not* happening. "Actually, I'm good."

"I don't think so. I'm afraid that, like most young men today, you've gathered information on this topic from your friends and television and movies. And, well, James Bond is not the best role model for a young man like yourself."

"Mr. S, come on."

"I'm embarrassing you, am I?"

"Yes." So much.

"Good. Because when you became a part of this organization, you signed a contract. And you agreed to abstain from sex."

"Mr. S, I didn't!"

"And yet the hope was there, wasn't it, when you decided to get on the boat?"

Oh, make it stop. "*Mr. S.*" I rubbed my hands over my face.

"We're the good guys, Spencer. And while everyone makes mistakes, and while I extend a great deal of grace to my students, I can't have my agents-in-training seeking out ways to take advantage of the opposite sex, be they friend or foe."

Like I would even know how. "I was only going to see what she wanted to do," I mumbled.

"Ah, spoken just like Adam in the Garden." Mr. S chuckled. "The 'It was Eve's idea' line of defense. But are we clear on this?"

"Yes, sir."

"Good."

Oh-kay. So, was that it? Would he stop now?

"How's your relationship with God, Spencer?"

I relaxed. He was shifting gears. "Uh . . . I think He answered one of my prayers?"

"Is that a question?"

"No. He did. Or maybe it was just a coincidence."

"There is no such thing as coincidence, Spencer."

"Okay."

"Do you know have a relationship with him?"

"Um . . . I've been going to think about that."

Mr. S seemed to be fighting a smile now, which knocked a load off my shoulders. "You're a busy guy, and I appreciate your honesty. But make time to think about it, okay? I'd hate to see you struggle like C. S. Lewis."

"The Narnia guy?"

"He remained a devout atheist until the age of thirty-one when, as he said, 'I came into Christianity kicking and screaming.'"

Oh. "I'm not really kicking or screaming. I'm just doing my own thing. I mean, when I have time I'll . . ." I took a breath. "I just need to think it through."

"And I know you will." Then he looked me straight in the eyes. "Spencer, you're bright and tenacious and strong. I respect you."

Okay, that was weird. "You do?"

Now he did smile. "Yes. In fact, I think you're pretty terrific. I'm glad to know you."

His words sent chills up my arms. Was he serious? Now he was complimenting me?

"I'd like to pray for you, Spencer. I pray for you every day already, in case you didn't know. But I'd like to pray a blessing over you, if that's all right with you."

Uh . . . "Okay."

He reached out and put his hand on my head. "Thank you, Lord, for my student, Spencer. May he come to trust you with all his heart and lean not on his own understanding. May he seek your will in all he does. You've promised to make his paths straight. Help him live a responsible life, a life of respect and righteousness. I know how special Spencer is to you, and today I pray that he'd know how special he is to me, now and forever. May he become all you intend for him to be. I'm honored to be his teacher. Bless him, bless his life, in Jesus' name, amen."

And on that note, I tried very hard not to cry me a river.

It's dark. I fumble, find a light switch near the door, flip it on. Beer cans pepper the kitchen and living room floor. Seventies rock music blares over the stereo system, urging me not to fear the reaper. The room reeks of alcohol, body odor, and mildew. It smells like death to me. I find the stereo and click it off. I move down a long hallway.

In a back room, a girl's body lies twisted in an unnatural shape just inside the doorway. Her blond hair is matted with blood. The room smells foul.

I crouch and brush the hair off of the girl's broken face. Her nose is bleeding and one eye is swollen shut. A sleeve of her blouse is torn half off, and her arm bends the wrong way at her side.

I shuddered awake and sat up, my hand over my rapidly

beating heart. I could feel the texture of my stitches though the thin fabric of my T-shirt. I was sitting in my bed at Grandma's house. Home sweet home. The clock read 8:22 p.m.

As soon as I'd gotten home from the airport, I'd crashed. That had been six hours ago.

Grace.

I got up and dug my journal out of my backpack and logged down the dream. I hated these dreams about Grace. Mr. S and Prière had better do something with this information. And fast.

I moved to my desk and flipped open my MacBook. The miniscule pile of mail that had accumulated while I was in Japan sat beside my keyboard. I flipped through it, humming the reaper song from my dream. Among the junk mail and bills I found a flyer from Coach announcing summer camp. Missed most of that. Guess I'd show up for the rest of it, though. See if I still knew how to play.

My class schedule held little excitement—same as last year only up a step. American History was now World History, Algebra I was now Algebra II. Blah, blah. I couldn't believe I was going to be a junior already. Time does fly.

The last piece of mail was a legal-sized envelope with no return address and a handwritten inscription. I ripped it open. It held one sheet of paper with a typed letter.

Jonas,

    I know it's been a while since you heard from me. I don't expect you to forgive me right away, but I want you to know that I'm a different person than I was all those years ago. I have a successful career now, and I own my own home. I know that Lorraine would forbid it, but I'd really like to see you. I'll wait for a call from you. If I don't get one, maybe I'll stop by sometime. I'd like to see my son.

Your father, Alex Wright

323-555-2375

A long silence passed, my mind blank. A lawnmower purred somewhere down the street. The neighbor's dog barked. I shook myself back to reality and re-read the letter in my hand. Was this some kind of sick joke? I grabbed the envelope and studied the postmark. Pacific Palisades? Wasn't that somewhere near the ocean, where the rich people lived? Actors and directors?

I don't expect you to forgive me right away? I own my own home?

In Pacific Palisades? And he's just writing now? All this time my dad had been living it up in Pacific Palisades? Forty minutes from here? Unbelievable. This I could not process.

I tore the letter into little bits. There was no way I was telling my grandma about this. Let the man come groveling if he wanted to see me so bad. I hoped he wouldn't. All my curiosity about my father had suddenly turned into hatred.

I don't expect you to forgive me right away. I'd like to see my son.

"Well, who's stopping you, *Dad?*" I mumbled aloud. "Come on by. We'll talk about old times."

I paced around my tiny room, trying to calm down. I had *not* seen this coming. Not by a long shot. I needed a distraction. My computer had booted up now, so I logged onto Facebook and clicked my messages. There was one from Gabe.

Hey. My youth group is having an all-nighter this Friday night at six o'clock. You should come. They're a lot of fun. We play games all night and eat pizza. Lukas is going. And I'm pretty sure Isabel, Arianna, and Grace are too. Text me if you need a ride. ~Gabe

Tomorrow was Friday. I bit my lip. I'd never voluntarily attended a churcher teen event in my life. And this one was hours long.

But Grace might be there.

I was worried about Grace, but I knew I had to be careful. She was like squirrel. Get too close, and she'd skitter away.

But if I'd learned one thing this summer, it was that making assumptions was stupid. I needed to learn the facts before I acted. And I couldn't do stuff on my own, either. Teamwork mattered. There was that quote Mr. S was always saying about multiple strands of cords being stronger than one. I recalled the three ropes that Beth had used to hook up our rappelling gear. We would have died if she'd used only one rope. And if I tried to help Grace on my own, she might die too.

So this meant that I needed to talk to Grace about stuff. And maybe talk to Arianna and Gabe too. And if all that backfired, Mr. S.

And, yes, I was fully aware that applying this same logic to the letter I'd just destroyed meant that I should talk to my dad too. Too bad I ripped it up.

THE END

Spencer will return in *Ambushed*

Grace's Origami Crane

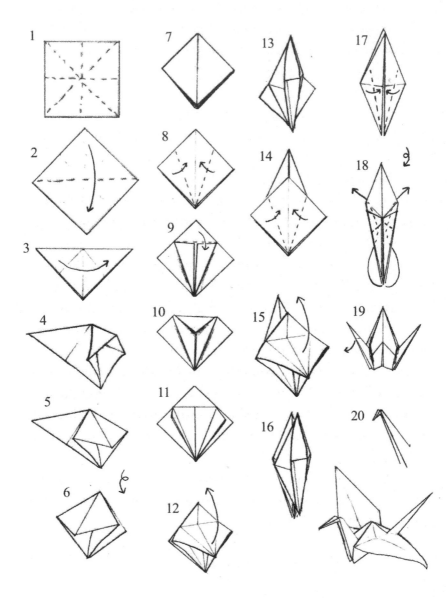

ALPHA GROUP:

Grace Thomas, freshman at Pilot Point High School, a gymnast and cheerleader with long blond hair and blue eyes. Grace hates Spencer.

Wally Parks, fifteen-year-old homeschooled junior, Wally inherited his mother's obsessive compulsive disorder and germ phobias. He loves reciting factoids.

Spencer Garmond, a six-foot-three sophomore; red-haired, varsity basketball player; grandson to Alice; sarcastic, impulsive, and gifted in prophecy.

Gabriel "Gabe" Stopplecamp, junior; black curly hair; glasses and braces; son of Mr. S and Kerri; honest, goodhearted; musician.

Jensina Han, senior; adopted Asian girl with dyed orange hair; loves to read; straight-A student; leader of Alpha group; plans to attend Azusa Pacific University and study business administration.

DIAKONOS GROUP:

Lukas Rodriguez, freshman at PPCS; Cuban native; dresses punk. Works at his mother's hair salon and as a lifeguard. Speaks fluent Spanish and English. Isabel's brother.

Arianna Sloan, sophomore; small, twiggy missionary kid; lived in France, England, and Japan before moving to the States; loves languages and medicine.

Isabel Rodriguez, junior; petite; Cuban native with curly brown hair; speaks fluent Spanish and English; loves to sing and work in her mother's beauty salon; Lukas's sister.

Nick Muren, junior; dark-haired, wealthy, arrogant pretty boy; father is a pastor at a mega church; dislikes Spencer; enjoys acting, partying, and chasing girls.

Jake Lindley, senior; black; bowtie-wearing, straight-A student with cornrows; loves academics and debate; seeking the Public Corruption post with plans to study law at Stanford.

Beth Watkins, senior; brown-haired; tough girl; former district champion in League Combat Training; leader of Diakonos group; plans to attend Mount Olive Special Forces Training Camp after graduation.

ADULT AGENTS:

Prière, mid-fifties; tall and thin with black hair; wears suits; native of France; never married, former field agent; now serves as a Level One intercessor.

Dave Kimbal, early forties; tall, pale, and muscular with red hair and freckles; never married; field agent assigned to protect his nephew, Spencer Garmond. His cover is a school resource officer.

Patrick "Mr. S" Stopplecamp, late forties; out of shape, pink-faced; bald; tiny double chin; thick glasses; serves as a Level One teaching agent in Pilot Point, California.

Jeannette "Kerri" Stopplecamp, mid-forties; short, round, with black curly hair and glasses; wife of Patrick; mother of Gabe and identical twins Mary and Martha; serves as a teaching agent with her husband.

Jean "Sasquatch" Sloan, late forties; tall, dark-haired, French. He is a Special Forces Project Gemini Agent assigned to track and protect Spencer Garmond. Father to Arianna Sloan. He has a twin brother, Christophe.

Hiroshi Toda, late forties; Japanese; slender with thinning hair. Serves as a Level One teaching agent in Okinawa, Japan.

Michito itou, late thirties; Japanese. Field agent assigned to Abaku-kai and to track and report Jun Uehara.

Dr. Maki, mid-fifties; Japanese; short, pudgy. Medical field agent assigned to Okinawa, Japan.

JAPANESE:

Jun Uehara, seventeen; Japanese; host brother for Spencer, Gabe, and Wally. Jun takes karate at Kimura Fitness and is working undercover as an agent-in-training to befriend Bushi Kogawa and become part of the Abaku-kai.

Keiko and Kozue Kimura, identical twins; seventeen; Japanese, host family for Grace, Isabel, and Arianna. Their father owns Kimura Fitness and Kimura Bank of Naha.

Hisoka Kimura, late forties; Japanese; owner of Kimura Fitness and Kimura Bank of Naha in Okinawa, Japan. He has twin daughters, Kozue and Keiko.

Bushi Kogawa, nineteen; Japanese; leader of the San Doubou and member of the Abaku-kai. Bushi excels in karate.

Shoko Miyake, late thirties; Japanese; leader of the Abakukai and Shizuka.

Glossary of Japanese Terms

Amerikan—American
Anata dare?—Who are you?
Aremaa!—Oh, my!
Arigato/Arigato gozaimasu/Arigato gozaimashita—Thank you
Baka—fool
Biiru—beer
Byooin—hospital
Daijoubu ka?—Are you okay?
Daijoubu—I'm okay/I'm fine
Damare!—Shut up!
Doko ni itteta ka?—Where have you been?
Donata desu ka?—Who is it?
Doshite sonna koto shi ta no?—Why did you do that?
Eigo—English
Eto—um
Ge—Gross
Genki desu—I'm good
Hai, so desu—yes, that's right.
Hajime—begin
Hajimemashite—Nice to meet you
Hayakushite!—Hurry up!
Heiwa—peace
Hottoite kure!—Leave me alone!
Ichi, ni, san, shi, go, roku, shichi, hachi—One, two, three, four, five, six, seven, eight
Iie—no/Don't mention it
Ikou/Ikuzo/Ikuwayo—Let's go
Isoginasai—Hurry up
Ja mata ne/Mata ne/Ja ne—See you later
Junbi dekitayo—I'm ready
Jyuuhachi—eighteen
Kaeru no ko wa kaeru—Like father, like son

Kariforunia—California
Kisu shi-te—Kiss me
Konnichiwa—Hello
Mishion Ligu—Mission League
Mo ichi do—One more time
Nandc? Why?
Nani o shiteru no?—What are you doing?
Nanika atta?—What's up?
Ne—huh
Odokasanai de yo!—you scared me!
Ogenki desuka?—How are you?
Ohayo—Good morning
Oitoma—I have to go now
Okasan—mother
Onegai shimasu—Let me train with you
Otosan—father
Panchi—punch
Seiretsu!—Line up!
Shinjirarenai!—I can't believe it!
Shiranai—I don't know
So desu ne—It is, isn't it?/I agree./That's right.
Subarashii!—Great!/Awesome!
Sugoi—wow **Taco**—octopus
Taifuu—typhoon
Tatakawa seru, Gojira!—Let's fight, Godzilla!
Toire—toilet/I'm going to the bathroom
Tori—chicken
Totemo—very **Waka/wakatta**—I understand
Wakaranai/wakarimasen—I don't understand
Yakiniku—Japanese barbecue
Yame—stop

Acknowledgements

Very special thanks to my husband, Brad, for helping me with this book, to Okinawan missionary Julie Woolery for answering my questions, and to Hilarey Johnson for your last-minute karate expertise.

Thanks and high-fives to the book creation team: Jeff Gerke, Kate Dunn, Keighley Kendig, Kirk DouPonce, Jeremy Gwinn, Kerry Nietz, and Luke and Kaitlyn Williamson.

And big hugs to my support team: Brad Williamson, Amanda Luedeke, Chris Kolmorgen, the Alliances—Melanie Dickerson, Shannon Dittemore, Stephanie Morrill, Shellie Neumeier, and Nicole O'Dell—for listening to all my stress and worries over this one.

Jill Williamson is a chocolate loving, daydreaming, creator of kingdoms. Growing up in Alaska led to a love of books, and in 2010 her first novel, *By Darkness Hid*, won a Christy Award. Jill writes fantasy and science fiction for teens and adults. She loves working with writers and blogs about writing at www.GoTeenWriters.com.

Jill is a Whovian, a Photoshop addict, and a recovering fashion design assistant. She now lives in the Pacific Northwest with her husband and two children Jill's full list of books can be found on her website, where adventure comes to life.

To be notified of new releases, subscribe to Jill's Sanctum ezine on her website and get a free short story.

Look for Jill online at:

www.JillWilliamson.com

www.facebook.com/jwilliamsonwrites

Readers of Jill Facebook Group: http://bit.ly/1RAwWuK

www.twitter.com/JillWilliamson

www.instagram.com/jill_williamson_author

www.pinterest.com/jillmwilliamson

Come hang out with us!

GO TEEN WRITERS

honesty, encouragement,
and community for writers

www.GoTeenWriters.com
And join the community of writers on Facebook:
http://www.facebook.com/groups/goteenwriters

FROM AWARD-WINNING AUTHOR

JILL WILLIAMSON

Achan has been a slave all his life. Worse than a slave—a stray.
He is consigned to the kitchens of a lord and forced to swallow a
foul potion every day. When an enigmatic knight offers to train
Achan for the Kingsguard, he readily accepts. But his new skills
with the sword do not prepare him for the battle raging between
the voices in his head.

TO LEARN MORE VISIT

WWW.JILLWILLIAMSON.COM

ONE CHOICE COULD DESTROY THEM ALL

THE SAFE LANDS
CAPTIVES
JILL WILLIAMSON

A young man must find
a cure for a deadly disease
by befriending a beautiful
woman who is his enemy.

www.jillwilliamson.com

Made in the USA
Monee, IL
03 December 2021

83819638R00210